The Apostates

V.E.H. Masters

NYDIE
BOOKS

Books by VEH Masters

The Seton Chronicles:

The Castilians
The Conversos
The Apostates

First Published in Scotland in 2022 by Nydie Books

A CIP catalogue record for this book is available from the British Library

Paperback ISBN 978-1-8382515-5-0

Also available as an ebook

Cover Design: Mike Masters

Map of Venice by Georg Braun 1572

View of Geneva, original drawing by Claude Chastillon (1559-1616), etching by Matthäus Merian, reproduced with kind permission of the Bibliothèque de Genève

www.vehmasters.com

For Mike

And our children Seth, Zoe and Adam

An Apostate – a person who renounces a religious belief or principle, sometimes reverting to a previously held religious belief.

The Players

Bethia, a Scottish Catholic who is married to Mainard.

Mainard, whose family are Conversos; that is, his parents converted from Judaism under threat of the Inquisition.

Will, Bethia's younger brother, a Protestant who was until recently enslaved on a French galley in punishment for his faith.

Katheline, Mainard's sister, who secretly practises the faith of her ancestors, Judaism.

Grissel, Bethia's servant, who came with her from Scotland and is suspected of disclosing information to the authorities about Katheline.

Part One

Antwerp

November 1549 to March 1550

Chapter One

Departure

Mainard surveyed his entrance hall, arms folded. The iron chests were piled three high leaving only a narrow passage between the sweep of the stairs and the front door. Fifteen in all, they contained a considerable part of the de Lange family wealth in cloth.

A thump from behind, and he turned to find his brother-in-law, who had the strength and size of Atlas, sliding another chest down the broad wooden staircase. Mainard was relieved to see that Will had placed a cloth beneath it to prevent scoring the floor, for he must get a good price for the house, but less happy when he noticed the *cloth* was a valuable rug come all the way from the Orient.

Seizing the handles, they lifted the chest together and piled it among the stacks. Will stood tall and rubbed his back. Mainard knew it pained him constantly and also knew that Will preferred not to speak of it.

'There's still so much left. How will you manage, and all alone?'

'I'll hire guards, just as I've done for your journey.' He looked Will in the eye. 'Most important of all is my wife's safety, and you carry that burden.'

'Hah! My big sister is as likely to say that she'll be looking out for me, indeed to complain that's what she's done all her life.'

Mainard laughed. 'Even when you neither needed nor desired it.'

Will knocked his shoulder against Mainard's. 'Aye, you know your wife well.'

The tap of footsteps on the stairs and they both looked up as Mainard's own sister, Katheline, descended. She was dressed in the plain clothes of a servant, although perhaps too clean for anyone setting fires, scrubbing floors and emptying chamber pots, the white kerchief covering her hair especially pristine.

'How will I do?' she said, giving a twirl within the confines of the baggage-strewn hall.

'Very well,' said Mainard. He glanced over at Will and didn't care for the look of admiration he caught on Will's face. Will was a fine man, but not right for Katheline.

He took both Katheline's hands in his and gazed down at her. 'Be very careful, my small sister. Attend to Bethia, remember you're my son's nursemaid, and do nothing to indicate otherwise or endanger the journey.'

Katheline blinked up at him and anxiety twisted Mainard's features. 'You did bury the Tefillot, as promised?' He chewed on his lower lip, knew it would've been wiser to deal with it himself but had succumbed to Katheline's pleas that she bury the book alone and with due ceremony.

He was conscious of Will watching – but Will was a Protestant and wouldn't understand it would cost Katheline dear to part with this sacred book of the Jews. He would, however, fully understand the peril it placed their small group in if the book was found in their possession.

Katheline shuttered her eyes and bowed her head. Mainard tightened his grip on her hands and shook them. 'Katheline?'

'The book has been safely disposed of,' she said stiffly.

A baby's cry, and Bethia appeared. Everything else

was forgotten. He went to his wife and wrapped his arms around her and his infant son; if he could only keep holding them all would be well. Bethia pressed her face into his chest and the baby let out another squawk. He released them and turned to practical matters.

'Have you brought plenty of blankets?'

'Yes, we're well supplied.'

There was a heaviness around her eyes and her normally smooth skin looked creased and pale, but then neither of them were sleeping well.

'If there was time I'd take you to Ortelius's home and show you the journey on his cartography. It's not so far really.' He frowned, envisioning the route. He'd suggested that they go to Augsburg but Will was set on Geneva. In any case, he was by no means certain where he and Bethia would end up. Florence was inviting Conversos to settle there, although he was drawn to Venice, or perhaps Ferrara.

He took his child from Bethia and held him close, rubbing his cheek against the soft skin. Samuel-Thomas opened his eyes, which were as blue as Bethia's, although Mama had said they were unlikely to stay that colour. Mainard thought of his parents on the way to Aachen, the explanation given to the authorities for the travel permissions that Papa was ill and needed to take the waters. Mainard had been surprised their application was successful, but Papa, truth be told, did look most unwell, although it was no wonder given the accusations levelled at the family by their treacherous servants.

The church bells chimed six. Will and his party had to go quickly now before the streets filled and the good burghers of Antwerp grew curious about their departure. Bethia held out her arms and he gently returned their son, glad that Samuel-Thomas was sleeping peacefully.

There was a loud knocking and he jumped. Will tugged open the front door before Mainard could prevent him. Moving forward to peer around Will's broad

5

shoulders, he caught sight of the pitted face of the leader amongst the guards he'd hired, and relaxed his shoulders.

The chests were loaded onto the waiting handcarts, Mainard checking that the padlock on each was secure as they passed. The men trundled the carts down to the small canal at the end of the street. Their shapes grew indistinct in the torchlight weaving in and out of the mist drifting off the canal. He watched, rubbing his arms vacantly, as the trunks were lifted onto the small barge from where they would be conveyed to the city gates and loaded onto carts.

Will, now dressed in cloak, bonnet, and thick scarf, set off for the stables by the southside gate. Mainard turned to find Katheline directly behind him and caught her shoulders to keep his balance. She was wrapped in her heavy cloak of fine English wool, a shawl tied over her shoulders and a further one tied over her bonnet. The knot of fear weighing down his belly grew heavier. His family shouldn't be undertaking any journey in the cold of late November, and it would only get colder as they drew closer to the mountains amongst which Geneva was said to be sited. He took his sister's face between his hands. 'Take care, Katheline... especially of Samuel-Thomas.'

'I will.' She gave him a quick one-armed hug, the other clutching a ceramic bottle of hot water to tuck beneath her feet, and hurried after Will.

The hallway felt remarkably warm. His son lay on the floor swaddled in blankets, only his buttoned-shut eyes and small nose showing. Mainard scooped him up. The eyelids fluttered open and then closed. He brought Samuel-Thomas's face close to his, could hear the soft whuff of breath.

A door banged and Bethia rushed down the passageway. 'I'll need to train Katheline in a servant's duties, for she was most remiss. She made herself a hot bottle but none for me and Samuel-Thomas.' She brushed her eyes with the back of her hand.

'You miss Grissel.'

'I do, and I still cannot believe that she betrayed us.'

'The evidence is incontrovertible.'

Bethia bundled herself in shawls, cloak, and bonnet. 'So everyone tells me, but I *know* she didn't like Coort. Certainly not at the end.'

Mainard stopped himself from saying *then where is she*? They mustn't part on a disagreement. 'Come, my love. Will and Katheline will be waiting at the gate and growing colder by the moment.'

'Is it not safer if you remain in the house?'

He knew she was right, better if she slipped away unnoticed. 'Let me at least see you as far as the city gates.'

Bethia, reaching up, draped Mainard's cloak over his shoulders, tying the tapes and tugging it up close to his neck. He felt the lump hard in his throat, couldn't swallow.

She held the front door wide and out they went, with their small son, into cold and danger.

Chapter Two

Grissel

The little light that penetrated the cellar faded. Grissel, curled up on her side, could no longer see the white of her breath. Once more she tried to rise but the spinning sensation was even worse than before. She dropped back onto the rough stone and lay still, drifting in a sinister otherworld of shadows.

Something scuttled up her leg with scratchy claws. She kicked feebly at it then whimpered. Her head hurt so much.

Why had no one found her? But Bethia was so smitten with her longed-for bairn that she could barely spare a glance for anyone, even that bonny man of hers. She wouldn't be thinking of her faithful servant Grissel, come all the way from Scotland with her. Probably hadn't even noticed her absence.

A tear leaked from Grissel's eye and she stuck her tongue out to catch it, her mouth as dry as the dust she swept up each day.

But if not Bethia, surely someone must have missed her. The potboy, where was he? He often came out to the yard and down into the cellar, fetching supplies. He'd no family and nowhere else to go... didn't even have a name.

Had Coort caught that innocent wee laddie too? A

sharpness of pain as she moved her head and, too dizzy to think, she descended into the darkness of an otherworld once more.

When she came to her senses again, a beam of light was stabbing her eyes. Her head throbbed still but the sick dizziness felt less. She crawled towards the brilliance, feeling around the cracks in the door where shafts of sun pierced. Rising slowly to her knees, she searched for the rope handle, hands patting over the wood. She snatched her hand away and sucked on her finger, the taste of blood salty on her lips. She ran her fingertips slowly across the wood once more, and then, feeling the coarse weave of the handle, tugged on it. It held fast. She staggered to her feet and leaned against it, rattling the door and shouting. But her voice was feeble and no one came.

She felt the back of her head, wincing as she probed with her fingertips. The hair was matted and clumped together. She pressed again and retched with the pain, although there was nothing in her hollow stomach to bring up. Her face felt tender too, especially around the corner of her eye where Coort first hit her. She curled her fingers in a fist. When she found Coort and his accomplice, Marisse, she would beat and beat and beat them till *they* were running with blood.

Grissel curled in on herself, tucking her hands beneath her oxters, knees up to her chest in vain search of warmth. She drifted, as though on a dark sea, then awakened to daylight once more. There must be an angle of the sun where it pierced the door and sent a shaft to illuminate a corner of this deep cellar. She huddled close to the thin beam of light, her teeth chattering uncontrollably. Surely by now Bethia must have lifted her head from the bairn and noticed that Grissel was not there to remove the soiled cloths, bring fresh water, change the linens and share a wee story or two. She once heard Bethia tell Master Mainard that *Grissel is more to me*

9

than any servant. It seemed that had all been forgot.

She lifted her face and spoke aloud. 'Well, Grissel, if nae bugger is coming tae help ye, then ye will just have tae help yerself.'

She crept around the cellar feeling carefully in front of her. There was a goodly pile of peat blocks and she crawled on top. 'A throne for Queen Grissel,' she said. Her head didn't hurt as bad, the thick haar clouding her mind slowly dissipating, but still she felt exhausted from this small effort.

Her hand rested on her shrunken belly – how many days since she last ate? She could picture Marisse, clothes straining at the seams, the stitching ready to burst. If it wasn't that Grissel knew of Coort's proclivities she'd have thought Marisse was with child instead of a greedy eater of the food left over from the master's board. Grissel licked her cracked lips thinking of the spit-roasted meats, marchpane, dates come from the Moors and the pomegranates of Spain. And she wondered again what had become of the potboy, for he was where all her troubles began – not that it was the wee laddie's fault.

When she'd first arrived in Antwerp, before she understood it was a house of secrets, she was determined to make Marisse her friend. It worked, once Grissel had some of the Dutchie language, which wasn't so very different from Scots. She remembered how they used to giggle together over nothing really: the milkcart losing a wheel and them rushing to save the churns from sliding off; a carrot grown with two legs all twisted together; the master's friend choking and the mouthful of claret dribbling into the white ruff at his neck. Yet, even in the moments when they were laughing so hard that the tears were running down their faces, Grissel knew she must be careful – Marisse thought Coort was hers. Coort, of course, thought he was his own man. And the nameless potboy only wanted someone to care for him.

Grissel watched as Coort used that smile of his,

bringing it out when it suited and then it would vanish, quick as the light from a blown-out candle, leaving heavy brows, chin thrust forward and a darkness about him. She stayed away from him then but sometimes he followed her saying cruel words. She came to understand that if Coort knew she was miserable then somehow he felt better. She knew she could be afraid of him, but she'd seen off better men, and women, than Coort. Bethia's mother for a start, sour-faced auld besom she was too.

Grissel shook with cold on her throne of turf while memories of the past two and a half years flashed across her mind. Antwerp – the size of it: busy, full and rich. The family, nae short of siller, but there was something strange about them. And that strangeness somehow leeched onto her. When she tried to make friends with a servant lassie that worked next door, smiling and talking in the best Dutch she could, the lassie sniffed and turned away even though the house she lived in was smaller than the de Langes. Grissel thought perhaps it was because she was from Scotland, but the girl was the same with Marisse. She asked Marisse about it but Marisse tossed her head in that way of hers, and Grissel was none the wiser. Eventually she uncovered that it was something to do with the family.

As time passed Grissel came to understand Dutch better, much better than Marisse or Coort realised as they blethered away in front of her. They spoke of a hidden chamber and strange prayers that Mainard's mama and sister made and Grissel decided it was best if she learnt the secrets of this home… and then one day she found the hidden room. It didn't look much with a few wee stools, a long-fringed shawl and a book with strange runes upon it and, although Grissel couldn't read, she'd seen enough of Bethia's books to know that this one was different. Was this some Devil worship that was afoot? And yet Mainard's mama was a kind woman; Grissel couldn't believe she would do anything bad.

11

And she was puzzled what Coort's intentions were with Marisse. He touched her cheek, he squeezed her waist, he pinched her fat arse, and from what she could learn he'd been doing it for years. So Grissel knew that Coort liked a wee squeeze and a flirt and a cuddle and, in the beginning, she was not averse to it either – especially when he favoured her with his smile. But she had eyes… there was never a bulge in his breeches be it her or Marisse he was cuddling. And it got her wondering. Marisse, it seemed, was wondering too… not about what was in the breeches but more thinking that Coort might choose Grissel instead of her.

Once Marisse got that fixed in her stupid head it seemed that nothing would dislodge it. Then Grissel needed eyes in the back of her own head, for Marisse became mean: sticking her foot out to trip Grissel up; nudging her so the tray of precious wine glasses smashed upon the flagstones; taking a knife to split the seams of Grissel's spare bodice. Yet Bethia blamed Grissel for the trouble, warning that she'd send her home to Scotland. Then it was as though a wee devil crept inside Grissel. She couldn't stop herself from taunting Marisse by making eyes at Coort… and he made eyes back.

Eventually, tired of Marisse's rancour, Grissel told her that Coort didn't work right. 'His pizzle is only for making water.'

She remembered Marisse's angry denial, tossing her head and marching away. Then Grissel caught Coort in the store, rubbing up against the potboy. The lad stood head hanging like there was nothing he could do to stop Coort. She gasped and Coort turned, face reddening. The boy took his chance and ran.

'You leave that wee laddie alone,' Grissel had shouted.

Coort growled back like a rabid dog and grabbed her wrist, twisting hard. He thrust his face close, his breath sour on her face. 'Stay away from me, you Scottish whore.'

'And you stay away from him.'

She hoped he'd be feart to touch the pot boy again. He was not. Grissel caught him once more as the lad bent to feed the fire, hand rubbing over the wee bum and reaching to tug down his breeks. Coort didn't see her. A skewer was lying on the board and she picked it up and prodded Coort's own arse with it, hard. He let out a groan, and it wasn't with pleasure. Turning, he rushed at her, fist swinging. She dodged the punch and stabbed him beneath the arm. He bellowed like a bull pressing his hand to his side, then charged again, but she was too rich with hot blood coursing through her to be scared. She picked up the flat iron lying to cool on the hearth and got ready to swing it.

He thrust his red face at her with thick black beard sprouting out of his chin and she wondered that she'd ever thought this ugly face bonny. 'Be watching over your shoulder, for I will get you when you least expect it.'

She stood there with the skewer in one hand and the flat iron in the other. 'I'm no feart o' you, ye wee runt. You'd better be watching yerself for I will come in the darkest hour of the night and prod this in, far as it'll go.' She jabbed the point at his face and he leant away from her.

Grissel sighed remembering all this, for Coort had caught her in the end. She stood up from her throne and swung her arms wide in a vain attempt to warm herself. She was shivering so badly she couldn't remember what it was to be still. She dropped back down onto the seat and tucked her face against her knees, her breath warming one spot on each. She knew something must've happened to the family because Bethia *would* have come to find her by now.

She crawled again to the cellar door and lay on the floor kicking at it rhythmically, like the beat of a drum. Perhaps a neighbour might come climbing over the back wall to investigate, but either the neighbours were all deaf or they didn't want to enter the yard of Conversos.

She woke up once more to the light creeping in around the door. It seemed brighter than before. Sitting up she could see the wood was cracked along the lower panel and felt a rush of hope. She kicked and kicked until a board splintered further. She could see the yard sparkling white with hoar frost in the sunshine. She reached her arm through, the jagged edges of the wood cutting into the soft flesh under her arm. Her fingertips brushed against the wooden bar which locked the door in place but, however hard she tried, she couldn't grip it. Now she truly feared she'd die in this cellar and the rats would eat her. She lay still. Then, suddenly, within her eyeline, she saw a pair of bare feet, patches of skin startlingly white through the dirt.

There was a fumbling and the door opened . She gazed up at the figure blocking the light.

'What are you doing Grissel?' said the diffident voice of the potboy.

Chapter Three

Capture

Grissel wandered through the house gnawing on the lump of bread, which was all she could find in the kitchens, hoping that it didn't break her back tooth worse than it was already broken. The house around her was heavy with silence, apart from the potboy following so closely behind she could hear his snuffly breath.

'Where have they gone?' she asked, but he didn't know.

'They left, all except the young master.'

'And where were you?'

'I was hid,' he said, and showed her his secret place, tucked under a shelf and lying on the flagstones at the back of the larder. He gazed up at her, eyes big in his thin face. 'I thought you'd left me too. I only found you cause I heard the banging.'

Grissel thought it was a pity he hadn't heard it sooner. 'Do you know where Master Mainard is?'

The lad shook his head.

Grissel went into each chamber in turn. The ashes in the grates were cold and there was a chill in the air like the fires hadn't been lit for days. No wonder no one had been to the cellar. The potboy's eyes grew bigger with each chamber they passed through, for he wasn't permitted above stairs and was such a timid lad he'd obviously never dared disobey.

They came to Mistress Bethia's chamber. It was in a great tummel: the armoire door hung open; the blankets strewn; where the kist usually sat at the bottom of the bed there was an empty space, apart from a few balls of fluff; and the cradle lay empty too.

Grissel stood before the armoire with the laddie close against her. Mainard's clothes still hung there. So it was true, he'd not left with the rest of the family. She folded the shutters back, and turning caught sight of herself in the big looking glass come from Venice. Her face was smeared with dirt, her hair hanging in great straggles from under her usually white cap, and her bodice filthy.

She sat down on the bed twisting her hands in her lap. Bethia had gone, and the bairn with her. She let herself fall back and stared at the droop of bed curtain above. The blankets had a faint scent of lavender and a much stronger smell of Mainard, which Grissel found strangely comforting. She rolled herself in them and curled up, ignoring the potboy, who stood by the bed, arms dangling. Drifting into a doze, she could hear the whisperings of Coort and Marisse as though she was following them through a long, dark, twisting tunnel.

A door banged and she sat up. Then she was running down the stairs straight into Mainard, the potboy at her heels, setting all three of them tumbling into a heap on the entranceway floor.

'Grissel!' said Mainard, once he'd disentangled himself.

'Aye, who else would it be?'

He took a step back.

Grissel knew she shouldn't be speaking to the master in such a tone but she was too angry to care. 'Where's my mistress?'

'More to the point, where have you been?' He looked behind her and then tugged on his ear. 'And where is Coort?'

'How would I ken where Coort is, the horse penis?'

Mainard's eyes grew large. 'We thought you'd run off with Coort.'

'What!' Grissel dropped onto the step of the stair behind, mouth open so wide it would catch flies, as her own mother would've said. 'Coort and Marisse hit me over the head and locked me up in the cellar out in the yard. I was there for days and days. I ken now why nae bugger came looking for me.' Yet a heaviness lifted from her to know that Bethia didn't just leave without a backward glance.

Now Mainard was gasping like a landed fish. 'But why...?'

Grissel became aware of the potboy sidling away down the passageway to the kitchen. She called him back. He crept reluctantly to her side. Mainard was waiting, head inclined to one side, but she wanted a moment to decide before speaking. Dinna let yer tongue run away with ye, Grissel. She knew what the punishment for sodomy was and little difference made between the sodomiser and their prey in meting out that punishment.

Anyway, she suddenly remembered, she'd some questions of her own that needed answering. Hands on hips, as though telling off some bairn who'd given her cheek, she said, 'Are you telling me that Mistress Bethia truly thocht I'd run off wi' Coort?'

Mainard blew the air out from between his lips, horselike. 'To be fair, my wife was most surprised. But when we couldn't find you anywhere,' he spread his hands wide, 'we didn't know what else to think.'

The potboy was tapping on Grissel's arm, unable to understand any of their exchange. She looked down at him and whispered in Dutch, 'We have to tell the master.'

The lad shook his head, tears filling his eyes.

Mainard watched them. 'Did you know that Marisse was going to make an accusation against us to the

17

aldermen? She has claimed we are secret Judaisers.'

'Wheesht! No! She didn't do such a terrible thing?'

Mainard's eyes narrowed. 'So if you do know anything that might overturn her testimony, out with it.'

Still Grissel hesitated.

'My entire family have had to flee because of the peril that Marisse has placed us in. I'm only here until I sell the property and sort out my father's business and then I'll follow. You're a servant of this house and must tell me what you know.'

Grissel's bones felt soft, as if they'd been boiling in the pot for hours and were on the verge of dissolving. 'What will happen to *me*?'

'That very much depends on whether you display loyalty to this family or not.'

The words poured out in a great jumble. 'Coort only pretends to like lassies. He was aywis at this wee laddie. I warned him to stay away, said I would tell the mistress. The last time, he had the laddie's breeks near around his ankles.' She paused for breath, watching Mainard's face anxiously.

Mainard walked across the hallway, turned and came back again.

'You are telling me that Coort is a sodomiser despite all the evidence to the contrary… all the flirting, pinching and giggling that your mistress had to speak to you about?'

Grissel nodded until it felt as though her head would spin off.

Mainard placed his hands under the potboy's chin, tilting the lad's head back. Grissel suspected it was the first time he'd ever properly looked into the boy's face.

'I didn't know you were still in the house, thought you'd left with the rest of them,' he said in Dutch.

The wee fellow shook with fear; even though he hadn't understood their previous exchange, it was clear he guessed what had been said.

Mainard patted his head. 'Don't be afraid. No one could blame you.'

Grissel let out the breath she'd been holding. 'See,' she said to the potboy in Dutch, 'the master is a good man.'

'I'm glad I've passed muster.' Mainard's face grew serious and he spoke again in English. 'You can give evidence against Coort and that should go some way to overturning what Marisse has told the aldermen.' He walked around the hallway once more. 'It all argues a case for malicious servants, but the question is, will it change anything? They may well arrest Coort for being a sodomiser and still come after our family as Crypto-Jews…' he glanced around '…the excuse to seize what we have most tempting to a debt-ridden Crown.'

Grissel touched the potboy lightly on the shoulder. 'What of him?'

'He can stay here. We don't need his evidence, yours is enough. Go and tidy yourself, and hurry. I want to get to them with this new information before they suddenly pounce on me like a cat on a bird.'

There was no hot water but Grissel scrubbed her face as best she could, dabbed her bodice, flipped her kerchief the other way round to hide the worst of the dirt and wrapped herself in her cloak. Mainard hurried outside as soon as she reappeared. Grissel lingered long enough to tell the potboy to lock the front door and not open it to anyone except them.

Master Mainard strode ahead, back straight and head held high, and Grissel scurried behind him, as a servant should. She saw a couple of women nudging one another and heard the muttered *Marrano*. It was nothing new, she was used to people turning away from her and the family but, was it her imagination, were there more whispers and backward glances than usual?

She noticed a couple of men slouching in a doorway watching the master, their leathers stained and well

19

worn, gloves on, and a glimpse of a cudgel half hidden behind a leg. As he passed they tucked in behind, so that they were between Grissel and him. She did a wee skip run to catch up so she might swerve around them and warn Mainard that he was being followed. But before she could, two other men came from the direction of the Grote Markt, their boots loud on the cobblestones. They were staring straight at Mainard; surely he would notice.

The men in front of her sped up, then all four surrounded him. He tried to push through, knocking one aside to take flight. But they were ready for him. The two behind grabbed his arms, hauling them back. Mainard kicked out but the man with the cudgel raised it; one swing and Mainard's right foot was crushed. He screamed in pain, still struggling to free himself. They stamped on his foot this time.

Grissel stood frozen, hand to mouth and stomach churning. A cart appeared and he was slung in it, the men jumping up behind.

She heard Mainard shout in English, 'Go to Shyud... Schyuds.' What was he trying to tell her, she couldn't make out the words?

The cart rumbled away. Grissel stood there for a long time, white-faced, her arms wrapped tight around herself.

Chapter Four

Floating Away

Bethia gazed across at Will, who sat hunched on the narrow seat, rubbing his lower back. Katheline next to him bent over the baby, the white kerchief around her head smudged with dirt.

She glanced up and caught Bethia staring at her. 'What?'

'I was only thinking how uncomfortable travel is.'

'Be grateful we're on the river and not on horseback,' said Will. 'At least it's quicker.'

Bethia tried to feel grateful as she shifted out of the way of a bargeman, for he was most verminous.

The captain was shouting to hold steady, for they were coming to a bridge. Another boat was making its way towards them, both barges keeping to the centre of the river. The captain had said the water was unusually low after little rain this winter so far and large sandbanks were constantly appearing in odd places. They drew close to the pillars of the wooden bridge, both barges determinedly keeping to the centre.

Ahead the river was no longer dark and smooth but had become tossed and white like there was a restless spirit below. The closer they drew, the angrier the spirit became. Bethia felt the timbers beneath her jolting as the water banged against them. Then water was forcing its

21

way in, swilling around her feet and soaking them. The captain was still roaring and swearing at the other boat to give way, but both barges held to their course.

'It's our right of way,' called Will, who was on his feet, sore back forgotten. 'We're the ones rowing against the current.' He too leant out, shouting at the other barge.

Their boat rocked violently and Will staggered, narrowly avoiding falling overboard. Bethia clung to the side, looking over to Katheline, whose face was as white as the rushing water, Samuel-Thomas held tight in her arms. Bethia dropped to her knees and crawled across the deck to reach her bairn but Will was in her way. He seized the inflated pigs' bladders from beneath the seat and tied one to each side of the wicker basket they used as a crib with a length of rope. Will held out his arms and Katheline handed the baby over. Will slid him under the rope bindings and tucked him into the crib. Bethia crept forward and sat at the other side of the basket holding it as steady as she could while being thrown around in the turbulence as though she was riding a bucking horse. Katheline too was now sitting on the deck and the women gripped the crib between them while Will made his way up the boat towards the captain.

Then they were beneath the bridge and the barges jostled and thumped against one another. The other captain was shouting that he had precedence because he had important passengers. Bethia saw one, richly dressed with long white plumes in his cap.

'Shame on you,' Will shouted back. 'We have a baby here and women too.'

The man covered his face, only the eyes showing, as they passed – as well he should.

The water grew calmer as they rounded the bend. Suddenly the boat came to an abrupt halt, lurching onto its side with such violence that they were all sliding towards the river. Bethia was dashed against the side and the crib was torn from her grasp. She screamed as the boat thumped further on its side and the crib flew through the air. Then she knew nothing until she came round to find Katheline's anxious face wavering before her eyes. She struggled to sit up.

The captain was shouting at the sailors who were running hither and thither and their guards were dealing with a kist which had broken free of its ropes and slid across the deck. All was confusion.

She rolled onto her hands and knees and rose dizzily to her feet. Katheline supported her arm, while gazing anxiously out into the river.

'Where's my baby?'

'Don't worry. Will has gone after him.'

Bethia looked out to see her wee lamb floating away in his wicker basket like Moses set adrift on the Nile, the swiftly flowing water carrying him back in the direction they'd come. Will, holding onto another of the inflated pig's bladders, and one of the guards swimming clumsily, chased the crib, but the gap was widening. Bethia screamed and went to climb over the side of the boat. Katheline grabbed her around the waist and hung on.

'Let me go, let me go,' shrieked Bethia, tearing at Katheline's hands.

'You can't swim,' panted Katheline.

Bethia fought Katheline, keening and weeping, pleading and gouging at Katheline's restraining hands, but Katheline did not slacken her grip. Leaning forward, Bethia strained with every part of her being to draw her wee lamb back to her.

The crib disappeared from sight around the bend in the river. Will and the guard followed – the guard's swimming becoming clumsier, arms flailing, with each stroke. All the air went out of Bethia, and after a few moments Katheline gently lowered her to the seat and sucked at the scratches Bethia had clawed across her hands.

Bethia rocked back and forth muttering, 'Mary Mother of Jesus save and keep him. God in Heaven watch over him.'

Her rocking slowed and she looked to her left. The riverbank wasn't far. Perhaps it wasn't so deep here, where they were stuck. She slipped off her cloak. The captain called out, telling them to get away from the lee side. Katheline moved and, freed from her restraining presence, Bethia scrambled over the side. She gasped in relief; the water rose only to her knees, her feet sinking into soft sand. She made for the bank, some distance away, each step a fight to break free from the suckering sand.

There was a shriek from above. 'Come back. Please come back. You'll drown and Mainard will never forgive me.'

Bethia kept going, but called back, 'Don't worry. It's quite shallow here.'

She heard a thump and looked over her shoulder to find Katheline's legs swung over the side, ready to drop into the river.

'Stay there. You can't swim.'

'Nor can you.'

Bethia screamed at the top of her voice. 'I am telling you to *stay there*.' She didn't wait to see if Katheline obeyed, didn't need this distraction. It must be near a quarter of an hour since her baby floated away.

The water was up to Bethia's thighs now. It was freezing but she disregarded it. Please Blessed Mary, let it not get any deeper. The water rose. It was at her waist, her skirts swirling around her. The riverbank, which had appeared close when the water was only up to her knees, now seemed very far away.

She could feel the tug of the current. She moved slowly, each step tentative as the river tugged, inviting her to its murky depths. The water cut across her chest now, like a band of steel. She was shivering so much she could hear the chatter of her own teeth. The water was at her collar tickling under her chin. Be brave, Bethia. Must go on… or drown.

She took one small step and then another. She was not imaging it, the Virgin had answered her prayer and it was growing steadily shallower. Move slowly… don't fall now… nearly there. There was a big stone in the water; she stood on it, wobbling. Behind her a sailor shouted encouragement. Katheline was screaming. Why didn't they keep quiet, she needed to concentrate.

Gathering her floating skirts in one hand, she managed to get a knee up on a dip in the bank and clambered out. She stood staring along the curve of the river for any sign of Will returning; nothing, apart from a heron gazing at her. She ran, the wet skirts wrapping themselves around her legs to trip her up; she fell, picked herself up again, couldn't breathe, kept going.

The river was wide and empty; where had all the boats moving goods and people gone? It felt as though she was the last person left in the world. She ran and ran, her breathe white in the chill air. The feeble sun dropped behind the trees lining the other bank. Bethia narrowed her eyes to scan ahead. Soon it would be dark.

Chapter Five

The Wee Lamb

Bethia glanced behind her. Another barge appeared, ghostly in the fading light. She shouted and waved. The passengers stared and the sailors waved back. The barge glided past and out of sight. She tripped and fell again, face down in the cold mud. She scrambled to her feet and staggered on, shivering uncontrollably.

Another bend in the river, a crowd gathered at the riverbank. Couldn't see what they were looking at. Please Blessed Virgin, please Blessed Virgin. She reached the group and pushed through. They stood, arms folded, muttering. What were they saying... something about *Moses in the Bullrushes.*

And there he was, her wee lamb, swaddled and white-faced, lying motionless in his straw crib amid the reeds, while the villagers muttered and crossed themselves.

Bethia leapt off the bank, not caring about the depth of the water, and splashed towards him. The cradle rocked in the ripples she was causing, and freed from the rushes began to float away. She lunged for it but each time she came near her movements sent the crib further on its way. Then suddenly one of the women was in the water – and shouting at her neighbours to close their mouths and help too. Quickly they fenced the crib in, although still it swirled out of the grasp of reaching hands.

'Stop!' shrieked Bethia, fearful they'd tip Samuel-Thomas into the river.

'Move slowly,' commanded her assistant.

They closed the circle around the baby, creeping towards him. The crib was caught, her baby could no longer float away. She lifted him into her arms. Two villagers, one on each side, steadied her. They moved as one to the riverbank. Her assistant clambered out first, reaching her arms for Bethia to pass the bairn up. Bethia held him tighter. Why was he so white and still?

The others clambered out, speaking at once, pleading with her to give them the baby. She could not let him go. But then she shivered and shivered, could barely grip him she was shaking so much; better to give him up than drop him. She passed the baby up and was herself pulled from in front and pushed from behind until she was sprawled on the bank.

They helped her to her feet, guiding her to the nearest cottage, where the men were chased away. Two women stripped her, rubbing her with a rough blanket, while another fed the fire and a fourth worked to warm Samuel-Thomas by massaging his wee limbs.

He gave a cry as weak as a newborn kitten, not the lusty sound he usually made, and Bethia wept in return. They wrapped the blankets around her, sat her on a stool, and passed him to her.

She held him against her skin, beneath the blanket. He felt as chill as ice and she rubbed him with frozen fingers. He wriggled and then latched on, sucking lethargically – but at least he was feeding. Bethia's head drooped. She was so very tired. She jerked upright… her brother, where was he? Must let him know Samuel-Thomas was safe.

Bethia pleaded with the curious villagers to find Will, explaining in quick bursts, impatient when they did not understand her Scots-accented French. She went to rise but her saviour pressed her hands down on Bethia's shoulders, insisting she wait and they would send out a search party.

'But it's dark,' Bethia wailed, and Samuel-Thomas began to cry in return.

'We'll take torches.' The woman stroked Bethia's face.

Bethia mumbled a silent prayer begging God to listen to her but she knew that she'd been given one miracle that day; would the Lord's great benevolence grant her a second?

She was left with the kindly householder, who brought her a bowl of broth. Bethia shook her head, could not eat while Will was lost and alone on the river. The woman insisted and fed her spoonful by spoonful while her bairn, growing warmer by the moment, insistently suckled. She brought Bethia's clothes, still damp but warmed from hanging by the fire.

'Better you are dressed with all the men around.'

The woman tied Bethia's skirt and laced her bodice – Bethia's fingers still too stiff to manage it herself.

There was a great noise outside and three villagers came in, with the captain of the barge following. He looked relieved to find her alive – and surprised when he glimpsed a rosy Samuel-Thomas.

'My brother?'

He shook his head. 'We've not found him yet. It's dangerous to travel in the dark, for we cannot see sandbanks or strong currents.'

Journeying by daylight didn't stop them getting caught on a sandbank, thought Bethia.

'I must warn you it's not hopeful.'

Bethia swallowed back the tears. 'Where's my good sister?'

The captain looked puzzled. 'Do you mean your servant?'

'Yes, yes, of course.'

She wanted to stay with the boat and search for your brother but I will send her to you.'

Bethia nodded. Katheline and Will were friendly but she hadn't realised Katheline was fond of him… so fond that she would keep to the boat… cannot think of that now. All that mattered was his safe return.

Katheline appeared soon after, ducking her head to enter. She pulled up a stool and sat down as close as she could to Bethia. And Katheline, who avoided touching anyone, apart from the bairn, wrapped her arm around Bethia, burying her face in Bethia's shoulder.

'I thought you were dead.' She lifted her head and gazed on Samuel-Thomas. 'And the wee lamb… he's unhurt.'

'Seems so. He's been feeding constantly since we were reunited.'

'God works in wondrous ways and does great, unsearchable and marvellous things without number.'

Bethia smiled softly. 'And the Virgin, I was praying to her the whole time.'

Katheline withdrew her arm and Bethia cursed herself. She'd spoiled the first real moment of unity with Katheline. Her head drooped, so tired. She didn't have the strength to deal with this now. All that mattered was Will be brought back safely.

She came awake with a start. By the darkness of the cottage, and the sound and smell of sleeping bodies all around, she must've been asleep for some time. She gazed down at her feet and saw Katheline there curled around Samuel-Thomas.

Rising slowly, she stepped carefully over the inert lumps around her, finding her way by the dim glow from the embers of the fire. There was a grunt when she knocked against someone with the corner of the door but then she was outside beneath the stars.

Chapter Six

Premonition

Bethia took a deep breath of cold air and gazed up at the sky above. She didn't think she'd ever seen as many stars twinkling so brightly before, and her so small beneath them. How could the Lord attend to her prayers for Will when there was such a vastness for him to oversee?

And it was as still as the dead standing beneath this sky. She shivered, afraid to look behind her in case the spectres were there… waiting. 'Begone ghosts,' she said, her voice loud in the stillness. She clenched her fists, fingernails digging into her palms, and somehow that steadied her.

She set off in what she hoped was the right direction for the river, and then it was before her: deep water moving darkly. She followed the path which shadowed it, the leaves from an overhanging branch whipping her face, then she tripped and was sent staggering. She found the broken branch and picked it up. It felt solid in her hands.

There was a dark shape ahead. She froze, then realised it was a barge moored alongside the bank. Indeed it was their barge, for she recognised the limply hanging pennant above the cabin. There was no sign of life; where was the watch? They should be guarding the many kists – the de Lange family wealth. Were they all out searching for her brother – or asleep? In a sudden fit of rage she took her stick and beat the side of the boat, wood banging against wood, shouting, 'Get up, get up.'

She turned and found herself looking down the long end of a matchlock. So there was a guard. Then her arms were pinned tight to her side from behind.

'Let me go, you fool.'

She was released with a suddenness that sent her stumbling.

'Where's the captain?'

'Out searching the riverbanks. It was better to go on foot. We found Lapin.'

'Alive?' But she knew the answer before she asked.

She steeled herself to ask about Will but the dark shape spoke. 'We haven't found your brother. There's still hope.'

The curve of the sky lightened, turning to a blue-green where it touched the horizon. She must return to the cottage soon, for Samuel-Thomas would awaken hungry, but she was determined to at least go a little further along the path. She walked fast, swinging her arms and wishing she'd thought to fetch her thick cloak from the barge. There was a mist sitting across the water and she watched as a boat glided through. She waved, opening her mouth to shout and ask if they'd seen anything, but there was no need. It turned towards the riverside where she stood beside a clump of reeds. She could see the men on board as it drew near, one among them head and shoulders above the others with a mop of yellow-red hair. She sank to her knees and gave thanks to the Blessed Virgin.

Will's face was grim when he leapt off and stood before her. He raised her to her feet and wrapped his arms around her. She couldn't ever remember her brother hugging her.

He let go and wouldn't meet her eyes. 'I am so sorry, Bethia. I couldn't find him.'

She squeezed his arm. 'But I did. He's safe and warm and with Katheline.'

Will let out a great shout.

Then she became aware of movement as another man jumped off, coming to stand next to Will.

'It is good news?' he said, looking from one to the other.

'The best,' said Will grinning. 'My nephew, it seems, has been safe with his mother while we searched. But let me introduce you. Bethia, this is my new, and very kind, friend Monsieur de Vaudemont, who, like the good Samaritan, turned aside from his own journey to render assistance to a fellow traveller in his hour of need.'

De Vaudemont bowed and Bethia curtsied deeply. She became aware that de Vaudemont was studying her and raised her hand to smooth the hair which had fallen out from beneath her cap, knowing she must present a tawdry sight: mud-smudged and dishevelled.

Will bowed to de Vaudemont. 'I thank you most truly for your assistance – I would've died in the water without it.'

'I did no more than anyone had they seen a fellow traveller in peril. But I must meet this young *voyou* before I depart.'

Will inclined his head. 'Lead on, Bethia.'

Samuel-Thomas was making his displeasure known when they reached the cottage. Bethia retreated to a corner to feed him while the men went outside. By the time she emerged all had been agreed. They were to journey together.

'For there is safety in numbers,' said de Vaudemont.

Bethia looked to Will, who was grinning down at the smaller man. She would've appreciated an opportunity to discuss it first in private. De Vaudemont was well-dressed, courtly of manner and had rescued Will, yet they knew nothing of him. But she was soon reassured. De Vaudemont was all concern for her well-being, even suggesting they join him on his barge, which was less crowded. Will demurred, saying they would stay with their possessions.

'Perhaps I may relieve you of some of your baggage then.'

Bethia looked startled and Will's smile faded. 'Best not.'

De Vaudemont took a step forward, anxious-faced, and spoke directly to Will. 'You have misunderstood. I'm only trying to make the journey with women and a small child more comfortable by creating space in what is a most cramped situation with a mountain of chests.'

Will's face cleared. 'That's most considerate of you and I thank you for your kind offer.'

Bethia tried to smile but somehow it wouldn't come. How did de Vaudemont know they had lots of kists when he and Will couldn't have been to the barge yet?

De Vaudemont hesitated. 'Of course, you may not be overfull of baggage, but since you're travelling with women, as well as a child, I should imagine it was unavoidable.'

This was said jocularly and Will responded with a laugh, clapping him on the shoulder. 'You have assessed the situation perfectly.'

She followed them back into the cottage and felt reassured when de Vaudemont picked up Samuel-Thomas and held him aloft, saying what a fine fellow he was. And soon they set off, both barges side by side. Indeed, as the journey continued, he regularly joined them on their barge claiming the company was more convivial.

'You allow your servant great familiarity,' he said one day, watching Katheline rebuke Will for tossing his cloak where she was about to sit.

Bethia thought of Grissel and her mighty spirit. She missed her, still couldn't believe it was Grissel who betrayed them. 'Our servants are part of the family,' she

33

said as Katheline covered her mouth to hide a giggle at Will's riposte.

De Vaudemont raised his eyebrows.

The days passed and Bethia had a strange, and growing, sense of foreboding. She chided herself – after all, de Vaudemont had saved Will. And yes, he had a predatory way of looking upon her but that was not unusual. Men often thought of women as their playthings; it was nothing she couldn't deal with. Yet the foreboding would not leave her.

Then de Vaudemont was suggesting that they could not reach Geneva safely in the winter months. He had an alternative plan to propose which perhaps he and Will might discuss.

Bethia's heart sank.

'We're not far from Lyon and you would do well to spend the rest of the winter there rather than trying, with a small child, to travel through mountains and snow.' He bowed. 'It would be an honour if you would stay with me. I'm lonely in my big house since my wife passed.'

Will looked to Bethia. 'My sister and I thank you for your kind offer. Please allow us time to consider.'

De Vaudemont nodded and moved away, although Bethia could feel him watching.

'Is it not dangerous for you to stay in the heartland of France so soon after your imprisonment in the galleys?' she whispered to Will.

'I served my time and was released. In any case, the chance of coming across anyone who knows me in Lyon is unlikely. And Scotland and France are, after all, allies.'

'I still don't feel easy about stopping there.'

But when they began to pass through countryside where snow lay and more fell that night, Bethia knew Will was right. They should rest in Lyon. De Vaudemont insisted they at least come to his home for the first few days. It was likely to be at least a month before they could move on, added Will, and so Bethia reluctantly demurred. She felt some reassurance when they arrived at de Vaudemont's home and were greeted by a trim, neatly dressed housekeeper and shown to a clean chamber.

Bethia slept that first night in Lyon curled around her baby, as ever. His small fingers gripped onto the long strands of her hair as though to tether himself to her. In the middle of the night she awakened to find Katheline patting her face and calling her name. She shook her head still caught up in the tangles of an evil dream. Then she sat bolt upright as though hauled by invisible strings and Samuel-Thomas let out a cry at the disturbance.

Bethia scrambled out of bed and ran around the chamber seeking her clothes in the dim light from the banked fire. Katheline slid out the bed too, leaving the baby tucked in its centre.

She caught Bethia's arm. 'What are you doing? Come back to bed and sleep while you can.'

'No, no. We must go back.'

'Go back! What are you talking about? Of course we can't go back – ever.'

'Mainard, it's Mainard. Something terrible has happened. I can feel it here.' Bethia crossed both hands over her heart and pressed hard. Finally she could name the gnawing dread, which was becoming a constant. She paced up and down while Katheline watched, arms dangling helplessly.

'It's only a bad dream.'

Bethia shook her head.

Katheline went to stand in front of her, and took hold of her arms, eyes wide. 'Bethia, my brother is a resourceful man and not without friends. And sister Geertruyt is in Antwerp. She, and more importantly her husband, will help should Mainard get into difficulties. Anyway, he most probably has left by now.'

'But why have we not heard from him? I've written to him so many times. And Geertruyt too – not a word from her.'

'Be sensible, Bethia, how would they know where to direct a letter?'

After a moment Bethia nodded – although she didn't feel any calmer, only wanted Katheline to let go and stop staring into her eyes. They both climbed back into bed. Katheline turned on her side facing away from Bethia and the bairn but Bethia lay on her back, hands resting on her chest, the sense of dread heavy. She *knew* something bad had happened to Mainard.

Chapter Seven

Het Steen

They took Mainard so quick he'd no opportunity to seek help or even resist. One moment he was striding along with a cleaned-up Grissel newly escaped from her own prison hell trotting behind, and the next he felt hands grab him and before he could react there was a cudgel swinging and he fell. Then they picked him up and flung him into a cart.

He bit on the back of his hand to stop himself screaming at the pain of his foot, had never imagined such agony. Please God, let Grissel have understood she was to go to the Schyuders for help. Will she even realise that these were no common ruffians but men sent by the alderman? He shouted before the sack was tugged over his head, stinking of the vomit and fear of its previous user, and suffocating as it sucked into his mouth. Even if she'd not heard surely that would be the logical thing to do – to go to his older sister's and seek help. Was he placing too much reliance on a servant? Bethia often said that Grissel had a spirit as mighty as the Valkyries yet it was not her spirit that mattered here but her powers of reasoning. Anyway, he could not think of his wife in this moment, the fear that somehow they got to her too rising up to choke him.

He came to, had no idea how long he'd been

insensible or what had happened. Most probably fainted from the pain in his foot. Slowly he pushed himself up, the stone floor, rough and gritty beneath his palms, and sat with his back resting against the equally rough wall. There was one window set high up in this narrow cell, the criss-cross of thick bars framing a hint of blue sky, but no sunlight could penetrate so deep. Yet it was as well that the light was dim, too dim to see the damage done to his foot... he could barely think for the twisting, stabbing, throbbing, burning pain of it.

He must have been taken to the Het Steen; didn't understand why he was being held in the depths of this castle prison. When his sister's husband was arrested he was kept in comfort in the upper quarters and Geertruyt was permitted to visit every day, bringing food and comfort. He prayed Grissel understood his shouts and Schyuder would come soon to render him assistance. He rubbed his eyes, hard. With Bethia and his parents gone, who else would intercede for him if Geertruyt and her husband did not.

Mainard had fallen into a restless sleep when they came for him.

'Why am I being subjected to such ill treatment?' he said, somehow keeping his voice strong.

But it made no difference. They dragged him out, foot scraping agonisingly along the rough stones, groans muffled by the rag they'd stuffed in his mouth. In the windowless dungeon yellow-red light leapt up the walls, illuminating the chains which hung from them. Branding irons were laid before the fire in the corner and the rack stood waiting in the centre. He tried not to look. Could not control the shaking.

They stripped him naked, tied him to the rack and examined his member, flicking it back and forward with their fingers.

'It looks to be untouched,' said one.

'That means nothing,' said the other. 'It's one of their

tricks to pretend they are true Christians. But this one is a relapser, a Marrano, a Crypto-Jew.' He leaned close, his breath foul in a mouth of rotting teeth, and whispered in Mainard's ear, 'The eyes leak fear.'

Mainard tried not to flinch but could not still the rapid blinking. The good Lord bless and keep me, Christ Jesus watch over me, he said to himself over and over, the Latin running behind his eyes as though, by conjuring it up, he might call down Christ to save him.

'Nothing to say for yourself, eh?' His tormentor poked at Mainard's broken foot.

Mainard's groan of agony was muffled by the gag. The fellow, watching him intently, leaned his elbow into Mainard's foot, slowly increasing the pressure.

The pain was white hot. Mainard writhed like a terrified snake. Oh Lord God Almighty, please help him… he'd always lived as a true Christian. Why had God abandoned him? He was cursed by his Jewish ancestry.

His tormentor suddenly whisked the gag out of Mainard's mouth. Mainard took a great gulp of air, then another, running his tongue around his dry lips.

The fellow spoke over his shoulder to his accomplice. 'This one thinks he's a fine fellow, with his great height and pretty face, although… ' he leant close and sniffed, 'there's a smell of Jew about him. And the look too. Where shall we start, at the head or the feet or anywhere in between?' He disappeared from Mainard's restricted view and reappeared brandishing tongs, snapping the jaws open and shut.

The terror rose up from Mainard's belly to choke him. His eyes felt like they would burst from his face.

'He has a goodly set of teeth. Let's begin with them.'

'Leave off, Zwijgers. You shouldn't be touching him till the Inquisitor gets here.'

Zwijgers withdrew, giving Mainard's broken foot a pat as he passed. The dungeon fell silent apart from the crackle of the fire, which burned ever brighter. Mainard mumbled to himself, 'I am a true follower of Christ and the Holy Father in Rome. I attend Mass, I go to confession, my son was baptised.' He wanted to howl with the unfairness of it all.

Zwijgers, clearly growing bored as they waited, was soon back leaning over him so that Mainard could see the dirt ingrained in the pockmarks which peppered the man's face. He closed his eyes and his tormentor stabbed one lid with a stubby finger, pressing down hard on the eyeball.

He jumped: a banging on the door. The pressure on his eyeball was released and he blinked rapidly. Zwijgers went to open it.

'What do you bastards think you're about? Since when did you become the hand of the Inquisition? Untie this man at once and get him out of here.'

There was sudden activity around Mainard and the ropes digging deep into his flesh were released. He sat up, knocking Zwijgers' hand away when he tried to assist.

'God's bones. Get something to cover him with,' bellowed his rescuer.

But Mainard only wanted out. He made it to the opposite wall before his strength deserted him. Zwijgers and his partner half carried, half dragged him down the passageway. He let out a guttural howl and then knew no more.

When he came to, he found himself clothed and high up in the Het Steen. It was of significance that they'd now incarcerated him in a chamber that could be considered comfortable, but of grave concern that he was a prisoner still. They were not done with him yet.

Chapter Eight

Johannes

Grissel was bargaining with a stallholder over the price of a scrawny chicken when she caught a glimpse of them. Since it was January the choice of wares was not great and she was loth to abandon her hen to the fat woman waiting to pounce, but what else could she do? Mainard would want her to follow them even if it did mean the meal she took to the prison for him would be sparse on meat and overfull of kale. In any case, she was by no means certain the guards were delivering his food. She had no funds to bribe them, only the few coins she'd discovered in Mainard's chamber, and she needed those to buy food for the potboy and herself, as well as Mainard.

She made her decision, gripped her basket tight, picked up her skirt and ran, swerving around a gossiping group of servants and tripping over a bucket of mussels. The mussel seller roared, grabbing at her shoulder. Grissel swung her basket at him and he tumbled over the fallen bucket, thick leaves of kale showering down upon him.

Grissel stumbled, clutching at the edge of a stall where a basin of lamprey was resting. The board tipped and the basin went sliding onto the cobbles, followed by the large and very ugly head of carp presiding over it. The eels untangled themselves, squirming away through the heap of fish guts under the stall, while people scattered shrieking. Grissel, legs moving faster than she knew she was capable of, left the market square followed by the cries, shouts and shaken fists of half the people in it.

She turned the corner into the fleshers market, slid on a patch of ice, pink with frozen blood, yet somehow kept her balance as parts of the dissected goat swinging from hooks above hit her full in the face. Up and down the alleys that led off the square she searched, but Marisse and Coort had disappeared. She sighed. If she could but have alerted the authorities to their whereabouts and they were arrested and questioned then perhaps it would be enough to secure Mainard's release. Eventually she gave up and retreated to the de Lange home. The potboy appeared the moment she entered the house, as though he'd stood by the door since she left.

'You didn't know it was me,' she chided him. 'I told you, you must stay hid. No one should know you're still here else they may insist you go before the scary men. And they'll put you in prison, or worse.'

The potboy hung his head. 'I'm sorry, mistress.'

Grissel straightened up. She liked being called *mistress*, however unlikely it was that she would ever be one. She surveyed what was left in her basket: a turnip, and a few leaves of kale slopping around in broken eggs – although remarkably one had survived intact. It would have to be a potage, and at least the dough had risen beside the fire which the lad had kept stoked. He stood, arms dangling, darting eyes watching her every move.

'What's your name?' she asked.

He looked puzzled. 'I'm Potboy.'

'That's what you do, not who you are.'

'I've always been Potboy.'

'You have no mother or father?'

He shook his head.

'Then we must give you a name.'

His worried wee face lit up.

'But what shall it be?' Grissel remembered another

small boy in faraway Scotland, a wild one whose spirit was never broken despite regular thrashings from his father. Perhaps naming the potboy after Bethia's cheeky wee brother might infuse this laddie with some of the same boldness. 'John,' she said. I shall name you John. He was one of Jesus's disciples, you know.'

'John,' said the potboy hesitantly as though his tongue didn't fit around the foreign sounding name. 'Johannes,' he mumbled. 'Johannes,' he said with stronger voice. 'I am Johannes.' He ran around the long board which dominated the kitchen shouting, 'I am Johannes,' over and over, while Grissel stood, arms akimbo, laughing.

But she wasn't laughing the next day.

They came before the sun had risen on a dreary January morning. Grissel had been up for some time, the habit of rising early to tend to the fire, get the water heating and the first meal of the day prepared too ingrained to allow her to lie on her pallet.

She'd taken to sleeping in the warm kitchen rather than the chill of the attics since there was no one there to prevent her. Johannes too had crept into the warmth from his usual lair. He drew close when the banging on the front door was heard echoing down the passageway.

Grissel bent down, gripping him by the arm and speaking in her fractured Dutch. 'Go and hide in your usual place. Do *not* come out for any reason. I will come for you once it's safe.'

She let go and the laddie scuttled away. The banging came again, louder and longer. Grissel crouched behind the front door, hoping she would hear voices and get some idea of who it was before she opened up. She didn't know why she was crouching, they couldn't see her, but it felt safer. The heavy door shook in its frame, sounding as though it was being hit with a cudgel. She drew the bolts with shaking fingers and struggled to turn the key.

There were four men on the doorstep and one waved a paper in front of her face. 'We've come to search the house and impound the goods of the Marranos who live here.'

He reached out his hand to knock Grissel out of the way but she stepped to one side and he stumbled over the doorstep, narrowly avoiding falling flat on his face. He raised his hand, but before he could slap her for her impudence, the other men filed in.

'Search the house. The alderman wants any ledgers or documents in particular. We're to make an inventory of all valuables and furniture. Any pilfering and I'll have you locked up in Het Steen, and it won't be in a comfortable chamber like the Crypto-Jew who lives here is occupying either.'

Grissel retreated to the kitchen. There was nothing she could do to stop them, and in any case, Mainard had told her all the ledgers went with Master de Lange. The kists that Will didn't take, Mainard had stored elsewhere.

She could hear the sound of their boots heavy on the boards, then the screeching of something scraped over the polished floors. Surely they weren't stealing the chairs and beds? She edged towards the door and then thought better of it. She was only one woman, however strong. She pressed her hands together and brought to mind her mother back in Scotland. It steadied her. She could hide with Johannes but that devil's spawn from the doorstep would most probably come searching for her and find him too; she would not expose the wee lad to any further abuse.

Instead, she busied herself around the kitchen preparing what little food there was. It was one way to control the rising fear. The knife slipped as she cut into the turnip and she narrowly avoided slicing her finger. She put the knife carefully to one side.

The kitchen door was thrust open and the Devil's spawn strutted in. Grissel, at the other end of the board, resisted backing away. She looked to the knife, couldn't get to it before him. She folded her arms and glared. She knew his kind and how they responded to weakness; must not show any.

'There's nothing worth taking in here.'

He snorted. 'Said by a rich man's servant. That pot alone is worth a considerable sum.'

Grissel glanced at the iron pot hanging over the fire. 'Take it, if you will.' And she hoped he would – and burn his hands in the trying.

The man moved around the board closer to her and she couldn't help but take a step back. 'You have a most strange way of speaking?'

'I'm frae Scotland, ye horse penis,' said Grissel, in Scots. The flat iron was within reach and she took hold of it, under cover of the board. Then in Dutch she said, 'And how well can *you* speak English?'

She edged away from him, staring into his face as she went. He was young with curly yellow hair, pale blue eyes, good skin and most of his teeth. He should have no need to force any woman, indeed was likely to be fighting them off. Why was he advancing on her with that sinister smile? He lunged but Grissel stepped back, twisting to avoid his grasp.

'Ah, so you want to play. But you may as well lie down and part your legs now, for I will have you.'

He lunged again as he spoke and Grissel swung her arm, the flat iron in her hand. But she tripped over the stool and the iron connected with his shoulder instead of the side of his head where she was aiming.

'Ahhh, you evil witch.' He rubbed his shoulder. Then grinned at her with such expectation of pleasure that, although she held the flat iron ready to hit him again, she couldn't help but shiver.

'So this is how you want it. I like a fight. It makes the enjoyment that much greater.'

She must control the trembling and let him near

enough, so she could at least hit him one more time. Hold strong, Grissel. He lunged. She swung her arm as hard as she could… but he was ready for her, catching her wrist in an iron grip. The flat iron clattered to the floor and she'd lost any advantage she had.

He hauled her towards him, twisting her arm cruelly. There was no escape. She heard herself, mewling like a newborn kitten before it's drowned. No pity shown to it, and none to her. He had her close now and reached out, tearing at her bodice. She punched him with her free hand, as hard as she could, full in the face. Her hand exploded with pain. Suddenly she found herself falling backwards, the crack of her head hitting the floor loud in her ears.

He crumpled on top of her, forcing all the air out of her body: a dead weight and she couldn't breathe. Frantically she wriggled to escape – the terror of being crushed much greater now than the fear of rape. A face appeared over his shoulder, and a hand holding the rolling pin.

'Get him off me,' she panted, as she pushed and squirmed.

She was trapped between the board and the wall. Couldn't breathe, couldn't get out, would suffocate beneath this beast. She was near to passing out when she felt the pressure on her chest release.

Johannes was tugging his legs and Grissel pushed. Then, between them, she was free. She scrambled to her feet and stared down at this foul creature, sprawled face down on the floor.

'How did you reach his head?' she asked Johannes.

'Stood on the stool.'

'Thank you.'

Johannes crept close to her. 'What are we going to do with him?'

Chapter Nine

Ortelius

Johannes looked up at Grissel and she placed her arm around his shoulders. He stood stiffly, holding his body away from her. Then after a moment he leant in and she held him tighter. She doubted this laddie had ever had a hug in his life. The only touch would be a clout for some wrongdoing or Coort's attentions, and she didn't want to think about that.

'Is he dead?' Johannes said in a small voice.

'Unfortunately not. It'll take more than a dunt on the head to kill that creature.'

'What are we to do?'

Grissel dropped her arm and bit her lip. 'Go back to your hiding place.'

Johannes stayed where he was, shifting from one leg to the other.

'Go,' said Grissel, giving him a light push on the back.

'But you'll need my help to move him. I can take one leg and you the other and we'll drag him.'

'Where? And even if there was somewhere to easily hide him, his fellows will want to know why he's disappeared. You go and hide *now*.'

Johannes went reluctantly. It felt good to have an ally, however small.

She gazed down at the fellow and gave him a kick on

the leg. He groaned.

'Wake up, you fool.'

His eyes flickered and he moaned louder.

Grissel ran to the kitchen door. 'Help, someone help,' she called. She tried to sound concerned rather than afraid.

The three men came thundering down the stairs. 'What's up, lass?' said the greybeard. He had a surprisingly kindly face for an officer of the courts.

'Your leader has fainted.'

Greybeard raised his eyebrows. They all went into the kitchen and stared down at the bastard who'd rolled onto his hands and knees. The other two men helped him onto a stool. He sat with his head in his hands. Grissel moved around the board out of his line of sight.

'What happened to you?' asked greybeard, who'd lingered by the door.

'I don't know,' he muttered, rolling his head back and forward between his hands.

'There's blood on the back of your head,' greybeard said, stepping forward and touching it none too gently.

'Get off.' Her attacker shook his head and then whimpered.

'I think we must go to the surgeon.' Greybeard winked at Grissel. 'He'll have your head off and then you'll feel much better.'

The bastard kicked out and then had to grab the board to prevent toppling off the stool.

'Calm down. You're only hurting yourself. Take his arms,' greybeard said to the other two.

They heaved him onto his feet. He knocked their arms away and walked unsteadily to the door. Holding onto it he turned and glared at Grissel. 'I don't know what you did, you bitch, but I'll be back.'

'Keep your doors locked,' greybeard muttered to Grissel as he followed them out of the kitchen. 'And find a stout fellow to stand guard at night.'

Grissel nodded but was thinking *and where shall I find funds to pay this stout fellow... and will I be any safer with him?*

They left pushing a handcart loaded with chairs, saying they'd be back soon. She barred the front door behind them and sat down on a stool in the kitchen, head in her hands. 'Think, Grissel, think. What are you to do?'

Mainard's sister and her husband, the Schyuders, were no longer in Antwerp, so far as she could ascertain. She'd gone to their house many times since Mainard was taken. It was all boarded up, and however often she returned that didn't change. They'd gone.

She stood up and fetched the remaining coins from their hiding place behind the loose stone at the side of the fireplace. Laying them on the board, she spread them out, but it didn't make their number any greater. There was only a small bag of flour left; that wouldn't last long. She rubbed her eye sockets with the palms of her hands, hard.

A memory came of once following Mistress Bethia as she in turn secretly trailed Mainard to a house of pillared doors in the Kloosterstraat. The door was opened by a pretty, young woman and Bethia had sunk to the cobbles convinced that Mainard had a secret lover. But then Mainard took Bethia to the house to show her the work he was engaged in with the yellow-hair's brother. Drawings it was; she saw one once: most strange. Bethia said it was important work... but it looked like a mess of scribbles to Grissel. What was it called, one of those Latin words, *carto* or *cosmo* or some such thing? She wished she knew the fellow's name, had only seen him briefly once and was not certain even what he looked like, but she did know his house. Perhaps he might be prevailed upon to help his friend. She would go there and watch and wait for him.

That night, whenever she closed her eyes, she came

49

awake again feeling the weight of her attacker on her once more. Next morning the greybeard appeared, with one man only this time, saying she must leave. The house was impounded in the name of Mary of Hungary, Governor of the Low Countries.

'We should have returned yestereve but I thought you needed time to recover from your ordeal,' he said, patting her on the shoulder.

Grissel brushed away the tears with the back of her hand, not used to any demonstration of care, and this from a man she didn't know.

'Do you have somewhere safe to go *mijn meisje?*'

Grissel swallowed and nodded, hoped it was so.

'Good. For unfortunately I cannot take you home. We've too many mouths to feed already and…' he said with a great bark of laughter, '… I don't think the wife would like it.'

Grissel looked at the man's honest open face and wished he was her father. She gathered her possessions into a small bundle, shrouded herself in the worn, but thick, cloak which once belonged to Bethia, took Johannes by the hand, and left. She would linger as close as she could to the house of the man who made the strange drawings and watch for him.

It was fortunate she didn't know how many days she'd be waiting before she caught a glimpse of Mainard's friend. The first night snow fell, light as flour through a sieve. The moon rose and all around them the ground sparkled with diamond dust. Grissel was eternally grateful for Bethia's old cloak, which she wrapped around both her and Johannes as they huddled in a doorway. But the watch soon moved them on.

Johannes led the way, whispering that he would take her to where he once lived, which turned out to a be an alcove in the city walls near the harbour gate. But Johannes's spot was long taken by a girl who snarled at them, ferocious as a stray dog, and they backed away.

'There is another place, but it's not so good,' said Johannes.

Grissel wondered what could be worse than a small indentation in a wall, with no roof. It turned out that the overhang at the back of an inn's stables, where the ordure was shovelled out, was indeed worse – although it was remarkable the heat emanating from the midden. Grissel decided that, on balance, she could manage to tolerate the stench, for the warmth. And if they sifted the muck there were some slops and bones to be found to eat. Yet when a second night outdoors came around she decided against the dungheap. Earlier in the day she'd given up waiting and knocked on the door of Mainard's friend's house. The yellow-haired girl answered but refused to listen to Grissel's story, wrinkled her nose and slammed the door in their faces. The stench of the privy obviously clung to them and Grissel would not risk offending further.

She went to the prison. They'd permitted her to bring food in the past; perhaps they would allow her to speak with Mainard.

She stood before a guard. 'I must speak with my master,' she said, forcing herself to stand steady, for another guard had wandered around behind her. He was so close she could feel his breath on the back of her neck and smell it too.

The guard facing her folded his arms. 'Entry could be arranged.' He waited.

'I have no funds with me. I could bring them later. Please.'

The guard behind ran his finger along the back of her neck. She hunched her shoulders but held her ground, staring pleadingly at the man before her.

'For a suitable payment we will let you in,' whispered the guard behind in her ear.

She turned, flapping her hands to ward him off. Both guards roared with laughter as she scurried away. She was not that desperate, not yet.

They were very hungry that night but, thanks be to the Virgin, found a pie dropped by a drunk man as he wavered away down the street, reaching it before any other beggar, or the rats. The next day, just as she was despairing, she saw Mainard's friend: long of face, high of forehead and stooped of walk, as though he was carrying a burden upon his shoulders.

He looked startled when she thrust herself in front of him and sidestepped her ready to walk on.

'Please,' she cried. 'It's Master Mainard. They've taken him prisoner. He's being held in the castle. Please can you help him?'

He stopped then and bent his head, listening most earnestly as the terrifying tale of Mainard's capture poured from her.

'I will go to him immediately,' he promised in his raspy voice.

Grissel shifted from one foot to the other. 'Please, master, they've impounded the house,' she glanced at Johannes standing huddled next to her, 'and we have nowhere to go and no food. Would you have need of a hard-working servant and potboy in your kitchen?'

He hesitated. She clasped her hands together and forced herself to fix her gaze on the ground. Most masters did *not* care to have a servant bold enough to look them directly in the eye. Johannes huddled next to her was, of course, meek enough for anyone.

She waited.

'Very well,' he said, brusquely.

He led the way across the street, and before she knew it, she and Johannes were installed in his kitchen, while the yellow-hair, who it turned out was called Mistress Elizabeth, huffed her complaints.

Grissel was called before the man the next day, whose name she finally discovered was Master Abram Ortelius. He had deep shadows under his eyes and Grissel doubted he was sleeping any better than she.

'I think they've decided de Lange is a relapser whatever evidence we may bring to the contrary. Charles of Hapsburg and his sister need funds, and what easier way to acquire them than impounding the possessions of Conversos,' he said.

Grissel blinked at Master Ortelius's manner of speaking to her, almost as though she wasn't a servant. She thought on what he said, had never understood the 'fuffle about Jews and Catholics and Protestants. When you were poor your only hope, and prayer, was a safe place to sleep and a warm meal once a day – as she'd most recently had ample evidence of. And whichever faith would give Grissel that was the one she'd stick with, tight as a small child to its mother's skirts – which was increasingly what Johannes was doing to her. He seemed to think of *her* as his saviour. It felt good to know there was one person in this world who depended on her, and would also watch out for her in return.

But for now she waited for Master Ortelius to hatch a plan to free Mainard, hoping that her trust in him was not misplaced.

Part Two

Lyon

February to March 1550

Chapter Ten

A Sick Child

Samuel-Thomas coughed all night. His wee body contorted, face red and swollen as he choked and fought for breath, choked and fought for breath. Bethia walked up and down the chamber holding him upright – she didn't know what else to do. And Katheline's normally serene expression was replaced by a wrinkled brow and bitten lips.

The constant feeling of dread, which had lain in the pit of Bethia's stomach while they travelled to Lyon, now filled her whole body with fluttering panic. But she'd got it wrong, it was not Mainard but Samuel-Thomas she needed to fear for. Her baby was sick and she couldn't help him.

The endless night was finally over and the early morning light crept beneath the shutters. Was it her imagination or was his breathing easier? She laid him in the bed, covering him lightly while she and Katheline stood together watching, hardly daring to breath themselves.

But soon the coughing started again. Bethia picked him up while Katheline slipped out. She returned quickly with a sleepy-eyed Will, his breeches pulled on over his nightshirt, tousled hair standing on end. His face grew fearful when he saw, and heard, Samuel-Thomas.

'I'll fetch a physician.'

Bethia muttered, 'Please' as she curled around her bairn once more.

Will was gone for what seemed like an eternity, eventually returning with a small, wizened man who carried a large pottery jar. The physician looked at the baby. 'Undress the child.'

With shaking hands she stripped her bairn, pausing each time he was engulfed by another coughing fit.

The physician stared down at him, laid naked upon the bed, and grunted. Then he dipped his hand in the pot and extracted a leech, pinching it between finger and thumb, dried blood caked in the creases of his fingers and under his nails, no doubt from previous patients. He lifted Samuel-Thomas's wee arm and placed the thick black leech in the smooth, pink-skinned and perfect hollow of her baby's armpit.

Katheline took Bethia's hand and they watched in silence. Samuel-Thomas's eyelids fluttered and he fell asleep. Bethia let go of the breath she was holding.

He slept for a while but soon was awake and coughing more than ever. The physician returned and again applied his leech – 'Only one is sufficient for the child is very young,' he said in response to Will's inquiry.

When he returned a third time and went for the same remedy it was Katheline who stopped him. 'Have you nothing else in your armoury?'

Bethia heard Will's intake of breath at Katheline's abruptness – and to a man of standing who had a diploma in medicine.

Katheline pointed at Samuel-Thomas. His skin was now grey, the healthy pink all gone. 'How is taking more of what little blood he has helping?'

Bethia gathered her heart's blood into her arms and nothing either Will nor the physician had to say about cooling the humours would persuade her to release him.

The physician, having made sure his bill was settled,

departed in high dudgeon. Bethia sat on the bed holding her gasping child while Katheline and Will watched helplessly and the housekeeper, Madame Dupont, hovered anxiously in the background.

Will rubbed his hand over his face, saying, 'I will find de Vaudemont and see if he knows of another, better physician.'

Bethia wondered that they hadn't seen de Vaudemont. He was usually with them constantly, but then it was his house, and he could come and go as he pleased. She'd wanted to remove to an inn but de Vaudemont had prevailed, saying that they, and their goods, would be much better protected in his home. And so, the guards, who'd travelled all the way from Antwerp with them, were dismissed.

'No point in paying them to sit around,' said de Vaudemont, 'and you can easily hire replacements when you're ready to travel onwards. Indeed, I have solid fellows I can recommend.'

Bethia felt much less protected and had wondered at Will, but his head seemed turned by all the attention that de Vaudemont bestowed upon him.

Katheline offered to take Samuel-Thomas into the parlour so that Bethia might get some rest. She shook her head, would not leave her baby – not for a moment. Only the strength of her will was binding him to her. How could she bear it if anything should happen and she not there – and how would she ever explain it to Mainard?

'It seems there is a physician famous for his success in treating victims of the plague,' said Will when he reappeared. 'De Vaudemont tells that this man lives in the south of France but is visiting Lyon at present.'

Bethia didn't care where the physician normally lived, only that he could be brought as soon as possible. Any man who could cure the plague must surely have some skills that would help a baby consumed by fever and slowly choking to death.

'Get him… quickly,' she pleaded.

A rosy-cheeked man, plump of face with a freshly combed beard and large eyes was brought. He studied Samuel-Thomas and shook his head when Bethia went to remove the baby's clothes.

'Leave them on, for I can tell all from the cough.' He pursed his lips as Samuel-Thomas hacked weakly. 'I need a bowl of water, hot as you can make it.'

Katheline hurried from the room. She returned with a servant by her side and Madame Dupont anxiously following. The servant carefully carried a large bowl of steaming water on a tray which the physician directed her to place on the washstand. He took a handful of dried herbs from a pouch and tossed them in the bowl. The stuffy chamber filled with the strong smell of lavender and an underlying scent that Bethia couldn't place. The smell was not only refreshing but somehow brought hope.

'Give me your baby,' he said softly.

Bethia passed her child to him reluctantly. The physician held the baby, face down, over the bowl, and Samuel-Thomas coughed and spluttered. Just when Bethia was about to snatch him away, convinced the cure would be his death, the physician returned him.

Leaving the pouch of herbs, he departed, saying, 'Do as I did when the coughing is bad.' He rested his hand on her arm. 'Your son is very sick but I'm not without hope.'

Her eyes filled with tears.

'Open the windows regularly,' the physician said from the doorway.

'Will that not allow the noxious air in?' asked Katheline in her calm voice, only her flickering eyelids betraying her.

'It's more important to let the noxious air within the chamber out.

'We will do it,' said Bethia.

'I'll come again tomorrow. Don't despair… your child has survived thus far.'

'What's his name?' asked Katheline as the door closed

behind the squat figure.

'I can't remember, Nostro something,' said Will. 'De Vaudemont will know.'

Samuel-Thomas had fallen asleep on Bethia's shoulder, his breathing noisy in her ear. 'Can you find out, please. He seems a kindly man, and I'd like to greet him properly on his return.'

Will nodded and disappeared. Bethia suspected he was glad of an excuse to escape the sickroom.

He soon returned. 'Michel de Nostradame is his name, although de Vaudemont says that he prefers the Latinised version – Nostradamus. De Vaudemont says that Nostradamus's first wife and two children perished of the plague and he has never quite got over it. He also has a reputation as something of a soothsayer.'

Bethia, and Katheline, stared at Will.

'You mean he can foretell what will happen?' said Katheline. 'Sounds like witchcraft to me.' She stood arms akimbo. 'What are you doing bringing such a man here? Are we not in enough peril already? And if he couldn't save his own family... I do *not* think we should follow his strictures about open windows.'

'Wheesht,' said Bethia, 'else you'll waken Samuel-Thomas.' She looked to Will. 'Desperate times call for desperate measures. I'm glad you brought him, risk of heresy for witchcraft or no.'

But it seemed Nostradamus had already been wanted by the authorities, or so de Vaudemont told Will in Katheline's hearing – and with much relish Katheline said, when she later recounted his words to Bethia.

Bethia, bending over her baby, who was sleeping more comfortably – or was it her imagination – after two more bouts of steaming, was not much interested, but Katheline continued regardless.

'De Vaudemont says it's rumoured that Nostradamus's grandparents were Jews. He is the descendant of Conversos, like us.'

There was a note of triumph in Katheline's voice but Bethia couldn't see what there was to be triumphant about. Nostradamus's grandparents were likely true converts whereas Katheline and her mama had secretly continued to practise Judaism. She grew hot with anger again at her sister-in-law but it soon faded. There were many reasons why they'd had to leave Antwerp, and Katheline's relapsing was only one among them.

'There is a story de Vaudemont recounted where Nostradamus was heard to say that the expression on the face of a statue of St Paul looked more like he had the belly thraw than was having his moment of revelation.'

'Truly? Those were his words?'

Katheline sniffed, looking annoyed to have her story questioned. 'Whatever his exact words were, there is no doubt he was ordered by the Inquisition to come and answer for them. Instead, he took to his heels.'

'Much as we have done.' Bethia felt a strong affinity with the man.

'He travelled in Italy for several years and only returned when he considered it safe to do so.

'He has the look of a Jew, I think,' said de Vaudemont, standing in the doorway. Bethia started, and wondered how long he'd lingered there, listening. Had he heard Katheline admit she was a Converso?

'His nose is so long it nearly touches his lip. And why must he visit again when it seems the child is recovering?'

Bethia ignored him, leaving Will, who'd appeared at de Vaudemont's shoulder, to respond. 'My nephew is most precious and we must be assured that he'll suffer no long-term damage from what was a most serious ailment.'

'I do not like that man,' she told Will, once de Vaudemont had gone, bowing and smirking, out into the streets of Lyon. 'I'd prefer to have our own lodgings.'

'We're vulnerable at any inn. Often the innkeepers are in cahoots with thieves and will pass on information about wealthy travellers. It's safer here, as I've said to you many times.'

'I pray you are right,' said Bethia.

Nostradamus returned yet again to check on Samuel-Thomas's well-being, which endeared Bethia to him even more. She asked him about his cures.

'Although it's not much lauded, I consider circulation of the air within a chamber of benefit in healing the sick,' he said in a voice which was surprisingly thin and reedy for such a squat, broad-shouldered man. 'And an infusion of rose hips is most efficacious. I would recommend it for you as well, since you're nursing the child.'

'Where would I find such a thing at this time of year?'

'I can provide it. I was once an apothecary.' A smile lit his face. 'Although that had me expelled from the study of medicine by the good bursars of the university at Montpellier. Never fear,' he said as Bethia frowned. 'I did finish the course elsewhere and am entitled to latinise my name.'

Bethia asked more about his remedies and Nostradamus replied, adding, 'If you want to understand the powders and infusions available, and more of my approach, then I'll happily bring you a copy of the translation I did of the works of Galen.'

Bethia smiled, pleased that as a woman she was being treated seriously by this learned man – and that he'd taken it for granted she could read. 'My husband frequently quoted Galen's works. I would be happy to peruse them.'

Samuel-Thomas grew stronger every day, although the feeling of dread remained heavy in the pit of her stomach. She was sending letters constantly to Mainard and still they'd not heard from him, even though he now had a settled address to direct any replies to.

She applied to Will. 'I know de Vaudemont said we must rely on bribing royal messengers for the transport of mail but surely at least one letter would have reached Mainard by now.'

'He will already have left Antwerp.'

'I've also directed several letters to his father in Aachen. At least one must've got through.'

'Mainard no doubt departed very soon after us. They're probably long gone from Aachen too.'

'But what if he reaches Geneva and finds we're not there.'

'Calm yourself, dear sister. He'll not reach Geneva any quicker than we – he too has snow and mountains in his way.'

She walked up and down wringing her hands. 'I think we should return to Antwerp now Samuel-Thomas is well enough to travel. I *know* something bad has happened to Mainard.'

Will took her hand and gently squeezed it. 'Your husband has tasked me with getting you and his son – and indeed his sister – to safety. I must not fail him, Bethia. And our father too is relying upon me.' He'd hunched over her protectively as he spoke; now he straightened his shoulders and stood tall. 'Think of the journey we've had to get here. Would you really want to turn around and retrace our steps, when we're so close?'

'Yes,' she said impulsively, but she knew it was unwise, even as the words left her lips. It was true the Blessed Virgin had watched over them, but her benevolence couldn't be limitless. And if anything more, or worse, should happen to Samuel-Thomas because she insisted on turning around, then how would she ever face Mainard?

Will looked down into her face and echoed what she was thinking. 'Mainard would be most unhappy were we to return.'

Bethia bowed her head in acceptance. Will patted her on the shoulder but it was of little comfort.

A thought came to her and she lifted her head. Perhaps Nostradamus might be persuaded to apply his soothsaying to her situation.

Chapter Eleven

Soothsayer

The weather grew colder day by day and Bethia was grateful for the large fires, rich provender and kindly housekeeper in this comfortable home. She wondered why de Vaudemont had not remarried.

'He and his wife live apart,' said the housekeeper when Bethia brought the conversation around to de Vaudemont's domestic arrangements. Bethia was certain that he'd told them his wife was dead, but Madame Dupont pursed her lips, as though to prevent any further words escaping them, when Bethia raised this.

Bethia studied de Vaudemont over the next few days but could see no obvious reason why his wife might have left. He was well-groomed enough with his smoothed black hair and tidy black beard flecked with white. But always he was watching, and she doubted much missed those darting eyes. And why was he being so friendly to them anyway? It was all very strange.

She applied to Will, who said, 'De Vaudemont lost his son to measles five years ago. He's only a kind man who wants to help.'

Bethia wondered if the son was another falsehood, like the dead wife, but Will looked weary and she let it go. The wee lamb's illness had put a strain on him almost as much as her, and Madame Dupont was so eminently

65

respectable it reassured her. Surely such a good woman would not work for a bad man.

She forgot de Vaudemont. Samuel-Thomas was in Katheline's capable care and Nostradamus had come. Ostensibly they were to discuss what she'd learned from reading his translation of Galen, and she did have questions, but she was eager to ask him about the sense of dread she carried within and what it might mean.

'How is the baby?' he asked as she guided him into the salon.

She turned, smiling, and found herself looking straight into his eyes, for he was no taller than she. 'I hardly dare say the words aloud in case the Devil hears me.'

'He is much better then.'

'Thank God.'

A servant appeared with refreshments and Bethia waited to speak until after they were served. She shifted in her high-backed chair, made again uncomfortable by the generosity with which de Vaudemont was treating them. It was almost as though she was the lady of the house and not a, previously unknown, visitor.

'And what did you think of Galen?'

'It was helpful to read more of how to restore the body's balance, and I hadn't understood how much writing he did. You say he authored almost three hundred texts.'

'Yes, he was prodigious, but then he lived to a very old age: past eighty when he died.' Nostradamus stretched his foot out and grimaced. 'We should all hope for such a long and productive life.'

'Your foot pains you?' She realised she was staring at him with raised eyebrows.

Nevertheless, Nostradamus echoed her thoughts. '*Medice, cura te ipsum*. But, unfortunately this physician has been unable, so far, to heal himself... I have yet to land upon a successful remedy for gout. Galen had much

66

to say upon the matter and little in the way of cure. We all have a cross to bear and this is mine.' He leaned forward. 'And what is yours, little Mistress Bethia, for I sense there is something that greatly troubles you still, even though your son looks to have made a full recovery?'

Bethia knocked twice on the wooden arm of her chair to ward away any evil spirits who might, having heard Nostradamus's words, carry away Samuel-Thomas. 'Yet still I carry a deep sense of disquiet here.' She patted her chest.

Nostradamus was silent, watching her intently.

'I fear for my husband. He stayed behind in Antwerp…' She stuttered to a halt, not wanting to reveal too much. 'There was family business to attend to.'

'And you sense all is not well with him.'

He stroked his long nose and she waited for him to speak. Instead, he came to stand before her and held out his hands. Hardly knowing what she was doing, she placed her hands in his outstretched ones. He held them loosely, staring down into her eyes as he rubbed his fingers across her knuckles. He let go, resuming his seat, and nose stroking.

'I can feel your agitation and may be able to assist. Are you willing to come to the inn where I reside, alone and at night?'

She hesitated but her instinct was to trust him. 'I am,' she said slowly. She was shaking, didn't know whether it was from terror or excitement.

Nostradamus said that the spirit only came in the depth of night and she should not set out till after the midnight bells had rung. Then he left. The day waned and darkness came early on this damp late-winter evening. Bethia, aware that Katheline was watching her as she moved restlessly around the chamber in the glow from the firelight, could not settle. She knew if she told Katheline what she was about to do then Katheline would tell Will – and he would insist on accompanying her, or more likely forbid it. She'd wait until Katheline fell asleep, slip out of bed and go... but what of Samuel-Thomas should he awake and need her?

But it was her bairn that soothed his mother rather than the other way around. He nursed, smacking his lips when he took a break, then fell asleep at the breast. She gently eased him into the bed, next to a snoring Katheline, and stood gazing down at the perfect curve of his closed eyelids and the pout of his rosebud mouth. But she must go, if she was to do this. He did sleep for longer at night now and, unless she was most unlucky, should not awaken until around five bells.

She slipped on her cloak and picked up the staff that Mainard had made for her, long ago, and taught her how to use. Creeping out into the blackness of the upper hall, she felt her way carefully down the stairs. There was a faint light shining beneath the front door and she could see the key was not in the lock. She lifted the latch but the door stood firm. She stood, uncertain, resisting the urge to bang on it with her fists. She'd have to find a way out through the kitchens, although one of the servants was likely sleeping across the back door.

Instead, she went into the chamber where they dined, shutting the door softly behind her. The shutters were closed tight and she stood on the window seat to open them. Leaning out, she saw the alleyway below; the mud looked ankle deep from the heavy rain today. She could climb down easily enough but doubted she could pull herself back in again on her return. She sat down on the seat.

The door opened slowly and the housekeeper's face appeared, in her nightcap, clutching a poker in one hand and a candle in the other. 'My dear child, what *are* you doing?'

Bethia's shoulders relaxed. Impulsively she rose and went to stand before Madame Dupont. 'You must help me, please.'

'Is it the baby?'

'No. No, he's well. It's my husband. I fear for him.'

'Yesss,' said Madame Dupont slowly, eyebrows raised. 'But he is far away – or so I understand.'

Bethia bit on her lower lip. 'Nostradamus may be able to give me news of him, but I must go now for it to work.'

'I would've thought that writing to your husband might be more productive than any visions, however convinced that man is about what he's seeing.'

'I *have* written and written. There's been no reply, and I'm afraid, very afraid.'

The housekeeper looked into Bethia's eyes. 'Very well, but only if I come with you.'

Bethia reached out and gripped her hand. 'Thank you.'

Nostradamus had said to come alone, but if the housekeeper stayed below, what should it matter? And she *must* see him.

'Wait for me here while I dress.'

Bethia retreated to the window and climbed up on the seat to close the shutters tightly against thieves, vagabonds and the night air. She had a moment of doubt and went to try the door which the housekeeper had closed behind her. It opened – what would be the point in locking her in anyway when she could climb out the window.

Madame Dupont quickly returned, key in one hand and a sheathed knife in the other.

'It belongs to the master,' she answered in response to Bethia's inquiring glance. 'Put it in your pocket. I have my own.'

'Lyon is a dangerous city?'

'No more than any other for two women walking through its dark streets after curfew. Are you sure you want to do this?'

Bethia, who'd faltered at Madame Dupont's words, felt a steeliness enter her soul. 'I am.'

The streets were so quiet it was as though all life had departed. The two women locked arms as much to support one another from slipping and falling in the muck as for protection. It began to rain again, making it even more unlikely that any except vagrants would be abroad, but added to the discomfort. Bethia was especially glad she had the housekeeper to guide her, for she was uncertain where Nostradamus was staying.

She knocked on the door of the inn and knocked again. Then suddenly it was flung wide.

'You're late.' Nostradamus, holding a candle high, looked to Madame Dupont. 'Who is this? I told you to come alone.'

'Don't be so foolish,' said the housekeeper. 'No young woman should be wandering these streets without protection, especially in the depth of the night.'

He grunted but stood aside, closing the door and then pushing past them in the narrow passageway. 'You can wait in there.' He waved his hand at a doorway then continued upstairs, turning when he was halfway up. 'Hurry up, if you're coming,' he said to Bethia, who was hesitating at the bottom of the stairs.

She went to give her staff to Madame Dupont then changed her mind and held it tight. This was not the kindly man, all concern about her son, who talked to her most earnestly about Galen's work. There was an angry intensity about him that she found most disquieting, and she was by no means certain that she wanted to be alone with him.

They were in his chamber now and he directed her to a stool in the corner. She laid the staff on the floor beside her.

'You must face away from me and cover yourself with your cloak, even your head, when I tell you.'

He bustled around the fire, lifted a steaming pot from it, and placed it on the hearth. 'I do not know if it can work, for I don't have my special stool made of brass to sit upon,' he muttered. Then he looked up, surprised to find Bethia still watching him. 'Turn away now, you must not look. Perhaps it were better that you were not here but then how am I to feel that which troubles you?'

Bethia, now shrouded under her cloak, felt the sweat bead her forehead and pool under her arms and in her cleavage. She sat for what felt a very long time. The weight of the cloak was suffocating, her heart was fluttering, and she could barely breathe. Just when she thought she must fling it off, the stuffiness was replaced by an unfamiliar, and most pungent, scent. Her breathing slowed, head drooping.

The smell was dissipating… how long had she been here… hoped Samuel-Thomas was still asleep. Her body responded to her thoughts, breasts tingling, and then a dampness. How much longer must she sit beneath this cloak, and what was Nostradamus doing?

Through the weave the light in the chamber grew brighter as the fire flared. Then she felt the strangest sensation, as though a heavy weight was pressing down on her from above. She gasped. It was crushing her. She waved her arms to ward it away. There was nothing there, but the pressure grew. She screamed, fell back off the stool, and her head banged off the floor.

Chapter Twelve

Attacked

When Bethia opened her eyes, Nostradamus was standing over her.

He reached down and helped her to her feet. 'You have a powerful energy and the spirit was much attracted to you. I've never seen such a thing before. Usually I must be in solitude… and secret.'

'I feel most peculiar.'

'And did the spirit speak?'

'There was no spirit, only this heaviness crushing me. What does *that* mean?'

'I don't know. I must think on it.'

He walked away from her and stared into the fire.

Bethia gathered up her cloak. 'Can you tell me anything?'

'I'll send you a message when I've had time to consider what this vision means.'

She bent to pick up her staff and left the chamber slowly.

Madame Dupont was waiting at the bottom of the stairs. 'I was about to come in search of you. You've been a long time.'

'It doesn't feel that long.'

'The fifth bell has rung.'

'Samuel-Thomas is likely awake and hungry. We

must hurry.'

Out they went into the street, Bethia running ahead and Madame Dupont calling to her to slow down. She allowed the housekeeper to catch up, suddenly conscious that they were both vulnerable and she shouldn't leave her trailing behind. She gripped her staff tighter, the wood reassuring in her hand.

'What happened?'

'It was most peculiar; I cannot quite comprehend it.'

'Could he tell you anything of your husband.'

'No, I am to come back tomorrow.'

'Huh! A charlatan then.'

'I don't know. Perhaps.'

Before she could speak further, Bethia found herself falling. She landed face down in the mud, the staff trapped beneath her, and felt the weight of a foot on her back. She cried out. The foot moved, pressing her face down… she couldn't breathe. Then she was as suddenly released, and lifted her head, gasping for air. She turned her head to see Madame Dupont pinned to the ground next to her.

'We'll have your money – and those fine clothes too,' a high voice said close to Bethia's ear in colloquial French.

Her hand was squashed beside her pocket. She nodded as though in acceptance, rolling onto her side as she slid the knife from its sheath. She got up, keeping it hidden in the folds of her skirt.

There were two of them, small and scrawny in their rags, the lower half of their faces masked.

'Take off your clothes, quickly,' said the slightly taller.

'How can I when you're holding my arms?' said Madame Dupont.

Bethia admired the calmness in her voice. The lad released her. Now both she and the housekeeper had their hands free – and were armed with knives, while their assailants, as far as she could ascertain, had only the stout sticks they were holding.

The moon appeared from behind a cloud and briefly cast some light on the dark street. Bethia saw Madame Dupont staring at her. The housekeeper inclined her head but Bethia was strangely reluctant to attack these two skinny waifs.

'You're only girls,' she said thickly.

'Do as we say.' Both raised their sticks threateningly.

Madame Dupont showed the dagger in her hand. It glinted in the moonlight.

Bethia showed hers too but spoke calmly. 'You'll be hungry. Come home with us and we'll feed you.'

'What are you saying? Have you lost your wits?' cried the housekeeper.

The girls moved closer, waving their makeshift clubs – which were little more than twisted branches from a tree. Madame Dupont thrust the dagger towards them in little darts, which made it plain she'd never used one before.

'Stop!' Bethia shouted.

Everyone ignored her. But she'd alerted the watch, who appeared suddenly behind the girls.

'Help! Help!' shrieked Madame Dupont.

One of the girls fled, but the other, not so quick, was grabbed around the neck by the brawny watch who towered over her.

'What's going on here?' he said to the women, as he slowly throttled his captive.

'We were attacked,' said Madame Dupont.

'I can see that. But what are *you* doing out during curfew?'

'She can't breathe,' said Bethia.

'You would have me let your assailant go?'

'Just don't hold her around the neck.'

The man took a grip of the girl's arm with the other meaty hand and released her neck. She took in great gulps of air.

'Bring her to our house,' said Bethia, 'and we'll

reward you for her capture.'

The watch didn't argue and followed as the two women led the way. Madame Dupont held Bethia's arm, leaning in close. 'That was quick thinking to say you'd reward him, but we cannot bring this thief into my master's home.'

Bethia knew the housekeeper was right but she felt a strong determination to at least give her attacker a meal. The desperation in the girl's voice had not been lost on her. She thought of Grissel run off with Coort and hoped Grissel was not being forced to resort to equally desperate measures.

They reached home and Madame Dupont unlocked the front door but told the constable and his prisoner to go around to the back. Bethia followed them. She felt oddly protective of their captive. The kitchen lad was standing sleepily by his pallet, which had been moved aside from the back door. The housekeeper bid the watch sit down at the board and, delving in the cupboard, brought him bread and cheese. The girl's eyes darted around the kitchen. Bethia doubted she'd ever been in such a well-appointed house – perhaps in a house at all.

'Here,' she said, passing a hunk of bread to the child. Seen clearly in the firelight she was young, dirty-faced and, what little clothing she had, ragged.

The girl held the bread tightly in her fist but didn't eat.

'Go on,' said Bethia.

The child shook her head. 'What are you going to do with me?' Her fear was greater than her hunger, it seemed.

'I will take you away to the gaol,' mumbled the watch, crumbs falling from a bread-stuffed mouth.

The child looked to Bethia. 'My sister has no one, please help us.'

'Don't listen to her nonsense. If you did a job such as

mine you'd have heard it all before. If I let her go they'll be back out thieving by tomorrow night.'

The girl said nothing, eyes fixed on Bethia.

'We'll keep her here with us.' She stared at the child. 'Would you like to train as my servant?' She could see Madame Dupont out of the corner of her eye, hands crossed over her stomach and the hard disapproving line of her lips, but the housekeeper remained silent.

The child nodded slowly but then swallowed. 'But...'

Bethia shook her head imperceptibly and the child fell silent. She passed a few coins to the watch, who noisily drained the trencher of ale the kitchen lad had brought him, wiped his mouth with the back of his hand and rose to depart.

Pausing by the back door, he turned and looked to Bethia. 'I hope you know what you're about and will not live to regret such benefice.'

I hope so too, thought Bethia, as the door closed behind him.

'You may fetch your sister,' she said to the girl.

'You will do no such thing. Are you mad?' said Madame Dupont, staring at Bethia.

Bethia raised her hand and kept her eyes on the girl. 'I have a small child and work enough for both of you. Are you prepared to travel – to leave France?'

'If you feed us well.'

Madame Dupont snorted.

'Of course you'll be fed.'

'And pay us too.'

Bethia raised her eyebrows at the child's audacity. 'If you work hard and obey me.'

'I'll work hard, I promise.'

'Wait until it's light and curfew over, then go and find your sister. You may sit at the board and eat and this lad will let you out when it's time.'

The kitchen boy looked to Madame Dupont, who sighed but nodded.

Bethia left the kitchen, anxious that Samuel-Thomas would be in need of her.

'Have you taken leave of your senses?' demanded Madame Dupont, following her into the hallway with a candle.

'I hope not,' said Bethia with a rueful smile.

'I must tell the master. We cannot have waifs, strays and thieves living within his house without his knowledge or permission.'

Bethia reached out and touched her arm lightly. 'You are quite right. What I've done is most improper, especially when he has been so hospitable. But let me tell him, or, more correctly, ask him. I would not have you placed in an awkward position – and I won't mention you were with me when I was attacked.'

The housekeeper looking relieved, passed Bethia the candle, and retreated to the kitchen saying, 'I dare not leave that child unsupervised else who knows what she'll steal.'

Chapter Thirteen

The Girls

De Vaudemont was from home when Bethia eventually arose. She'd crawled, chilled and shivering, into the warm bed, and fallen asleep while Samuel-Thomas suckled contentedly, only waking once it was full light on this grey winter morn, and Katheline long up. She dressed and wrapped Samuel-Thomas tightly in her shawl, tying it around her so the baby was held close and calm, and her arms were free.

Will stood, arms folded, in the hallway staring at her while she descended the narrow stairs. 'How could you be so daft?'

She saw Madame Dupont whisk away and chewed on her lip. But she wasn't going to be told off by someone whose actions had him spend nineteen months as a galley slave.

'What did the housekeeper say?'

'That you've given employ to some waif off the street to be a nurse to Samuel-Thomas.' He stared at her. 'Why, what else are you hiding?'

Bethia could feel the colour flood her face.

His eyes narrowed. 'What have you done?'

She tossed her head. For a moment she nearly confided that she'd met with Nostradamus last night – would like to talk it over with him, but suspected all she would get was a scold rather than a discussion.

'What are you smiling at?'

'Nothing,' she said, sliding her arm through his. 'Come, let's go and see if the new nursemaid has returned with her sister.'

'What! You've taken in more than one stray? We cannot impose on de Vaudemont further. He's been more than generous.'

'I know,' said Bethia. 'And yet I do not understand why he is *quite* so generous.'

Will sighed. 'Not this again, Bethia, please. Why should it be anything more than he is a good Christian.'

'He's always watching. Every time I turn around he's there... watching. Sometimes it feels as though I'm back in Antwerp among the watchers and whisperers, eyes on me wherever I go.'

Will, towering above her, placed his arm around her shoulders. 'Don't worry, wee sister. I'll take good care of you.' He tilted his head. 'And if I don't, I'll have your husband to answer to, not to mention our father.'

The front door opened and de Vaudemont slid through it, almost as though he was trying to catch someone out. Will and she stepped away from one another.

'All well here?' he said, rubbing his hands together.

Will looked to Bethia, who stifled a sigh. He was clearly not going to help.

'I hope you'll have no objection but I've employed a servant to assist me in caring for my son.'

De Vaudemont smile faded. 'My servants are not helpful to you? Let me call my housekeeper and make it clear that you must be given every assistance.'

'No, please,' said Bethia, touching his arm. 'Madame Dupont has been kindness itself. But we cannot impose on your hospitality further and I must train up a servant for when we depart.'

A smile crept across de Vaudemont's face as he looked at her hand resting on his arm. Bethia gazed upon it too.

It had a disembodied look as though it didn't belong to her; the fingers soft and white – signalling a wealthy woman, albeit with dirt still under the nails from when she was face down in the mud last night.

'You must not consider leaving until spring is fully here,' said de Vaudemont, patting Bethia on the arm where the sleeve of her dress fell away exposing bare skin.

She slid her hand away, clenching and unclenching her fingers. 'You are too kind,' she said, eyes downward.

A hand was placed under her chin, tilting her face to look up. She saw Will out of the corner of her eye, raising his own arm to swipe de Vaudemont's away. But it was Samuel-Thomas who created the diversion, letting out a roar of complaint and giving Bethia reason to murmur she must tend to him.

Katheline was on the stairs watching. She turned and followed Bethia back into their chamber. 'I do not like that man.'

'Nor I.' Bethia undid her shawl and handed Katheline the baby. 'Take care of him while I go and see to my newest responsibilities.'

'What have you done now?' hissed Katheline.

'I'll tell you all later.'

The kitchen lad had both sisters before the fire and was regaling them with a long tale. Madame Dupont appeared, knife in hand, and chased him back to his duties. 'Time for a clean-up,' she said grimly.

Standing well back, she grabbed a handful of filthy matted hair in one hand and sliced it off with the knife. Bethia was surprised that neither sister resisted while their hair was sheared and flung sizzling onto the fire, the fleas broiling in the tangle. A similar fate followed for the few rags they wore. The stench of burning hair and cloth made Bethia's eyes water and she stepped well away from the fire. The sisters and Madame Dupont were made of sterner stuff. The girls sat sharing a blanket to cover their nakedness watching bright-eyed to see what

Madame Dupont would do next, and clearly revelling in the unaccustomed warmth. She passed them a bowl of water and a rag. The girls sat gazing into it then the older one tipped it back, drank half, gave it to her sister, who drank the rest. Both girls wiped their mouths with the backs of their hands and looked expectantly at Madame Dupont.

Madame Dupont raised her eyebrows at Bethia and pursed her lips. Bethia, holding in the laughter, thought it no surprise that Madame Dupont had such deep lines radiating from her mouth given how often her disapproval was incurred.

'Give me the bowl,' the housekeeper demanded.

The girl meekly passed it to her. There was a glint in the child's eye that had Bethia wondering if she understood all along she was meant to wash, but then it was unlikely these wee vagabonds had ever seen clean water, for the river here was as filthy as the Scheldt in Antwerp, and this home fortunate to have its own well. It had meant she'd been able to bathe Samuel-Thomas regularly and without risk, rather than relying on cleaning him only with fresh linen.

Madame Dupont finally got the girls washed, dressed, scarves around their shorn heads, and looked to Bethia. 'They're all yours.'

Bethia led the way upstairs with a confidence she didn't feel. The girls crowded into the chamber behind her.

Katheline was walking up and down rocking a grizzling baby. 'Who are they?'

'New nursemaids for Samuel-Thomas.'

'What!' Katheline stared at the girls, then sniffed. 'Where did you find them?'

Bethia looked to the girls. 'Have you ever taken care of a baby?'

'Bit late to be asking that now,' muttered Katheline.

'Yes, mistress,' said the taller. 'We were a big family

until the plague came.'

'Are your parents still alive?'

The girl shook her head. ''Tis only us left.'

The younger child leant against her sister, looking up into her face.

The older held out her arms for Samuel-Thomas. Katheline wrapped her arms around the baby more tightly.

'Give him to her,' said Bethia.

'And what would Mainard say, if he learned that his most precious child was being cared for by street urchins?'

'Mainard isn't here.' Bethia lifted her bairn out of Katheline's arms and placed him in the girl's. She had cleaned up to be a pretty wee thing, whose darting brown eyes didn't miss much.

'Will is, though,' said Katheline, whisking out the door.

'What are your names?' Bethia asked, looking to the smaller girl.

'I am Suzanne and she is Ysabeau,' said the taller one stoutly.

Bethia watched as the girl walked up and down whispering in Samuel-Thomas's ear, the younger one stuck to her side as fast as flour paste. 'Is there something wrong with your sister?'

Suzanne shook her head vehemently and Samuel-Thomas whimpered. The girl tickled his cheek with her finger. Bethia watched in wonder as he gave his first smile. And it was more than just the curve of the lip that she'd witnessed before. It was a full, gummy grin as he gazed up into the face gazing down at him. The door burst open and Will rushed in followed by Katheline. Bethia shushed them.

'Look,' she said, pointing, and they all fixed their eyes upon the baby, who was still smiling widely at the waif. 'See how he likes her.'

Will humphed and shook his head. 'Very well, have it your own way.'

Even Katheline could not help but soften at the expression on Samuel-Thomas's face.

Still, it wasn't easy having four people sleeping in one small chamber, and the smell of bodies and used pot was soon overpowering at night. Bethia appealed to the housekeeper, who was not to be moved.

'It's enough to have them in the house, but I cannot allow them to wander. They're your responsibility and must bide with you.'

Bethia shrugged and desisted. She was waiting each day, as patiently as she could, for a message from Nostradamus to learn the outcome of his cogitations, but none came. The weather grew colder again and late snow fell dampening all sound under its white coverlet and turning the dirty streets a brief pristine white. But the sense of dread grew stronger. When she hadn't heard from him by the fourth day, Bethia determined she must brave her way out into the streets and demand of Nostradamus that he reveal what he knew. And at least she could go during daylight this time.

She took Suzanne, leaving Ysabeau to tend to Samuel-Thomas. She was fairly certain the younger child was simple, but since Ysabeau never took her eyes off the wee lamb, Bethia felt a confidence that she hoped was not misplaced and, in any case, Katheline would oversee all.

They went out into the crisp white, daytime streets, the air burnishing their cheeks rosy red. Bethia strode along, staff in hand, while Suzanne trotted behind: a matron with her servant. At least that was the impression she wanted to give but, still, a group of young men nudged one another and moved to block her way. She had no patience for their nonsense today and waved her staff to clear a path. One of them went to grab it, receiving a wrap across his knuckles that had him shouting, probably more in surprise than pain.

The men scattered then fell in behind her. Bethia feared she'd thrown down a challenge she didn't intend.

She kept her eyes fixed on where she was going, walking faster and faster, but that was a mistake, as they closed up until she could feel a foot tripping at her heel. She didn't know where Suzanne had gone, hoped it was for assistance – that was if anyone would listen to one wee lassie. She swerved around the corner and found herself amid a group of women coming from the opposite direction, talking and laughing. She passed through them and when she glanced back the men had vanished. She leant against the wall to still the shaking. Suzanne appeared by her side touching Bethia's arm.

'Shall we go home, mistress.'

'No, we're near the inn.' Bethia stood up and continued.

'Nostradamus is unavailable,' said the rotten-toothed servant who answered her rap on the door.

'Then I will wait,' said Bethia, pushing past, which was no easy feat since the woman was of a girth that made it likely she was the innkeeper's wife. Suzanne lent her weight from behind and they tumbled in.

The woman pointed to the settle. 'Wait if you will, but he works late into the night and rarely rises before noon.'

Bethia sat down upon the settle and folded her hands in her lap while Suzanne crouched at her feet. The woman returned, surprisingly, with a glass of wine. The stink of her breath had Bethia drawing back. It seemed that Nostradamus, famous for his breath-sweetening potions, didn't provide them for those who served him – either that or they didn't work.

Just when Bethia had decided she could wait no longer, the woman returned and ushered her into Nostradamus's presence, Suzanne trailing behind. The chamber was brightly lit by the sun and, looking around, Bethia found it hard to believe this was the smoky place of dark shadows she'd sat terrified in a few nights ago.

'I cannot control my visions, they come and go as they will,' said Nostradamus before Bethia could speak. 'I needed to carefully consider what I saw so that I might present the truth, as far as I can ascertain.'

He waved Bethia to the stool that he'd sat on the other night by the fire. She dropped down, eyes fixed on him, hands pressed together in her lap. His grey hair stood in a wild curly halo around his head, lit by the sun streaming through the small windowpane, and there was a drop of moisture hanging from the end of his long nose. In the bright light of day, he looked less like a learned prophet and more like a frantic old man. Was she a fool to place so much reliance on him? But when she remembered the sensation of the weight pressing down upon her… he did have some strange power.

'I've been busy about my almanac,' he said portentously. 'And I must soon return home to Provence and my medical practice, for I've tarried too long in this unwholesome city.'

She wanted to scream at him to get on with it but instead gripped her hands tighter together. She could hear Suzanne, standing hard by her shoulder, breathing heavily.

'There's an evil presence surrounding you. I see a tall hooded figure, a shadow hanging over you. Even in the bright light of day he hovers near.'

Bethia instinctively twisted on the stool to look, and Suzanne too turned.

'What does it mean?'

Nostradamus wiped his nose with the back of his hand, yet the drip hung on still. 'My almanac is soon to be published. You would do better to read it. I do not give quatrains to individuals, it's more that I can see the shadow cast over many.'

Bethia had had enough of his dissembling. She stood up. 'Have you anything to tell me, or not? Is my husband in peril?'

'All are in peril in these dangerous times, especially Jews.'

Bethia started. 'He's not a Jew.'

Nostradamus stepped forward and clasped her hands. She looked into his woolly face and then quickly glanced down again. His eyes were intense, burrowing into her like a weevil into biscuit. 'My family were once Jews who converted.'

She tugged her hands out from his. 'Your family were indeed fortunate to be believed when they converted. My husband is a true follower of Christ and yet is beset by suspicion and accusations of being a Crypto-Jew.'

'I suspect my people didn't have the wealth that yours do. 'Tis too tempting to find a reason to seize it.'

Bethia felt a deep weariness. 'Have you anything to tell me that is specific to my situation – or is it all generalities? Is my husband in imminent danger? Do I need to return to Antwerp?'

Nostradamus rubbed his hand over his face, which finally removed the drip from the end of his nose. 'Your husband is at great risk. I sense a time of incarceration.' He held up his hand as she gasped. 'Wait, let me finish. He has friends who are helping him and a loud servant girl.'

Grissel, thought Bethia, how can that be? But her heart was lighter... for a moment.

Nostradamus again took possession of her hands. 'It's not your husband you should worry about, but yourselves. What do you know of this man within whose house you reside?'

'He was a traveller we met along the way. A kind man who offered us shelter.'

'Humph!' said Nostradamus and dropped her hands. 'Not so much kind as self-serving. You must get far away.' He waved his hands at her as though to chase her. 'And check every possession before you go. Danger presses hard upon you. That is all I have to say.'

It was more than enough. Bethia drew her cloak tight around her, beckoned to Suzanne, and hurried back to what she must call home, for the present.

Chapter Fourteen

The Bad Samaritan

Bethia wanted to be back in this house that was not so welcoming with her baby in her arms, overseeing their packing as quickly as possible. But, as they left, Nostradamus had counselled caution.

'In my trance I saw a vision of a man rising over you like a great beast, his foul breath upon your neck. But still, do not act hastily,' were his final mumbled words as he followed her down the passageway.

Bethia shuddered, picked up her skirts, and ran down the street.

Suzanne tugged on her arm and she slowed. 'Mistress, we must be calm when we enter the house or that man will suspect something. I see the way he stares at you.'

And then they were again surrounded by the fellows who'd chased her earlier.

'La belle étrangère,' said the handsome one reaching out to touch her face.

Bethia had had enough. She thrust the staff, poking him in the scrotum. He howled as he crumpled. The rest of the men dispersed and Bethia was proud of herself.

A tall figure came up behind her. 'God's blood, Bethia, have you not the sense you were born with,' said Will. 'What are you doing wandering these streets alone?'

'I'm not alone, Suzanne is with me, and I needed to speak with Nostradamus.'

'That teller of tall tales. I swear he's more like a prophet of Satan than that any words from the Lord flow through him.'

Bethia pulled on his sleeve. 'Listen to me, Will. Nostradamus warns we are in danger. He implied that de Vaudemont's hospitality is naught but a ruse to steal from us, or worse.' She turned to Suzanne, slight as a firefly next to Will. 'Did he not?'

Suzanne nodded emphatically.

'Where does de Vaudemont store the wools and linens we carry – which, as you well know, represent a great deal of the de Lange family wealth. The gold coin is hidden safe, at least it was when I checked last night.' Bethia went to chew on the skin around her thumbnail, forgetting she had gloves on.

'I think you're overreacting. De Vaudemont is clearly a man of wealth himself. As I've said many times, he's a good Samaritan and nothing more.'

'How do you know? Even men of wealth invariably are in need of more. And where did his wealth come from?'

Will rubbed his forehead then dropped his hand and glared at her. 'We will return home and empty every kist. I have the inventory. Will that satisfy you?'

Bethia hesitated. 'It'll be a beginning... but Will... it's not our home, we have only been beguiled into thinking it so.'

Will raised his eyebrows and took her arm.

But de Vaudemont was out when they returned and Madame Dupont didn't hold the key to the strongroom.

Bethia went to feed her baby and answer questions from a perturbed Katheline, who insisted on being told all. 'I share in whatever may befall us,' she said fiercely to Bethia, 'and you should not keep secrets from me.'

De Vaudemont returned and appeared most

surprised to be applied to for the key and for all the chests to be emptied and the stock cross-checked against Will's inventory.

They found nothing missing.

Will was furious with Bethia. 'We've treated a kind and considerate man with grave discourtesy. This was badly done, my sister. And I forbid you to go near Nostradamus again; he's like an old woman, the tales he feeds you.'

But Bethia was not convinced. 'Samuel-Thomas and I are leaving this house. You do as you see fit.'

Will snorted. 'Leave the house – you can't walk down the street without coming under attack by a group of popinjays. How far do you think you'll get without my protection? And I *will not* permit you to take Samuel-Thomas if you do leave.'

Bethia's face grew red with rage. 'Where I go, my son goes.'

'I am the man of this party and your son goes where I permit him to go.'

Bethia, ready to fly at him and scratch his eyes out, had to take a deep breath to calm herself. 'We cannot stay here forever. When *do* you plan on leaving?'

'When we can travel without risk of being buried alive in snow.'

'And even if I'm wrong about de Vaudemont, how much longer do you think we can impose upon his hospitality? After the snow comes the mud, indeed we're better to travel while the ground is ice hard.'

Will stroked his beard, in a way that was so reminiscent of their father that Bethia gulped. Would Father have attended to her fears any better than Will was doing… probably not.

'I promise we won't tarry here much longer. We'll find a town to bide in closer to Geneva as we wait for the mountain pass to open.'

And with this Bethia had to be satisfied, for the

moment. She tried to settle – to smile at the quips from de Vaudemont, to stay steady when he found reason to take her hand and hold it between his soft, pulpy fingers – but the modest bend of her head drooped lower and lower as she hid her distaste. She could only grimace privately and quickly withdraw to the safety of her chamber. At least de Vaudemont would not venture there, so overfull was it with Katheline, the wee lamb, Suzanne, and her sister. Suzanne, of course, was fully aware of Nostradamus's warnings. Bethia hoped she could be trusted. And Ysabeau – a fanciful name for a child of the streets – Bethia had still not heard her utter a word. Ysabeau watched, oh how she watched, and did whatever she was told and was devoted to Samuel-Thomas and really was no trouble, but still Bethia sensed there was something not right with her. They had enough troubles without the added burden of a wrong-in-the-head child.

Suzanne came to her one morning as she and Katheline were bent over Samuel-Thomas, who was responding to having his toes tickled with most satisfying glee. Glancing up, Bethia saw Suzanne, forehead wrinkling so that the white headscarf rode up, small nose as sharply pointed as a dagger, head tilting, round brown eyes rolling. Bethia slid away from Katheline and, grabbing the poker, riddled the fire while Suzanne came to stand next to her. Suzanne whispered so softly Bethia struggled to hear.

The attempted conversation came to an abrupt halt when Katheline spoke, her voice loud in the room. 'You'll kill that fire if you don't stop. And anyway, why are you touching it when we have a surplus of servants?' She raised her eyebrows as she looked from Suzanne, leaning in to speak to Bethia, to Ysabeau crouched in her corner.

Bethia didn't want to continue the conversation in

front of Katheline: didn't entirely trust her. Will and Katheline were great allies these days. But where else could she go to speak privately with Suzanne in this house of watchers?

Before Suzanne could fully explain the urgency, there was a knock on the door and Will came in. 'We must leave at your earliest convenience.'

Bethia stared at him.

'Aye, aye, you were correct.' He raised his hands to halt the exclamation. 'De Vaudemont has just presented me with a bill for the stabling of the horses. It's doubly annoying, for I would've sold them rather than pay for their maintenance over the winter but he persuaded me to keep them, saying as long as we paid for their feed – which was expensive enough – then I could have the stabling for nought. He now claims he never made such an offer. And he's also saying that the cost of all food has risen and we must pay for that too.'

'But we *have* been paying for our food.'

'He wants more money.'

'Where are we going?' said Bethia, wondering why she was even debating payments for food instead of immediately packing. Yet now they were finally to leave, she felt a reluctance to be exposed to the perils of the journey once more.

'Towards Geneva of course. I must hire some men to guard us and we may depart, I hope, by first light tomorrow.'

De Vaudemont was all regret when he learned they were to go. He bowed, drew close, said how much he would miss her and, clearly emboldened by their imminent departure, reached a finger out to stroke the side of her face. Bethia tolerated it. She didn't see any need to offend the man now she was to escape his most unwelcome attentions. They packed with great efficiency. Bethia saw Suzanne's fearful face and placed her arm around the child.

'You will come with us of course.'

'And Ysabeau,' whispered Suzanne.

Bethia suppressed a sigh. 'And Ysabeau,' and was rewarded with a small twisted smile, as though the smiler was unused to forming her lips into such a shape.

Their kists were released from the strongroom the next morning and de Vaudemont stood, arms folded, watching as Will and Bethia again looked over the wools and linens. He drew close to Bethia, smelling strongly of garlic. But in this instance, he seemed more interested in scrutinising the contents of the chests than in touching her.

They all breathed a sigh of relief once the carts were loaded with goods and servants. Bethia climbed aboard the carriage with her well-swaddled baby in her arms and Katheline followed. Will mounted his horse, the three stout guards took charge of the carriage and carts, and the procession began.

The mud was frozen solid and the road hard-rutted, which meant it was an uncomfortably bumpy ride, but at least they didn't get stuck. They made good progress, Will saying they'd covered more than three miles in the first hour, but the state of the highways were not their only difficulty. At the next village the dogs were waiting.

Chapter Fifteen

The Guards

It was as though the dogs had forewarning. One moment they were plodding steadily along the track with Samuel-Thomas sound asleep and the next the beasts were upon them, barking and growling, leaping and snarling, full mouths of teeth whiter and sharper than any man's, and the bairn was howling.

The enclosed carriage, sitting higher off the ground than the carts, did not deter them, and they leapt at the windows, which were covered only by flaps of leather. The guards surrounded the carriage leaving the carts unprotected. Through the torn flap Bethia saw Suzanne standing on the cart behind with Ysabeau crouched at her feet, fending off the feral beast which had leapt up beside her, with only her hands to protect them.

'Will,' screamed Bethia, leaning out and pointing.

Will spurred over to the cart, kicking to free himself from the small dog which had sunk its teeth into his leg. Suzanne flung her cloak over the beast attacking her, and she and Ysabeau fell on top of it. Bethia was opening her mouth to cheer when there was a commotion at the other side of the carriage. The muzzle of a huge dog appeared at the aperture, legs scrambling to climb in, mouth wide and slavering, eyes fixed on the wee lamb who Katheline was holding. The giant beast clamped its teeth on

Katheline's arm, and Bethia, with no weapon to hand, hauled on one ear with all her strength. The dog let go and snapped at Bethia. Will was there, struggling to control his terrified horse, its ears back, eyes rolling in fear. He stabbed at the dog but the dog was too quick. It ran, followed by the rest of the pack.

Bethia took the baby from Katheline and laid him on the seat. He gazed up at her, calm now and seemingly unperturbed by how close he'd come to being dog fodder. She gently took hold of Katheline's arm and pushed the sleeve up. There was a perfect half circle of teeth marks on either side of her forearm from which a small amount of blood was seeping.

'Fortunate that the beast didn't get a good grip. The bite marks are shallow.'

Katheline slid her arm out of Bethia's hands, covered it with the ripped sleeve and cradled it.

Will opened the carriage door. 'All well here?'

'Katheline's been bitten.'

Will looked concerned. 'Let me see.'

Katheline shook her head, holding her arm tightly across her middle. 'It's nothing. A minor injury that'll soon heal.'

'Is Suzanne hurt?' said Bethia.

He grinned. 'Suzanne soon saw off her attacker, with my help. But we must get moving before the pack regroups and returns.'

She gathered the bairn in her arms while Katheline sat hunched in her corner. Bethia could see the arm was paining her. She tugged out the leather bottle of wine from the bag at her feet and handed it to Katheline, who took small sips.

'Your colour is improving.'

Katheline smiled wanly.

The passed through a village, a poor-looking place with a few rags spread over bushes to dry – a vain hope in the damp air – and puny bundles of firewood stacked outside the homes. Not like Lyon, Bethia reflected, where the alleys were often blocked by great wood piles. The carriage suddenly lurched to one side and she and the baby went sliding into Katheline, who cried out in pain. Bethia pushed herself away with one hand while keeping a tight hold on young Samuel-Thomas, who was howling his outrage at this second disturbance. The carriage door opened and Will reached in and took the baby from her, passing him to Suzanne, who was standing anxiously by.

'What happened?' Bethia asked, as he helped her and then Katheline out.

Will pointed to a deep hole. 'The driver tried to skirt around it but the wheel caught.'

'Why would anyone dig a hole in the middle of the lane?'

Will shrugged. 'Why not? They look to be too poor here to own carts, and if you need sand and clay to repair your house then you'll dig in the nearest available place without a care for any traveller who may pass by.'

They had to unload the carts so they could be pushed over the hole without incurring damage. Then the carts had to be restacked again. Will paid a few of the suspicious locals, who were silently watching, to assist, and they found themselves waved on their way with considerably more cheer than greeted their arrival.

It was mid-afternoon now, a watery sun hanging low in a grey sky. The villagers had said there was a town with a comfortable inn not more than four miles away, but it would be a push to reach it before dark. Bethia wondered what such poor people considered to be *comfortable* but soon she didn't care. It grew chill as the light failed, and the hot bottles they'd tucked into the coach this morning were now as cold as stone. Samuel-Thomas was again howling and Katheline had shrunk even further in her corner. She was profoundly grateful when they made their way beneath the town gate and heard the clank of it closing firmly behind them.

Bethia stood quietly reading a broadsheet which the innkeeper had laid before her. It was in French, but she dreamt in French these days, even sang wee Samuel-Thomas lullabies in French, interspersed with bawdier Scots songs. He didn't care, it was only her voice he wanted to hear.

She studied the broadsheet trying to make sense of why the man had given it to her.

A traveller has need of a falcon's eye, an ass's ears, a monkey's face, a merchant's words, a camel's back, a hog's mouth, a deer's feet and, for the traveller to Rome, a conscience as broad as the king's highway.

It was all very true, she thought, although she couldn't comment on the traveller to Rome's conscience. And she didn't want to be a traveller any more, only to reach her destination. She looked up, sensing the innkeeper was awaiting a response.

'Funny, eh?'

Bethia nodded. 'Most amusing.'

The inn was better provisioned than she'd expected. There was only one central hall open to the rafters but it was warmed by a large fire and the provender was generous. A chamber was available to them and they all piled in, while Will went to sleep in the hall with their guards. Katheline suggested Suzanne and Ysabeau might also sleep there.

'I would not leave them so unprotected,' said Bethia.

Katheline snorted. 'How do you think they survived before you took them in? They'd no protection then.'

'By dressing and behaving as boys – that disguise is no longer available to them. The guards know they're lassies.'

They rose early and were ready to leave as quickly as carrying all the kists from the hall to the carts, feeding and saddling the horses, breaking their own fast, and tending to the baby would allow. As they emerged through the town gate, people were streaming towards them: men leading packhorses; men and women balancing baskets on their heads – kale waving out the top as though they'd grown an extra head of hair; carts as overfull as their own carts were but with sacks of grain and bundles of hay; a small flock of sheep and even a couple of pigs. It must be market day, and with a surprising quantity of produce and animals for sale at the tail end of winter. The hordes flowed around them, their breath misting in the air and creating a brief illusion of heat from warm bodies as they passed.

Bethia had wrapped Samuel-Thomas in her shawl and drew her cloak over them both. He was near five months old now, and having survived his first bout of serious illness, she prayed he'd been born under a lucky star. She touched his nose with her fingertip and he smiled.

They made good progress that day. The way was less rutted than before and followed the valley of the river Rhone; all too close to it for Bethia's liking. There was little traffic on the road, too early in the season yet. As the sun disappeared behind the towering snow-capped mountains and the valley fell into shadow, they'd yet to find an inn or even reach a settlement large enough to support one. In the end Will knocked on the door of a hovel that was slightly less tumbled down than its neighbours and offered coin, which had the woman peeping out in answer, flinging her door wide and bidding them enter.

It was a single room with beds set in the wall. The woman tumbled her children out and sent them to neighbours. A soup was served, watery and lacking much substance, but at least it was hot. The woman then slipped away too. Bethia settled on a stool by the fire to feed her bairn, with Ysabeau crouched at her feet, while Katheline tended to her bitten arm in the gloom and Will was out with their guards seeking secure shelter for their goods, and taking care of the horses.

'You must at least wash it,' said Bethia. 'And perhaps the cottar woman has some herbs that may help the healing.'

Katheline ignored her, and Bethia, handing the now sleeping baby to Ysabeau, rose to insist Katheline let her see the wound.

The door burst open. Suzanne rushed breathlessly in and grabbed Bethia, looking imploringly up into her face. 'I heard them. They were whispering when I was in the privy and didn't know I was there. They're going to do bad things.'

'Sit down,' said Bethia, pointing to the stool she'd just vacated. 'And calm down. Who did you overhear and what bad things are they planning?'

Suzanne perched on the seat. Ysabeau, while still rocking the baby, watched her sister intently. Bethia looked from one to the other and thought how carefully Ysabeau studied facial expressions and gestures.

'Our guards – they were whispering about stealing from us. They say there will never be a better chance and it's too difficult in the towns, for there are too many people, but here there are only a few houses mostly of women and old folk. They can take everything and no one can prevent it. They said something about the river hiding all evidence.'

Bethia looked to Katheline. 'We must get Will.'

'I'll go,' said Katheline. 'He's more likely to come immediately than if Suzanne asks.'

'Go with her,' Bethia said to Suzanne. 'You can watch out for one another.'

Suzanne tugged a branch out of the wood piled beside the fire and Katheline, after a moment, did too.

'Bar the door behind us,' she said. 'We'll knock three times when we return.'

Bethia slid the length of wood in place after they left. The door was old with cracks running down it and a large gap at the bottom where the wood had worn. It wouldn't long withstand anyone determined to gain entry.

She paced up and down holding Samuel-Thomas tight in her arms, then looked for somewhere to lay him down so that she had both hands free to defend herself. She made a wee nest of blankets for him in the corner close to the warmth of the fire, but not so close that sparks might land upon him. He lay quietly lifting his hands and twisting them before his eyes, captivated. Ysabeau settled beside him, watching.

There was a soft tap on the door and she rushed to it.

'Let us in,' a voice whispered.

She put her hand to her heart. 'Who is it?'

'Me, you fool. Let us in quickly.'

It was her brother's voice – and words. She fumbled to lift the bar, catching her fingers between it and the door frame. Will and Katheline pushed in.

She looked behind them as Will closed and barred the door once more. 'Where's Suzanne?'

'She disappeared.'

'And you let her?' said Bethia, the rising tone of her voice causing a grumble of dismay from the bairn in the corner.

'She slipped away before we could stop her,' said Katheline, bending to soothe the baby by stroking his belly.

Bethia frowned. 'I never thought she'd desert us – and especially Ysabeau.' She glanced at Ysabeau, who had stood up and was staring at her anxiously.

'I don't think she has deserted us,' said Katheline slowly. 'I think she's our eyes and ears outside.'

'And if she's caught she may well be our undoing,' muttered Will, who was poised, sword drawn, by the door.

Bethia faced Ysabeau. 'Suzanne back soon.' She waved her arm towards the door and then gestured towards them. Ysabeau watched her intently. A strange, twisted groan issued from her lips, loud in the small cottage. Bethia jerked her head back at the sound, the first she'd heard Ysabeau make.

'Definitely a deaf mute,' muttered Katheline.

Bethia picked up the baby and placed him in Ysabeau's arms, directing her to the bed corner. Then she slid the dagger that Madame Dupont had gifted to her on their departure from Lyon from her pocket. Bethia thought it a curious gift at the time, but then travel was dangerous. Still, it worried her. She wondered if de Vaudemont was somehow behind this attack.

They all stood silently, waiting. Will at his post by the door, Katheline behind it, and Bethia, uncertain where to position herself, standing in the middle of the hovel. Nothing happened for what seemed a very long time. Bethia felt the fear tight in her belly. Where was Suzanne?

There was a light tap on the door and a whisper. Will hesitated.

'Let her in,' hissed Bethia.

Will pressed his ear against the door, then slowly opened it.

Chapter Sixteen

Treachery

'They were harnessing the horses and arguing about how best to get you out,' said Suzanne, the moment she was inside. 'One says they should leave, taking everything with them, and there's not much Master Will can do against many.' She blew air out through her lips, pouff. 'But they should not discount us women.'

'What do the other two say should be done with us?' asked Katheline.

Suzanne shuffled her feet on the earthen floor. 'They want us killed. They say dead men tell no tales. There's talk of smoking us out.'

Bethia looked to Will.

'Like we did with Cardinal Beaton,' he said softly. Then he straightened up to his full height, head brushing the low beams. 'Where are they now, Suzanne?'

'In the stables. One was watching the cottage, but when they started to argue what should be done he was distracted and I took the chance to come. He may have seen me enter.'

'Are there any at the rear of the cottage?'

Suzanne shook her head. 'All three were by the shed where the horses are.'

Will went to the back wall and poked at the daub and wattle with his sword. It crumbled easily and soon there was a hole large enough to escape through.

'Bethia, you get out first. Take the bairn and go to the neighbours. See if there are any men in the settlement who can be prevailed upon to help us.'

Bethia hesitated. She thought it would be better if Suzanne took the baby and then she could stay and fight. Both she and Katheline knew how to wield a staff enough to beat off an attacker, for Mainard had taught them. Their guards were armed with cudgels only, no one had a sword except Will – although they might have knives. Better she stayed here to help. Yet she knew there was not time to debate it… and Samuel-Thomas must be her priority. In any case the villagers were more likely to respond to an appeal for help from her than Suzanne. She loosened her shawl and Suzanne held the baby against her back. She tied him on tightly.

'We'll follow,' said Will.

Bethia squirmed on her belly through the gap Will had created, aware of Suzanne's hand protecting the baby's head. Suzanne passed her the staff and, bent double, Bethia scurried through the darkness, sending up a prayer that Samuel-Thomas kept quiet.

She could hear voices to her right, raised in argument, and turned in the opposite direction. There was a dim light visible on the hillside above, and she climbed breathlessly, hoping it was another settlement. She stumbled and nearly fell. Samuel-Thomas grunted at the disturbance and Bethia spoke softly to him, pleading that he *haud his wheesht*. The Scots words seemed to soothe and he fell quiet.

It *was* a cottage, the light of the fire creeping out around the flimsy wood of the door. Bethia tapped on it. There was no response. She knocked again, louder, tensing for any sound from within.

The door was flung wide and a young lad stood before her, a burning stick of wood in his hand. He looked startled to find a well-dressed young woman before him.

'Please help us,' Bethia said, hands held out in supplication.

The lad looked behind him. 'It's a gentlewoman. She says she needs help.'

He was pushed aside and a woman came, arms folded and lips narrowed in her thin face. 'What do you want? Can you pay us?'

'Yes, yes. It's our guards, they're threatening us. Can you hide my baby please? I must go back and support my brother.'

The tiny woman's face softened as Bethia untied the shawl drawn tight across her chest and belly and swung the baby off her back.

'Of course we'll help,' she said, holding out her arms for Samuel-Thomas.

'Maman?' said the young lad.

'On this occasion I'll break my own rule,' she mumbled, cradling the baby in her arms. She looked up. 'Don't stand there gawping. Go and fetch the men to assist this poor young woman.'

The boy darted away, and Bethia having directed the woman to where they were, and with one last look at her son, hurried down the hill to the cottage by the river. She could barely still the shaking, knew she could argue that she must remain with the baby – especially as she was his source of food. But she couldn't leave her brother and good sister unaided. And where were they? Surely they should've followed her out? She gripped the staff tighter as she ran towards danger. She could hear shouting now and the acrid smell of smoke was bitter in her nostrils. She tripped, falling flat on her face. Scrambling to her feet, she ignored the stinging pain in palms, knees and forehead. She could see the yellow-red lick of flame as she drew closer. She ran faster and bumped into a small figure, knocking her over.

'Ysabeau,' she whispered. She gripped the child's

arm, rotated her and pointed up the hill, gave a push in that direction and then she was off again.

She slowed as she neared the flames. A dark figure appeared and grabbed her arm. 'Mistress, they have Katheline,' Suzanne whispered.

Bethia could hear Suzanne's small rapid breaths and feel Suzanne's hand shaking where it clutched her arm.

'And Will?'

'He's holding them off with his sword but I think he must give up else they'll kill Katheline. I got away while all eyes were on him. Is there help coming?'

'Pray to the Blessed Virgin there is,' mumbled Bethia. 'Go to the cottage above, Ysabeau should be there with Samuel-Thomas. Tell the woman whose cottage it is what you've told me.'

Suzanne stumbled away, and Bethia, gripping her staff even tighter, set off once more. She moved warily, uncertain what she'd find. There was a figure silhouetted in the light of dying flames stamping the fire out, then it disappeared inside. She reached the cottage and, creeping around it, heard Will's voice.

'You must let us go – people know where we are. They'll come after you and you'll hang for this.'

A man responded. 'If you mean Monsieur de Vaudemont then you'll wait a long time before he sends any assistance. He's most interested in acquiring your goods.'

There was a note of triumph in the sneering voice. It must be the biggest of the three – who always took the lead. And it was as she had long suspected: de Vaudemont was indeed false. Yet Will had hired these guards without the proffered assistance from the man; trickery upon trickery.

She picked up her skirts ready to run back up the hill and bring the boy and whatever men he had gathered back here to surround the cottage and, in the dark, walked into the wood stack sending a log rolling.

'Quick, go and find out what that is,' the leader's voice ordered.

Bethia, in her desperation to escape, had caught her skirt around a chunk of wood and was trying to free herself when the man appeared. She was still gripping the stave but in the wrong hand. She swung it awkwardly yet managed to hit him. It had little effect and he swung his fist in return. She doubled over, collapsing face down on the ground, all the breath knocked out of her by a punch to the belly. He grabbed her by the back of her dress and hair, dragged her into the cottage, and tossed her on the floor. Bethia lay there, bile rising in her throat, belly burning and gasping for breath.

'Where's the child?' demanded the leader.

'How would I know? At least I caught her.'

The leader growled.

Bethia was aware of Katheline bending over her but stayed curled up, eyes closed and panting noisily. She heard a thump, then a cry from Katheline.

'Leave her alone,' shouted Will.

Then her own back flooded with pain from a booted foot. She bit on her tongue to suppress the groan and lay as limp as she could with a back and belly that were on fire. Her knife was lying on the floor nearby; must've fallen from her pocket. She reached her hand out, fingers creeping slowly towards the knife.

A foot pressed down on her arm; she could see where the boot leather needed restitching along the side. Her tormentor leant down and picked up the dagger, grinning into her face as he did.

'Tie them up,' ordered the leader.

'With what?'

'Rope, of course. Go and fetch some from the shed. Use the horses' harness if necessary.'

'But we'll need it.'

'Once we've caught those two scrawny little girls then we can get rid of them all, and recover the harness.'

105

Bethia tried to still the shiver of fear that ran through her and felt for the staff beneath her, which somehow she'd kept a hold of. There was the sound of a scuffle outside and the guard sent for the harnesses cried out.

The leader directed the other man. 'Find out what's going on.'

'You go, I'll stay here,' he muttered.

'Get out there, now.'

Bethia half-opened her eyes. She saw the leader's feet and the tip of the sword he was waving towards his fellow: Will's sword. The other man slipped out the door.

The leader swung back to Will. 'Stay where you are.'

Later, Bethia could never explain how she did it, but she went from lying upon the floor to standing in one move. The leader, his back to her, was turning as she swung, cracking him across the head, and the sword dropped from his hand.

Will seized the sword and stabbed him in the belly. The man looked down as Will tugged it out. He folded to his knees and Will thrust again, through the chest. He fell at Will's feet and they all stared down on him.

Katheline, hand over her mouth and eyes wide, looked to Will. 'Surely we could have taken him prisoner?'

'No,' said Bethia slowly as she gazed on the dead man at her feet who, eyes wide open, stared back. 'They were intending to kill us. This was not a time to show mercy, especially when there are two more of them to deal with.'

Will was already on his way out the door. 'Stay here,' he hissed.

Bethia ignored the command and followed him out. The fight outside was over and the local worthies stood over a man who lay senseless on the ground.

'Where's the third one?' said Will.

Bethia didn't wait for the reply. She was off running back up the hill to her bairn.

Chapter Seventeen

Suzanne

Suzanne was cradling the baby while Ysabeau leant against her, eyes fixed on his face. He was laughing when Suzanne tickled him and grizzling as soon as she stopped. Bethia stood in the doorway, her heart overflowing with tenderness for all three. She didn't yet know it, but this scene would stay with her for the rest of her long life.

Suzanne looked over, face fearful until she realised it was Bethia.

'Will killed one, one is captured and one got away. We're safe.'

Ysabeau tugged on Suzanne's arm, looking up anxiously. Suzanne smiled and nodded at her, and Ysabeau smiled in return. Samuel-Thomas, indignant that he was no longer the centre of attention, cried.

'He's hungry now,' said Suzanne.

Bethia held out her arms and Suzanne passed him over.

The cottar woman, ignored in the corner, stared open-mouthed. 'I never thought to see this,' she muttered. 'A gentlewoman giving her own milk to her child. Do they not have wet nurses in your country?'

Bethia frowned at the woman's familiarity, then reminded herself of what they owed her this night. 'My

107

husband says 'tis better for our son, and Galen agrees.' She knew she was being pompous referencing Galen but couldn't quite help herself. 'And,' she said, her voice softening, 'it has saved us much trouble on this journey. We never once had to worry about his sustenance.'

'A wise husband,' said the woman. 'You are indeed fortunate to have such a one.'

'I am,' said Bethia, bending over her child, who was suckling with loud pleasure. In this moment she missed Mainard so desperately it was as though she'd been stabbed in the belly.

She heard voices outside and Katheline appeared, ducking under the low doorway. 'I see all's well with his lordship.'

'Aye, I wish all our needs could be as easily met. Has the other guard been discovered?'

Katheline shook her head.

Will came in, his eyes passing quickly over Bethia. 'The men here tell me we can be in Geneva in four days. They know a quicker path and will guide us.'

'How do you know we'll be any safer with them?' said Bethia, and bent over her child, who gave a cry of complaint at how tightly she was holding him. Suzanne held out her arms and Bethia gave the bairn to her and fastened her bodice up.

Will knelt in front of her, never so humble before. 'Bethia, these men helped us. Of course it is a risk, but what else can we do? The river here is unnavigable, we must stick to the road.' He stood up, towering over her. 'The good Lord watched over us and they were returning to their homes from guiding other travellers when our need was greatest.'

Bethia smoothed her skirt, eyes cast down.

Will waited, but only when he took a step back did she nod agreement.

'We'll depart tomorrow. Get what rest you can. I'm going to stay with the horses and guard our goods, along with three stout fellows from the village, and a further three will remain with you.'

'What'll happen to the one you caught.'

'He's under guard and will be taken to the nearest town jail first thing tomorrow,' said Will, on his own way out the door.

The woman of the house laid a pallet before the fire which Bethia, Katheline and the baby shared. The sisters cooried in the other corner, wrapped in blankets, and were both quickly asleep, with the normally silent Ysabeau snoring. Katheline soon fell asleep too and Samuel-Thomas snuffled as he slept. Bethia hoped he wasn't getting another fever. She couldn't rest anyway. Her head hurt where she'd been dragged by the hair, her back throbbed where she was kicked, and her belly was tender to the touch from the punch.

She shifted again, trying to find a position that didn't cause pain. Katheline grunted and turned over, taking most of the covers with her. It was no good, Bethia couldn't lie still. She crawled out and Samuel-Thomas rolled onto the warm spot. Already he liked to sprawl across the bed, just as his father did.

She sat on a stool by the fire and poked it with a stick to encourage the embers to flare up, then fed it. Her eyes fluttered closed. When she awoke she was leaning against the rough stone wall, her back so stiff that Suzanne had to help her up. Each step she took was agony and she could do nothing beyond feed her baby and watch preparations for departure.

Will appeared in the doorway saying they'd buried the dead leader and the horses were saddled ready below. Bethia called Suzanne to her and gave her the baby. Then she moved slowly, biting the inside of her lip to contain the groan. She waved to Ysabeau to come lend her a shoulder to lean upon and the procession set off down the path to the cottages below, Will leading the way as he leant in to speak to Katheline.

109

Soon they were well ahead as Bethia limped behind with Ysabeau's support. She glanced over her shoulder to make certain Suzanne was near. Suzanne walked slowly, placing each foot down with care as she carried Samuel-Thomas. The sun sparkled on the snow-capped mountains before her, the river snaking through the valley was of deepest turquoise and, although she was still fearful of the journey and in pain, Bethia was surprised to feel a rising sense of well-being amid this glorious day.

A muffled sound came from behind and she glanced over her shoulder again and gasped. She swung around, all pain forgotten, and stumbled back up the hill towards Suzanne, Ysabeau alongside.

'Stay where you are or they get it,' said the man, who was holding a dagger – her dagger – to Suzanne's throat.

'Please, let them go. I'll give you whatever you want.' She kept moving slowly towards him as she spoke. 'Your leader is dead, your other accomplice captured. I have coin. Let her and the baby go. I will give everything I have.'

The man tightened his grip, pressing the blade into the skin. Bethia saw droplets of blood, bright against Suzanne's white collar. Suzanne whimpered, terrified brown eyes staring at Bethia, and Samuel-Thomas let out a cry in sympathy.

'Do not move or else I'll kill her, and your son.'

Bethia slid her hand into her pocket, and he wrenched Suzanne's head back, exposing the small neck further. 'I told you not to move.'

'I'm getting my purse,' said Bethia withdrawing her hand slowly. She held the coin-purse out, moving closer. Where was Will? She prayed to the Blessed Virgin that he'd notice they were no longer behind him. Ysabeau suddenly took to her heels, off down the hill. The man roared at her disappearing back.

'It's no good,' shouted Bethia, waving her hands

frantically to calm him. 'You know she cannot hear, or speak. Take my purse and leave now before she returns with my brother – and his sword.'

The man hesitated.

Bethia took a further step towards him, holding the purse in her outstretched arm.

'Put it on the ground.'

She bent and slowly laid it down.

He edged nearer, pushing Suzanne before him. Suzanne winced as the knife bit deeper. Bethia could see his face clearly now: dirty, scrawny beard, cracked lips, scared eyes – had never paid much attention to him before.

'Move away,' he said.

Suzanne stared intently at Bethia, as though she was trying to tell her something. Then suddenly she flicked her arms, tossing the wee lamb in the air. Bethia leapt forward, her breath loud in her ears, chest feeling as though it might explode. She sank to her knees reaching out her arms and caught her child, who howled at such treatment.

Suzanne had thrust her body forward to throw the baby. Taken by surprise, the man's hand jerked, his dagger slicing deep into the side of Suzanne's throat. The blood spurted, splashing her attacker across the face, a spray of richest crimson. He let go and Suzanne collapsed on the stony ground. He stood over her for a moment; Bethia saw the look of horror on his face.

There were shouts from below and the attacker fled. Bethia placed the bairn on a swarth of grass. He was screaming but all her attention was on Suzanne's white face, terrified eyes, and the blood pulsing from her neck. Bethia crawled forward and pressed her shawl against the wound, trying to stem the bleeding. Will rushed past in pursuit of their attacker. Katheline sank to her knees on the other side of Suzanne and Ysabeau stood over them, making a terrible mewling noise and tearing at her face and hair.

Bethia released the pressure momentarily to check the wound and the blood spurted higher. She'd never seen so much blood, didn't know a body held all this... why would it not stop? She pressed harder yet the blood still came. Her shawl was soaked. Blessed Virgin, please make it stop.

Ysabeau fell to her knees, narrowly avoiding crushing the baby. She rocked back and forward, still making the unearthly sound, hands held out in supplication to her dying sister.

Katheline muttered over and over. 'What can we do, oh the Lord save and protect her? What can we do?' She passed Bethia her own shawl and the two young women applied pressure together.

Suzanne looked to Ysabeau and tried to speak. The blood pumped harder.

Bethia stared into Suzanne's dulling eyes. 'I will take care of Ysabeau. I promise.'

Suzanne's eyelids flickered and closed. The flow of blood slowed.

Will returned and picked up his howling nephew. 'He got away but we'll get a search party out. He won't get far.'

Bethia clambered stiffly to her feet and placed her arm around Ysabeau, drawing the child close. Ysabeau resisted at first then leant into Bethia.

'Suzanne is gone then,' said Will. It was a statement not a question.

'She is gone,' said Katheline wearily.

'A brave lass.'

Bethia held Ysabeau tight and wept and wept, while Suzanne's body lay at her feet, still and white.

Chapter Eighteen

Faith

Mainard turned in the narrow bed. They brought him soft sheets last night and he'd managed a few hours' sleep without the coarse blankets rubbing against the raw places and his damaged foot. He wondered who delivered the sheets. And the wine which was used to revive him.

His foot was bound now and he regularly bent forward to sniff it, forever fearful that he could smell rotting. And then he was hot and sweating, and remembered little of the next few days. He was dimly aware of the bandages being changed and his face bathed with cool water, but he drifted off into a world of spectres – for it seemed the Lord had truly forgot him. He came to, after what could be weeks for all he knew, to see the large grey eyes and long face of his good friend Ortelius bending over him.

'How are you, de Lange?' said Ortelius, his voice unusually soft.

Mainard blinked. 'I've been better.'

Ortelius's lips curved into a smile.

Mainard struggled to raise himself onto one elbow. 'Help me up. I've lain here too long.'

Ortelius tugged him into a sitting position. Biting his lip to contain the pain, Mainard swung his legs around, head low.

'They used the iron boot on you?' Ortelius knelt, touching the bandaged foot lightly with his fingers.

Mainard tried to smooth the knotted hair at the back of his head. 'No, they didn't need to apply the boot. A cudgel sufficed. Although, truth to tell, I was so much surprised when they confronted me in the street I didn't think to resist. There would've been no point anyway.'

Ortelius inclined his head. 'No one escapes the Inquisition when they're determined to get you. But let me look at your foot.'

He took the wrappings off slowly. 'I had a poultice of herbs applied. It'll have drawn the poison out and prevented suppuration.'

Mainard let out a sigh of relief.

'But it's much twisted.' Ortelius looked up at Mainard. 'We'll find a surgeon to set the bones.'

Mainard shook his head emphatically. 'No surgeon. You know what they are. He'll likely have the foot off.'

'Let's at least get you out of this bed and into a chair so the blood may move within your body.'

Ortelius supported him and, wincing, Mainard hopped over to the chair, still not quite believing there was such an item of comfort here after the privations of his previous cell. Ortelius sat down on the stool opposite as Mainard leant back, eyes closed, swallowing hard to contain the bile rising up his throat.

'How did you find me?' he asked, when he was eventually able to speak.

'You have a most persistent servant.'

'Ah, Grissel. But I told her to seek help from my sister and her husband.'

'I have spoken with their neighbour and The Schyuders have gone, I believe to Germany.'

Mainard sat up. 'Did they know I was taken?'

Ortelius tapped his nose. 'I am sure your sister did not, but I think it likely that Peter Schyuder did – and it was that which precipitated his departure, which the neighbour said was sudden.'

Mainard snorted, thinking of the considerable sum his father expended to secure Schyuder's release when he was similarly imprisoned and which had yet to be repaid. Nevertheless, he could not entirely blame his brother-in-law for taking Geertruyt and his children to safety, especially when the stigma of Crypto-Jew might spread to them. Yet Schyuder could've done something to render assistance before he slipped away. The injustice burned but really it was as nothing to the unfairness of being accused of apostasy when he'd faithfully adhered to Christ. He reminded himself Christ was tested on the Cross but it didn't much help.

'It was clever of Grissel to find you.'

'Find me! We thought the Inquisitors had come for us and were breaking the door down – at least so Elizabeth told me. I was from home, which was unfortunate else I would've come immediately.'

'Did Elizabeth send you a message?'

Ortelius stared at the floor and gave a slight shake of the head. 'My sister didn't know your servant and threatened to call the watch. Grissel waited, so she tells me, every day close by our home looking out for me. I was stopped on my return, before I even entered the house. At first I couldn't understand her, for she contorts English most peculiarly and speaks very fast, but when we reverted to Dutch I realised why she was so desperate. And I may say it was all concern for you and none on her own behalf. She is a most loyal servant.' He raised his eyebrows. 'And a pretty one at that. Has quite the look of the Norse woman.'

Mainard shifted, to relieve the throbbing in his foot. It didn't help, indeed there was a sudden sharp pain as though he'd been stabbed as well as cudgelled. Ortelius half rose but was waved to sit down. 'Grissel is my wife's servant… or more correctly was. Bethia should be well on her way to Geneva by now.'

'It was most fortunate for you that she left the servant behind,' Ortelius said with raised eyebrows.

'The tale is more complicated.'

'Then we will save it for later since the guards are likely to come soon and escort me out.'

'So what's being said; have you discovered what the charges are and what I must do to secure my release? There are funds which my father left that I can draw upon, and no doubt a large ransom will be required. Then there's my living expenses while I'm incarcerated. What can you tell me?'

'Slow down.' Ortelius leaned forward and tapped Mainard's knee. 'Whatever happens be assured of one thing, my friend, I will focus all my efforts on rendering you assistance.'

Mainard dipped his head. 'And for that I most truly thank you.'

'One thing though, your house has been impounded.'

Mainard dropped his face into his hands. Weary, he was so weary.

The guard came then and Ortelius insisted they help Mainard back onto his bed. Mainard was too pain-ridden to care that they lifted him like a child.

He watched as they bent to shuffle through the low doorway, and felt bereft as Ortelius disappeared. The door shut with a clang, followed by the scraping of bolts pushed into place. Then there was silence, so deep it was as though the dense walls were suffocating all noise. The agony in his foot intensified, pulsing and throbbing and filling his head so he could think of nothing else. He twisted and turned on the bed but couldn't escape, indeed any movement increased his suffering; his whole world was pain. Oh God, why hast thou forsaken me?

Darkness fell and a hunched woman with a straggle of hair came to feed the fire, which Ortelius had made certain was burning well before he left. The soft glow of the embers was briefly soothing, but when she left there was only pain. The night was long. The fear that he would lose the foot pressed in on him hard. It could've been worse, he reminded himself... the torture might have continued, he might still be in a cell so cold that icicles formed on the dank walls, Grissel might never have found Ortelius. But such reminders didn't help when the white-hot agony of Satan's hammer blows culminated in the darkest hours. He wept then, and didn't care that he showed such weakness, for the Lord truly had forsaken him – he, who had always been the favoured child, beloved and indulged, even to the point that, when he turned up with a Christian, and not a Converso, as his bride his parents accepted her. And now he couldn't even cry out to the God of the Jews for he had no words, no prayers, no rituals of comfort and protection. He'd been abandoned by both his adopted God and his ancestral God. He was alone, and the Devil would claim him.

Chapter Nineteen

Options

Finally, the grey light of day seeped through the narrow window and Mainard's demons receded. By the time Ortelius came he was restored enough to greet him with equanimity, although the shadow of his long night had not completely dissipated. Ortelius was laden with supplies, bringing food, fresh clothes, medicine, bandages, a cushion and stool to rest Mainard's foot upon. Mainard was quite overcome and had to swallow several times before his voice was steady enough to speak. Fortunately Ortelius was bustling around.

'I can discover little,' said Ortelius. 'You there,' he shouted to the slatternly girl tending the fire, 'bring some warm water.'

Mainard lay back, eyes closed and teeth gritted while Ortelius removed the wrappings around his foot. The best outcome would be that he walked with a limp for the rest of what days he had, the worst he didn't care to consider.

'What little *have* you discovered?' he asked when Ortelius finished his ministrations and the pain faded enough for him to speak.

'Here, let me help you to the chair. You need to eat. You'll not gain strength to resist infection without sustenance.'

Mainard picked at the plateful that was passed to him

but the smell of meat made him want to vomit.

'I'm in discussions with our guild and there is much outrage that one of their own has been treated thus,' said Ortelius.

'And what can they do?'

'Representations are being made to the aldermen in the strongest of terms, make no doubt about that. However, it was perhaps not wise for your parents to leave as precipitously as they did.'

'They were given the permissions to travel.'

Ortelius rubbed along his hairline. 'I understand the official who signed those is being questioned. It's said that their journey to take the waters has a similar ring to Gracia Mendes's escape route several years ago, and she was a rich prize for Antwerp and the emperor to lose.'

'Indeed she was, a ready source of borrowings for him and other kings of Europe.' Mainard raised his eyes from the lump of bandages covering his foot. 'Her nephew Don Juan Micas, he might help.'

Ortelius sucked air in through his teeth. 'I already thought of him, but he was recently, during a visit to Antwerp, arrested himself which will no doubt swell the emperor's coffers further when the ransom is paid. No, my friend, it would be best if your parents returned, and quickly, which would most certainly strengthen the case that they'd not fled the city and go some way to removing any questions about their religious practices.'

Mainard shook his head vehemently, and then wished he had not. God's blood, was there no part of him that didn't hurt.

Ortelius held up his hand. 'I thought that would probably be your response. There's something else that may assist. I take it that your Scottish servant has told you what happened to her.'

'Yes, of course. Poor Grissel, she was trapped in the cellar.' He gazed around him. 'Certainly a much worse imprisonment than this. We all thought she'd run off with our manservant, but she had not.'

'And did she tell you why he hit her on the head and bundled her into the cellar?'

'He has a fondness for young boys, as I understand it.'

Ortelius stood up and walked around the chamber, running his fingers along his high hairline again. It reminded Mainard forcibly of Bethia touching her own hairline to check whether it needed plucked. He swallowed, but it was difficult with the lump which seemed to be again forming in his throat.

Ortelius stopped pacing and turned his piercing eyes on Mainard. 'You are my good friend and I think you know me well.'

'We are good friends to each other,' Mainard said slowly. He suspected what might be troubling Ortelius and decided to forestall it. And, although he had his suspicions about Ortelius's affections and could never but shudder when he thought of it, he was certain that Ortelius would never prey on young boys – his friend had a good heart despite his Florenzer tendencies. 'Coort, while professing a desire for women, in reality has a fondness for defenceless young boys – or so Grissel told me, and I have no reason to doubt her, especially after what she's suffered.'

Ortelius stared at him. 'What I wanted to tell you is that your pretty servant is bound and determined to go to the aldermen and tell all of Coort, thus overturning the accusations that have been made against your family.'

'Yes, I thought of that before but have considered it further – I've had ample time to think in here.' Mainard spread his arms wide. 'It cannot work. It was Marisse who made the accusations, not Coort.'

Ortelius blinked. 'And who is Marisse?'

'Another of our servants.'

'Christ's tears, what a collection of servants you do have.'

A glimmer of a smile appeared on Mainard's face.

'You're not wrong, my friend. Marisse has been with us the longest and has always considered Coort to belong to her – a misconception that he fostered with much touching and smiling glances. But then Grissel came and he played them off against each other, while all the time, unbeknownst to any of us I may say – but, as long as they do their work, our attention is not greatly focused on the servants – forcing himself on the potboy. What Coort failed to take account of is that Grissel is no fool, and she, discovering his deception, threatened to reveal all if he did not desist. But I don't see how this sorry tale can help my case.'

'But of course it does. We can say it was malice and lies.'

Mainard tugged on his earlobe. 'I hoped so, and it was where I was going when I was taken, but I think now it's too great a risk. If Coort is arrested he may build on Marisse's tales of apostasy further, which will only strengthen the case against me.'

Ortelius sighed. 'Then I do not know what to suggest.'

Chapter Twenty

A Plan

Ortelius returned promptly the next day, bringing Grissel this time. He paced up and down while Grissel knelt and tended to Mainard's foot. Mainard could see, from the way Grissel kept glancing over her shoulder, that she was trying to contain her annoyance, for with each pass Ortelius made, he trod on the back of her skirt.

Ortelius suddenly stopped pacing and picked up from their conversation the previous day. 'I think you're correct. It matters not if we discredit your manservant. If they capture him he'll be punished as a sodomite and the claims against you will still stand. They'll find other ways to show that you're an apostate. The temptation of holding onto your property will be too great.'

Mainard rubbed his tired face with his hands. 'It is most unfair. For I swear to you I *have* been a true follower of Christ Jesus and have never engaged in any nefarious practices.' He glanced at Grissel and noticed she was gazing up at him with a most peculiar expression... almost in adoration he would've said, were that not ridiculous.

Ortelius spoke again and Mainard forgot about his servant.

'And I believe you, my friend, but 'tis not me that you have to convince. And the punishment is worse than only having your property confiscated. If you're found guilty of relapsing, then *dictatoriam postestatem* will prevail.'

'What do you mean?'

'There is no appeal against any verdict.'

It was hopeless. Ortelius was right, whatever he did they would have him. He wanted to open his mouth and howl. He was young, vigorous, had a family, wanted to live. And *he* had done nothing wrong... nothing! He sagged in his chair, hadn't the strength to hold himself upright.

After a moment he said, 'I am sorry to involve you, Ortelius. T'would be better if you forget about me, for it's dangerous for you to be seen as a friend to a Converso. Go back to your maps. I've interrupted your work too long and you should distance yourself from me.'

'I will not,' said Ortelius. The words burst from him and he pressed the sides of his forehead between thumb and middle finger. Mainard could see his friend was near tears.

Then Ortelius lifted his head and his eyes gleamed in the pale light from the high window. 'I think we must find a way for you to escape.'

Grissel rested back on her haunches and looked from one to the other.

Mainard leaned forward. 'You mean like Francisco de Enzinas did from prison in Brussels.'

'Who?'

'You remember, the Spanish Protestant who translated the New Testament into Castilian?'

'Ah yes. Exactly like him.'

'How did Enzinas escape?'

'His cell door was left open and he walked out,' said Ortelius. He slapped his knee. 'All we need to find are some guards willing to look the other way for generous recompense.'

Grissel rose to her feet, her ministrations finished. 'Ye canna walk,' she said in her usual abrupt manner. 'Your foot's buggered,' she added in Scots for emphasis.

'I will bring a crutch.'

'Aye, and how will he walk out of here on a crutch without awbody knowing it's him?'

Mainard would've laughed at the expression on Ortelius's face to be spoken to so directly and in such a manner, and by a servant. He was fortunate to have escaped thus far; Grissel didn't generally hold back.

'Grissel is correct. Even at night and in disguise, given my stature and shape it's likely that I'd be recognised.'

'Then we'll disguise you so that even I won't recognise you. Some padding, different clothes, and a lot of dirt could do the trick.'

'He still canna walk far,' said the ever-practical Grissel. 'Even with a crutch.'

'We'll give it some thought,' said Ortelius as the noon bell was heard. 'I must away, I have work to do.'

Mainard tried to smile as they left but knew it was simply a distortion of the face that he was managing. Grissel wanted to stay behind but he wouldn't allow it. He knew he was fortunate to have books and writing materials around him as distraction; should not be made despondent by the amount of time he spent alone with his fears. He settled down to pen a letter to Bethia but it was difficult to know what to say. To write that he was in prison with a foot he might never walk on again – no he could not do that. He knew his wife… she would insist on turning around and coming back. Yet there was a risk she might return anyway. The only letter he'd received from her spoke of her uneasiness, wondered why he had not left Antwerp already, urged him to follow them, said he should forgo selling the property to reach safety. How he wished he had done so.

He shifted on his chair, reminding himself that Diogo Mendes was held prisoner for many months before being freed – although Mendes had kings petitioning for his release as well as the merchant community of Antwerp. The de Langes did not have his reach, and in any case, Mainard, in becoming a map colourist, had distanced himself from his father's peers. He was fortunate to have the loyal support of Ortelius, but he, although increasingly known, was still young and not especially well connected.

Mainard struggled to his feet. If escape was ever to be an option then he must practise walking. White-hot pain shot across his foot as though burning pokers had been applied. He stood on one leg, would not allow himself to collapse back on the chair. He hopped one, two, three, four, five hops across the cell. It was spacious, he knew, and comfortable – for a prison. There was a fire burning brightly in the wide fireplace, the remains of the meal brought by Grissel spread across the board, the book he was reading lying next to it, and his writing materials reproaching him. A guard, big, burly and clearly well fed, came in to tend the fire and looked surprised to see Mainard standing.

'Let me help you to your seat, young master,' he said, offering a muscled arm.

'I thank you but I must move, else my other foot may drop off from inactivity.'

The guard grinned then edged closer, stretching his neck up to whisper in Mainard's ear. 'Should you require anything you must tell me. I will attend to all your needs.'

Mainard gazed at him thoughtfully. 'For a price.'

The man shrugged. 'Of course. We all have families to feed.'

'You may take the leftovers from my meal but please make sure at least some goes to the poor wretches incarcerated below.'

The guard rubbed his hands. Mainard doubted any of it would reach the cellars where there were so many who must rely on charity. On impulse he grabbed the bread from under the guard's reaching hand. Later, when that wretched creature dragged her way in to empty his pot, he gave the bread to her. She glanced up at him from under the tangle of hair falling over her face, tucked the bread furtively into her bodice, the other hand frozen into a permanent claw by the webbing grown between the fingers – a devil's hand – hanging by her side.

'Thankee, sir,' she whispered.

He was left alone again and hobbled around the corners of the cell, the stone rough beneath his hand as he used the wall for balance. Even with the aid of a crutch, never mind bribing someone to leave the cell door unlocked, he knew he would struggle to walk out. Yet waiting and hoping for release was not a sensible option, especially when he was leaving Antwerp forever anyway. Diogo Mendes, he seemed to remember, was held for near twelve months.

'I've been pondering further how you might escape,' said Ortelius when he arrived the next day.

'I've thought of little else,' said Mainard, gripping the crutch which Ortelius had brought. 'But where is Grissel?'

'I told her to stay at home, with her brother.'

Mainard raised his eyebrows, unsurprised to learn that the potboy had been adopted as a *brother*.

'My sister has need of her, for Grissel proved useful in mixing paint.' Ortelius gave a snort of laughter. 'Although she refers to the work as *guddling*.'

It was a relief to have a reason to smile. 'You're no doubt learning a range of Scots words to fit every occasion.'

'But down to business,' said Ortelius rubbing his hands together. 'Here's what I've been thinking.' He counted his suggestions off on his fingers. 'One, we bribe a guard to leave the door unlocked…'

'Remember I cannot walk more than a few steps, although this should help.' He patted the crutch.

Ortelius held up his hand. 'Let me say my list and then we can discuss the merits, or otherwise, of each.'

He began again. 'One, we go the Enzinas way; two, we disguise you; three, we leave a substitute in disguise; four, you are carried out by some means…'

126

'Most likely in my coffin,' Mainard muttered.

'That's not a bad idea,' said Ortelius slowly. 'I wonder if there is some draught we could have the apothecary make up that would have you sleep so deeply it could feign death?'

'Hah, that sounds like the script from a bad play.'

Ortelius squeezed his eyes shut then opened them wide. 'Nevertheless, I will investigate the possibility further. In the meantime, is there any guard who may be prevailed upon to render assistance for a substantial sum – perhaps the one with the thick arms who is forever hanging around hoping for a few more coins?'

'Maybe. I'll find a way to discreetly raise it with him.'

But in the end it was the Devil's daughter with her claw-hand who came to Mainard's assistance.

He'd given her money to prepare an evening meal to supplement the food that Grissel brought, and this was also a way he could make sure that she received some sustenance, for his heart was wrung with pity for her. As she moved around him to fulfil this task, he realised she was much younger than he initially thought: the dragging walk and tangle of hair permanently shrouding her face no doubt to disguise her youth. She fussed between the cooking pot, which was set over the fire, and the array of tableware that Grissel had left. The first time she picked up the ceramic jug she held it in her hand with an expression of wonder on her face, as though it was the finest thing she'd ever seen.

'What's your name?' Mainard asked.

She started, quickly replaced the jug on the board and hung her head. He realised he'd never heard her speak.

He waited and eventually she whispered, 'Hanneke.'

'That's a pretty name.'

She said nothing, but he glimpsed a smile through the hair.

The burly guard disliked Mainard's new friendship, glowering at her and telling Mainard to 'Watch that one because she'll steal what she can.'

But it was him that Mainard watched. He heard the guard waylay the girl as soon as she left the cell and the squeal of pain that followed.

'Hanneke, come back here,' he called.

There was silence, then she reappeared, head hung lower than ever.

'What did he do to you?'

But she shook her head and would not speak, while Mainard puzzled over how he might pass payment to her without the guard stealing it – and hurting her in the process.

When Mainard told Ortelius that he didn't want to approach the guard to assist with his escape, Ortelius's high forehead wrinkled mightily.

'So what are you going to do?' The words burst from his mouth like a spray of water from a pump.

'I'm sorry, my friend. I know that you devote much time to my care and visiting every day is taking its toll.'

Ortelius frowned, but, after a moment, he walked over and squeezed Mainard's shoulder, as was his wont. 'My concerns are all for you, de Lange. I fear we must get you out, and soon. There are rumours that they do intend to try you… and if not, it seems they may hold you indefinitely.'

There was movement in the corner and both men started.

'Hanneke, I didn't know you were still here.'

Ortelius glared at her as she scuttled away.

Mainard flapped his hand. 'Don't worry, she's an ally.' He hoped he wouldn't be proved wrong.

'What does she do here?'

'Cleans… and I have her prepare some food for me.'

'After she empties out the close-stool?'

'I suppose.'

Ortelius's nose wrinkled.

Later, Hanneke sidled up to Mainard, whispering about cesspits and disguises.

He stopped her, saying, 'Speak plainly, for I cannot understand you.'

'There is a cart which comes early every morning to

take away the night soil and tip it in the river, just outside the prison.' She shivered, glancing around her.

'How will I reach the cart?' he asked softly.

She leant in closer, staring at the ground as she spoke. 'I am here before daybreak. The guards are often asleep and I can creep in and get the keys.'

'And if they catch you?'

'I'll say I wanted to start work early. They may beat me but I doubt they'll suspect me. No one does, you know.' She waved the claw-hand at him. 'You'll need to walk down the stairs. Can you do it?'

'I will, even if I have to slide down on my arse. When can we do this? I must have time to arrange a boat.'

''Tis better on a Sunday. The guards are given ale on a Saturday night.'

'That explains why they're more pungent than usual on a Sunday.'

She hunched, and he guessed she didn't understand the word. 'Smelly, I mean. They are very smelly.'

Her shoulders shook and he realised she was laughing, but only as a poor downtrodden girl will dare to laugh… silently.

Ortelius approved the plan, saying he had the easy part if all he need do was arrange a boat. 'I may even join you on it myself. I've been planning to go to Italy for sometime.'

Mainard's face brightened. 'That would be most satisfactory, although I have a wandering journey ahead as I must collect my parents from Aachen and thence to Geneva where Bethia is.'

Ortelius gazed at the rough stone floor. 'You have many family responsibilities; perhaps another time,' he mumbled.

Mainard felt a great weariness. 'I will write to you once we're in Venice, or wherever it is that we end up, and you must visit us there.'

Ortelius inclined his head. 'I'll away and arrange a boat for Sunday.'

Chapter Twenty-One

Escape

Mainard rolled over and came up to sitting, stifling a groan as he swung his legs to the floor. The pain in his foot changed from a twisting ache to a regular throb, like the rat-tat-tat of a drum beating inside it. He heaved himself off the narrow bed, holding onto the back of the chair which he'd hauled over to the bedside last eve for just this purpose. He was fully dressed apart from his cloak. He draped it over his shoulders. Hanneke was in the doorway beckoning and he grabbed his crutch and hobbled over, ignoring the pain that shot up his foot with each movement, although he couldn't hold in the gasp when he stumbled.

He held onto Hanneke's shoulder as they moved out into the passageway; she was shaking beneath the thin shawl. All was dark and silent, apart from the odd snore emanating from behind closed doors. Yet Mainard could sense the sleeping bodies all around, pressing down like a great weight upon his own shoulders. They reached the first set of stairs and he paused, gathering his strength, and courage, to descend.

'Quickly,' hissed Hanneke.

There was a moment with each downward step on this worn and uneven spiral of stairs where he had to place weight on his injured foot. Then he tried gripping the rough stone wall and hopping. Hanneke moved slowly in front of him, presumably to prevent a tumble, but if he fell he would take her with him. He shook his head impatiently, but she only moved one step lower, turning to watch him through her veil of hair.

There were voices from below. Mainard halted, mid-hop. A door slammed, and then there was the unmistakable sound of heavy footsteps clomping up the stairs; he could hear the man huffing and puffing as he climbed. Mainard turned, the agony of his foot all but forgotten, and tried to run back up the stairs. His foot gave way and he fell heavily, sprawling across the steps. Hanneke climbed over him, took hold of his arm and hauled, but Mainard was a tall man and she small and slight.

Someone called from below and the climbing man responded, then his footsteps receded. Mainard felt his heart begin beating again.

'Hurry,' begged Hanneke, for Mainard had frozen, uncertain. Perhaps he should return to his cell and attempt this when his foot had healed further. Yet he saw his wife almost as though she was before him and knew he must go to her. He began hopping again, as fast as he could. They reached the level below and the one below that. His left leg was screaming from the unaccustomed movement, almost blocking out the pain in his right foot. Then suddenly the stairs came to an end and Hanneke led him along a narrow passageway, the ceiling so low he had to lower his head to avoid hitting it. There was the usual powerful malodour of unwashed bodies but that was soon overtaken by the stench of latrines. Mainard swallowed again and again to stop himself retching. The corridor twisted and turned, grew lower and narrower till his shoulders brushed each side, up a few uneven steps, down another few. Finally, it came to an end.

He stared into a deep channel thick with slurry moving sluggishly beneath an iron grill. Through the grill

131

he could see the grey waters of the River Scheldt drifting by.

Mainard looked to Hanneke. 'I am to get in this? I thought there was a cart in which I could hide?'

Hanneke shook her head.

'Why did you not tell me of this?'

'It's the easiest way for you to escape.'

'I will drown in shit. I cannot swim, and even if I could, this stuff is too thick to swim in and will suck me down.'

Hanneke turned and fumbled at the low wall behind. A rat came scuttling out and Mainard went to kick it away, forgetting he had only one usable leg. He groaned and the rat escaped.

'You can hold onto this,' said Hanneke, flourishing a length of board. 'I hid it down here yesterday, for you.'

She was clearly expecting praise for her cleverness. Mainard looked to the board in her hands and then gazed at the channel of foetid sludge beneath him.

'I will need to kick my way out to the river.'

'Only a little way. Jump in close to the grill.'

He could not stand debating this further. Bethia's father would take her back if he drowned. Mainard had seen the love in his eyes when he looked upon his daughter, and Master Seton seemed most taken with his namesake and grandson. He gave Hanneke his cloak and the bag of coin agreed for her help – she took both gratefully – dropped his crutch, grabbed the board and jumped.

The soup was so thick he rested momentarily on top then slowly began to sink. Desperately he hauled himself half onto the board, leaving his legs dangling, and kicked with his good foot. The board swirled and he was facing backwards. Hanneke raised her arm in farewell and disappeared back up the passage. He felt destitute. Was he to drown here alone and unrecorded?

The muck swirled once more and he was beneath the

bars. His jerkin caught on the prongs. He tugged to free himself but he was caught fast, like a badger in a trap. He tried to wriggle out of the jerkin but was pinned down between grill and board, indeed could feel the spike pressing hard into his back. His hands, slippy with slime, were sliding… could not hold on… would drown here, alone… would never see Bethia again.

There was the sound of material ripping, beautiful to his ear. The board floated lazily into the river. The sludge mingled with the clearer water and he began to move with greater speed. He sent up a prayer that the promised boat was waiting downstream.

He was moving inexorably towards the middle of the broad river as the sun slowly rose, the long rays dazzling his eyes and casting a yellow glaze over everything. The water grew colder as the board pirouetted further out. He thought how ironic it would be if he survived near suffocation by shite only to die of cold in the cleansing river water. He turned his head this way and that searching desperately for a boat, any boat, but the river, normally so overfull of craft, seemed empty.

'Help!' he shouted, over and over.

Then a small rowing boat was upon him. A man reached out an oar, urging him to grasp it. The board slipped away from beneath him and he was sinking, his hand too cold to grip the oar.

A hand grabbed his wrist, another hand the back of his jacket.

'Kick, man, kick.'

It was Ortelius. Mainard opened his mouth to tell Ortelius he shouldn't have come, it was too dangerous, but instead he took a mouthful of river water. He was choking on it, coughing and spluttering, as Ortelius and the other man heaved him into the boat while a third stayed on the far side leaning his weight out to prevent them being overturned and all ending up in the river.

Then he was in the bottom of the boat, in a great

tangle of arms and legs. Ortelius took off his cloak and flung it over Mainard.

'Stay down. We must get past the prison.'

And Mainard heard it now. The bells ringing long and insistent to signal a prisoner had escaped. Peering out from beneath the cover, he saw the oars pulled with deep strokes and Ortelius's big feet in their stout boots resting in the prow while the clamour of discordant bells grew louder; they must be adjacent to the castle now. He hoped Hanneke got away safe. It seemed to take an eternity to row past the city and he was shaking so hard with cold he doubted he'd ever be still again. Finally the noise diminished. They slowed and Mainard saw the edge of a grassy bank. He was helped out of the boat with the cloak draped over him and, bent double like a hunchback, supported along the stone-strewn track then loaded onto a barge. He turned once he was safely aboard and looked to where Ortelius stood.

'Farewell, my friend. I would come with you but it's known I visited you often in prison, and if I disappear too then it may be difficult for me to safely return to Antwerp.'

'But you'll be in danger anyway. Is it not wiser for you to depart, at least for a while?'

'My servants are loyal. They'll confirm that I've not left the house today.'

'Then go, please. And I thank you from the bottom of my heart – no one could have been a more faithful friend.'

Ortelius brushed his eyes with the back of his hand. 'I almost forgot. Take this.' He handed a purse to Mainard. 'And there are bills of exchange in the chests. I have brought all that you stored with me; everything is accounted for. Clothes for you too.'

Before Mainard could reply he turned and hurried away, without a backward glance.

The tears came to Mainard's own eyes. He could not

have had a more loyal friend.

The barge cast off and then Grissel was on one side of him, her *brother* on the other, and he was helped into the small cabin.

It was the last time he was aware of much for many days, apart from his fraught dreams, which were filled with firelight dancing on thick walls, Zwijgers' face thrusting close, spike in hand coming at Mainard's eyes, and always a desperate anxiety as to where his wife and child were. Then one turbulent night, when he thrashed and cried out, of being held. A cool hand stroked his forehead as his head was cradled in a woman's lap.

'Bethia…' he whispered.

The hand paused.

'Don't stop, my Bethia.'

He turned his head and pressed his face against her soft belly.

One day he opened his eyes wide. He was alone. His foot throbbed, but not with the same agonising pain as before. The door opened and Grissel's face appeared around it. She came into the chamber but wouldn't look him in the eye. This was not the bold servant he was used to. She looked… embarrassed. But he was more concerned about his foot than what was going on for his servant.

'Did you have to take it off?' he asked bluntly in English.

'Take what off? I never took nothing off. I'm a good girl, like my mother aye telt me to be, nae matter what that Coort may have said.'

'Grissel, what are you talking, or as you would say blethering, about? Do I still have my foot or not?'

'Oh, aye, right,' mumbled Grissel, shifting from her own foot to the other, face flushing as though she'd thrust it close to the burning embers in the grate. Mainard didn't think he'd ever seen anyone go such a deep red, even Bethia at her most embarrassed.

'Aye ye still hae it. We thought it would have to come off but the physician says you are young and well fed and the blood coursing through you did not become full of poison.'

'Was Bethia here? No, that was in my dreams, wasn't it?'

She nodded, eyes sliding away.

'Where are we? An inn?'

She nodded again, head bent.

'Ask the innkeeper to come to me. And where is the purse Ortelius left?'

'I have it here.' Grissel dug deep in her pocket and thrust it at him. 'I can tell you all I spent.'

'I'm sure you've managed the funds wisely, Grissel.'

She stopped kicking at the bedframe and looked him fully in the face for the first time. Dipping a small curtsy she said, 'Thankee, sir.'

Mainard sighed as the door closed behind her. Then, lifting the covers, he swung his legs out and used the bedpost to haul himself shakily up. He stood weight on one foot and gazed down on the lump of bandages. Enough lying around, it was time now to put what strength he had into retrieving his family and getting them to a place of safety.

Part Three

Geneva

April to June 1550

Chapter Twenty-Two

Will's Geneva

They saw the city state of Geneva from a distance, its walls rising from green pastures, the patchwork of new stone mixed with tarnished stone showing where the defences had recently been strengthened. Even the walls of Antwerp couldn't compare to the massive building work achieved here; Geneva was a fortress. The citadel rose even higher behind its walls, like a giant overseeing all around, having recently and most determinedly asserted its independence from Bern, Fribourg and the Dukes of Savoy.

Will, gazing upon it for the first time, understood that his home of St Andrews was comparatively a safe town, its walls intended more to delineate the boundaries for trade rather than to provide protection for its citizens. He wondered what it would be like to live where the threat of attack was constant; would soon find out as he hoped to make Geneva his home, at least for the foreseeable future.

The Genevans had cleverly diverted some of the river so it formed an additional layer of defence and flowed part way around the walls, creating a broad moat. Not only that, there was a second defensive waterway dug some distance out from the first. As they descended the hillside and drew closer, he saw that houses extended on both sides of the broad river with an island conveniently in the middle, which meant the span required of the bridges linking one side with the other was not so great. The bridges themselves looked to be solid wooden structures with a jumble of buildings sprawled across them. Beyond them, through a break in the pall of smoke rising from the thousands of chimneys peppering the rooftops, Will glimpsed the lake, spreading out and so large it looked to have no end. In front of the bridges, great chains were stretched loosely across the river ready to be hauled tight, preventing any enemy from rowing up the river and breeching the defences and by such means creating another line of protection for this city of wealthy burghers.

As they rode along the broad path leading to the gate, the mountains rising all around in serried peaks turned a glowing pink from the setting sun. Will didn't think he'd ever seen anything so beautiful. It touched his soul deep inside; he prayed it was a good omen for his life to come in Calvin's city.

They soon crossed the wooden bridge over the moat and passed through the high, but narrow, entrance to the city. Indeed, so narrow there was barely a finger breadth between the carriage and the stone of the gate, and Will called a warning to the women to tuck their elbows in. Following behind, he was surprised to find a broad space opening before him. The track wound through fields and then there was another layer of defence, this wall not so high as the outer one.

He gave instructions to one driver to take his precious cargo to a reputable inn, and hastened off with the rest of the carts to find safe storage for the many kists. Their saviours from the terrible attack, who both he and Bethia had grown fond of and found to be most kindly men, advised and assisted his negotiations with a small, grizzled wisp of a man who Will doubted could see off any determined thieves. However, when two strapping sons, almost as tall as Will, appeared and flanked their father, he was reassured.

The driver returned as they finished offloading the carts and Will waved farewell to their saviours with many thanks. They in turn were most grateful for the gift of the horses, for Will had determined there was no need to expend funds on stabling them, especially when he hoped to remain in Geneva. When Mainard came he could purchase new mounts.

Strolling across the green swath towards the centre of the city, he studied the spires of a church rising high above the cluster of rooftops: two lower spikes and a third much higher one with a great ball perched atop the cone of its roof. It looked strangely foreign and… unchristian. Yet Geneva was known as the Protestant Rome, for all Protestants in Europe looked to John Calvin now Martin Luther was dead.

He found his sister, as directed, already settled in the inn opposite the cathedral which dominated the town.

'There's no shortage of inns to choose from, there seems to be an abundance in this city,' said Bethia, while Samuel-Thomas sat on her lap watching everything around him with a quiet intelligence that Will found disconcerting in such a young child. 'But I'm satisfied and think we'll be most comfortable while I await Mainard. And all even better now I've a settled address to give him.'

He saw her swallow, knew she was anxious that she hadn't heard from her husband but decided to say nothing, for he'd no more information as to Mainard's movements than she. Suddenly many bells rang out and they all started. The baby's face puckered but he didn't cry – why would he, sheltered as he was in his mother's arms.

'This inn is perhaps not such a wise choice after all,' said Bethia.

'I doubt if any other would be much quieter. Geneva

141

seems to be blessed with an abundance of bells.'

'It's convenient for worship I suppose.' Bethia looked to Katheline. 'I'll go to Mass this evening, if you'll look after Samuel-Thomas.'

Will looked from Bethia to Katheline and sighed. He was finally in a city where he could espouse a true faith without fear of a charge of heresy, and he was here with a Catholic and a secret Judaiser.

'There is nowhere in this city you may attend Mass. Do you not understand, Bethia? Geneva chased its bishop out twenty years ago and most of the nobles with him. The electors determined the city would become Protestant. Knox told me that Geneva was falling apart and known as the smelliest city in Europe, the people poor, until Calvin came. He said the priests even ran the brothels.'

'Will!' Bethia said, glancing at Katheline. 'That's most inappropriate.'

Will rolled his eyes.

'Is there truly no place of worship I can attend in all of Geneva?'

'There are several churches in Geneva, but you're not listening, Bethia. Anyone found to be a follower of the Pope will be expelled from the city. I thought you understood that when you insisted on coming with me, rather than returning to Scotland with Father. I told you – you cannot have paid attention.' Will cast his eyes down, knew he'd perhaps not been as clear as he should, so desperate was he to get here and with no funds to do so until Mainard provided them.

He opened his mouth to speak further but the bells were off again, followed by the loud beating of a drum. 'Most probably the signal that the gates have closed for the night and curfew begun,' he said in answer to their inquiring looks.

'What an unquiet city. But surely there must be a priest somewhere in a place which looks to have many thousands of souls.'

'At least ten thousand I believe.'

'Ten thousand people – and all Protestants!'

'Close your mouth otherwise you'll catch flies.' He scratched at the soft flesh on the inside of his elbow. 'Why not see this as an opportunity to understand better a faith that is true to Christ?'

Bethia humphed. 'Katheline and I will stay quietly in our chamber of a Sunday.'

Will soon learned this would be most unwise. Early next morning he was on Calvin's doorstep, wondering if he would gain entry. But Calvin had heard of him, indeed was expecting him, for John Knox had recently written to John Calvin expressly to recommend William Seton. Will was touched that his former counsellor had thought to do so and appreciative that Calvin gave him a warm welcome.

The two Johns looked not dissimilar to one another, with long noses, long thick beards and bulbous eyes, although Calvin was shorter in height than Knox, which meant Will felt even more like the steeple rising above the nave than usual.

'You're not the first Scot I have met. You may not know but George Wishart was with me for some time before his sad end,' Calvin said.

He fell silent and Will thought of poor Wishart.

After a few moment Calvin spoke again in his gravelly voice. 'John Knox seems to be a fine man of sound doctrine. I've heard of him, of course, but this was the first time I'd heard from him. I believe you once acted as his secretary.'

Will shifted on the chair he'd been offered. 'I learned much working for Master Knox, especially when he was dictating his thoughts so that I might scribe for him.'

Calvin stroked his nose with his forefinger. Will didn't think he'd ever seen such long white fingers on a man before.

'What made you undertake this journey?'

'I've read your work and was eager to understand more.' Will tried to be still but was twitching as though he'd a nest of ants beneath him. He hoped he'd given a sufficient, if not entirely truthful, reason to be in Geneva – was not going to explain that he mainly left Berwick and Knox's service because Knox was to marry the fragrant Marjorie Bowes.

'I believe you're travelling with a large party and much baggage.'

Will gulped. Calvin was well informed. 'My sister and her child are with me. Her husband will follow soon and they'll continue on to Italy, where he has business.'

Calvin inclined his head. 'Ah, so your sojourn here is to be brief.'

Will leant forward. It was very hot in this chamber and he could feel the sweat running down the side of his face and into his beard. 'I hope, I very much hope, to remain here and study under you.'

'Well, you've most certainly demonstrated commitment to a true faith after what you, and Knox, endured on the galleys.' He leant back in his chair, steepled his fingers and smiled at Will's expression. 'It's my duty to know what takes place within the synod. I'd hope to see all your family at church with you tomorrow morning.'

Will swallowed.

Calvin stood up. It was clear the meeting was at an end. He went out into the crowded streets, didn't want to return to the inn yet, needed to have space to think. He crossed the long wooden bridge over the river, weaving his way between the booths, tall houses and people which crowded it, and into the other half of Geneva. From there he could see ships sailing up the lake and more anchored close by. It had nothing like the busyness of Antwerp but still it appeared likely there were many Genevan merchants who made a good living. He wandered up and down through narrow streets and even narrower alleyways trying to determine what was best. There were no doubt Catholic visitors come to Geneva who were left to pursue their faith in private, but that was a different matter from his own sister doing so. Will desperately wanted to become one of Calvin's close associates but doubted it would happen if Bethia didn't espouse Calvinism. If he could be certain she would be gone soon then it wouldn't matter, but it might be many weeks before de Lange arrived. He would just have to insist, as the man of the party, that both Bethia and Katheline showed true meekness and attended the evangelical services.

But when he returned to the inn, full of purpose, all was in uproar. Katheline had uncovered an infestation of bedbugs and Bethia vowed she would spend not one more night in this place.

Chapter Twenty-Three

Persuasion

'Bethia,' said Will earnestly, the next day, in the private chamber of a less pestilential but equally noisy inn – there was no avoiding the many bells of Geneva, be they a harmonious chiming or a great clanging. 'Please at least come to a service. John Calvin is a clever man of sound doctrine who men all over Europe are following.'

Bethia flapped her hands at him. 'Stop towering over me.'

He took a step back and waited, determined to secure her agreement. There was little purpose in remaining in Geneva if she refused.

'I've heard John Knox preach, is that not enough?'

'When?'

'He came to Holy Trinity while you were in the castle.'

'Ah yes. It was his first time in the pulpit as a Protestant priest. I wish I could've heard him.'

'You could – if only you'd given up the siege.'

Will chewed on his lip to prevent a sharp retort. He tried to reply calmly. 'We each made our choices.'

Bethia sniffed. 'You think women have choices?'

Will folded his arms and grinned at her. Perhaps if he introduced some levity she might be more amenable. 'Not usually, but you somehow managed when you chose to marry Mainard.' His smile faded, as he considered what the marriage had meant for her. 'Do you ever regret it?'

'It's not been easy, yet I'm fortunate to have such a loving husband,' she said slowly. 'But we're allowing ourselves to become distracted. In answer to your question about attending church... I was quite wrung out after listening to John Knox. He spoke, or, more correctly, shouted for four hours, barely drawing breath. I've never seen anyone so convinced of his own rightness and with so much to say about it.'

'And that's what makes him a great man.' The words burst from Will's lips and then he was annoyed with himself for being so emphatic. Now they were teetering on the verge of another argument.

Bethia stood up and smoothed her gown, her expression as serene as any portrait of the Blessed Virgin. He hated when she enacted this unnatural calmness; it was so provoking. He clenched and unclenched his fingers; a shouting match would gain him nothing. He could see her watching him, knew that she realised full well he was trying to contain himself.

'You've grown in wisdom, brother,' she said, nodding.

He found this more provoking than her false serenity.

'But I will come with you and listen to Calvin, once at least.'

Will's shoulders relaxed. 'And Katheline?'

'I cannot speak for Katheline, she must decide for herself.'

Katheline, when applied to, was unconcerned and willingly concurred. Yet there was something in her expression that made him suspect she was toying with him as much as his sister. He wandered out of the chamber and went to return to ask which service today they planned to go to. Hand on the latch he overheard the discussion within.

'I've feigned worship in church for many years, what

difference if it is a Protestant or Catholic service when the true faith is with the rabbi and the synagogue,' said Katheline.

'Hush, you shouldn't say such words aloud, even to me. If it was known they would torture and burn you.'

'I believe they favour a quick drowning here,' said Katheline lightly. 'Come, Bethia, whatever faith you profess, what matters is where you are. If we were in Lyon still, it's Will who would likely be burned or drowned, if caught.'

Will sucked the air in through his teeth, although she was probably correct.

'Nevertheless, take care. This is not something to treat lightly.'

'I think it's the only way to treat it, else I'd be crushed under a heavy rock of fear,' said Katheline. 'But I'll heed your words.'

Will was about to charge into the chamber and insist that no services should be attended with such cynical intent when Katheline's next words had him pause in shock.

'Speaking of different faiths, did you know that Calvin's wife was previously an Anabaptist?'

'God's blood, how can that be?' Bethia had spoken aloud what Will was thinking. And how did Katheline know of this and he did not?

'How I wish I could forget the burning of that poor Anabaptist in Antwerp,' he heard Bethia say. 'But how strange that Calvin should have married one. Actually, how strange that a priest can now take a wife; I cannot get used to it.'

'I know,' said Katheline, giggling. 'You'd think their minds would rise higher than their nethers.'

He heard his sister's laughter and beat a hasty retreat.

He puzzled over this unexpected information about Calvin's wife, but dismissed it as an irrelevance when he learned that Calvin was now a widower.

They all went together, shepherded by a solemn and stiff-backed Will, to the cathedral. He couldn't help but glance frequently at Bethia during the service. Surely she could have no complaints about the level of Calvin's voice, for there was no shouting. Indeed, Calvin lovingly exhorted them to follow him as he worked his way through the Scriptures, drawing his congregation into right-thinking rather than putting the fear of Satan first and foremost. He ended the service with simple words of direction. '*Let us fall before the majesty of our great God.*'

They came out blinking into the early spring sunshine and Will couldn't help himself. 'Well?'

'I'll resist the temptation to tease you, brother, for it's all too easy.'

Will rolled his eyes, unseen.

'You know, he reminded me of our father. The same yellow-red beard, pale blue eyes and frown lines. He's much less of the fire and brimstone than Knox. Indeed, I warmed to the man and have no objection to hearing more of what he has to say.' She took his arm and smiled. 'I hope that satisfies you.'

'It does,' he said simply.

Katheline too seemed drawn to Calvin and went each day to listen to him. Will was most curious until it dawned that Calvin devoted his weekday expositions to an examination of the Old Testament. He said nothing, better to leave her and hope that some of Calvin's right-thinking was being absorbed.

He was now meeting with Calvin regularly, and one of the benefits of his known association was an invitation for his family to reside with a Madame Bernier and her husband, *until you're settled more permanently*. He was delighted by the inference that his presence was sought in the longer term but masked his pleasure, simply bowing and thanking Calvin for the recommendation.

Bethia was reluctant when he put it to her. 'We

accepted de Vaudemont's hospitality and look what happened.' She sighed. 'Poor Suzanne. And Ysabeau awakens every night, whimpering in terror, for all she's a mute.'

It was Will's turn to sigh. Did he have to take every waif Bethia picked up into consideration as well? 'This is different. Madame Bernier *is* known. She's a pillar of the church and a devotee of Calvin's. Let's at least go and meet her.'

They went that very day. The matron of the house bustled around, their comfort of great concern to her, and especially since Will was already known to be an assistant to Calvin. She was a woman of middle years, rosy-cheeked and well-cushioned. Master Bernier must enjoy resting his face on her large bosom – Will blushed fiery red at the impropriety of his thoughts. He distracted himself by studying the picture hanging on the wall behind her. She turned and gazed at it.

'That is Monsieur Bernier's favourite. The woman is…' her voice faded away.

'Very old to be displayed naked,' Bethia whispered as their hostess moved to stand before another painting. Will covered his mouth to prevent the laugh escaping.

Madame Bernier said briskly, 'I prefer this print of two squirrels myself.'

'It is… unusual,' said Bethia.

Will gazed on it for several moments silently. 'I like it very much. It has a plainness that's appealing and is executed with great attention to detail.'

Madame Bernier looked gratified. 'The artist of both paintings, a man called Albrecht Durer, studied the texts of Luther before he died. Monsieur Bernier and I consider his work a most suitable adornment for a Protestant household.'

Will could see Bethia smirking out of the corner of his eye but he no longer considered the Berniers choice of art a matter for levity. He felt great respect for them that faith

150

was central to every action they took; they were indeed true believers. By the following day he and his charges were established at the Berniers. Bethia seemed satisfied and Will felt the burden of responsibility lighten.

The next thing that happened had him so overfull with joy he felt he might burst. He hastened home to tell Bethia, and Katheline, his good news. 'Calvin is preparing another commentary for publication and has asked if I will assist in his endeavours. Until recently he always wrote his papers and letters by himself, can you imagine? And with his prolific output.' He saw Bethia and Katheline exchange a glance but was too buoyed up to care that he was amusing them. 'Farni has been helping but he grows arthritic and is in need of an assistant.' Will curled his fingers to demonstrate. 'Farni cannot well control his movements. His writing has become erratic and often illegible, and Calvin feels that I, especially since I've a sound understanding of doctrine, would do well to take over.' He shifted from one leg to the other. 'It's quite a responsibility and I pray that I may live up to his expectations. Farni has promised to be by my side to render his advice and guidance.'

Bethia smiled and he realised it was affectionate rather than sardonic. 'Our father would be proud of you, Will. You've grown into a fine man.'

'Do you truly think I'd make Father proud?'

'I believe Father thought well enough of Calvin's work… although I doubt he'd ever renounce the Pope.'

'Who knows,' said Will. 'If Scotland were turned from the Antichrist then I'm sure Father, ever the pragmatist, would follow. But as long as our queen is among the French I cannot see that happening.' He paused. 'Did I tell you that I saw her, even spoke to her briefly, our wee Queen Mary of Scotland?'

'Yesss. You have mentioned it once or twice.' The

sardonic expression he so disliked was in evidence, and Katheline too was smirking behind her hand.

'Calvin does do great work,' said Bethia.

He stared at her suspiciously; was she trying to mollify him?

'It's good to see all children go to school each day, girls as well as boys.'

His suspicions were wrong, Bethia did understand what a good man Calvin was. 'Did you know he established a tribunal where any man who beats his wife, or any mother who neglects her children, is brought before a jury of neighbours and held to account?' He frowned. 'Although I understand there have been some abuses and it's not entirely successful, yet.'

'Well, I salute the man for trying,' said Katheline, and Bethia nodded her approval vigorously.

Going each day to scribe, he was privileged to listen as Calvin expounded the foundations of his doctrine and the basis of his leadership.

'We have restored the church to biblical purity through sound preaching of the gospel and clear debate on what that means. This is the first cornerstone of a strong religious foundation, for we can all truly now be saved and enter the kingdom of heaven, provided we follow right-thinking.' Calvin paused, clutching at his belly, wincing as he did.

Will looked to Farni to check if he should be writing Calvin's words down. Farni shook his head and whispered to Will, 'We have all this. Our master is reminding and reassuring himself.'

'And to follow a true path we must be shown to live right, and that means all men, even the rich, must work. But never,' he slapped the board with his hand, 'never lust after wealth. All work is sacred and all gains should be continually reinvested. Wealth should never be for its own sake but only to make more and demonstrate correct living.' He slapped the board again and paused for breath. 'When we stand before the Lord we will be held to account for how we have lived.'

Calvin nodded to himself. 'Our lives may be predestined but that does *not* mean we shouldn't try our hardest to follow the true path and live a good and holy life.'

Again he nodded to himself, and Will was suddenly reminded of his small brother John and how his wee head would bob like a duck on the sea when he was enthusiastic. He felt an overwhelming rush of longing for his home and dipped his head to hide the tears, wondering if he *was* predestined never to return.

Chapter Twenty-Four

Ameaux

Will glanced sideways at Bethia. She sat elbows resting on knees, chin resting in hands, gazing up at the pulpit with an expression of rapt attention which he found most appropriate... and gratifying. Calvin was telling of the joy of motherhood, of what Mary would've felt in caring for Jesus, and then, when she must return him to the Lord, of how Jesus sent John to be her substitute son.

When they rose and filed out of the church, she was silent. They walked together. She was small beside him, the buxomness which had bloomed after the bairn's birth all gone in the anxiety of the journey and the constant fear that something had happened to her husband. Now she was like a squirrel, head turning here and there to constantly check all around her, her movements quick and darting. She was still pretty though; he clenched his fists as a couple of men nudged one another and stared as they passed. Will sighed. Between Bethia and Katheline he could spend all his time on guard duty. He must find a stout fellow to watch over them whenever they left the house.

'And what if we both want to go out and to different places?' said Bethia when he brought it up. 'Will you hire two men? In any case, one man alone can hardly fight off a determined onslaught – we'll need at least half a dozen.'

154

Will could feel the bile rising at being wrong-footed so easily. And when he was only trying to show loving care for their welfare. But the laughter faded from Bethia's face and she made some attempt to pacify him.

'It's a good thought, but Geneva's not as Antwerp, where always the whisper of *Marrano* and *relapser* followed us. Here we're doing our best to fit in. I've even joined a good wives group where we read our Bibles and discuss what Master Calvin has preached.'

'Is there a man to guide the discussion?'

'Madame Pasteur is our leader. Her husband is a pastor, I believe.'

Will walked around the chamber and the agitation he felt settled. 'He's a man of sound thinking, and if he approves of this group then I'll not gainsay it.'

Bethia dipped a small curtsy. 'Thank you, my lord.'

Will decided not to rise to the bait, this time.

Bethia's face softened. 'Thank you for always taking such good care of us, Will.'

'Humph! Enough of the honeyed words.'

She looked up at him through her eyelashes and fluttered them.

He tried to remain po-faced but the laughter burst out. 'Please, Bethia, do take care.'

'I promise we'll carry our staffs with us whenever Katheline and I venture forth.'

And with this he chose to be satisfied. In any case, other troubles were soon filling his head. Several times he heard someone calling *Calvin*, over and over, from beneath his casement. Perhaps there was more than one Calvin in this city. He opened the window and leant out. Below he could see the broad back of a well-dressed woman. He shrugged and forgot about it. But that evening again he was disturbed by much shouting of *Calvin*, the master from next door adding his deeper tones to the wife's shrill ones.

He applied to their hostess for an explanation. She

patted her bosom with her lace-trimmed handkerchief saying it was all nonsense and Will should ignore it. Then she hurried away because the servant couldn't be relied upon to prepare a posset correctly unless overseen.

When the calls started up again that night Will went down himself, determined to establish, once and for all, what was going on. He saw the master from next door scoop up a squat, flat-nosed dog and stroke its head, saying, 'Good doggie, you're a good *Calvin*.'

Will felt the indignation rise up like a fountain.

'Master Seton,' Madame Bernier called, most insistently. She came and took his arm, turning him back to the house.

'That whelp was called…'

'Shush, I know. People are most cruel to good Master Calvin.'

'But why?' said Will, genuinely astonished. 'I thought he was much loved here.'

'He is, but there are a few who resent the power he has. Yet he has done so much for our city: an end to gambling, drunkenness and houses of ill repute. But there are those who lost money and position as a result, so inevitably he has his detractors. Our neighbour is not the only one who has named his dog thus, and many miscall Calvin *Cain*.'

'But a dog!'

'Ah,' said Madame Bernier, 'some say that animals have souls.'

'Nonsense,' said Will, and his hostess blinked. 'What I mean is animal's souls are not rational, and disappear when the animal dies.'

'That's an interesting point, young master, and one worthy of further debate. Perhaps you would join our good wives meeting one evening and we may discuss it?'

A smile crept over Will's face to receive such an invitation.

She rested her hand on his arm and looked up into his face. 'We both know that Calvin is a good man and his soul is pure. For every one of his naysayers there are at least five yeasayers who revere him.'

But sometimes it seemed as though the naysayers outweighed those who valued Calvin. When Will next met with his mentor the shadows under Calvin's eyes were so dark as to be almost black and the skin beneath them furrowed and dried out.

'You didn't sleep well, master?'

'I rarely sleep well. My mind is often busy in the midnight hours.' Calvin smothered a yawn. 'But 'tis made worse by the discordant noise of handbells ringing outside my window in the deepest darkness of night.'

'Why would there be handbells ringing?'

'Hah! Why indeed. Tis another petty scheme to undermine me.'

'But where's the watch? Can't they stop the destroyers of your peace?'

Calvin raised his eyebrows, great bushes disappearing into his hairline.

'Then I'll stand guard.'

'That's kind of you, my young friend. Yet my enemies find many ways in which to cause disquiet; that midnight jangling is a minor irritant only. Here, I have some work for you.'

Calvin glanced out of the casement as he passed. 'Hah, I see I have a visitor, *Caesar Comicus* is on his way up to give me the benefit of his opinion and no doubt again complain about the flow of French refugees into Geneva.' He winked at Will, who gave an uneasy smile back. Somehow it seemed wrong that Calvin should bestow a nickname on such an eminent citizen as Ami Perrin.

Later that same day, walking into church to ascertain that all was well before the congregation entered to hear Calvin preach, Will saw a flutter of paper and went to investigate. He found a notice pinned to the pulpit, writ in large letters for all to read… *Calvin teaches God to be the author of sin*. Will puzzled over its meaning, but when he

157

understood the gross insult to a good man he crumpled the paper in his hand. His instinct was to burn it, but he knew Calvin would want to know of the content, however painful.

He hurried back to Calvin's home. Calvin's face flushed as he perused the notice. He looked up and stared at Will as though he wasn't seeing him.

'This is not the first such epistle,' he said, his voice thick with rage. He rummaged in his desk and passed Will another notice with a hole in the paper where it had been pinned.

'*It is he who feels himself itchy who scratches himself,*' Will read aloud.

'The writer infers that I have the same frailties as that serpent Servetus.' Calvin sighed deeply. 'I can bear an attack on me with equanimity...' he flapped today's notice, '... but *this* is too much. I'll not tolerate an attack on the right-thinking which is at the foundation of my teaching.' He rubbed the line of his eyebrow. 'Do you think you could uncover who the foul writer of these wicked words might be?'

Will was wondering who Servetus was, but forgot all about him at this request – to be so trusted, he could barely contain his smiles. 'I'll do my best.'

He was up before sunrise the next day and keeping watch outside the cathedral. He thought of the forbearance that Calvin showed to any personal attacks on him, tolerating the handbells at midnight, the dog naming and the scurrilous insinuations, but when the rights of the church or sound doctrine were the subject of vileness, then he became a lion in defence of God.

Will leant against the wall of a house opposite, grateful that it wasn't raining, and wiped his nose with the back of his cold hand. He saw no one go near the cathedral, not that there were more than a handful of people out and about so early. He was back again the next day and, just when he was ready to give up and take his chilly bones home, he saw a man slip into the side entrance. He waited a moment then edged through the door after him.

The transept rose high above in great grey arches and his footsteps sounded loud in his ears in the echoing space, but the perpetrator was fortunately too intent on pinning his paper to the pulpit to notice. Will tucked himself behind a pillar. The miscreant, hurrying to leave, came past, and Will reached out a long arm and seized him by the collar.

The man screamed, a curiously high-pitched sound, which bounced off the stone. He was small, round and furious. 'Let go of me, you malapert,' he cried, fighting to free himself from Will's unyielding grip.

It was like holding onto a wriggling child. 'You're the malapert. Why are you impugning Calvin?'

'I'm only doing what any godly citizen would do and visiting the cathedral for early morning private prayer.'

'Aye, and I'm a lemon.' Will stared down into the man's chubby face. 'I know you, you're Ameaux.'

Ameaux twisted and turned. Will let go of his collar and grabbed him by the arm, dragging him outside, but he was as slippery as wet seaweed. Will lost his grip and Ameaux was off like a cannonball birling along the street. Will let him go; there was no need to chase after him. He would tell Calvin, who'd let the Council know. The gates would be closed against Ameaux and he could not stay long hidden within the confines of the great walls of this city.

Will was proved correct, and within a few days Ameaux was apprehended. He watched as Ameaux was led away bellowing to all who would listen, 'John Calvin is a wicked seducer who wants to be our bishop. Genevans beware; if we're not careful, Frenchmen will rule our city.'

Will went immediately to tell Calvin that Ameaux had been captured. 'What are we to do with him?' he said, rushing into Calvin's chambers.

Calvin looked startled by the interruption.

Will blushed. 'I think we need to act quickly and stop this calumny against you.'

'It's not only up to me. The pastors will meet to determine his punishment. And sadly Ameaux is not alone... You do know he was a maker of playing cards and lost his business when we closed all those dens of iniquity?' Calvin rubbed his face. 'Half the members of the Council are against me for such reasons and they may choose to overlook Ameaux's crimes.'

But punishment was swiftly meted out and Ameaux was required to make a public apology. Will watched as he trudged the streets, bareheaded with a burning torch in his hand so that all eyes would be drawn to him. Soon a crowd was following, ready to be entertained by one of their richer citizen's public humiliation. Ameaux knelt first outside the cathedral and mumbled the words.

'Louder, you pig's snout,' shouted a fellow, and the crowd took it up, chanting *pig snout* over and over.

'I beseech Calvin's forgiveness for my transgressions and apologise most abjectly to the Council for the error of my ways. May God forgive me,' bellowed Ameaux.

Will thought it a mistake that he allowed himself to be provoked but the crowd loved it. 'Beseeeeech,' a fellow copied, and soon they were chanting that.

Next were the offices of the Council, the sweat beading on Ameaux's forehead from the heat of the torch and, Will hoped, the shame. After the third repetition close by the city gates, Ameaux had served his punishment and tossed the torch down at the feet of his taunters, who soon dispersed when the entertainment was over.

Will hoped that Calvin could now get on with his real work of communicating the Word of God to the citizens of Geneva without further distractions, but it was Will's family who caused the next upset.

Since they'd arrived in Geneva Will had felt... what

had he felt? It was pride. There was no other way to describe it. And the Bible has much to say about the sin of pride. But he couldn't help himself. His sister came to church most days, sitting face rapt and nodding her agreement to much of the sound doctrine she was hearing. There was the small matter of the veneration of the Virgin which she seemed reluctant to relinquish but, given time, he knew she would see sense. She was a member of the good wives group, and Madame Bernier, a stalwart of Calvin's Church, approved mightily of her. Even Katheline was spending much time in church, albeit with a focus on the Old Testament, but still, she was attending services. Will was the head of a most devout family. Then, invited to a gathering at Perrin's home when Will, unfortunately, wasn't present, Bethia broke one of Calvin's basic tenets. And Will suddenly realised how fragile his world was.

'What were you thinking?' he raged at her, after Madame Bernier had informed him in a whispered aside of his sister's transgression. 'You must've known it was forbidden.'

She stood her ground, arms folded and face flushing with an equal anger, which did nothing to calm him.

'God's blood, Will. We were dancing. Dancing! Everyone invited to Perrin's house was doing so.' She was shouting now at the top of her voice.

'Calm down,' he shouted back. 'Do you want to bring the whole street in here.'

'Since when did dancing go against God's laws.'

'It's a breach of Genevan law. And I don't blame you, not really, for we've been here barely a month. But those that you were among did know and should set a better example. They've arrested the ringleaders and I'm to be called before the Consistory to answer for *your* actions.' He slumped down on a chair, head in his hands.

After a moment Bethia came and rested her hand on his shoulder. 'I'm sorry, Will. I didn't mean to shame you.

161

I'll go myself and take responsibility for my *crime*.'

She couldn't quite disguise the contempt in her voice. He twisted his head and looked up at her.

'I'm truly sorry that you're upset. But I cannot be sorry I danced. I've never done those dances before, you know, and I liked it greatly.'

He groaned.

Calvin was indeed most displeased. 'You must teach your womenfolk better than this, else how can you become a pastor to others?'

Will bowed his head and left for the church, where he prayed long and hard and would have gladly done so on his knees – if it were permitted. But there was some small corner of him delighting to know that Calvin considered he had the potential to become a pastor.

Chapter Twenty-Five

Preaching

Calvin had given Will a task which he was in equal measures excited and terrified by. He was to speak to a congregation, albeit in the smallest of the churches of Geneva, but still it was the first step along the path that he so eagerly sought to travel down.

'There is a great and constant need from the villages around this city for preachers, which we cannot meet. If you do well then this can be your beginning,' he said.

As ever the kind teacher, Calvin helped him prepare – although Will suspected it was also a distraction from the demands of the magistrates, for Will was learning that Calvin was not the determiner of all that happened in the city state and there were constant attempts to undermine his authority.

He worked hard, each word carefully selected and balanced against other options to make certain his meaning was clear and his doctrine sound. He'd initially chosen a passage from Matthew… *Then was Jesus led up of the Spirit into the wilderness to be tempted of the Devil.* But Calvin directed him to expound on predestination, a subject close to Calvin's heart.

'I think you should seek an appropriate verse from Jeremiah,' he said, taking the Bible out of Will's hand.

Will was not averse to using the Old Testament. It

gave him good reason to debate his discourse with Katheline and perhaps turn her from the wrong path she was most determinedly following.

'Here are God's mighty words,' said Calvin, speaking softly but with great feeling. *'Before I formed you in the womb I knew you, and before you were born I consecrated you; I appointed you a prophet to the nations.'*

Will wondered what it was about the Prophet Jeremiah which drew these reforming preachers, for Knox too aspired to be a latter-day Jeremiah.

Calvin had fallen silent, his finger tracing down the page. Then suddenly his voice boomed out, much louder than he normally spoke. *'See, I have this day set thee over the nations and over the kingdoms, to root out, and to pull down, and to destroy, and to throw down, to build, and to plant.'* Calvin stared at Will, as though Will had challenged the text. 'And this is why I must act as the rod of God and do the necessary, however little I may desire it.'

Farni had little to say on the discourse Will was preparing, although he listened patiently.

'You know Calvin has been much persecuted by the Libertines?' he said when Will had finished.

Will shook his head in puzzlement. 'I know he's constantly being challenged but was not aware of this particular group.'

'Of course, you'll not know the history and how put upon Calvin has often been. 'Tis Calvin who called them *libertines*, for they think it's the Council who should control the spiritual affairs of Geneva.' He shook his head. 'Very wrong thinking, very wrong indeed.'

He fell silent and Will waited, hoping to hear more, for if he was to make Geneva his home then he should understand its story.

'The Libertines resent Calvin because he insists religious matters are not the provenance of a secular authority.'

Will remembered John Knox arguing with the Bishop

164

of Durham that no king, queen, government, nor university should determine matters of the faith, only the synod.

'But I think they resent Calvin most because he's not Genevan, asking why a foreigner should rule their city, and sometimes even claiming it's under French control because Calvin hails from France – which makes no sense, since Calvin would be in mortal danger were he to return to the country of his birth. For nine years Calvin has lived thus, expecting every week to be expelled from Geneva, a city he has guided as though it's a vessel on fire. Once he gave up and went to Strasbourg and the councillors were immediately pleading for his return.'

'I'm sure many cities in Germany would wish to have him,' said Will earnestly.

Farni winced and rubbed his clawed fingers. 'I don't mean to imply Calvin doesn't have his own demons but he is in constant battle against them. And, of course, now there's the matter of George Buchanan, which has us all gravely concerned.'

'Who's George Buchanan?'

'Ah, I thought you would know of him for he is a great scholar who hails from Scotland.'

Will shook his head.

'He was invited to speak at the university in Lisbon and went – perhaps not entirely wisely – where he was taken by the Inquisition.'

'He's a Protestant then?'

Farni inclined his head. 'He's been accused of Lutheran and Judaistic practices, as well as eating meat during Lent and other anti-Catholic behaviours. We're praying for his release.'

Will was concerned about the well-being of a fellow Protestant but his mind was very full of his sermon. He retreated home to practise and spent considerable time speaking to the wall in his chamber, much to the amusement of the whole household who were soon almost as familiar with his words as he.

When Will began what he hoped would lead to his first ministry, Bethia and Katheline were there at the front watching and listening. He spoke without notes, holding his closed Bible in one hand, only stumbling a few times, and losing his way once. And the important thing was that he quickly found it again.

He looked out from the pulpit at the white faces beneath, topped by caps and bonnets, who were gazing back up at him... mostly. There were a few with eyes closed, all the better to listen, Will hoped, but when one head drooped forward with an alarming suddenness, it was plain that sleep had overcome the listener. Nevertheless, Will felt uplifted when his part of the service was over and he went to join the congregation, although it was difficult for him to sit still, his leg twitching as though ready to run a race.

When the congregation streamed out of the church, it was raining heavily and everyone hurried away, eager to get home and dry for their midday meal. Will trudged back through the streets with Bethia and Katheline by his side, heads down as the rain drove into their faces. Once in the house they all scattered to their respective chambers to change out of their damp clothes. Bethia was absent from the board, tending to the bairn, and Will had only their hostess, her husband, and a silent Katheline, for company. No one mentioned his sermon. Will slumped on the settle, all the joy draining out of him. He escaped to his chamber as soon as the meal was over and lay on his back gazing at the ceiling, where the outline of the fresco of angels painted upon it, and now considered entirely unsuitable for a Protestant household, was still visible beneath the layer of whitewash.

He fell asleep; what else was a man to do after the most important day of his life, so far.

Chapter Twenty-Six

Apostasy

It was time for Calvin's daily service and Will followed him to church, resting quietly in the corner as the word flowed over him. His composure restored, Will emerged to find Katheline among the throng, shadowed by the mute servant girl.

'Come, Ysabeau, walk behind us,' said Katheline, gesturing and watching for the girl's reaction.

Katheline took Will's proffered arm. 'What do you think of Calvin's assertion that the Old Testament is part of the Christian Church because Christ is present within it?' he asked.

She glanced up at him, face unreadable. 'Indeed, Christ is present – he was after all a Jew.'

Will stiffened. 'Hah! It's one of Calvin's abiding concerns, this Judaising of the Old Testament.'

'How can something which was written by Jews be Judaised?'

Will detected no anger in her voice, which remained soft and well modulated.

'Christ Jesus re-interpreted and re-informed all our thinking on the basis of what was written in the Old Testament. It *is* a *Christian* document.'

Katheline let go of his arm. 'Something does *not* suddenly belong to others simply because they appropriate it. The Jewish people had been studying the Bible for hundreds of years before Christ was born. And now Calvin, after only a few years perusal, considers himself its absolute authority.'

'Wheesht, Katheline. These are not wise words, especially spoken aloud in the street.' He looked behind but there was no one nearby and he couldn't resist continuing such an interesting discussion. 'Yet I think when Calvin speaks of the Judaising of the Old Testament he is referring to the work of the Anabaptists rather than the Jews. He has said that the Jews misread their own Scriptures because they do not understand the unity of the Old and New Testaments. And really the main issue with Jews is their refusal to believe that the Messiah has indeed come. But *I am* interested in your thoughts. Let's discuss this further in private.'

When Bethia returned, the bairn wrapped in her shawl and small face peeping out, to the comfortable home in which they had been given refuge, Will saw her eyebrows shoot up at what she encountered. For he and Katheline were deep in debate.

Katheline was looking prettier than ever. Her eyes bright, face flushed, as words tumbled from rosy lips. He knew they could never be a match, their differences were too great. And yet, if Calvin could marry an Anabaptist, surely Will could marry a Converso... provided she again converted, this time from Catholicism to Protestantism. She'd make a good wife too, if this intelligent debate they were having was anything to go by.

Will resolved to ask Calvin his view of the Jews. The next day he was emboldening himself to do so when Calvin spoke.

'I had conversation with many Jews while I was in Strasbourg.'

Will was startled. Had Calvin read his thoughts?

'They have no reverence for God and show this very clearly because not only did they hate Jesus Christ, who ought to rule over them, not only did they shun and reject him, but they crucified him, despising God, and they turned away from the salvation which had been promised them.' Calvin's voice rose as he spoke then grew softer. 'And they, in turn, have been rejected by the Lord, who has blinded them so that they are no longer able to see the truth.'

Will smoothed his beard thoughtfully. He would lay this before Katheline. And the very next time they'd an opportunity to speak privately, out it poured. They had a most spirited debate over who it was that redeemed Adam's sin, with Katheline an emphatic proponent of Moses, and Will fighting the corner that it was Jesus Christ.

'Tis a pity you do not follow the true faith,' said Katheline, eyebrows raised.

He frowned, and wanted to say the same to her in response. What a partner in life she would make, if only she followed the right path.

But then a matter of even greater consequence arose which caused Will distress and sadness, all seemingly brought on by Easter.

Sitting next to Bethia in church one day, and feeling a deep sense of rightness in his heart while the whole congregation recited the Lord's Prayer aloud, he became aware that Bethia was quietly saying something different. He went silent and listened, catching the final words...

Sancta Maria, Mater Dei,
ora pro nobis peccatoribus,
nunc et in hora mortis nostrae.
Amen.

They were as familiar to him as the calloused hands he was gazing down upon. The anger flowed hot within him. What was his sister playing at? She sat as calm as could be, head bent, saying words that were so very wrong.

Holy Mary, Mother of God,
pray for us sinners,
now and at the hour of our death.

Bethia had grown more and more thoughtful as Easter drew near but he'd assumed that she was absorbing Calvin's doctrine, not questioning it. As soon as they reached the safety of their chambers, he turned on her, but got no further than a few words of reproach before she exploded in return. It was all most unexpected.

'This is not Easter. Where is the pageantry, the street plays, the celebration? Where is the abstinence of Lent? Easter is a time of joy and rebirth, not sitting in a church denuded of all colour and ornamentation, listening to endless diatribes on doctrine. I find your faith to be a most dour one.'

'You are a relapser,' said Will in shocked tones. 'An apostate.'

'Do not look at me like that. There's no requirement for you to turn as pale as a ghost because I cannot follow *your* religion. And how can I relapse from something I never fully embraced in the first place? What is this anyway, a Protestant Inquisition, and all because I've recited the Ave Maria?'

'I don't understand. You reject Calvin and all his good works because there is no street theatre and the walls of the church are bare?'

'No, no. How can you think me so facile? It is this constant attack on Mary that I find the most unacceptable – worse, I find it unbearable.'

'What constant attack?'

'Perhaps not constant, but you heard Calvin – he insists the veneration of the Virgin is wrong. He said that

170

the Blessed Virgin is nothing but an idol who diminishes the importance of Jesus. He said to call her the mother of God is mere superstition. He forbids us to pray to her.'

'You have misunderstood. Calvin has said Mary is a model of faith. He has genuine respect for her as the mother of Christ.' Will rubbed his head as he thought how best to explain. 'It's true that Mary cannot intercede on behalf of the dead, that we should indeed *not* pray to her, but she has her place in Calvin's heart.'

'But it is a *lowly* place. He has reduced her.' Bethia crossed her hands over her heart. 'I know the Blessed Virgin watches over me. Who else can women seek to love, care and understand them so well but another woman? It's as though the Lord has turned his back on us if we are to be denied our beloved Mary, Mother of God.'

Will flinched as though she'd slapped him. He wanted to shout at her not to call Mary the *Mother of God*, she was the mother of Jesus. He turned his own back on her and gazed out of the casement trying to find the words to bring Bethia to a true faith. Katheline, well, there was never great hope she could be turned having already relapsed – he'd been a fool there – but Bethia! What kind of pastor was he if he couldn't even guide his own sister to right-thinking? He caught movement below; there was the wretched neighbour calling for the ugly wee dog she had the effrontery to name Calvin. This was unendurable.

Chapter Twenty-Seven

Tefillot

When Will arrived home, Madame Bernier was waiting.

'A word, if you please,' she said, drawing him into the salon.

Will stood, arms dangling. She folded her arms, one small foot peeping out from below her appropriately dark, yet still voluminous, skirt, tapping loud on the floorboards.

'I know you're a godly young man, and Monsieur Bernier and I are most proud of the work you do with Master Calvin, and to know that we have contributed in some small way to your success.'

Will flushed. 'I thank you most truly for your kindness. I've only taken the first step on a long journey and will always remember your assistance with gratitude.'

She paused and took a deep breath. 'I am reluctant to speak of this.'

Will wished she wouldn't speak of it then, but held his tongue.

'I am most concerned about Mistress Katheline. I'm not entirely clear on her relationship to you...'

She's my sister-in-law,' said Will, hoping to forestall whatever revelation was coming.

Madame Bernier continued as though he hadn't

spoken. 'As the head of your small party I think you should be made aware that she is often to be found studying a most peculiar book. She claims it's the Old Testament in Hebrew. But the cover,' Madame Bernier's eyes flicked to the right, 'I've never seen the like. There's even a jewel set therein, and that is *not* a sign of a good Protestant Bible.'

Will felt himself grow cold inside. Katheline had kept *that book*. He stilled the trembling and replied as calmly as he could. 'I will speak to her, madame, as a matter of urgency.'

'Please make sure you do. Otherwise I must refer the matter to the Consistory.'

The flush faded from Will's face as quickly as it came. 'Good madame, I implore you, do not. I can assure you Katheline is most devout.'

She nodded curtly.

Will walked about the chamber after Madame Bernier whisked out. He was furious with Katheline. How dare she risk the family like this? How dare she keep that book when she promised her brother it was disposed of? He rubbed his face hard. He already knew how stubborn Katheline could be, especially about matters of faith. That she'd somehow kept hold of this book of the Jews even though it had already placed the family in mortal peril was truly unbelievable. First Bethia and now Katheline. God was surely testing him. His chest felt tight and there was a great sadness within him. He liked Katheline. He truly did. They'd had such excellent debates and she would make an excellent wife, forever challenging her husband's thinking... could it work. And as he was turning this over and over in his mind, wondering if there was a way to reach her, Katheline drifted into the chamber where he sat.

She stood before the Durer print of the naked old woman which Monsieur Bernier liked and his wife was embarrassed by.

173

'I think Albrecht Durer is from a family of Conversos,' she said, stroking her upper lip.

Will's head shot up. 'What on earth makes you say that?'

'Do you see the rings on the old woman's finger?' She pointed.

Will drew close, leaning in to peer where the tip of her finger touched the print. 'Yes,' he said slowly.

'Those are the wedding rings of a Jewish woman.'

He drew his head back quickly and glared at her. 'What nonsense.'

She sniffed. 'It's true. You think I do not know about my people, but I do.'

Will was ready to weep. What a fool he was about women. He sat down abruptly and covered his face with his hands.

Eventually when he looked up he found Katheline gazing down on him. There was a tenderness about her expression that he could not bear to look upon.

He stood up and said abruptly, 'Madame Bernier is going to report you to the Consistory'

'And why would she do that?' She responded stoutly, but he could see her blinking. 'I worship every day and am probably the most godly person in this house. And what of Bethia and her continued cleaving to the Virgin – where does that sit?'

The despair had gone; Will felt only exasperation. 'Bethia's piety is not the issue here, so please don't complicate matters.' He seized Katheline's hands, clasping them together as though about to pray with her. 'Please, Katheline, for the sake of our small family do *not* provoke the *seigneurie*. They'll require that you repent publicly and will punish obstinacy.'

Katheline tugged her hands from his and moved towards the door. 'This is not obstinacy. This is about following the faith of my fathers.'

'It is *apostasy*. Don't you understand, it could lead to

your death?' Will took a deep breath to calm himself. 'In any case, you must bring me the book.'

'It is well hid.'

'Aye, so well hid our landlady has seen you reading it.'

She looked shocked and came close to him, staring up into his face. 'I promise you she'll never catch me again. This is a sacred book of the Jews and you cannot ask me to destroy it. Imagine if I was to order you to burn your Bible, could you do it?'

No, he could not. He bowed his head in defeat.

She touched his arm lightly. 'Can we not leave this dreary place.'

Will didn't want to leave Geneva – it was his spiritual home. 'We await your brother.'

'We could journey to meet him.'

'And risk missing him.' But as he spoke, Will realised that he might soon have to weigh up what was the greater risk: missing Mainard or staying in Geneva.

Bethia came into the chamber carrying Samuel-Thomas and saying he was a wee varmint who wouldn't settle. Her voice trailed away and she looked curiously from one to the other.

'Katheline was suggesting that we go to meet Mainard,' said Will wearily, certain that Bethia would want to set off now summer was near. But she surprised him.

'We do not know where Mainard is. It would be different if he'd written confirming where he's going.' He watched her brow furrow, knew how worried she was that she still hadn't heard from him. 'We could wander around these mountains for months without finding him. Here there's a settled address he may come to.'

Katheline had knelt on the floor and was playing with the wee varmint, who could now roll over and over with great speed so that the women were forever running to remove anything of danger in his way.

Bethia mouthed *church* at Will and he shrugged. She crouched down. 'Please, Katheline, come to more than the Old Testament discourses. You don't have to actually listen, only be seen.'

Aghast at such cynical pragmatism, Will opened his mouth to protest, but before he could speak, Katheline scooped up a squirming Samuel-Thomas and left the chamber.

Will looked at Bethia, eyebrows raised. 'Did you know she still has that book of the Jews which we all though disposed of before we left Antwerp.'

'How do you know about that?' He saw, by the way she was picking at the skin around her thumb, that she knew, or had guessed, what Katheline was up to.

'Our hostess informed me,' he said, voice as dry as hard biscuit.

'Right!' Bethia whisked out the room after Katheline but soon returned. 'She refuses to give it up and I don't know where it's hid.'

'Then let us pray that Madame Bernier doesn't again discover it.'

Katheline attended church the next day, the very picture of a pious young woman. Relieved, Will let the demand for her to relinquish the secret book go, for the moment.

A few days later and Will entered Calvin's chambers to find him on his knees at prayer. Will thought of John Knox in Berwick demanding that his congregation rise and sit to take Communion, and the consternation this departure from the Book of Common Prayer caused. Christ Jesus sat for the Last Supper was Knox's reasoning and soon all prayers were conducted with him standing in the pulpit and his parishioners sitting. It felt good to remember Knox and his certainties. But Calvin didn't approve of kneeling any more than Knox did; what was going on?

Calvin rose and looked wearily at Will. He winced, holding his stomach, and began to speak...

It seemed Katheline's book was not so well hid, for their hostess had again discovered it – and handed it over.

Chapter Twenty-Eight

Banished

By the time Will reached home, Katheline was gone.

'Where is she?' he asked Bethia, making no attempt to lower his voice. Didn't care if that Judas, Madame Bernier, heard.

Bethia spread her arms wide. 'I don't know.'

'How can you not know? You're the elder, you should be overseeing all that's happening within your small domain. Is it too much to ask that you do that? What else can occupy you all day?'

He felt his face grow redder with each word and saw his sister flushing in response. He knew attacking her was not helpful and was made even more furious with Katheline for making him lose his temper, when he was every day working to be more measured. And it was Bethia bearing the brunt of his rage, who every day he saw grow sadder and more fearful because her husband had not come. Will wondered if de Lange would ever appear. Perhaps he was an apostate now too, like Katheline, and no longer wanted his Christian wife and son.

Will pushed up his sleeve and scratched at the soft skin of his inner elbow, until it was raw and painful. Of course his good brother would come – he'd never seen a man more smitten by his wife and child. And the pressing matter was Katheline and that wretched Tefillot. But what could they do?

The wee waif came into the chamber as he deliberated, and ran to Bethia, tugging on her sleeve.

'What is it, Ysabeau?' Bethia rocked her arms back and forth as though cradling a baby. 'Is there something wrong with Samuel-Thomas?'

Ysabeau shook her head and began to gesture wildly, face tight with concentration. Bethia leant over asking questions. Will was most impressed, for he could make no sense of the girl's movements nor much of Bethia's exaggerated gestures in return. At least Bethia spoke her movements aloud.

'Mistress Katheline is gone from Geneva?'

Vehement shake of the head from Ysabeau.

'Mistress Katheline is still in Geneva?'

Vehement nod of the head.

'She's hiding somewhere?'

Ysabeau again shook her head and moved her arms while staring at Bethia with great intensity.

Bethia looked up at Will. 'I think Katheline may have been arrested.'

'I've guessed right, have I not, Ysabeau? Katheline is in prison.' She made a fist as though her hands were holding bars and she was peering through them.

There could be no mistaking Ysabeau's confirmation.

Will stood, arms dangling helplessly. He saw his sister was tying on her bonnet over her cap while Ysabeau stood ready to pass Bethia her cloak.

Bethia looked to Ysabeau. 'You must stay with Samuel-Thomas,' she said, staring into Ysabeau's face, rocking her arms and pointing to the chamber in which the bairn slept.

Will came to life. 'Not so hasty, Bethia. It's better if you remain here and I'll ascertain where Katheline is being held.'

But she would not be gainsaid. They moved out into the hallway to find Madame Bernier standing arms folded.

'Judaisers,' she hissed. 'I've been duped, the very air within my house poisoned by Marranos.'

Will drew himself up to his not inconsiderable height. 'Are you suggesting that I, secretary to Calvin and soon to become a pastor, am not a true Protestant and follower of Christ? Tread very carefully, madame, or I will have *you* called before the Consistory And especially since you have a painting by a Converso hung upon your wall.' He waved in the direction of the naked old lady.

Madame Bernier's eyes grew wide and then her hands were fluttering, and she stuttered, 'No, no. I didn't mean you, Master Seton. But you have a most ragtag collection of followers.'

'We'll arrange to leave your house this very day.'

'There is no need for excessive haste.'

Will ignored her and opened the front door. Once out in the street, he gripped Bethia by the elbow. 'Let me ascertain Katheline's whereabouts. It'll be easier without any reminder of my *ragtag*. You go and seek an inn for us, and preferably without bedbugs.'

He expected an argument but was relieved when Bethia acquiesced. He walked swiftly away, by no means clear how to go about finding Katheline and having no wish to ask Calvin if he knew. What if Ysabeau was wrong and by asking questions he set hares running? He faltered, uncertain where to turn. But Madame Bernier had clearly been up to something. He set off again at a great pace and then Calvin's servant was before him saying Calvin had need of him.

Calvin sat at the board turning the book in his hands. 'It has a most beautiful cover,' he said, looking up at Will. 'Where did your family get it?'

Unprepared, Will did not know how to respond. He stared at the floor, noticed his foot was tapping wildly and stilled it. Perhaps an honest reply was best, with only a little prevarication. 'It came from Antwerp.'

'So I had supposed. But why would a book of the Jews be in your possession?'

'You yourself say 'tis better to read and understand for sound doctrine.'

'I meant the Old Testament, not just any book in Hebrew you may acquire.' Calvin frowned. 'In any case, I thought you couldn't read Hebrew.'

'I have been learning.'

'We have the young woman – she is a Converso I now learn. And what of your sister?'

'Bethia is a Christian, of course.' Will clenched his fists to control the shaking. He sent up a prayer that Calvin would not suspect Bethia of being a Catholic still.

'Who married a Crypto-Jew, most curious,' murmured Calvin to himself. 'I've no appetite for any interrogation of this young woman, Jew or apostate, whatever she may be. And since she's not a citizen of Geneva we may simply banish her from our city. I'll have her released into your care. Leave Geneva and go quickly.'

Will felt the heavy weight of sadness descend upon him. He was so close to becoming a pastor and now his dream was over. And to be dismissed by the great man; it hurt.

Calvin gazed at him thoughtfully. 'I know you're a true follower of Christ. Dispose of this girl among her people and perhaps you may return in the future. In the meantime, go to Frankfurt or Strasbourg to continue your training.'

Will bowed. 'I thank you for your kindness and pray that I may return soon.'

Calvin waved him away.

As he wandered out into the street, bereft, Will wondered what Calvin would do with the book – wouldn't be at all surprised if he quietly read it, for he

181

was a most erudite and learned man.

He heard his name called and Farni came running after him. 'I am sorry you're leaving but would hope to see you again. You'll find the young woman in the old convent of St Clare which is now a refuge for the worthy poor.'

Will, unfamiliar with the distinction between being worthy or unworthy in terms of poverty, looked puzzled.

'Orphans, widows, the infirm and the old are involuntarily poor, but able-bodied beggars are simply lazy, and the Catholic Church is very wrong to give them succour.'

'And why is Katheline being held there?'

'Better than the prison.'

'Thank you,' said Will.

Farni shook Will's hand. 'I wish you well, my friend. You have the making of a good pastor.'

The heaviness in Will's heart lifted to be so described.

Waiting in the entrance hall of the old convent, Will gazed around, the damage from when it was stormed and the nuns expelled still visible. Doors pitted and scored from axe and hammer, the embrasures, where images of the saints once stood, empty, and blackened streaks up the muralled walls where no doubt there was a burning of pulpit, books, breviaries and any other items of Catholic worship precious to the nuns. The weight of their fear and the destruction wrought lay heavy across his shoulders; surely they could have been quietly invited to leave and not attacked by a great mob of men, however correct in their thinking.

Katheline came then, her arm held tight by a pinched-face woman. The woman nodded to Will, released Katheline, and dragged open the large entrance door, which screeched as it scraped over small stones. It reminded Will forcibly of his old home in St Andrews and the need to open the front door with care if he was to escape without Father's notice. He blinked rapidly but

Katheline spoke as they emerged into the busy streets and he forgot about his home.

'They shut me up in the correction chamber with two madwomen and a verminous beggar. There was a pile of straw in the corner to sleep on and a single bucket for the necessary that was emptied only once a day.'

Will bit his lower lip and shook his head slowly. He could feel his face flushing with anger. 'What did you expect? That they would give you a feather mattress, your own chamber and a commendation for stubbornly holding onto a book which you'd promised your brother that you'd buried. Be grateful you were there barely one day. And now I've been banished, along with you.'

She slowed her rapid walk and half turned. 'I am sorry, Will. I know how much it meant to you.' She paused and then spoke more brightly. 'But there are other Protestant city states nearby that you may go to.'

'Not until we've found your brother and I can place Bethia and you in his capable hands, poor man.'

She patted him on the arm. 'It *is* difficult for us both to follow our faiths.' She added quietly, almost to herself, 'And a pity we do not share the same true path.'

The lump came back in his throat then and yet he felt some solace that Katheline too had sensed a connection between them. He'd been about to say that his chances of becoming a pastor were now considerably lessened because of his association with her, for gossip travelled easily between cities – and what was more delightfully shocking than a would-be pastor associating with a secret Judaiser – but was glad he'd not spoken. Better to leave without any further harsh words between them.

Chapter Twenty-Nine

Bern

By early the next morning Will and his small family were packed up and boarding one of the boats that plied between Geneva and the far end of the lake. He didn't look back, couldn't bear to, as they sailed away. Better to look forward and pray for a future that involved a return to Geneva and Calvin.

The wind blew strong, gusting down the mountainsides and capriciously changing direction. Soon the sails were lowered, the oars out, and the passengers huddled beneath inadequate shelter from the increasingly high waves. The whole party was profoundly grateful when they stopped at Lausanne overnight.

Will found the innkeeper talking with a wiry, white-haired fellow in travel-stained clothes and inquired of them both the quickest route to Venice.

'Ah, you would've done better to head for Augsburg and through the Brenner Pass,' said the traveller when Will mentioned they'd originally come from Antwerp, while the innkeeper nodded his agreement. 'But still, Brenner is the most accessible and lowest of the passes through the Alps. The Eisack Gorge is a good road well maintained by the local people and it's a straight line onto Venice.'

'But we are far to the west here in Lausanne,' said the innkeeper. 'Perhaps you should retrace your steps, go down through France to the coast and enter Italy via Genoa. That way,' he nodded to the traveller, 'you would mostly avoid the high mountains.'

'That is very true,' said the traveller. 'A long way around though. You could go south from here but the roads are few and not so good. There *is* a route you might follow which means jumping from one lake to another. Travel by water is invariably quicker.' The traveller tapped his finger against his lip as though imparting some great wisdom instead of stating the obvious.

'Except when there are storms. Then travel by water may only be the shortest way to encounter St Peter at the Gates of Heaven,' interjected the innkeeper and laughed, making his large belly shake like jelly.

Will retreated from this outpouring of advice and went to find his sister.

'I think we're best to go through the Brenner Pass,' he told her.

She looked even more birdlike and anxious than before. 'Do you think that's the way Mainard will come? Do you think Venice is where he will make for?'

'I do,' he said stoutly.

She stared at him then dipped her head. He saw how badly she wanted to believe him.

They got back on the boat the next day and were at the Vevey by early afternoon. The market was just winding up, the traders packing away a few unsold cheeses and dragging a sickly looking calf homeward, but otherwise not much was left except a few tired yellowed cabbage leaves.

'Take care,' Will heard Bethia say sharply to Katheline, who had narrowly missed treading in dung.

He wondered what Bethia had said to Katheline about her arrest and their subsequent banishment. Not much, he suspected, but Bethia was clearly irritated by

185

the very sight of Katheline. He stood studying a group of workers creating shingles in a courtyard. And very pretty the shingles looked too once on the roofs, although they must be a great fire risk. His sister nudged him, and they set off to arrange horses and carts for all their baggage and persons.

They made good progress over the next few days beneath a bright blue sky, but the following day it rained heavily, the road soon grew muddy, and all in all it was miserable travelling. The party were most relieved when they saw Bern, a city tucked within the bend of a river, much like Lyon. The river curved around so that Bern was protected on three sides by broad, fast-flowing water, and on the fourth a moat had been dug. They crossed its only bridge, solid beneath their feet, the tall spires rising high above their head. Will felt a sense of peace as he passed through its gate, for Bern was as stoutly Protestant as Geneva.

He told Bethia they would rest here for a few days before making the next push onwards, and she looked relieved.

'Thank you,' she said, smiling at him. 'Samuel-Thomas will be as grateful as I for some respite.'

Will felt ashamed to be lauded for his thoughtfulness when really it was only that he wanted to attend church, pray, read his Bible and immerse himself, albeit briefly, in good Protestant environs. It was a pretty city too, he thought, as he strode along its streets with the half-timbered buildings and many examples of the beautiful painted glass, for which it was justly famous, glowing in the sunlight. He felt the burden of familial responsibility lighter on his shoulders today.

Ahead he saw Bethia, with Ysabeau carrying the bairn, standing at the famous bear pit in the centre of the marketplace. Bethia was leaning over the side, talking to Samuel-Thomas and pointing while Ysabeau watched. Then Ysabeau was leaning over so Samuel-Thomas could see. Will felt a tightening in the depth of his belly. What was Bethia thinking, to be so careless. He prayed that Ysabeau had a good grip on the bairn: would not drop him where the bears restlessly ranged. He hurried to them.

He saw the back of a man also moving towards Bethia as fast as he could given he was using a crutch. He was tall, broad-shouldered, with dark curly hair, and his right foot heavily bandaged. Will slowed. There was something very familiar about him.

Bethia drifted away from the bear pit now, Ysabeau following. Will could see her expression as she caught sight of the hirpling man. Now she was running towards him, her face lit up as though the sun had come out after months of rain. She slowed as she reached him. He could see the man holding his arms wide but with palms face out to stop her leaping upon him. Mainard, for Will *was* certain it was him, would likely not want a public display of affection, however understandable. And he looked to be unsteady on his feet. Bethia stood before her husband gazing up into his face. She'd got hold of one of his hands. Will rushing towards them himself, saw Mainard free himself from her grip and turn to his son.

Suddenly Will felt a blow to his back and forgot all about the family reunion. He stumbled, arms flailing, to regain his balance. He turned ready to defend himself and found a grinning young woman before him. His mouth dropped open.

'Grissel? What are you doing here?'

'I'm with Master Mainard.'

'But...'

'Dinna tell me that you believed all that nonsense about me an' Coort. I thocht *you* would hae mair sense.'

'Ach, Grissel, it's good to see you.'

He glanced over his shoulder to see Mainard weaving his way along the street through the passers-by, Bethia following, carrying Samuel-Thomas, while Ysabeau trailed behind. Will offered Grissel his arm and she made a little curtsy and took it, nudging him with her hip. They hurried after the small family party, for he was eager to greet his good brother.

Once at the inn Will, Mainard and Bethia sat before a plate of bread and cheese with a glass of claret to hand, while Ysabeau took the bairn off for his nap and Grissel hovered behind. Will gazed at Mainard, thinking how very weary and old he looked. There was a deep twin furrow between his brows and he shifted constantly, clearly in pain from his injured foot – which he refused to speak of, saying only it was a foolish accident when Will inquired. Nevertheless he'd greeted Will effusively enough; indeed with more genuine pleasure than he seemed to be according his wife.

'I said that Grissel could not have run off with Coort, was sure you didn't even like him any more,' said Bethia, looking from Mainard to Grissel. She frowned. 'Although, if you hadn't caused so much trouble between Coort and Marisse in the first place, perhaps none of this would've happened.'

'That had nothing to do with it,' said Mainard abruptly. 'And without Grissel's assistance I'd still be languishing in prison. She's taken great risks on my behalf, for which I am most grateful.' He smiled at Grissel and she flushed and hung her head, although Will could see she too was smiling.

He gazed at his sister, who was staring at Mainard, a hurt look upon her face. Will was surprised that Mainard should speak so sharply and when he remembered Bethia's anguish that she'd not heard from Mainard, he felt like giving him a good clout.

'Why did you not write?' Mainard said, before Will could ask the same of him.

'I did, constantly,' said Bethia, 'but it was difficult to know where to direct my letters, especially as I'd had no communication from you.'

Will gulped. 'It seems there was much confusion,' he said cheerfully. Then realised by the way they both stared at him that perhaps he was being overly hearty.

Thankfully Katheline appeared at that moment and the subject was dropped as she exclaimed joyfully at the sight of her brother.

They packed quickly the next day. Mainard was eager to be off, and Will not any less so now that he was freed from the burden of familial responsibility. A small corner of him worried away that his sister and brother-in-law were not more joyful to be restored to one another. He could not but observe the strained look on Mainard's face and the hurt on Bethia's. Surely her husband should be more loving towards her or at least look happy to be reunited? He thought back to how de Lange was in Antwerp; devoted to his wife. This disharmony was most probably nothing more than the necessary adjustment after a long parting. But in any case he could do nothing to interfere between man and wife. No doubt they'd soon grow familiar and comfortable together once more.

He parted company with them soon after they'd crossed the town's bridge together. Now he was for the north and Strasbourg and the rest of the family for the east and Venice. Will reined his horse once he'd climbed the first hill and turned to look back. Mainard was determinedly riding, although his injured foot was dangling out of the stirrup in a most awkward fashion. Will thought of how he might never see them all again, and especially his sister, and felt a great sadness. Yet they would be parted by more than distance: a confusion of not only two but three faiths. And it wasn't simply a difference of perspective. Heresy was a moral blight which, if left unchecked, had the power to corrupt everyone it touched. He could not be among Catholics, Conversos nor Crypto-Jews any longer. He must be with true thinkers, his head unclogged by sentiment.

He watched until the last moment before they

disappeared, raising his hand in salute as Bethia's shawl streamed out on the breeze in farewell.

Then he headed for Strasbourg and a godly life.

Part Four

Venice

July 1550 to October 1553

Chapter Thirty

A Beautiful City

Venice was a city of flowers and gardens and trees and, of course, water. All the rest of her life Bethia would remember that first morning arising and gazing down onto the narrow streets, with the even narrower hump of bridges over the canals, and everywhere another wonder.

It had been dark and she very tired, and concerned to settle her baby, when they arrived, all attention on reaching the home where Mama and Papa would be waiting. But when she opened the shutters the next morning and the first thing she saw were the pots of flowers on the windowsills opposite, she knew she would love this city.

'What are they called?' she asked Mainard.

He shrugged and gazed over her shoulder.

'Carnations,' said Mama, coming into the salon.

'We must get some,' said Bethia joyfully, 'for our new home.'

Mama and Mainard looked to one another but Bethia chose to ignore it. She would take not one step further east, or north or south for that matter. In Venice she would bide.

Mainard limped across the chamber. He refused to use a crutch, and days of riding with his foot awkwardly dangling had not aided his recovery. There was a haunted look about him which she assumed was to do with the constant fear the foot might need to be amputated. She'd watched as Grissel changed the bandages nightly while they were travelling and, although she was no physician, the flesh looked to be a healthy pink. But the foot was misshapen, the bones not set properly. He would never again walk with that loose-limbed, easy gait she had loved – most probably would always limp. Her heart felt wrung out with pity for him, but she mustn't show it. He grew gruff and withdrew even further at any sign of tenderness. She pushed it from her mind and smiled at Mama.

It was almost as good to see Mama again as to be with Mainard. Her sweet-natured face was more lined and there was a great weariness about her, but she was still the same kind woman. Initially Bethia struggled to remember Judeo-Spanish, for it was the only language Mama spoke fluently, but soon it came flowing back in from the deep recesses of her mind. And now she must learn Italian, which she hoped would not be difficult with her knowledge of Latin. She was surprised that her heart sank at the prospect of a new language. What was happening to her… she used to love any opportunity for learning?

'Let's go out,' she said, linking her arm through Mainard's. 'We'll take the wee lamb to see his new city.'

Mainard's face softened at the mention of his son, although he disengaged his arm from Bethia and sat down. She knelt to lift his leg onto the footstool.

'Leave it, Bethia.'

She stood up and moved away, trying not to let the hurt show that he should be so brusque. 'Come out with us, please.'

'You forget that I came for you after I'd settled Mama and Papa here. I've already seen the city.'

'I thought you could show me its wonders, be my guide. We'll find a carriage.' She spoke with a brightness, as chirpy as any small caged bird.

He rubbed his hand over his head and his curly hair sprung out further. 'I've business to transact. Mama will go with you, and no doubt Katheline.'

Bethia thought to cajole further but could see by his frown that it would be unsuccessful. He was in a strange mood these days, and she didn't want to embarrass either him, or herself, in front of Mama… wasn't sure she could take another rejection without falling to her knees and howling. She'd tried to speak of it with him but he grew angry and told her she was mistaken. She had briefly considered asking Grissel what was going on with him but quickly rejected the idea. She would not so demean herself by speaking to her servant about her own husband.

'Bethia,' he called as she was slipping from the room. 'Leave Samuel-Thomas with me.'

'Certainly.' She tried to contain the smile in case he saw it and changed his mind. It vanished anyway as she thought on how reluctant the bairn had been to go to Mainard, hiding his face in Bethia's bosom and refusing to look at his father whenever Mainard came near.

'And Bethia,' he called again, 'you should know that there's recently been an edict issued in Venice which directs that all Conversos must leave within the next two months, so do *not* get too attached to this city.'

'Don't worry, my dear,' said Mama, as she followed Bethia out of the room. 'The Christian merchants don't want to lose us. They're fighting the edict and we're confident it will all come to naught.'

Bethia, who'd again felt close to collapse at such tidings, and so carelessly given, decided to put it from her mind. There was nothing she could do anyway.

She found Ysabeau on hands and knees chasing the wee lamb as he crawled at speed across a floor, which was constructed of thousands of pieces of coloured glass and tile. She'd never seen anything so intricately made, of such a puzzling joy to the eye, so highly polished yet smooth and cool underfoot. Grissel was watching from the corner, face twisted with longing… jealousy… hurt. Whatever it was, Bethia neither wanted to see nor deal with it. Couldn't understand herself why she felt so resentful towards Grissel, but perhaps it was because Mainard seemed far more comfortable in Grissel's presence than her's.

'Ysabeau?' She tapped her on the shoulder, ignoring Grissel. She looked much better than when Bethia found her destitute on the street and, although her skin was remarkably pale to go with the near white hair, she was rounder of face and with a pleasing plumpness to the flesh. Of course, the sadness was always there, how could any of them forget brave Suzanne.

'You will attend to Samuel-Thomas while the master plays with him.' Bethia spoke for Grissel's benefit, but she accompanied the words with gestures and Ysabeau watched her every movement with great concentration.

'I can do that,' said Grissel.

'We don't need you,' said Bethia, eyes on Ysabeau.

Bethia led Ysabeau into the chamber where Mainard sat, plopped the baby on the floor in front of him, tugged Ysabeau into a corner to show her where to stand, and then left swiftly. It was fortunate that Mainard seemed to have taken to the lass and was untroubled by her impediment.

'We're two damaged souls together,' he said when Bethia explained about Ysabeau and the death of Suzanne.

'Katheline is tired and didn't want to join us,' said Mama, reappearing with her hair caught up in a most elaborate headdress: tightly fitted behind the ears and then rising to bulge out like a smooth bowl at the back of her head.

'I like your bonnet,' said Bethia, for it had great style.

Mama raised her hand self-consciously to pat it.

'I must get some new clothes made.' She glanced down at her sober black dress, so suitable for Geneva and so very dull amid the vividness of Venice.

They descended the broad curve of stairs, past a fresco depicting entwined sea creatures on a massive scale. A servant brought up the rear with heavy steps so that the sound echoed up the stairwell. They emerged under the portico and before them the waters of a narrow canal danced and sparkled in the sunshine.

Bethia turned to find Grissel at her elbow, smiling and hopeful of face. She didn't return the smile. 'Go about your business, Grissel. I'll see you on my return.'

Grissel's face fell. Bethia knew she need not be so sharp. But she was angry with her, somehow felt it was Grissel's fault that they'd to flee Antwerp so precipitously. She'd been told about Coort and the potboy but if Grissel had not flirted with Coort, and if Grissel had not enraged Marisse, perhaps none of this would've happened. And if she and Mainard had not been parted for so long then there would not be this great abyss between them.

One of the strange high-prowed boats of Venice was waiting and Mama took the hand of the rower who stood respectfully at the bottom of the steps to assist her in.

Bethia faltered. 'Can we not walk? I don't much care for boats.'

'You must get over your fears. You can go nowhere in Venice except by gondola.'

Bethia bit down on her lower lip as she, in turn, was helped into the boat, or gondola, as she must remember to call it.

Mama gave directions to the rower and Bethia was impressed that she had some words of Italian, given that Mama never troubled to learn French during all the time she lived in Antwerp, although her Dutch was passable. But of course the few people Mama engaged with there were Ladino speakers – Conversos like herself. What else was Mama to do given that the Christians of Antwerp seemed either indifferent or actively unfriendly? She shivered, could almost hear *Marrano* hissed behind her back again. Would living in Venice be any different from Antwerp? She prayed it was so, wanted to stay in this city of light, water and the Blessed Virgin, whose face she saw looked down from many buildings.

They moved out of the side canal and turned into a wide expanse of blue, sparkling water lined by many grand houses. She turned her head this way and that, didn't know what to look at next, and all so magnificent.

Bethia became aware that Mama was speaking. 'Please excuse me, Mama,' she said, touching her hand to her heart.

'I was saying how beautiful the newly constructed palaces are along the Grand Canal.' She waved her arm encouraging Bethia to look upwards. Bethia tilted her head back and gazed at the marble facades which glistened like hoar frost in the sunlight, framed by the deep blue sky. So bright were they that she was dazzled and dropped her gaze to find herself looking directly into the eyes of a woman of such startling beauty that Bethia gasped.

The woman rested back in her seat and inclined her head at Bethia, while the man sitting half turned next to her, so he too could gaze upon the beautiful face, lightly kissed her fingertips.

'Who was that?'

'Don't look,' said Mama, for Bethia had swivelled around to stare over her shoulder.

'Do you know her?'

'Of course not. She's not… a good woman.'

Bethia blinked. 'But how can she show herself so openly?'

Mama shrugged. 'This is Venice, and the normal rules of behaviour do not apply. You see these courtesans everywhere; they're even to be found in church.'

Bethia was curious at the mention of church. 'Which church do we attend? I'm much in need of Mass after the austerities of Geneva.'

'We'll go later,' said Mama, avoiding Bethia's eye.

Bethia was relieved to hear it, and wondered if Katheline would come.

Chapter Thirty-One

Ghetto

The waters were lapping at the top step when they returned.

'Why does the water rise and fall?' she asked Mainard who she found lolling in a chair, while Grissel stood beside him, eyes sliding away when Bethia glanced at her. It was clear they'd been blethering.

Mainard yawned, mouth gaping most unattractively. 'Probably because of the tides.'

'How can it be tidal?'

'You crossed by boat yesterday. Didn't you notice you were on water?'

'I thought it was a river.'

'Venice is by the sea. How did you not know this?'

'How should I know? I have not been a colourer of maps.' But her heart was lifting. 'Is there a beach nearby? Oh, Mainard, let's go there, please.'

He smiled at her and, for a moment, her world brightened. But the smile faded as quickly as it came. 'I must rest my foot,' he said abruptly.

'It's nae so bad today,' said Grissel.

Bethia looked at her.

'I just did the bandage.' Grissel dipped her head, but not before Bethia caught the smirk upon her face.

'That'll be all, Grissel. You may go.'

Grissel wandered from the chamber as Bethia stared at Mainard. She opened her mouth to ask what in the name of the Blessed Virgin was going on between him and Grissel, but he forestalled her.

'I think I'll be better lying down. Can you help me to my chamber?'

Her face softened as she offered him her shoulder. Once he was in bed she elevated the foot and stood gazing down at him. She hoped he might invite her to join him but he closed his eyes, saying, 'I will rest for a time.'

She went in search of her son and found both Katheline and Ysabeau dancing attendance on him. He was pulling himself up onto a nearby chair and she exclaimed at his cleverness while Ysabeau clapped her hands.

'Did you enjoy your trip on the gondoola?' said Katheline.

Bethia thought to correct her pronunciation and then decided not. Katheline and she hadn't had much discourse, especially friendly discourse, since they left Geneva so hurriedly. She'd been very angry with her good sister but it had faded now they were within this remarkable city.

'I did.'

Katheline leant forward, her face alight with excitement 'There's a place in Venice wherein Jews live. I want to go very much. Will you come with me?'

Bethia felt an unutterable weariness. There was Mainard, distant, remote, unapproachable, and mostly silent, and here was Katheline, whose relapsing placed them in such danger in Geneva, and indeed in Antwerp. But then it could not be so perilous in Venice else why would Jews be permitted to live openly?

Katheline echoed her thoughts, saying, 'This is the first place I've ever been where our people can practise their faith freely.'

'Will Mama and Papa not go with you?'

Katheline shook her head so vehemently a lock of her

dark curly hair broke free from its snood. 'We must be seen to live as Christians. It seems that, unlike Antwerp, Conversos are treated no differently from any other Christian – but there must be no suspicion attached to us. And you know Papa, like Mainard, considers himself a Christian anyway.'

'Then we should not go,' said Bethia firmly. She wondered if it was true that Mainard was a Christian still. She sighed. In the old days she would just have asked him.

'But if you come with me then we're simply going to tour it.'

'But why are the Jews all gathered in one place and not allowed to live wherever they wish in this city?'

'I don't know.'

'I'm not sure about going; I'll think on it.'

Bethia applied to Mainard for information but he closed his eyes, saying, 'I'm tired, Bethia,' and she forgot about the place of the Jews in her anxiety about him. His behaviour reminded her of when she was pregnant with her first child and lost it, and how she fell into a deep dark space which she was unable to climb out of, and no amount of coaxing helped.

But information on the place of the Jews came from another source: two ladies most wondrous, one in brocade shot through with gold thread, the other with a pattern of pearls sewn into her bodice and carrying an ermine muff even though the weather outside was warm enough for them both to be wielding a fan. They were dazzling, especially the most unnatural yellow hue of their hair, and so very different from the solemn folk of Antwerp. It seemed they already knew Mama, who introduced them as Signoras Guistina and Pelegrina. They were all eagerness to meet her daughter and her son's wife.

'Ciao bella!' they said to Katheline and Bethia, in turn, then rattled away to the girls in French. 'We are so happy to meet the *bellisimas*, the daughter and son's wife, of

202

whom we have heard so much. My dears, we're going to the Ghetto, such fun, you must come.' Guistina leant forward. 'There is a play, you know, of Esther. Such, *such* fun, and then we will wear a disguise and dance in the streets. The Jews are very good at this sort of thing and we'll leave before they shut the gate.' They both covered their mouths and giggled. 'But even if it *is* after their curfew, they always let us out.'

Katheline leant forward, eagerly accepting before a frowning Mama could prevent her.

'Do not fear,' Pelegrina said to Mama. 'We *will* make certain to leave before the gate is closed.'

'Always,' nodded Guistina.

Mama didn't look reassured. 'Bethia, you will accompany Katheline, and I'll stay here with the baby.'

'A bambino,' the women shrieked. 'We must see the bambino.'

And so Samuel-Thomas was brought out and had his cheeks pinched, which he didn't much care for. He was removed, kicking and screaming, by the combined efforts of Ysabeau and Grissel, who it seemed were forming an alliance. And then there was the potboy, or Johannes as Mainard now insisted he was called, who was forever lurking in the background when surely he should have pots to wash and spit roasts to turn. Bethia shook her head; what a grump she was becoming.

Down the curve of stairs they went and out into the sunshine. The water slapped against the wooden sides of the canal as they clambered into the gondola. They'd some distance to cover, their guides cried, for the Jews lived crowded into a marshy area at one end of the island.

'Why is it called the Ghetto?' Katheline asked.

The women shrugged and looked to one another. 'There used to be a foundry there, I believe,' said Guistina.

'Then it would be called *fonderia* not Ghetto,' said the Pelegrina, with a trill of laughter at her own wit.

Her friend sniffed, clearly annoyed to be wrong-footed. She wrinkled her pert little nose. 'I think it comes from *geto*, you know, to cast iron.'

'I know nothing of such things,' said Pelegrina. 'Girls, I hope you have brought your pomanders,' she wafted her hand, 'for the smell can be very terrible.'

Bethia pointed. 'What's going on over there?'

'That's the Rialto, where everyone, Jews, Christians and Mussulmen, Greeks, Armenians, Arabs, Germans and Turks gather each day to trade. My dears, you can get anything there, but remember,' Guistina waggled her forefinger, the nail coloured a disturbingly bright red, 'never accept the first price you're offered.'

The Grand Canal was busy here with boats crisscrossing as they went back and forth from one side to the other; one gondola drew too close and they were splashed by the oar. The women shrieked and the boatman shouted.

'How much longer can it be before the new bridge is begun,' Pelegrina complained. 'It's taking forever.'

'Forever!' echoed her companion, drawing out her syllables. 'But we've arrived, girls.'

They disembarked and crossed the narrow bridge into the Ghetto. The buildings rose high above them, all looking inward, and the streets were densely packed with people.

'Why do the men wear yellow hats?' Bethia whispered to Katheline.

'To show they're Jews, of course,' said Pelegrina, loudly enough that Bethia flinched. 'They're required to, you know, so there's no confusion between them and us.'

'The Jews make very good physicians,' fluted Guistina twirling her pearls. 'It's the only time I would permit one within my home.' She stared at Katheline as she spoke but then a passing man bumped into her and her servant grabbed him by the throat.

'Apologise,' he grunted.

'Sorry, mistress,' the man said. The guard released

him and he backed away, bowing.

Then they were amidst a market, the flies rising off a new slaughtered calf, the blood from its cut throat dripping onto the ground and pooling beneath their shoes. And Bethia was suddenly made ill, could not stay one moment longer. The crowds, the smell of blood, the sight of the sliced throat and these exhausting women.

'I must go home,' she whispered to Katheline.

'You've turned quite white,' said Katheline, taking her arm. 'What's wrong?'

'Suzanne,' whispered Bethia.

Katheline gulped. 'We will leave you here,' she called to their new acquaintances.

There was a great flutter around them. They should not go home unescorted, everyone must leave together. Bethia didn't attempt to remonstrate but was guided out of the Ghetto and back to their waiting gondola. The women chattered incessantly but she considered her moment of ill health enough of a reason that she was not required to speak – or listen.

'They think you may be with child,' said Katheline once they were safely inside their tall cool home. She gazed curiously at Bethia. 'Are you?'

Bethia shook her head. It would be an immaculate conception if she were, for Mainard and she had not been intimate since they were reunited. Indeed, he seemed barely able to touch her when once he couldn't keep away. The sadness washed over her. It was not that she was eager to be enceinte, but she missed conjugal relations – and really it was his foot which was injured, which shouldn't interfere with the workings of other parts.

'You're certain?'

'I can absolutely assure you that I am not with child.'

Katheline raised her eyebrows and Bethia turned away to hide her annoyance.

When her menses came a few days later, she was tempted to take the evidence and show Katheline, but really there was no need, for the servants would've chattered amongst themselves, and it'd be known to anyone in the household who cared to discover it.

The house was so large that she and Mainard, for the first time in their married life, had been given adjoining chambers. Mainard suggested he sleep alone, for he was made restless with pain during the night and would not want to disturb her sleep. And when Bethia remonstrated, he wouldn't hear her out. It was as though the shutters closed tight across his eyes, as tight as she closed them each night to keep out the night air.

However, on one thing her mind *was* at rest, for she was most relieved to receive a letter from Will fairly soon after her arrival in Venice.

I found Mainard's sister and her husband in Strasbourg, was that not a remarkable coincidence? They were most welcoming when I called and immediately invited me to stay with them.

Bethia was relieved, for she knew Will was perpetually short of funds and, although Mainard had been generous when they parted company, the money would eventually run out. She bent back to her letter.

Geertruyt grew tearful when she learned that Mainard had been arrested in Antwerp, and angry with her husband for leaving the city so precipitously. I told her that Schyuder could not have known. I do not think she entirely believed me but she's heavy with child and I didn't want to cause her any further distress.

Again... already, thought Bethia, aware she was breaching the tenth commandment by coveting what Geertruyt had – more children. But at least her own husband had more honour than Geertruyt's. Mainard would never slip away and leave a family member in peril as he had done.

She told Mainard the news of Geertruyt. 'At least we know where they are and they us,' he said, although his eyes narrowed at the mention of Schyuder.

One day they were bid to a masked ball and she ran excitedly to show him the invitation scrolled elegantly across the parchment. 'They say the Doge is to attend,' she said eagerly, hoping that the opportunity to meet influential people would rouse him. 'And I've never attended a ball, never mind a masked one.'

He lay back in the chair and sighed. 'There's no need. Papa has met with the Doge several times.' He waved his hand at her. 'You may go if you wish, with my parents.'

Bethia shrugged and left him to his misery.

It was very exciting for the first hour to wear a mask and have unknown masked men inviting her to dance – although her Italian was limited, she understood enough for this, helped by the bow and extended hand. But she was a married woman, and in any case didn't know how to dance much – especially these elaborate formal movements and patterns. She wandered the edge of the great ballroom with the frescos on the vast ceiling, large paintings above the fireplaces at each end and carpets hung from its walls. Then she tucked herself away in one of the alcoves, where Papa found her. She'd not had much conversation with him since she arrived here, not that she ever did, and was surprised to be singled out and offered his arm.

'There's much talk of the designs for new Rialto bridge. It's to be of stone this time and will hopefully survive better than the previous ones made of wood. Michelangelo himself has been invited to submit a design,' he said.

They strolled the length of the ballroom and out into one of its antechambers while she tried to ask intelligent questions about the new bridge.

He invited her to take a seat and pulled up a chair next to her. 'I wanted to ask you about my son,' he said, leaning in confidentially. 'And it's impossible to speak in our house without everyone knowing.'

Bethia looked him fully in the face for the first time in a long time; frank appraisal being something that was normally neither encouraged nor permitted of one's husband's father. He did *not* look well.

'What can you tell me?' Papa continued.

Bethia opened her mouth to voice her concerns and then stopped herself. Mainard was her husband; she would manage him and not add to Papa's burden, although she had no idea how.

'He only needs time,' was all she said.

Chapter Thirty-Two

Ridotto

It was Bethia who pointed out to Mainard that Papa looked most unwell. Initially he ignored her, so caught up was he in his own miseries. He wondered why Mama hadn't mentioned it but Mama's worried frown whenever she gazed upon him was reason enough. Poor Mama, a crippled son and now a husband who was looking old beyond his years.

Mainard determined he could no longer lie in bed with his foot throbbing and his mind bursting with the memories of being taken, beaten, humiliated, threatened with torture and imprisoned. How could he be a man to his wife after such emasculation? And yet he was at a loss, for his feelings towards Bethia fluctuated and sometimes he wanted her very much. Anyway, he excused himself, 'twas better if he did not get her with child until the family were established in Venice, which was what he must now exert himself to do, for it seemed the merchants had prevailed and this new edict against Conversos would indeed be disregarded.

Papa looked relieved when Mainard limped into his workroom and offered assistance. 'I would be most grateful,' he said simply.

And Mainard, looking at Papa's tired face, felt ashamed. He knew that his father had indulged him over the years, indeed Don Juan Micas when he last visited them in Antwerp had been most critical. 'All this colouring of maps is a distraction and not a proper life. How will you support your family in the manner required through such indulgence?'

'Ortelius's family make a good living from it and soon there will be a Theatrum published.'

'They are not Conversos.'

'But they may be secret followers of Luther,' Mainard had countered.

Don Juan had shrugged. 'These Christians, surely they can all worship Christ without going to war over matters of doctrine. Jews may disagree but at least do not resort to burning those they disagree with. In any case, you should stick with your own kind, it's always safer.'

Mainard had disregarded Don Juan's counsel then but now resolved he would provide a shoulder for Papa to lean upon. Don Juan had written an introduction for the de Langes to the da Molinas, an old noble family of Venice who the Mendes family did much business in partnership with.

'Why do we need them?' Mainard asked his father.

He suspected that Papa was trying to contain a sigh when he responded. 'We cannot conduct business without them. Venice has laws that protect its citizens...' Papa held up his hand as Mainard went to speak. 'And we cannot be citizens until we've lived and paid taxes here for at least twenty-five years. We're not permitted to use Venetian galleys to transport our goods, even to Constantinople, which is the biggest market for us now.'

And so Mainard was sent to the customs office with Niccolo da Molina, the son of the Venetian noble, to arrange for the release of a shipment of sugar and pepper. Da Molina was small next to Mainard, but he made up for that with his snapping black eyes, rich black hair and youthful face. His clothes too, the pink satin cloak lined with leopard skin, the long ostrich feather waving from

210

his rich red bonnet, the black velvet doublet, all drew attention, and Mainard became aware they were the subject of interest as they lolled at their ease in the gondola, especially from a couple of courtesans who leant over a balcony, with much bosom on display. He caught da Molina watching him speculatively, as he twirled his long hair around his fingers.

'Beautiful women,' said Mainard, for da Molina seemed to be waiting for him to say something.

'Pretty enough, but I can introduce you to the queen of courtesans, who is skilled in ways you cannot imagine.'

Mainard's curiosity was piqued, but he wasn't sure he trusted da Molina. 'Perhaps I may take you up on your offer, once my foot is healed.'

Da Molina responded with a lascivious smile that Mainard found deeply unattractive. He reflected that there were many benefits of his friendship with Ortelius, including that his proclivities tended towards Florenzers and he thus never challenged Mainard to partake of prostitutes, high class or otherwise.

'I don't think any injury to your foot is much impediment to a night with a courtesan, but then I understand you have a very beautiful wife.'

Mainard stared at him and da Molina shrugged.

'Tell me more about the business you're engaged in?' Mainard said after a moment, although he was furious that da Molina dare mention Bethia in the same breath as a prostitute.

Da Molina leant back. 'You may find the *ridotti* of interest.

'And what are they?'

'We'll conduct our business and then I'll show you.'

Mainard shrugged. He didn't know what was the matter with him; was consumed by a terrible lethargy. He should be embracing life having escaped prison but the weariness was overwhelming and the single thing that brought him any joy was his son – and even then he could tolerate Samuel-Thomas's exuberance for a short time only before he found an excuse to escape. And so, once they were finished at the customs house, he allowed da Molina to lead him to this *ridotto* which he soon discovered was held in a house of courtesans and involved gambling with dice and play with cards. He briefly grew energised as he bet on the throw of the dice, but when a courtesan with the most unnatural red hair, wearing breeches and those strange high platform shoes they called zoccoli, leant over and touched his ear with the tip of her tongue, he rose abruptly from the board. Da Molina was watching from under heavy lids and, curling his tongue across his upper lip, smirked. Mainard rolled his eyes and then wondered why he was playing along with the man when what he really wanted to do was punch him in his self-satisfied face. He shook his head; he was the one who needed punching for the way he was treating his loyal and loving wife.

The weeks passed and Mainard quickly learned the manner in which business was done in Venice. And he appreciated the manner in which he was dealt with. In Antwerp there was a willingness, of course, amongst other merchants to trade without concern for background or religion. As many English merchants as Conversos were to be found there but it was all about business. Outside the Bourse and the quays there was no mixing between groups, no meeting of families. Here in Venice it was very different and they were invited everywhere. He saw that Bethia was far more content. In Antwerp she'd been accepted by neither Christians nor Conversos and he suspected was often lonely, although she'd put a brave face on it. And yet her obvious pleasure in keeping company with noble Venetian families left him feeling more estranged. He should never have married her; it was cruel and her life would've been better if he'd not wrested her away from Gilbert Logie, especially since

Christ had forsaken him – no doubt a sign he *should* cleave to Judaism.

Yet whatever Bethia wanted he indulged – dresses, jewels, bonnets, furs – apart from the one thing she wanted most, a loving touch. One day she lifted her skirts to show him the pair of zoccoli she'd recently had made, saying she'd need his arm when she went out else she'd fall off them.

He couldn't disguise the disgust he felt. 'Take them off and burn them,' he shouted.

She stared at him in bewilderment. 'But everyone wears zoccoli…'

'I don't care, *my* wife will not. Get rid of them, now.'

Afterwards he was ashamed of his behaviour and knew that his disgust was at himself.

And then one day, two things happen which lifted his spirits greatly.

The first was his son, who of course he loved but had struggled to connect with. Mama had reassured him saying that men do not generally take great interest in their children until they're weaned and able to speak. Bethia still fed Samuel-Thomas, which Mainard knew was at his insistence, for he believed in Galen's strictures on the matter and distrusted any wet nurse, but hadn't realised the downside. He didn't find the damp milkiness conducive to congress, even before they were parted. But now his son was walking he was become of more interest, and when he arrived home this day Samuel-Thomas came tottering towards him on his fat little legs shouting 'Papa.'

Mainard caught him up, swung him high and his boy gurgled with laughter. From that moment he was as smitten as the coterie of women who looked fondly on the boy's every move. And in feeling that surge of love, he drew a little closer to Bethia, although not enough to resume intimacy.

The second was that Ortelius suddenly, and without

213

forewarning, appeared. Mainard was happy to see him, happy to resume a connection that was based on friendship without any of the undertones that dogged his every conversation with the good men of Venice.

'We always planned a trip to Italy together,' said Ortelius, clapping Mainard on the back. 'You just got here before me.'

'How long are you here for? I'll take you to our church to see the work by Bellini and the paintings, oh such paintings, by these fellows Tintoretto and Titian...' He trailed off as he saw a smile cross Ortelius's face. 'Please excuse me, I am just so very pleased to see you, my friend.'

'And I too am happy to be in this city from which topographical cartography of the greatest excellence comes and especially to see you looking considerably better than the last time we were together. How's the foot? You are able to bear some weight upon it?'

'Indeed,' said Mainard, suddenly aware it was throbbing from standing for so long to greet Ortelius. 'But I'm ready to sit down now.'

He led the way into the salon while Ortelius gazed at the walls, ceiling and mosaic floors, his eyes wide with wonder. Before Mainard could speak, Bethia came into the salon holding Samuel-Thomas by the hand. His son toddled to him and Mainard was delighted to show what a fine boy he was. Bethia greeted Ortelius with every expression of courtesy, which Mainard was grateful for.

'How was your journey?' she asked.

'As tolerable as could be expected.'

'Yes, it's not something to be done for enjoyment: the destination is the thing.'

Ortelius inclined his head in agreement.

'And the plague? It was bad for a while when we were travelling from Antwerp to Geneva.'

'The worst is over, I believe.'

Mainard thought of the stories come from Ferrara.

The Conversos who'd recently fled there from a now unwelcoming Antwerp, being forced into quarantine outside the city and much preyed upon by the guards who were supposed to protect them in their temporary island home. Always it was the Jews who were the whipping boys.

He watched as Ortelius drew back when Samuel-Thomas gripped his leg to pull himself back onto his feet with, no doubt, sticky fingers. Bethia was quick to swoop in and seize their son and Ortelius looked relieved. It had been on the tip of Mainard's tongue to invite their guest to stay while he was in Venice but he realised it would likely suit neither of them. In any case, with Papa growing frailer almost daily and Mama increasingly anxious, it was probably best not to have guests.

Bethia soon took Samuel-Thomas away and Ortelius questioned Mainard about his work, and whether he was a colourist still.

Mainard shook his head. 'There are probably as many printers here as in Antwerp but I don't think I can pursue this calling further.'

Ortelius waited, head inclined.

'And my friend, it's not the same without you. I'd need to make new connections, and my heart's no longer in it. I've a duty to my family, especially now my father has grown frail.'

Ortelius gazed at the floor. Then he looked Mainard straight in the eye. 'You choose rightly, my friend. Family must come first. But in the meantime perhaps you might have a few days in which to show me the wonders of Venice.'

'It would be my pleasure.' Mainard stood up. 'Let's begin now with the work of Tintoretto.'

Ortelius rose and clapped Mainard on the shoulder. 'Lead on.'

In the event he had only one week with Ortelius before Papa announced they must go to Ferrara. Mainard gazed at him while he spoke, wondering when Papa became so sickly. Once a tall man, he was now shrunken, as though his frame could not support his weight.

Mama scuttled behind him like a worried crab until he sat down. 'Why do *you* have to go?'

Papa blinked at her and Mainard wanted to laugh at his expression. Mama was normally so meek. It seemed she was learning boldness from Bethia.

'I must see Gracia Mendes and report to her on the latest outrage her sister has perpetrated.' He glared at his wife. 'You know our business is dependent on the goodwill of the Mendes. No effort must be spared where they're concerned.'

'And why will a letter not suffice.'

'Hold your tongue, woman.' Papa rose from his chair, but he staggered, and both Mainard and Mama leapt forward to catch him.

'Enough, enough,' he roared, although he leant on Mama's shoulder as he left the chamber.

Mama found Mainard as he was about to slip out to meet Ortelius. 'Papa has agreed – you are to go to Ferrara alone.'

But it seemed Bethia had other ideas. 'I will join you.'

He raised his eyebrows. 'I think not. You have Samuel-Thomas to care for and you'll slow me down.'

She looked pointedly at his foot but refrained from saying the obvious, for which he was grateful. 'Perhaps you didn't know but Samuel-Thomas is weaned. He'll be very well cared for between Mama, Katheline and Ysabeau.'

'And what of Grissel?'

She stared at him, rolled her eyes, and swept from the room.

But it was Mama who next interfered. 'Take Bethia.'

Mainard shook his head. ''Tis better I go alone.'

Mama reached up and took his face between her hands. He stood stiff and resistant, although he couldn't remember the last time his mother held him this way.

'You need to repair whatever has gone wrong between you. Bethia gave up much to be with you. She's been a devoted wife and loyal to this family, indeed has taken great risks for us. She doesn't deserve to be so disregarded.'

And so Mainard found himself, a few days later, travelling in a carriage over remarkably smooth roads with his wife opposite him, and nothing to say to her.

Chapter Thirty-Three

Ferrara

Bethia talked about the smoothness of the roads, the beauty of Venice, but only when she spoke of Samuel-Thomas did she get more than a grunt out of Mainard. His eyes lit up and his whole aspect changed at the mention of his son. It was a dull late autumn day but the sun came out briefly then as quickly hid again behind the clouds. Mainard's mood was like today's weather but she was determined they would not sit in silence for three days all the way to Ferrara. If only he would exert himself, but he refused even to look at her, keeping his face turned towards the window. She knew she was blethering on to fill the crushing silence… felt a fool and hated him for it. Eventually her voice trailed away and she slept. When she opened her eyes she found Mainard gazing at her. There was a look of anguish in his eyes but he quickly turned his head again towards the window, and she doubted herself.

She determined to ask him what was happening with Gracia Mendes; surely this was a safe topic on which to dwell. And all Venice had been talking of the sisters Gracia and Brianda and their fight for control of the Mendes fortune.

'Why did Brianda claim to the authorities that Gracia is a secret Jew? I cannot ever imagine doing such a thing to your own family.'

Mainard stretched out his foot, and she could see it was, as ever, causing him pain. 'Money and power do strange things within families.'

She waited, hoping he would elaborate without prompting, but he did not.

'It would be helpful if I understood more fully before we reach Ferrara and then I might not inadvertently say the wrong thing.'

His eyes narrowed and she suspected he wasn't intending she should be present for his meetings with Gracia. She felt the tears come to her own eyes that he would treat her with such disrespect.

'It'll look most odd that you should come here with your wife and not introduce her.'

'It was not at my behest you came,' he muttered. Then said loudly, 'You're right. I will tell you what I understand to be the cause of the ruction, although who knows, perhaps the sisters were never close.'

He leant back and tugged on his ear. The gesture was so belovedly familiar that Bethia had to restrain herself from flinging her arms around him. Back in Antwerp she would've done so without a moment's hesitation, but her world had changed since then.

'Gracia married her uncle Francisco Mendes, head of the Mendes trading empire, so rich that the kings of France, Portugal and England have all, at various times, been in debt to it. Francisco was in partnership with his brother Diogo, and after Francisco died some thought Diogo would marry Gracia, but, of course, Christians are not permitted to marry their brother's widow. Instead, Diogo married Brianda, who, as you know, is Gracia's sister. When Diogo himself died, it was not his wife but Gracia who was named as his successor and, what is more, she became the personal and financial guardian of Diogo and Brianda's daughter. This meant that Gracia has entire control of the Mendes trading empire.'

Bethia nodded slowly. 'I can understand that Brianda would resent having to apply to her sister for funds.'

'It's more than that though. Brianda can take her daughter nowhere without Gracia's permission.'

'I would very much dislike having to apply for a permit from my sister before I took my own child anywhere. It would certainly not be conducive to sisterly love.'

Mainard rubbed at his ear. 'Brianda is a most extravagant woman by all accounts so perhaps it's as well that Gracia controls the purse strings.'

Bethia sniffed.

'And she's a confirmed Christian who is aware of the large amount of Mendes money that Gracia has expended on assisting Conversos to escape from Antwerp, and on to the Ottomans, mention of which, I'm told, has had her frequently fly into a rage.'

Bethia sat up. She didn't care about Brianda Mendes, only wanted to know more of the Ottomans and what Mainard might be planning for their future. 'And is it any safer for Conversos among the Turks?'

'Yes. I'm told they allow Jews, and Christians, the freedom to follow their faith.'

Bethia smoothed her hair under her cap. 'Perhaps it's the place for Katheline then.'

'Perhaps.'

Bethia felt an odd fluttering in her chest, as though she couldn't quite breathe. She wanted to ask *and you*? But the words wouldn't form in her mouth. Yet Mainard had always claimed he was no relapser… although she didn't recognise this withdrawn man slumped opposite her.

There was a sudden bump and the carriage rocked widely.

'Potholes,' said Mainard. 'Not so smooth a road after all.'

By the next day Bethia began to regret that she'd insisted on coming. When they finally arrived, jolted and shaken, at the palazzo in Ferrara which Gracia Mendes had rented from its duke, she was exhausted.

Dona Gracia greeted them most graciously and Bethia was quite humbled to find the Duke Ercole himself visiting from his castle, barely twenty steps away. She wished she'd had time to refresh herself and change her clothes, for she was dusty and stained from travelling. She curtsied so low she near overbalanced, which flustered her even more. The duke was a man large of eyes, long of nose, and protruding from under the sides of his bonnet were the biggest ears she'd ever seen. He had a haughtiness of demeanour as he stared at them down his prominent nose and yet spoke pleasantly to both her and Mainard, asking of their journey and turning to Gracia, who he called Dona Beatrice, much to Bethia's confusion, saying she must be glad to have such handsome young visitors come from Venice.

Their audience was brief and Gracia soon called for servants to show them to their quarters, where Bethia gratefully accepted assistance to remove her travelling clothes. Mainard had suggested they bring Grissel but she refused and in the end they travelled lightly with only one cart following with their kists and two well-armed guards.

She washed and was helped into her heavy red brocade dress with the black bodice sewn with seed pearls and the equally heavy headdress with the veil cascading down her back, for she was now a fine Venetian lady too. She thought of her home in St Andrews and how her old neighbours would gasp if they could see her now.

Mainard appeared from the garde-robe in his black velvet doublet slashed with red, the plume in his cap fluttering with each move he made. She reached up to smooth the feather, which was from a most peculiar long-

221

legged bird and come all the way from Africa; another small wonder of her new world.

He bowed, saying, 'My lady looks very well tonight.'

She took his arm with a sense of well-being and hoped that they might finally be turning a corner.

But he disentangled from her almost immediately. 'I can barely keep myself upright never mind support another,' he mumbled as he limped from the chamber.

She followed in his wake, shoulders slumped, but when she entered the hall she straightened. This was only a temporary setback and she would overcome it. Nevertheless, she was aware of Dona Gracia watching them as the interminable meal progressed. Dish after dish was brought to the long board of polished wood where they sat along either side with the duke at one end, Dona Gracia on his left and Mainard next to her. Bethia was disappointed to learn that the duchess was from home, for she'd heard tales of Renée of France and had been curious to meet her.

Seated opposite Mainard, and next to a gruff greybeard who directed all his conversation understandably towards the duke, Bethia had ample time to observe her husband in conversation, most enjoyably it would seem from the smiles that flitted across his face, while Gracia leaned in to whisper in his ear. Then she was aware of Gracia watching her, in turn, and tried to still her face – uncomfortably conscious of the look of distress she was directing Mainard's way.

Eventually Bethia turned to the man on her other side, who was wearing a most alarming headdress, consisting of a number of these ostrich feathers set in a metal ring around his bonnet. They were dyed in alternating red and green, drawing all eyes to him and making him seem much taller than he was. Each time he turned his head the feathers brushed against the side of Bethia's face.

'Your plumes are most wondrous,' she said.

He preened, proud as any cock. 'They are come from Matthaus Schwarz, for he is the king of such designs.'

Bethia smiled politely.

'You don't know of Master Schwarz? I thought you were recently living in Antwerp, and he works for the Fuggers, who are much in evidence in that city.'

'I do know of the Fugger Brothers, for they are great merchants but I didn't go out much while I lived in Antwerp.'

'You must be very happy to have left then,' said her companion, and she couldn't stop the bubble of laughter escaping.

They discussed ostrich feathers, and the delicate task of dyeing them so they weren't damaged, until the subject was exhausted, at which point he moved onto codpieces, standing up to display the thrust of his.

'Look, I had my jeweller provide a few diamonds to make it sparkle and the tassels are of my particular design. It even cunningly holds this,' he said, fiddling at his package.

Bethia knew she should avert her eyes but somehow could not. She waited to see what would emerge. He tugged out a handkerchief, flourishing it to the applause of those around them. She caught Mainard's eye and he smiled but, as ever, it quickly faded. The duke rose then, indicating the repast was over. Bethia scurried around the board to Mainard's side so he might make use of her shoulder to lean on, which he for once did without resistance.

They gave thanks to their hostess, said they would not stay for the music tonight, and moved slowly off to their chamber through the crowd, nodding and bowing to they knew not who.

Mainard slumped on a chair when they eventually reached the privacy of their chamber.

'Why does Gracia have two names?' she asked as she knelt to unwrap the bandages around his foot.

223

'She is Beatrice de Luna and Gracia Mendes. The first was her birth name, the second is her Spanish name and the one she wishes now to be known by.'

'Is this like Katheline?'

'Perhaps,' said Mainard, 'and perhaps she liked the name Gracia.'

He shrugged but she didn't believe his insouciance. Katheline had lately announced that, since she was no longer living in Antwerp and did not have to adopt a local name to disguise her origins, she would revert to the Spanish version of her name. She now refused to answer to Katheline, saying she was henceforth Catarina.

'Do you have a Spanish name?'

Mainard sighed. 'Let me to bed, Bethia. And leave the foot unbound.'

'What of the noxious night air upon it?'

'I'll keep it beneath the blankets.'

He climbed into bed and lay down with his back to her. Bethia gave a sigh of her own and, once eventually divested of her clothes, followed him.

Chapter Thirty-Four

Gracia

When Mainard went to meet with Dona Gracia and Don Juan alone, a servant was sent to fetch Bethia.

'The decisions we take will affect you,' said Gracia when Bethia shyly appeared. 'And so it seems fair you should be party to them. It's interesting to me that you hail from Scotland and the Scots are great allies of the French. Perhaps you might have some insights to give since our discussions are about how we might recover the debt owed us by the French king.'

Bethia bowed her head respectfully and sat down, although truth be told she had had no dealings with Frenchmen. Father did, of course, but she was never party to them. But Gracia was most interested in what Bethia knew of Father's trade, asking many searching questions about his contacts and goods exchanged. And when she learnt that Bethia kept Father's ledgers Gracia looked at her with what felt like respect. Eager for this powerful woman's approval, Bethia realised she was saying far more than was wise or that her father would want disclosed. She comforted herself later – Scotland was far, far away. But of course, as Mainard pointed out when she confided her concerns, it was not so far from Antwerp where Gracia had connections still.

Mainard patted her hand, telling her not to be overly

concerned, and she forgot her worries in the pleasure of this rare gesture of affection from her husband. But seeing her flushed and hopeful face, he quickly withdrew, leaving her cursing herself for a fool at her overeagerness. She felt like a small dog leaping at her master's legs and grateful for just one wee stroke.

Dona Gracia, too, it seemed had observed that all might not be well with her young guests. 'Your husband has suffered, I think,' she said to Bethia one day when they were briefly alone.

Bethia was silent. She barely knew this woman and was by no means certain it was safe to confide in her.

'It is difficult for a man to know terrible fear and to speak of it.'

Bethia leant forward. 'He will tell me nothing. I've not even learned how the injury to his foot came about.'

'You're not a Converso and cannot understand the constant cloud we live under, never knowing which way the authorities will turn and what new edicts they may bring in to deprive us of our liberty and, especially, to seize our belongings.'

Bethia shifted on the low scoop seat and gazed at Dona Gracia sitting upright in her high-backed chair with the carving of a wolf's face gracing the end of each arm. 'I'm not unfamiliar with religious strife,' she said stiffly.

'Ah, the siege in which your brother was heavily implicated. I understand he suffered greatly as a consequence.'

The woman was a giant spider sitting in the centre of its web, ever tugging on threads and spinning new ones… and information was what fed her.

'My brother did suffer, as did Mainard, but he too is free now.'

'And still in pursuit of heresy, I believe.'

Bethia thought of the recent letter come from Will. He'd been greatly relieved that Calvin had not held the issue of the Tefillot against him overmuch and quoted

Calvin's words…

'You cannot be held responsible for the transgressions of your sister's relatives. If your own sister was the transgressor then that's an entirely different matter, but I observed Mistress Bethia to be most devout in her prayers, to show true piety and be well on her way to a proper understanding of doctrine. Indeed, I would hope she is using her time in Venice to persuade others to follow the Protestant path.'

Bethia had snorted reading it. She'd clearly disguised her beliefs well if Calvin thought she'd ever desert the benevolence of the Virgin and the gentle rhythm of Mass for his cold doctrine.

Yet, regardless of Calvin's wrong thinking, she valued Will's correspondence and wrote him long letters in return. They'd developed a closeness in this way that they never quite managed when they were together and intolerant of one another's foibles. It was as though the letters allowed them to show their best to each other. And for a taciturn man he wrote with surprising skill and occasional jocularity.

Like John Knox, Calvin suffers from severe pains in his belly and is often to be found doubled over, stifling his groans. Privately I wonder if belly thraw is a clerical requirement.

Bethia had laughed aloud. Her brother was at long last developing a joyous humour to counterbalance his great seriousness.

But such levity is inappropriate in a man who is becoming a most solemn cleric himself. Perhaps I too will end up with a constant sore belly to add to my unrelentingly sore back.

Poor Will, the mark of the galley would never leave him…

Bethia suddenly became aware that Dona Gracia was

waiting for an answer. 'My brother is a follower of Calvin's and has recently returned to Geneva.' She smiled ruefully. 'And it's my faith that would be considered heresy there.'

'You are a true Catholic?'

Bethia hesitated, thinking how to describe her beliefs. 'I'm a true follower of the Virgin.'

Dona Gracia raised the thin line of her plucked eyebrows high. 'And that makes you a Catholic. Yet I understand you've given up much to follow Mainard de Lange. I believe there was another more suitable claimant for your hand.'

Was there nothing this woman did not know? No detail so small that it was beneath her notice?

'I love my husband.'

'And will follow him anywhere?'

Bethia inclined her head. 'As I've more than demonstrated.'

Dona Gracia rose to indicate the audience was at an end. Bethia curtsied low, like a subject taking leave of her queen, and departed.

'Do you think Gracia will remain here?' Bethia asked Mainard as they took the air a few days later in the quiet of early evening, along the cobbled alleyways of Ferrara. 'It is a most impressive city with its new laid streets, printing houses, artists, music, physicians and university, but it seems too small for her. Venice is much the bigger board on which she may paint.'

He winced and she glanced anxiously towards him, but he waved her on, having already said that he must use the foot more when she questioned the wisdom of this outing. 'I think we can safely say that the Mendes family has an impeccable sense of timing. They got out of Portugal when it was still easy, they slipped away from Antwerp before Mary of Hungary could seize them, and

Gracia obtained the invitation to reside in Ferrara just as her sister laid charges against her and the Venetian courts issued a writ for her to come before them.'

'It must be exhausting having to be so constantly on her guard.'

'Although Gracia has more to lose and so is pursued relentlessly, it's not so very different for us.'

Bethia felt a great sadness. It was true of course. She'd been on her guard since the early days in Antwerp, and yet it was not fair to lay this at Mainard's door – even secretly inside her head. The siege in St Andrews was the beginning of it all and also the end: the end of quiet, safe days in her town. They paused before the colonnaded doorway that marked the entrance to a synagogue.

'You never spoke truer words.' She stepped forward and gripped his arm, gazing up into his face. 'All must be about our family, protecting our child and those to come. We shall be as Gracia Mendes: ever watchful, ever seekers of information and quick to act upon it.'

Mainard reached down and stroked her cheek with his forefinger. Bethia was so earnest she forgot to be self-conscious as she stared into his eyes. After a moment, ignoring the curious looks from the kosher butcher working away opposite, he wrapped his arms around her.

'We must not be parted again,' he whispered.

'Never again,' she murmured.

That night he turned to her and their long abstinence was over.

Chapter Thirty-Five

Papa

The journey back to Venice seemed shorter than the outward one. They were both anxious to return to their son: five weeks away too long, and Bethia grew tearful with longing whenever she spoke of him. Mainard was equally anxious to see Papa, for they'd received a letter from Katheline – he must remember to call her Catarina, even in his head – saying that Papa grew frailer day by day. *He is not sick exactly* she had written, *more as though he has no vigour or even the will to go on.*

Mainard worried over those words. Papa had moved from Spain to Portugal to Antwerp and now to here. He knew the Conversos of Papa's generation; their hearts had never left their beloved Spain. Mainard himself felt no such allegiance, was in any case born in Portugal to parents who'd already converted. But Papa seemed tired, weary that he must again adapt to living in a fourth country, build connections, understand new ways. Nothing had happened with the edict that had been enacted last summer requiring Conversos to leave Venice, the Christian merchants had seen to that, but always the fear lurked that Venice might turn on its Converso population at any time and they would have to flee once more.

Mainard gazed at his sleepy wife opposite, and felt a

softening deep in his core as he watched her. Perhaps they could remain in Venice, his antecedents might be forgot, his wife and children true Catholics. He sighed. It might work if he were the Christian and Bethia the Converso, but as the head of their small family it was his forebears who counted, for the Christians at least. And, in any case, if he looked deep in his heart the pull he felt was back to the faith of his ancestors, although he promised himself he would never act upon it. How could he when his wife and, most probably, children could never be accepted by the Jews. The safety of his family was paramount.

Bethia gave a soft snore and Mainard smiled. She was a good woman, as Gracia Mendes had firmly reminded him when she drew him aside before he and Bethia finally were again man and wife, saying she wanted to speak to him most seriously.

'There is discord between you and your wife.'

It was said as a statement, not even a question. Mainard had stiffened, saying, 'The connection between man and wife is most sacred, and private.'

Gracia gave the smallest of smiles. 'Let us walk outside. The gardeners have been hard at work and I would see this new structure, against which climbing plants will be trained, closer than through an open window.'

She'd taken Mainard's arm and turned him towards the doorway. He couldn't free himself without discourtesy, yet went with the greatest reluctance. It was warm outside in the heat of the day, although the gardens were dull and winter dormant. She was diminutive next to him and yet he felt like a small boy about to receive instruction from his magister. He hoped she would quickly have done and release him.

'I would not seek to interfere between a man and his wife…' she began.

Then don't. Mainard chewed on his lip to prevent the

words slipping out. Dona Gracia was not a woman to antagonise.

She stopped and released his arm, turning to look at him. 'You have a child, and God willing more will come. I've watched your wife…'

I am sure you have, thought Mainard.

She reached out and tapped him on the arm. 'I know this discussion is not to your liking, so I will say this one thing and be done. Your wife is most loyal. I, more than anything, value loyalty – look how I'm being dragged through the ringer by my own sister, and if I don't resolve our dispute she may take our entire family down with her malice. Bethia is, of course, a difficulty for you should you wish to return to the faith.' She narrowed her eyes and stared at him, and Mainard had to resist the impulse to glare back. 'But I hear no whispers that this is the case. So I say to you, do *not* squander the loyalty, and love, your wife has for you.' She turned away from him then and went to speak with the gardener. Knowing himself to be dismissed, Mainard left.

He gazed over at Bethia and found her watching him. 'Did Dona Gracia say something to you?'

'She said many things to me.'

Bethia sat up and rearranged herself on the seat. 'And about me?'

'Let's just say she made her opinion known as she does on all things.'

He thought of Grissel and hoped that now that he and Bethia were reconciled, Bethia would treat her with a gentler spirit.

'There was nothing between Grissel and I, you know.' He spoke reluctantly but better to clear all their differences once and for all.

'Grissel is most familiar with you.'

'Grissel is spirited with everyone who does not dampen her.'

'Are you suggesting I dampen her?'

Mainard swallowed. Harmony had just been restored and they were verging on a disagreement already. 'No, I'm saying that Grissel is a part of home for you. She is loyal and that loyalty should be valued.' He knew he was repeating Dona Gracia's words to him, but they bore repeating.

'And nothing inappropriate happened between you and Grissel?'

The sensation of turning his face into a soft warm belly rose up – but it was only a dream, he was sure. He brushed away Grissel's self-consciousness with him for weeks after he'd regained his senses.

'No, nothing,' he said firmly.

Bethia opened her mouth to speak as the carriage jolted violently and they were flung together. By the time they'd sorted themselves the subject was let go and Bethia never once raised it again. He was most grateful that she so generously forgave his unkindness to her – yet more evidence that she was like to an angel – but then any reminder of their long estrangement was no doubt as painful to her as it was to him.

It was a relief when he saw the spires and basilicas of Venice rising in the distance. Soon they were climbing into a boat. The boatman passed them a rug to place across their laps. Mainard wrapped his cloak tight around him and tucked his hands inside. The water between the mainland and Venice's islands was crowded with ships – the large galleasses, which Venice could produce at such great speed, interspersed by the smaller galleys of France and the Ottomans – and much activity as cargoes of people and goods were loaded and offloaded, for winter brought little cessation of trade. Beyond them, fishermen cast their nets from their small craft, catching the anchovies and sardines that his family had much enjoyed since arriving here.

A purple haze sat over the lagoon by one of the islands where the weed of the sea grew in profusion. The boatman navigated the channels with care and they rowed past the towering houses that made up the Ghetto, smoke rising in the still air from the hundreds of chimney cones dotting its roofs. He couldn't believe how high they were built and all facing inwards. He'd yet to visit the Ghetto, although he knew his sister spent much time there. He felt a strange reluctance to go, yet there was no reason he should not, as many Christians went, not only for trade, but also to watch the plays the Jews produced which were said to be most entertaining. But he knew the Jews despised Conversos – especially those who secretly returned to Judaism while still retaining all the benefits of being ostensibly Christian, including much lower taxation. Relapsing Conversos straddled both worlds – all the privileges of appearing to be Christian in this life while often embracing Judaism sufficiently to make sure they were Jews at the point of death. Could he do that? Certainly his adherence to the Christian faith had been gravely tested over the past year.

He took Bethia's hand in his as they drew near to their palazzo just off the Grand Canal and squeezed it, happy to know they were of one mind once more, happy to have this beautiful woman, who men's eyes followed, as his wife, and happy to have a partnership where they could be comfortably silent together. He felt a great sense of well-being as they drew up at their palazzo's mooring but that dissipated in an instant when they entered the house. It was in darkness, every window shuttered, mirrors and paintings shrouded.

'What's happened?' said Bethia, breathlessly climbing the stairs in front of him. He climbed as fast as he could, ignoring the twinge of pain in his foot, and stepped on the trailing hem of her dress. He heard it rip but neither of them heeded it. In they went to the salon to find Mama and Catarina sitting on stools, rocking back and forward, their heads covered with black shawls. Mainard covered his face with his hands. He knew before they spoke a word that Papa had left them.

'It was very sudden,' Mama said, when the first tumult was over and they had wept and hugged, and wept some more.

'Yet he seemed better only the day before,' said Catarina, shaking her head in disbelief.

'He was up and walking around, but very bent over,' said Mama, standing to demonstrate and shuffling over the mosaic marble floor.

Bethia reappeared with Samuel-Thomas in her arms. She held him close but the boy struggled to free himself. Mainard felt his overfull heart ready to burst as his son was put down and ran to him. He swung him into his lap. He wanted to hold the boy tight, to seek comfort in his warmth and closeness, but he stopped himself, instead jiggling him up and down on his knee while Mama and Catarina described Papa's demise in short bursts.

'He ate a hearty meal.'

'Well hearty for him, who'd been eating so little.'

'Then he said he was tired and would rest.'

'You know how he had taken to resting in the afternoon.'

Mainard nodded. Bethia opposite, had her face cupped in her hands, wide-eyed still from the shock, head turning back and forward between Mama and Catarina.

'I was busy with Samuel-Thomas. It's not good to leave him so much with Ysabeau when she cannot speak.'

'And Grissel was attending me as I went to look at lace.' Catarina covered her face and sobbed. 'How could I be engaged on something so trivial.'

Mama rocked back and forward, hands covering her face.

'Sad,' said the wee lamb, and Mainard was too sad himself to evince any joy at his son's increased vocabulary. The boy squirmed down from his lap and tottered to Bethia. Mainard brushed the tears from his eyes with the back of his hand while Bethia allowed them to run unchecked down her face.

After a few minutes Catarina dropped her hands and continued the story in a voice thick with tears. 'When I returned home I assumed Papa had risen, perhaps he'd gone out. I didn't think to look for him, or even to ask his whereabouts.'

Mama picked up the story. 'Catarina returned and I left the baby with Grissel. I looked for Samuel. I too thought he might have gone out, he seemed so much better. But then I knew.' She thumped her chest with her fist. 'I knew that he would not have left the house without telling me. I knew,' she hit herself again, 'that he was gone. I could feel it here, deep inside.'

Bethia was sobbing uncontrollably now and Samuel-Thomas touched her face with a child's erratic pats. When she didn't stop, he grew frightened and began to cry himself.

'How long?' said Mainard.

'Three days,' said Mama.

'The day we left Ferrara. If only we'd left sooner,' he muttered, looking accusingly at his wife, which he knew was entirely unreasonable when it was he who had ordered the date of their departure.

'I must see him. Where is he?' He looked from his mother to his sister. Mama avoided his eyes, staring at the hands resting in her lap, but Catarina gazed at him. It felt as though she was challenging him. 'You have already buried him,' he said slowly.

Catarina nodded. Mainard got up and left the salon. He was too angry to look at her.

He was aware of Bethia hurrying after him, a distressed Samuel-Thomas in her arms. 'Stop, Mainard. What's going on? Why have they buried Papa so quickly and without awaiting our return?' She tugged on his sleeve and he came to a halt.

'It is the Jewish way. The dead are not left to

suppurate but interred within a day of death.'

'But... but...'

'Papa is, was, a Converso. And as a convert to Christianity he should've been buried according to Christian rites and not Jewish ones.' Mainard rubbed his face. 'It seems my sister determined otherwise.'

'And Mama?'

'I suspect it was Catarina's doing but Mama clearly didn't prevent it. They *should* have waited for my return.' He slapped the banister and set his son to howling once more.

Mainard climbed the stairs to his chamber. It was too dark to see much with the shutters tight closed. He opened one and stood gazing out. It was dusk outside, lit dimly by the soft glow of a rising crescent moon. On the balconies opposite a few late flowers bloomed and banderole fluttered in the gentle breeze. It must be a feast day tomorrow. He felt an utter weariness and turned from the window to the chair, where he sat down and removed his boots. He rubbed his twisted foot. Bethia appeared, candelabra in hand, the candles flickering as she moved.

'Where's my boy?' he asked hoarsely.

'Grissel and Ysabeau have him.'

He was relieved. Did not want his son near Catarina, was too angry with her. Bethia closed the shutter. Mainard stood up, stripped off his clothes and crawled into bed. It was early but he couldn't bear to sit gazing into space. He lay on his back, arms behind his head, aware of Bethia moving around the chamber, picking up his clothes and folding them. He thought of when he last saw Papa. He should've taken more of the burden from Papa's shoulders sooner; he had been the indulged son – but no more. Bethia slipped into bed next to him and he wrapped his arms around her, pulling her close. The need for comfort was sudden and overwhelming. They were intimate with such an intensity that they were both left

237

gasping – but it didn't fill the void. The emptiness was there, deep inside, and it was right that it should be, for his father was a good man and Mainard had loved him.

He awakened next morning, his head aching as though he'd drunk a bottle of brandy, tongue cleaving to the roof of his mouth. Bethia was gone but soon reappeared with Samuel-Thomas wriggling in her arms like a stumpy eel. It was of immeasurable comfort for him to hold his son and play hiding beneath the covers. But the stuffiness of the darkened chamber and the heaviness of the house soon had him so oppressed he could barely draw breath.

'I must get out.'

'Let me quickly dress and I'll come with you.'

He tapped her wrist, while Samuel-Thomas disappeared beneath the bed. 'You know there's no such thing as you being able to dress quickly. And what about your mourning clothes? We must take care to do nothing out of the ordinary, to fit in – especially given the inexplicable haste with which Papa was buried.'

He got down on his hands and knees to entice his boy out but the bed was high enough that Samuel-Thomas could stay beneath it without hitting his head, and he sat and stared at Mainard.

'I've a dark skirt and bodice I can pair, from when I was in Geneva.'

Mainard squirmed beneath the bed and hauled his son out. Samuel-Thomas squealed, and as soon as Mainard released him, he disappeared beneath the bed once more.

Mainard took Bethia's hand and squeezed it. 'I need to go alone, for now. I'll come back for you soon but I must have some time to think on what has happened.'

She nodded understanding. 'This wee varmint and I will be ready upon your return.'

Chapter Thirty-Six

Ark of the Covenant

When Mainard ventured out, he didn't find the calm he sought, for the streets and canals were even more crowded than usual. He was in time to see the Doge borne high in his golden chair surmounted by the Virgin Mary, and dressed magnificently in robes of purple with a white ermine collar and bright crimson hose. The eight squires who bore him aloft were equally vividly coloured in yellow, green, and red. Musicians led the procession, playing silver trumpets of such length that they required boys walking in front to hold the trumpet bowls up. Following behind the Doge were a phalanx of men carrying high his badges and insignia of office, as if there could be any doubt of his importance.

Mainard pushed his way through the crowd and headed for the Jewish quarter. He would visit Papa's grave later, with Mama and Bethia – and would prefer if Katheline or Catarina or whatever she was calling herself stayed out of his way. He knew he would need to confront his sister sooner or later but found it hard to forgive her for making decisions that were not hers to take. And what of his other sister Geertruyt living in Strasbourg, had they written to her? How would she have felt about the speed and lack of Christian ceremony surrounding their father's death? It appeared her husband had Lutheran leanings after all; Bethia had been right to suspect him. He wondered how Geertruyt felt to be a Converso moving from Jew to Catholic to Protestant. A smile crept across his face; she was robust enough to take anything in her stride. The smile quickly faded. He felt sad that he might never see her again and the news of Papa's death would hit her as hard as anyone.

He hesitated outside the Jewish quarter. All was quiet in comparison to the streets around San Marcos; no procession celebrating a saint would pass through here. He walked over the hump of the slatted wooden bridge, down through the low dark gate and into his family history, for the first time in his life.

The clusters of buildings rising high above left him feeling more oppressed than he already was. In a courtyard he came across workmen chipping away at the decorative shield of one of the deep wells, which were such a familiar sight all around Venice. The shield was made of marble and removing the heraldic insignia was clearly a difficult task.

'What are you doing?' he asked in Italian. They stared at him and shrugged. He asked again, in Ladino, and one responded.

'We're scraping off the old Christian insignia and replacing it with the lions of Judah as we already did over there.' He waved his hand behind him.

Mainard passed through the crowd of women holding buckets and discovered a further two wells in this courtyard. He was surprised there should be three so close together, but then so many people lived here that water must be in great demand. He stood studying the Jewish lions but soon realised he was in the way as the women huffed and puffed around him.

He pushed through the narrow alleyways looking for one of the synagogues. The synagogue of the Ashkenazis he'd heard tell was the richest and most ornate, but then that was no wonder since the Jewish merchants originating from Germany had special privileges to trade that others did not. Everything was so densely packed there was even a rumour that in some homes people had to take it in turns to sleep because there wasn't sufficient space for them all to lie down at once. He peered in a window, which had a second window set slightly higher to the right, and realised that the ground floor had been split horizontally and a new floor inserted to make a second apartment. The ceilings in both levels were so low that, if he lived there, he'd have to walk with his head bent and no doubt develop a permanent stoop to add to his permanent limp.

He wandered expecting any moment to come across a synagogue, for he had knew there were three: one for the Ashkenazi, one for the French, and a very small one for the Italian Jews. He was looking for a grand facade, pillars, a dome, something that would proclaim that this was a place of worship like the churches and cathedrals he was familiar with, but he couldn't find one. He really wanted the French or Italian synagogue. The Ashkenazi and Sephardim didn't care overmuch for one another, but then, although his family originated from Spain, he was a Christian and not a Sephardi Jew, so it what did it matter. And would any group allow a Converso within their sacred place anyway?

In the end he asked and was quickly directed to a synagogue. The entrance was unprepossessing: a row of five windows and a small plaque but otherwise nothing to distinguish it from any other cramped house in the Ghetto. He stood uncertainly before it. There was a simple doorway with an inscription set into the wall next to it. He bent forward to read the Hebrew; it was a long time since he was at university in Louvain and studying these bold strokes. He translated slowly, murmuring the words aloud.

Much ill will befall the wicked, but he who puts his faith in God is surrounded by compassion.

241

Mainard became aware that he was standing motionless, hand on heart. He gave himself a shake and opened the door to the Tedesca Synagogue, any moment expecting to be challenged.

Facing him was a steep staircase. He climbed it, his heel hanging off the narrow step and his knee hitting the riser in front, and at the top a low doorway which opened into a wide space. On the floor an intricate marble mosaic, in the centre an octagonal kind of pulpit... he searched his mind, *a bimah*. Directly above it there was an octagonal opening in the ceiling through which bright sunlight was pouring, and which would illuminate the preacher, but would also soak him when rain fell. He sat down on one of the benches, a polished walnut carved with flowers and beasts, the arms in the form of a lion's paws, before an ornate gold-embossed armoire – was it an armoire?

There were other men also sitting but they left him alone, only casting the occasional glance at him. He gazed up at the red border painted around the walls bearing an inscription in gold. Eventually he deciphered it enough to recognise the Ten Commandments.

One of the men came and sat down next to him. He spoke to Mainard in what Mainard assumed was Yiddish. Mainard shook his head.

'Francaise?'

Mainard inclined his head.

'I was welcoming you,' said the man. 'But also wondering what brings you here since you are clearly not one of us.' He inclined his head towards Mainard's bonnet, which was not the yellow hue betokening a Jew.

'My father has died.'

'It's difficult to lose a parent.'

Mainard swallowed. 'He was a good man,' he said huskily.

'You are Conversos?'

'We are, although truth be told, my parents never

242

fully gave up the old ways.'

'Conversos are as a ship with two rudders, twisting and turning in whatever way is beneficial in the moment.' He stared at Mainard intently. 'And you, where is your rudder steering you?'

Mainard shifted in his seat, the wood hard beneath him. He'd said enough, admitting that his parents, or certainly his mother, were apostates. But there was something about the way this man looked at him that had Mainard saying more than he meant; he hoped those kind eyes were to be trusted.

'I was baptised. But in Antwerp I was tortured and imprisoned. It seems that Jesus Christ has forgot me and now I don't know where I belong.'

The man patted Mainard on the arm. 'You're sitting before the Ark of the Covenant which faces Jerusalem and contains our sacred Torah.' He paused and stared intently into Mainard's eyes. 'There are those who think they may move between Christianity and Judaism as it suits. When they're mortally sick and want to save their Jewish souls, Conversos think they may rejoin the fold. But it doesn't work like that. The Lord will only welcome you if you come with a true and faithful heart. Return once you *know* your way and are ready.' He stood up and Mainard followed him to the entrance, where he opened the door and, with a dip of the head, let him pass.

Mainard drifted out into the busy street, past women darning clothes and stalls selling the unleavened bread of the Jews. Here were the Jews struggling under the degradations imposed on them by the Venetian state, locked in at night and forever limited in the trade they might do by the yellow clothing which marked them out. And then there were his people, the Conversos, who, stateless, could not trade freely either and were forever in peril of expulsion. Yet neither Jews nor Conversos had much compassion for the other's plight.

He stood motionless mid-square gazing at the

243

synagogue while people flowed around him like a river around a small boulder. The Christians built churches to face Jerusalem and the Jews pointed their Ark of the Covenant in the same direction. Faiths united in so many ways, and yet so desperately divided.

How could he know where he belonged?

Chapter Thirty-Seven

The Fortesa Lad

It was the beginning of summer, and Bethia had been in Venice for near on twelve months. She expected to find this second summer more tolerable than the first but it seemed even hotter, and the family were warned to stay away from the mouths of the rivers which fed the lagoon.

'The air becomes bad and people get the sweating sickness,' Mainard told Bethia. 'Da Molina also says there's an insect which breeds there, so small that it can bite without you ever having seen it.

'Most probably a midge,' Bethia said. 'The bites can drive you as mad as the maddest dog. We have them aplenty in Scotland during the summer, especially beneath the trees after rain.' She swallowed a sigh. There were times when she missed her home so much she ached. Even if it meant being bitten all over by midges she would gladly bear it for a few days back in her ane country.

'I think they may be called mosquitoes, but in any case it's the air which causes the malady and we should keep all windows shut by day as well as at night.'

Bethia stroked her belly and caught the smile that crept across Mainard's face as he watched her. Their second child was underway. She had not been confident it would take after the troubles she'd had before Samuel-

Thomas was conceived, but as each week passed hope grew.

She bent to her task again, for she was now assisting Mainard, as she once helped her own father, to keep the ledgers. She loved this work, was happy that she was an integral part of making the family successful and no longer consigned to its fringes. Mama had fluttered about, especially when she knew Bethia was again with child, but Mainard had gainsaid her. Mama didn't persist once she'd said her piece, which Bethia was grateful for, nor did she berate Bethia behind Mainard's back. When Bethia remembered her own mother, querulous and demanding, she was every day grateful for the blessing of Mama.

The water levels in the canals dropped and the stink rose, as summer deepened. Bethia was larger now, the child most probably due in late autumn. Samuel-Thomas grew sturdier day by day. Whatever connection there had been between Mainard and Grissel had faded and they behaved towards one another as a master and servant should – at least as much as Grissel ever did behave as a servant. Often, Bethia, coming into the darkness of the basement kitchens, heard a door quickly slammed and caught that bland expression on Grissel's face which meant she was up to something, although Johannes stuck tight as her shadow, so there was a limit to what she could get up to. Nevertheless, Bethia suspected Grissel of a flirtation with one of the gondoliers. She didn't entirely blame her for they were most handsome in their black-and-white-striped pantaloons and blouses – and skilled charmers.

Catarina, who gave them such cause for concern – and fear – in Geneva could slip into the Ghetto and consort with Jews whenever she cared to, as long as she left by curfew when the gates were locked. Indeed, few of the people that she and Mainard regularly met with were aware he had a sister, for she was rarely with them. And

Mainard, after his brief brush with Judaism, seemed to have returned, like one of Jesus's lambs, to the fold. Together they attended a small church under the benevolent gaze of a Tintoretto masterpiece, they took Mass, they knelt to pray, they took confession – Will would've been most unhappy if he could see her. She loved this city, its vibrancy, beauty, and the sense of being watched over by the ever-present symbols of the Madonna. All felt well in her world.

Then one day da Molina came to warn Mainard that the family were under suspicion. Catarina's activities were not so secret after all. And there were questions about Papa's burial. Neighbours had reported the unnatural speed with which he was interred and even worse that the corpse was wrapped in white linen – a most foreign and unchristian act. The sense of being constantly watched again grew until Bethia was glancing all around whenever she left home.

'I've found Catarina a husband,' Mainard said a few weeks after da Molina's disclosure, as she bent over the ledgers, tongue between her teeth writing in her careful copper plate. 'It's more than time she was married but I will need your support to prepare her.'

Bethia looked up, rolling the pen between her fingers. 'Who is he?' For some reason she felt afraid for Catarina, yet surely Mainard, of all people, could be trusted not to marry his sister off to someone repugnant, however suitable the prospective groom's credentials.

Mainard took a turn around the chamber and stopped abruptly in front of her. 'He's the son of an old acquaintance of Papa's. The family recently arrived in Venice.'

'So he's young?' said Bethia hopefully. She would find it more difficult to support Catarina's marriage if it were to an old man.

'Yes.' Mainard rubbed at the furrow between his eyebrows. 'Very young.'

Bethia placed the quill carefully in the inkstand. 'I assume he's at least out of short coats?'

'Yes, yes. He's sixteen.'

'That is youthful indeed: four years younger than Catarina. Why do his parents want him married at such an early age?'

'Oh, the Fortesas are old, frail, and most of all in need of funds. He's their only surviving child and they want his future secured.'

Bethia let out a great puff of air. 'Is there no one else?'

'I did make inquiries but Catarina's frequent visits to the Ghetto, as we've recently discovered, have been remarked on. No one wants to align their family with an apostate.'

Bethia rubbed the thumb of one hand across the palm of the other, back and forth. She paused and gazed up at Mainard. 'Can we not find a husband for her among the Jews? I think she'd much prefer that.'

'I've considered it, and it's of no benefit to our family, indeed might well cause us considerable harm even if we could find a Jewish family willing to make a match with Conversos. No, she must marry another Converso else it brings our position into question. My sister has already placed us in enough peril. I may yet be called before the Council to explain the speed and manner with which Papa was interred.'

Bethia went back to rubbing thumb into palm. 'I'll do my best to bring Catarina around to her duty.'

Catarina, being Catarina, didn't appear to resist the proposal, but Bethia, by now, knew well the strong will which lay behind the mild countenance. Fortunately, the Fortesa lad was comely enough, although gawky as a young colt that has grown overfast with only a fluff of hair covering his chin. At the first meeting, his parents sat on the edge of their seats nodding in agreement to whatever Mainard was saying. Catarina kept her eyes fixed on the floor and Bethia grew annoyed – surely her good sister could at least have the manners to engage the lad in conversation, especially as he kept glancing towards her. Eventually Bethia caught Mainard's eye and inclined her head at the young couple, who now both sat eyes fixed on the floor. He suggested that they remove themselves to the other side of the large salon where they 'might have quiet speech together.'

Catarina rose and glided to where Mainard directed and the lad followed. His parents sat back in their seats and Fortesa began a conversation with Mainard seeking an introduction to Don Juan Micas while the mother confided to Bethia about her hope that Catarina would be happy living with them 'for our home is not as fine as yours.' Bethia, struggling to follow the Ladino spoken in the mother's whispering voice, was grateful when Mama interjected reassuring her that Catarina would be delighted with her new home. Bethia, glancing over at Catarina, who caught her eye and winked, did not share Mama's confidence in her good sister's amenability. But Catarina, as ever, surprised her.

'He will do well enough,' she said when applied to by Mainard and Bethia, while Mama, in the wings, stopped wringing her hands and smiled as bright as the shafts of sunlight dancing over the mosaic marble floor.

Bethia smiled too and Mainard said privately later to her, 'I feel as though the weight of the world has slipped off my shoulders.'

Next there was a dinner, stilted and uncomfortable, although the young couple giggled behind their hands. Bethia wished they would share the jest and bring some levity to this interminable meal. Eventually it was over and Mainard took the father to his workroom to discuss settlements while Bethia and Mama entertained the mother, and the young couple whispered away in their corner.

When Grissel came in answer to the bell, Bethia looked expressively at her, and Grissel, for once, caught on, gave a slight nod and, after serving the wine with smooth efficiency, left the room, returning a few minutes later to say Bethia was needed for the bairn. She rose with alacrity but Catarina had sidled over with the lad in tow and was asking if they could together attend the carnival tomorrow. Bethia sat down again, watching Catarina intently while the mothers discussed the request. Eventually it was agreed provided they were chaperoned… but by whom was then the question. Bethia left them debating, with Catarina insisting, since they would be masked, no one would know who they were, and it was carnival time when the normal rules did not apply, so no chaperone was necessary. Privately Bethia thought Catarina would've been better to have kept that thought to herself, but her prospective new mother already seemed so in awe of her future daughter it appeared she would agree to anything Catarina suggested. Yet it was most curious. Catarina had never before evinced any desire to join revellers but was quiet and devout, much like Will.

A week later, Bethia, with Ysabeau carrying Samuel-Thomas, walked through the market emerging into the Piazza San Marco to stand below the clock tower. She often came here, for she found the golden and blue astrological signs, which marked the passing of time as much as the giant Moor bronzes beating out the hour above the clock, very beautiful. She could've stood and gazed upon it for a long time but Samuel-Thomas was wriggling to escape, and when she signalled to Ysabeau to let him down he shot off across the square as fast as his little legs would go. Bethia watched as Ysabeau chased after, but, before she could catch him, he ran straight into the back of a woman, near oversetting them both. Bethia hurried over. It was only when she reached her son, she realised it was Mistress Fortesa with whom he'd become entangled.

'I must apologise. My son can be over-exuberant. I should not have let my servant put him down. Are you hurt?

'No, no, the fault is all mine. I was distracted, you see.'

Her voice, always soft, faded away on the last words and Bethia had to lean forward to catch them, thinking as she did that the lady looked even more flustered than usual.

'You have no one to attend you?'

Mistress Fortesa shook her head, her eyes unaccountably filling with tears.

'Then let me escort you to your house.'

She directed Ysabeau to take Samuel-Thomas home then took Mistress Fortesa's arm and turned back beneath the archway and into the Merceria. They walked past the caged nightingales swinging outside the apothecaries but were soon halted by a crowd blocking the street.

'What's going on?' muttered Bethia.

'It's a punishment,' said a woman in front of them, turning to explain, with evident satisfaction, that a man caught selling pamphlets printed without permission was being whipped from the Rialto to San Marcos.

'We must get away,' pleaded Mistress Fortesa, hands fluttering as much as the wings of the poor caged nightingales.

The poor woman looked on the verge of having a seizure and Bethia felt most concerned for her. They escaped up an alleyway that twisted and turned until they found themselves crossing a bridge over one of the minor canals.

Mistress Fortesa gripped Bethia's arm so tightly she was sure the blood was constricted. 'I hate these steep bridges without sides. Every moment I expect to find myself knocked into the water and drowned,' she mumbled.

'You'll soon grow accustomed. I barely notice them

now,' said Bethia, but the grip was not relaxed. She was thankful when they arrived outside the Fortesa's home, saying that she would leave now. Mistress Fortesa wouldn't hear of it and was so insistent that Bethia come in that Bethia grew embarrassed, especially when the neighbour opposite hung out of her window and joined in the entreaties.

The house was narrow and dark, plaster chippings dusting the stairway giving a general air of neglect, and Bethia's heart sank; this did not look to be a suitable home for Catarina. Fortunately, the salon, reached once they'd climbed two flights of stairs, was bright with sunshine, well furnished, and with the obligatory portrait of the Virgin smiling benignly over them.

She was invited to sit on what she suspected was normally the master's chair and Mistress Fortesa called for wine. A servant came, neat and tidy, and, although her bodice was worn at the seams, Bethia felt further reassured. The mistress of the house sat down but rose again as soon as the servant had served them, oscillating around the chamber like a trapped moth.

Bethia sat watching her, at a loss. Eventually she said, 'You seem most perturbed. Is there anything I can do to assist?'

Madame Fortesa sat down on her much lower seat pressing her hands together. 'My husband says it's all nonsense and he would be very angry if he knew I was speaking to you of this, and perhaps you *will* think I'm nothing but a foolish old woman, which is what he calls me, but I've sought an astrological prognosis for this marriage and it is not good. Not good at all.'

Chapter Thirty-Eight

Prognostication

Mistress Fortesa's hair had come loose under her cap and hung over one eye, which she appeared unaware of, and with her scratchy voice and dishevelled appearance, she did look, and sound, crazed.

But Bethia, the memory of her encounters with Nostradamus still present in her mind, didn't dismiss her. 'Is it written down; can I see it?'

Mistress Fortesa shook her head. 'My husband burned it. He said it was the work of a charlatan.' She rose and came to kneel before Bethia, hands clasped imploringly. 'It said that if he married now, my son would not long survive, would be dead before his eighteenth birthday. Please, he's my only child; ten children I bore and only he is left. I cannot lose him.'

Bethia stood and, raising the poor woman up, guided her back to her seat. 'I'm not sure what I can do.'

'Persuade your husband to give up the betrothal. I see how he attends to you. He'll listen if *you* tell him it cannot go ahead.'

'But I have no reason to give. Where did you get this prediction from – at least if I'd something to show him it would help. And how can you be certain that it *isn't* some nonsense from a charlatan, as your husband claims?'

'I *know* it's true. A mother knows here.' She hit herself

on the chest with her fist. And once started she couldn't seem to stop, hitting over and over.

Bethia remembered the constant feeling of dread while she was in Lyon, and her instinct that something terrible had happened to Mainard – and she'd been correct. She couldn't dismiss Mistress Fortesa's fears.

'I'll speak with my husband,' she promised. And was relieved when the poor woman ceased beating her breast and looked hopefully up at her.

Bethia raised her hands, palms outwards. 'I can do no more than that. I give you no certainty that he'll listen.' Indeed, she doubted Mainard would take her seriously, more likely to consider that she'd taken leave of her senses, which is indeed what happened when she raised it with him.

'You want me to renege on a marriage settlement which I'm on the verge of signing?' was his response. 'And what of Catarina? It was hard enough to find any family willing to take her, and word will soon fly around that she's some sort of death knell for any man. And all on the basis of some prophecy... prognostication... whatever it is.'

Bethia hung her head. Nevertheless, the more he dismissed her fears, the stronger her conviction grew that Mistress Fortesa could not be ignored. 'You shouldn't disregard a woman's instinct. We know things.' She thumped her chest with her fist much as Mistress Fortesa had. 'Deep inside, we can feel it.'

Mainard snorted. 'Any clever fellow can make up some story and sell it to a foolish woman. Let me think... here's my prognostication based on the alignment of stars and the next comet that is to shoot across our skies... some prince will die before the end of the year, great conflicts will take place, famine will affect those who have no livelihood, people will die in the spring, pregnant women will give birth to either boys or girls, and if the harvests are good there will be plenty. Oh, and

I almost forgot, if Catarina marries the Fortesa boy, she will, Medusa-like, turn him to stone – or do the astrological charts foretell that his death is to be bloodier and more gruesome?'

Bethia, red-faced, stared helplessly at her husband.

After a moment his face softened and he took her hands. 'My love, I know you're concerned, but whatever this story Mistress Fortesa has been persuaded of, it is a banal fallacy, I am certain.'

'I pray you may be right,' said Bethia.

Catarina was to wed her lad in two days. Samuel-Thomas seemed to have been infected by the excitement and ran around squealing, crawling amid the new clothing laid out across the kists and bed and getting in everyone's way. There was a moment of panic when all went quiet and Bethia was convinced he'd fallen down the stairs and broken his neck. Ysabeau quickly became tearful, which a frantic Bethia considered most unhelpful. It was the preternaturally calm Catarina who discovered him asleep behind Papa's large chair in the salon, which sat mostly unused, left as though the master of the house still occupied it, at least in spirit.

'What a wild one he is,' said the fond father when he found the women of the house gathered around his sleeping son and was told the story of the disappearance. 'I'll stay with him now and we'll keep Ysabeau busy with us until she recovers from her fright.'

Bethia considered that she was the one most in need of recovery but Catarina took her arm, saying, 'Good sister, I need your help.'

It was a rare demonstration of affection which warmed Bethia's heart. She couldn't resist asking, 'Are you happy, Catarina?' And then cursed herself for a fool as the mask of serenity came down over Catarina's face.

'I want to try on my headdress and need your assistance to affix it, is all.'

'Come to my chamber, it's peaceful there,' said Bethia

as Grissel bustled in to join the throng, having just returned from the lacemaker with the trim for Catarina's new underskirts.

Bethia lifted the headdress from its stand, the material woven in a great roll, fixed to the frame with gold thread, and the whole creation heavy with pearls. She settled it carefully over Catarina's head. Catarina lifted her hand to steady it and her sleeve slid down exposing her arm. Bethia went still, for she could see the ring of teeth marks pink against the skin, from when Catarina was bitten by the dog. Catarina dropped her arm and quickly covered it.

'Grissel, come and help,' Bethia called.

Grissel held the other side of the headdress in position, and between them, after some manoeuvring, they got it at an angle all were satisfied with.

'Now I'll pin it in position so you don't end up with it hanging over one eye.' Bethia smiled at Catarina in the mirror and, after a moment, Catarina smiled back. 'You may go now, Grissel, I can do the rest.'

Grissel left and Bethia gathered her courage. Mistress Fortesa hadn't spoken to Bethia again but then she'd made certain they were never alone together. Yet every time they met, the woman seemed more agitated: hands twisted together and lifting her head only to gaze reproachfully at Bethia.

Mainard had forbidden her to say another word about it to anyone, but she was afraid. Fearful that if something did happen to the Fortesa boy and she hadn't told Catarina of the prophecy, then she herself would be culpable.

Catarina said nothing as Bethia told the story, only dropping her gaze to the hands lying in her lap. Bethia finished and awaited a response. None came. Catarina remained very still, apart from the slight rise of her chest as the breath moved within her.

'I felt I must tell you. Then you'll understand better

Mistress Fortesa's behaviour.' Bethia knew she was babbling but Catarina's unnatural stillness was most disconcerting.

'Can you take the headdress off now. I think we're clear how it may be best sited and attached.' Catarina's voice was without expression.

Bethia slid the pins out as quick as her fumbling fingers would permit, eager to leave Catarina to her thoughts. She held little hope that Catarina would act on her words, but there was some relief, as well as shame, in having passed the responsibility for the survival of young Master Fortesa onto Catarina's rigid shoulders. She slipped from the room and it was to be a long time before she could meet Catarina's eyes again.

Mainard came to her two days later saying that the marriage would not go ahead. Bethia jumped and the pen dripped ink over her calculations, but he didn't look angry, more resigned.

'What happened?'

'Catarina happened.'

'What did she do?'

Mainard took Bethia's hand in his and kissed it. 'There's no need for such alarm, my love. I suspected it was almost too good to be true that we'd found her a husband amongst a respectable Converso family, who were willing to overlook her activities, and whose son was not repugnant to her.'

'What excuse did the family give?'

'The not unexpected one that Catarina was corrupting their son. She'd taken him to visit the Ghetto and suggested that they might convert. Apparently she even discussed circumcision with him.' He looked heavenwards. 'I ask you, is that a suitable subject for a young woman?'

Bethia considered that, given Catarina was to wed the lad, perhaps it wasn't entirely unsuitable but, determining now was not the time for levity, she held her tongue.

'Curiously Fortesa seemed almost glad to have a reason to withdraw. I'd noticed a reluctance to finalise the settlement, even as the nuptials drew near.'

Bethia suspected Mistress Fortesa had eventually sown doubt in her husband's mind, but simply nodded.

Mainard rubbed the back of his head and exhaled. 'Now what are we to do with her?'

Chapter Thirty-Nine

Old Eleni

Bethia was with Mama, Samuel-Thomas playing at their feet, when Grissel came to say that their neighbour was below with a gift for the bairn.

'Which neighbour?' asked Bethia.

'Ye ken, that weirdie one.'

Bethia, raising her eyebrows as much at Grissel's way of speaking of her betters as the description, was glad Grissel spoke in Scots and Mama didn't understand her words.

Bethia stilled her face and turned to Mama. 'Mistress Eleni is below.'

Mama rose. 'I'll go and speak with her.'

She knew that Mama was too kind to turn the old woman away but would rather not have her invited into the salon. The last time Bethia saw Eleni in the street, she was shouting and erratically waving a stick as she stumbled after pigeons. The pigeons rose up and then landed again, barely out of reach as though deliberately provoking her.

She heard voices and was about to go out and peer down the deep stairwell when the door opened and Old Eleni shuffled in followed by Mama. She felt a rush of love for her good mother, for her kindness and sweetness of nature. But then Old Eleni came from Spain long ago and was a Converso too. Mama gathered all to her bosom, thought Bethia, even her – a Christian from faraway Scotland.

Old Eleni made straight for where the wee lamb was sitting on the rug, for once playing quietly with a set of clay dolls which Mainard had brought him yesterday, instead of his more usual activity of charging around the chamber and climbing onto chairs to reach what he should not be touching. She sat down on the floor beside the bairn, legs splayed wide and grey hair falling over her face. Mama and Bethia looked to one another and raised their eyebrows.

'See what I have brought you, *my baba,*' Old Eleni said, extending her hand. A piece of pottery lay in the palm. Bethia inclined her head, squinting to work out what it was…

'A pig,' said Mama. 'How… unusual.'

Old Eleni shook it and it rattled.

Samuel-Thomas giggled. 'Again,' he cried.

Old Eleni gathered him in her lap, holding him close. Bethia half rose, was sure she could see beasties crawling in the old woman's tangle of dirty hair. Eleni clutched Samuel-Thomas to her breast and rocked him back and forward singing in her cracked voice. Soon he'd had enough and struggled to free himself, but Eleni gripped tighter, bending her head to sing croakily in his ear.

Bethia and Mama leant over Eleni, insisting she let him go. She kept singing, as though they weren't there. Samuel-Thomas was roaring now, but Eleni was oblivious. Bethia grabbed the old woman's arm, tugging on it, but Eleni held on all the tighter.

'Eleni. Let him go. Now,' shouted Mama, in Ladino.

Old Eleni released Samuel-Thomas and Bethia caught him before he hit the floor. She hurried away, leaving Mama to deal with the old woman. It took her, Ysabeau and Grissel until the noon bell to settle him. Eventually he fell asleep, still red-faced with indignation. Bethia left

Ysabeau to watch over him, sending Grissel out to purchase some *golosessi*, the sweet biscuits of Venice, to restore her and Mama.

'She's not right,' said Mama. 'Her head is confused. I'll speak with her son, for he seems to be a good man and kind to his mother. It's not wise that she lives alone.'

But before Mama met with the son there was more trouble.

One day Bethia went to Mass, accompanied only by Grissel. Grissel walked demurely behind, eyes down and hands crossed over her belly. Bethia knew this because she kept turning to catch Grissel out in her more normal practices of gazing all around and exchanging a wink and some banter with any eligible lad she passed. Grissel's assumed meekness did not reassure. Bethia sighed. She'd hoped Grissel would mend her ways after what happened in Antwerp, but Grissel was incorrigible.

Once in church, Grissel stood at the back while Bethia settled near the front gazing at the painting by Tintoretto that sat high above the altar table. There'd been much discussion about this art, for Titian also painted the same subject, *The Presentation of the Virgin Mary*, near twenty years before. All Venice had debated the merits of each painting and Bethia herself had compared both. In each, her eyes were drawn to the child Mary, so small and humble, bathed in the light of the Holy Spirit as she dedicated herself to the Lord while the watching men rose like giants over her. The vulnerability of this Virgin child never failed to smite Bethia's heart and she felt filled with light and love herself as the priest began to recite the Credo, which she effortlessly translated in her head.

> *I believe in God,*
> *the Father Almighty,*
> *Creator of Heaven and Earth,*
> *and in Jesus Christ, his only Son, Our Lord,*
> *who was conceived by the Holy Spirit,*

born of the Virgin Mary,
suffered under Pontius Pilate,
was crucified, died and was buried;
He descended into Hell…

'You son of a harlot,' a voice muttered from behind. Bethia hunched her shoulders. She knew that voice: cracked yet insistent. She glanced over her shoulder to see Old Eleni, hair more tangled than ever and her few teeth showing yellow against the dirt of her face.

Fortunately, the priest hadn't heard, and continued.

on the third day He rose again from the dead;
he ascended into heaven,
and is seated at the right hand of God the Father
Almighty; from there He will come to judge the living
and the dead. I believe in the Holy Spirit…

'You lie in your teeth, you bastard,' shouted Eleni.

The priest's voice trailed away. Bethia was on her feet as he came down the aisle. People were half rising and turning to look as Bethia pushed her way to Eleni before the priest reached her.

'I am sorry, Father. She's unwell. I'll take her home and fetch the physician.'

The priest glared at Bethia, eyes bulging, as though it was she, and not the old woman, who'd spoken such terrible words in his church. For a moment she thought he wouldn't let her leave, but then he spoke. 'Take her away,' he said, the spittle bubbling in the corner of his mouth. 'But I am *not* done with her.'

Bethia dipped her head but it didn't seem to mollify him. He turned on his heel and marched back up the aisle.

Together she and Grissel led Eleni from the church followed by the rising rustle of whispers. Fortunately, the old woman didn't resist but came willingly, her expression vacant.

Mama called on the son, and all hoped that it would be dismissed as the rantings of a mad old woman. But the priest would not let it go, for a month later Bethia was called as a witness at Old Eleni's trial.

The priest stood up, implacable in his accusations saying Eleni swore while he was reciting the Credo. He spoke her words loudly for all to hear.

'You lie in your teeth, you bastard.'

There was a twittering of excitement around the court and people leant into one another repeating the words with pleasurable outrage.

The old woman looked bewildered as she stood before them. Today she was at least clean and her hair tidied beneath her cap, thanks to Mama. Bethia's eyes shifted to where the son sat, leaning forward, brow furrowed beneath his tight black cap. He was dressed soberly and looked every inch the respectable Venetian citizen.

Bethia was called to give her testimony, and she rose slowly, the weight of responsibility to persuade the court of Eleni's innocence heavy upon her. She was asked if she too heard what Eleni said and was made to repeat it, causing a further twittering around the court – the spectators almost ecstatic that such words should come out of the mouth of a young woman, and one heavy with child too. She was dismissed before she could explain that Old Eleni was not right in the head.

She moved towards her seat reluctantly, must at least try to speak, have the court listen to what she knew. 'Please, she's an old woman. She doesn't know what she's saying,' she said, clasping her hands together and gazing at the judge.

The guard stepped forward but the judge signalled that she should continue.

'Eleni is our neighbour.'

She could see Mama nodding encouragement, but Mainard sat next to her, his face impassive. She knew it wasn't wise to show they'd any connection with Old

Eleni beyond happening to witness her strange behaviour in church. Mainard had counselled she should say only that, and she understood he was responsible for their family's safety, for her safety. Always the spectre of being Conversos hung over them, but she must help Eleni, it was her Christian duty.

In the end, all her descriptions of Old Eleni's erratic behaviour, of her visit to their home, and her conviction that Bethia's own son was her child came to naught. Another neighbour testified that Eleni lit candles before sunset on a Friday, rested on a Saturday yet swept her house on a Sunday, and had an image of the Virgin Mary by the front door where a mezuzah would normally sit. Bethia wondered how the neighbour knew so much about Jewish practices, but it seemed the judge didn't think to question it. Old Eleni was sentenced to be imprisoned in the Piombi as an *unrepentant Jewess*.

'Be thankful it wasn't a burning,' said Mainard when Mama wept at the old woman's fate. 'And at least her son can afford to pay for her accommodation.'

'That may not be such a benefit. I've heard tell the wealthy are kept at the top of the prison.' Mama turned to Bethia, who was crying freely too. 'And their cells are beneath the lead roof. 'Tis said to be bitter cold in winter and unbearably hot in summer.'

'Enough, Mama.' Mainard swivelled Bethia around, holding her face between his long fingers and gazed down into her eyes. 'You did as much as you were able, my love. No one could've saved her, for that priest was determined.' He dropped his hands and stared at his feet. 'A most unchristian act for a follower of Christ.'

'Hush,' said Mama. 'Someone will hear you. I fear much of what we do and say is reported. Our servants cannot be trusted.'

There was a grunt from Bethia.

'Apart from Grissel, Johannes, and Ysabeau, of course. Not that Ysabeau could tell anything.'

'Yes,' said Mainard in a strangely deep voice. 'Grissel, as she's already more than demonstrated, is loyal.'

Bethia stopped crying and looked up into his eyes. He met her gaze without any consciousness. She still wondered what did go on between them all that time ago.

'Go home and rest, my love.' He touched her belly lightly. 'I would not have this one distressed.'

Bethia's second child was born in the chill fog of the short Venetian winter. Mama had hung amulets all around the chamber which rattled whenever anyone brushed against them, much to Bethia's annoyance. The Venetian midwife insisted that she stayed in the birthing chair throughout, but Bethia swatted the pressing hands away and got up frequently to move restlessly around. Nevertheless, her labour, although long, was, in the main, bearable. Of course, she knew what to expect this time and there was not the same fear that accompanied the birth of Samuel-Thomas. If anyone was fearful it was Mainard, who Mama said paced outside the chamber all night.

'Another big fellow,' said Mainard, gazing down as Bethia cradled the babe in her arms. She could see the tears in his eyes and guessed he was remembering how he celebrated Samuel-Thomas's birth with Papa, and indeed Will. Papa's death had left a gaping hole in their life and the burden of responsibility for the family now fell on Mainard, but more than that they both missed Papa's deep voice, tall presence, and even his not always entirely successful forays into new business.

'What will we call him?' she asked.

'Jacopo,' said Mainard decisively.

'We're giving him a Venetian name?'

'Yes.' He spoke abruptly, as though it was a foolish question. Bethia didn't think it was at all.

'But *we* do not have Venetian names.'

'I've been considering if I should revert to my Spanish name, as Catarina has done.'

Bethia shifted on the bed and winced.

'You're in pain, my love.' He stroked her hair.

'Not so bad.' She tilted her head back and looked up into his eyes. 'It'd feel like I was married to another man if you were no longer Mainard. And what does Jacopo mean in English?'

He pursed his lips. 'James, I believe.'

'Then he shall be my wee James.' She bent to kiss the little face peeping out from the swaddling, then hesitated. Her head felt like there was a fog as thick inside it as that pressing against the tall windows of the chamber. 'Isn't Jacopo also Jacob?'

Mainard stepped back from the bed and shrugged. 'Possibly.'

She wasn't fooled by his nonchalance.

The baby cried and she rocked him in her arms. When she looked up Mainard had gone. She frowned, feeling ashamed that she didn't know her husband's Spanish name. Yet why should she? His family were already in Portugal when he was born. The great longing amongst Conversos for Spain left her confused. She didn't understand why they should hanker after a place that so ill treated them.

A shiver ran through her, as though a ghost was near. She chided herself – it was only the chill damp from outside creeping in – and bent to her new babe once more.

Chapter Forty

Brianda

Her lying-in over, Bethia was again taking up the reins of family life. One day, working on copying a long and complex contract about importing Venetian cloth to Constantinople which each merchant involved required a copy of, and which she was required to translate from Ladino into French, she felt her head ready to burst. Laying her quill down, she went in search of some light relief and found Mainard in deep discussion with Don Juan Micas.

'It is most wearing,' Don Juan was saying in his high fluting voice. 'We've been welcomed in Italy for some time, and now, even here, there's a constant push against Jews and Conversos. I blame these Protestants. Were it not for them, the Pope would deal with us as he always has: privileges in return for regular donations to his purse.'

He caught sight of Bethia standing in the doorway shifting from one foot to another. She wondered if Don Juan knew about Will and his fervent espousal of Protestant doctrine; probably, for he thrived on secrets – and, of course, Dona Gracia knew, so he would too. She caught Mainard's eye as Don Juan rose to greet her. He gave a slight shake of the head but she didn't feel reassured.

Don Juan bowed low, flicking his green satin cape

over his shoulder. He'd never survive in the Ghetto with the dull clothes and limited colours that the Jews were restricted to. Next to him, her husband looked much the wiser and steadier in his dark clothes, although both men were around the same age.

'It's good to see you,' she said in response to his greeting. 'And how is Dona Gracia?'

'My aunt is in good health. I've just escorted her from Ferrara.' He looked to Mainard. 'We have hopes of finally resolving the ongoing dispute with her sister which has been so injurious to our family fortunes. Perhaps we may discuss further how the work is going with recovery of the many debts due to us.'

Bethia knew this was her cue to leave and retreated. After Don Juan had gone, Mainard came seeking her. 'Ah, me – those sisters. There are enough troubles in this world for Conversos without making further within your own family.'

'There are troubles in all families, Conversos or no,' said Bethia, who'd been moving restlessly around her chamber feeling most anxious that it might become known who her brother was. She'd recently met a traveller from Geneva who spoke of the young Scot working with Calvin and saying he was like to become as fiery as the infamous John Knox. 'His name is Seton,' the man had said, staring at Bethia. 'You're a Scot, do you know of him?'

Bethia, whose heart had stopped at the 's' of Scot, felt it begin beating again.

'There are many people in Scotland,' was all she said, and the man turned away to find someone of more moment to gossip with at this *ridotto*. Her pleasure in the evening was spoiled, for now all she could think of was her brother's most recent letter about a man called Servetus. She supposed it was her own fault, for it was she who'd asked who he was and Will had replied at length…

The first I became aware of Servetus was when Calvin

threw the letter he was reading upon the board, exclaimed loudly and rushed out clutching his belly.

Who is this Servetus?' I said to Farni.

'A most unwise man.'

'What has he done?'

'He's a Spanish Protestant practising as a physician in France who's determined to make his own, often strange, interpretation of the gospel and has been foolish enough to commit those thoughts to paper and publish them. They challenge many of the principles on which the word rightly espoused by Calvin is based.' Farni stretched his fingers as much as he could, for you will remember that his hands are like that of a bear's claws and he is forever rubbing them to ease the pain.

Then he said, 'It's most unfortunate that Servetus didn't stick to what he's good at. By all accounts, he's a most able physician – which Master Calvin has great need of at this time.'

Calvin returned at this moment and affixed his eyes upon us. There's not much gets passed Master Calvin. I quickly bent my head to the task, the ink blotting, and Farni by my side tutting and instructing me to take a fresh sheet, although he winked at me behind Calvin's back. I do like Farni; he's a good, kind, and learned man.

He told me later that Calvin and Servetus knew one another when they both lived in Paris eighteen years ago. 'I think Servetus has had his eye on Calvin for a long time and wants Calvin as his follower, not the other way around. Although, curiously, when they arranged a meeting to discuss what they might do to prevent the burning of any more evangelicals – for France was having a fair old torching at the time – it was Servetus who didn't show up. Calvin said he waited for more than three hours.'

'What is he like, this Servetus – apart from being a sound physician,' I asked Farni.

'Certainly 'tis a pity he did not stick to physicking. Do you know he tells that it is the heart which drives the circulation of blood around the body?'

Can you believe that, Bethia – such wonder to think of this movement within us while we go about our days all unaware.

Then Farni had more to say on the subject… 'but I fear the blood within him is altogether too hot. He's Spanish and naturally has the look of the sinjoren, with a clipped beard, trimmed hair, and way of flinging his cloak over his shoulder.'

I smiled then, for of course Farni does not know that your husband is a sinjoor, and I haven't noticed him flinging his cloak about his person overmuch.

Reading this, Bethia had laughed aloud. Her brother could be charming!

Farni says that Servetus loves nothing better than a fight. 'I think he may be envious of Calvin and how he has become the spiritual leader of Geneva. For that is what Servetus aspires to be. He seeks followers, and especially Calvin.' Farni snorted. 'As if that were ever possible.'…

'Though Gracia *has* been much put upon,' said Mainard, bringing Bethia back to herself.

She blinked, then said, 'I thought many months were spent in Ferrara reaching an agreement between the sisters.'

'Joao claims it had no more validity than the previous agreement reached here in Venice.' Mainard looked at her intently. 'He's asked if you might be willing to assist him in gathering information.'

Bethia sat bolt upright. 'Yes, of course.'

Mainard laughed. 'You don't yet know what he requires of you.'

'I do know that you'd never accede to a request that would place me in any danger.'

Mainard rubbed his hand over his face. 'I would hope that were always so.'

'We're safe enough in Venice?'

'As long as we're seen to observe the rituals of

Christianity and our wealth is of benefit to the Council of Ten. I wish that Catarina would stop her activities in the Ghetto but, short of locking her up, I can do nothing.' He paused, 'Although it may come to that since finding a husband to take responsibility for her now seems impossible. But I digress. Don Juan has asked if you will visit with Brianda and try to uncover what devilment she's planning next.'

'I've only seen her at a *ridotto*, never actually spoken to her.' Bethia chewed on her lips. 'But I'll find a way in. Why *do* the sisters fight so?'

'You know some of the story – their dead husbands left wills which overturned the agreements made in their respective marriage settlements.' He picked up her hand and squeezed it. 'Few are as fortunate as we to choose whom we should marry.'

'Yet our parents were made unhappy.'

'My father came to love you.'

Bethia swallowed. She missed Papa; couldn't believe it was more than a year since he passed.

'But again I digress. You should understand the family relationships for it will help for you to have the background in any meeting you may engineer with Brianda.'

'You already told me when we were in Ferrara.'

'I gave you the bare bones.'

'The bare bones were complicated enough, I can't believe there's more.' She picked at the skin around her thumb absent-mindedly as he walked slowly back and forth.

'Gracia's mother had a brother named Francisco, whom Gracia married, meaning her husband was also her uncle. When Francisco died he left half his fortune to his trading partner, his brother Diogo and half to Gracia. Diogo subsequently married Brianda, who we know is Gracia's sister.'

Mainard stopped to draw breath, then continued. 'Diogo left the guardianship of their daughter to her aunt

271

and not to Brianda, so, as I told you in Ferrara, Gracia controls what funds Brianda has – which does not promote sisterly love. And then there is Don Juan, who is the son of a third Mendes brother. He protects the interests of the Mendes family above all but has chosen to side with Gracia, perhaps because his father also left a will that put Gracia in control of his side of the family fortune too – and which his own mother Ana seeks to overturn. So Gracia is beset on all sides and most determined to hold onto as much as she can.'

He paused to draw breathe and then continued. 'Brianda didn't help her case by sending an agent to France to claim the many debts owing to the Mendes trading empire and saying they should be paid to her since Gracia was a Crypto-Jew. The king of France promptly had the funds frozen saying they need not be repaid at all, since the funds were borrowed from a Christian and not a Jew. Gracia was incensed and is working still to have them returned.'

Bethia shook her head, made quite dizzy by the new complications she was now hearing of. 'But what can I do?'

'All you need do is befriend Brianda and find out, if you can, what she plans next so Gracia is forewarned.'

'But will she not be suspicious? She must know that you're working with Don Juan.'

'Of course. And she'll in turn seek to extract information from you. Joao is prepared for this.'

'So I'm to extract what I can from Brianda and in turn set her a false trail. I doubt she'll be so foolish as to believe me.'

'Oh she'll be careful, but she'll also be curious, for there's no contact between the sisters.'

Bethia thought of Don Juan with his high fluting voice and over-fussy dress and realised that there was a man of steel hidden beneath the girlish exterior. 'I do not think I much like your Joao.' She sniffed. 'But then I doubt that he'd much care.'

Mainard crouched before her. 'We need him, Bethia. Our contacts, trade, and debts are now inextricably tied up with the Mendes. They are more powerful than you could ever imagine, and, for a young man, Joao has networks and spies everywhere. Some say he's even sending information back to the king of Portugal. The Mendes never close a door behind them if they can help it.'

Bethia shivered. 'And just how treacherous are they?'

Mainard rose and rolled his shoulders. 'I trust him because we share the same fate. We're all Conversos together beset by enemies wherever we turn, both Christian and Jew. And the one thing that Dona Gracia and Don Juan have shown is a remarkable loyalty to our kind… with the exception of their immediate family.' He laughed and then quickly grew serious once more. 'It's only thanks to their efforts so many Conversos were saved from Portugal.'

'Then I'll do my best for Dona Gracia.'

Chapter Forty-One

Intelligence Gatherer

Bethia went to visit Brianda in the company of Guistina and Pelegrina. 'Yes, yes, *mia cara*, we know Signora Brianda very well. Charming woman, much put upon by the sister.'

Pelegrina nodded slowly up and down, up and down. 'We visited the sister once but she was unavailable. We didn't go again for we are busy women too. But Brianda is most welcoming.'

'Most,' echoed Guistina.

And so indeed she was. Bethia, once the first introductions were over, sat quietly studying Brianda, while Guistina and Pelegrina spoke. She was prettier than Gracia, her features less pinched-looking in a long face, her hair dark and lustrous whereas Gracia's was shot through with grey which she made no attempt to darken.

'I believe you have met *my cruel sister*,' Brianda said, in her surprisingly mannish voice, to Bethia.

Guistina and Pelegrina leaned forward, eyes alight, eagerly awaiting the answer.

'I have had that privilege,' said a startled Bethia. Then thought she should have worded it differently.

'And how was she?' Brianda continued without awaiting an answer. 'Busy about all her many trading activities, I should imagine.'

Bethia nodded, glad to move onto what seemed safer ground.

'I understand your husband works for her.'

Bethia shifted in her seat. 'He performs some small services, yes.'

Brianda narrowed her eyes at such dissembling, but, after a moment, turned to her other guests with a comment about a *ridotto* they'd all recently attended. Bethia felt like a fish whose line had been let to run loose.

They rose to leave soon after. Mainard was waiting when Bethia arrived home but she had nothing of note to tell him beyond the *cruel sister* comment. It had felt most inappropriate that someone she'd only just met should speak thus – and of her own family too, and it made Bethia feel better about her spying activities.

On her next visit she was introduced to Brianda's daughter, who was around twelve years old. The girl curtsied and sat down, eyes on the hands lying her in lap. Bethia moved to sit close to her, asking about the book La Chica, as the child was mostly oddly referred to by her mother, had laid aside when the visitors entered.

'I love to read still,' said Bethia, 'although I have little times these days. Are you enjoying this?'

'It's exciting,' said La Chica, smiling brightly. Catching her mother's eye, she dropped her gaze once more.

'What's it about?'

'Oh it's very sad. They love one another but cannot be together. I'll give it to you when I've finished.'

'Thank you. I'd like that very much.'

But when Bethia read the novel she was shocked. 'It's called *La Celestina*,' she told Mainard. 'And is entirely unsuitable for an innocent young girl. Why, the man starts an affair with a girl not much older than La Chica – he procures her through this evil old woman Celestina – and the innocent thinks she's in love. I cannot think what Brianda is about to permit her daughter to read such…

such... bawdiness.'

Mainard burst out laughing at her outraged expression, but after a moment he grew serious. 'It is of concern. I will tell Don Juan.'

'No, no. Please don't do anything to infer that Brianda doesn't care for her daughter, for she does. She's openly affectionate towards her on occasion; I've seen her stroke her daughter's hair and pat her gently on the arm.'

The more often Bethia met with Brianda the more she began to sympathise with her invidious position.

'I hear only about the wickedness of Brianda, never about the reasons for her actions. And really, what could she do, since Dona Gracia, as she says, keeps such a tight hold on the finances?'

'I think, my love,' said Mainard, 'that there are actions and actions.'

Bethia couldn't help but giggle.

'And to accuse your own sister of Judaising takes it too far.'

Bethia grew serious again. 'But don't you see, Mainard, Dona Gracia is the one who controls the Mendes' vast fortune so no one dares speak against her. Everyone speaks ill of Brianda because she has few funds and so it's in no one's interest to defend her. You've seen Dona Gracia, she is truly formidable.' Bethia grew thoughtful. 'Although Brianda has her scary moments too.'

'So what *have* you learned from these regular visits you make?'

'That her daughter is the sweetest-natured child you could ever hope to meet. And she's named for her Aunt Gracia – how strange is that family – although known as La Chica.'

'You don't make much of an intelligence gatherer, my love.'

'Should I cease my visits to Brianda?' She smoothed her hair as she spoke. 'Actually, I quite enjoy them.'

He shrugged. 'Then you should keep going.'

Brianda seemed to like her in return, for now Bethia was invited to a noon repast, along with Guistina and Pelegrina, and many others. She found herself placed next to Brianda's physician and adviser. She'd met Tristan da Costa before, during her visits but this was the first time she'd conversed with him.

'You're an Old Christian married to a New Christian, I understand,' da Costa said, leaning in to speak to her.

Bethia stared at him, but he had a twinkle in his eye and a genial cast to his features that she couldn't help but find appealing.

'I am, but in a match of like minds it's of no consequence.'

He inclined his head. 'Then you're a fortunate couple indeed. My family are in Thessaloniki, where I hope soon to join them once Dona Brianda no longer has need of me.'

He waved away the bowl of goat kid's blood potage that the server was placing in front of him.

'You don't like potage?' Bethia asked.

He grimaced and shook his head. 'I don't eat food which involves raw blood. It's both unhealthy and wrong.'

She supped her potage, made curious about his assertion; why would it be wrong to eat blood? The fried chicken was brought next.

'Was this chicken purchased from the market in the Ghetto?' he asked the server.

'I do not know, signore. I'll ask.'

The server returned soon, saying that it was, and da Costa set about his plate with enthusiasm.

'You only eat meat come from the Ghetto?' she said when their plates littered with chicken bones were removed.

He nodded slowly. 'Only from the Ghetto.' He patted his belly. 'I am most careful about what I take into my body.' Again he leaned in to Bethia and they had a conversation in low voices that she found most surprising.

When she reached home she went in search of Mainard and found him playing horse to Samuel-

Thomas, who rode upon his back with shrieks of laughter.

'How was your feast, my love?' he asked, detaching his son and rising to his feet. He dusted his breeches down while the boy hung around his legs begging for more play.

'Later,' he said, smiling down at the upturned face. Grissel, Jacopo in her arms, stepped forward and gestured to Ysabeau, who removed the squirming child.

Bethia wandered around the chamber. Picking up the bronze statuette of a Venus whose foot rested on a large fish, she twisted it in her hands.

'Well?' he said, eyebrows raised. 'I can tell you have learned something of value today.'

'Perhaps,' she said slowly.

Mainard leaned forward eagerly and Bethia hesitated, feeling most mean-spirited. But in the end her family's fortunes were dependent on Gracia Mendes's continued well-being.

'It's most odd. Brianda accused Gracia of Judaising and yet da Costa lives in her home, is her closest adviser, wears the black hat of a Christian but will only eat meat that has been purchased from the Ghetto. I asked him about it and he told me that he's intrinsically a Jew but extrinsically a Christian. How can that be?'

Mainard stroked his chin. He'd recently cut off his beard, as many young Venetian men were doing, and she still found the smooth skin of his chin strange to look upon.

'This could be helpful. I'll speak with Don Juan.' He patted her shoulder as he left the chamber. 'Don't worry. Brianda would have no scruples about using similar information against Dona Gracia. And Joao is probably already aware of all this; not much surprises him.'

'Still, I don't think I like being an informer after all,' said Bethia slowly. 'I think I'll stay in the nursery in future.'

Chapter Forty-Two

Caterina

Mainard rubbed between his eyebrows where two furrows had appeared. He could see them clearly in the large Venetian glass which adorned the wall of the salon. Even when he stilled his face they didn't vanish but were a badge of the perpetual weight of anxiety he carried. Sometimes it was a small knot, some days it grew larger, and on bad days it was so big it choked him, rising up into his chest so he could barely breathe. Bethia was with child once more, which was a joyful prospect, but really he should not have attended to her so soon after Jacopo's birth. There would less than a year between Jacopo and this next child, although his wife had winked at him when he expressed his concerns, saying she would rather he spent time with her than a courtesan. Mainard thought of da Molina's encouragement to do just that; it had been tempting, but in the end the connection with Bethia was restored and he would do nothing to damage it.

He turned away from the mirror, shaking his head to free himself from the tangle of his thoughts. There was a message come from Joao. He wanted Mainard's presence immediately even though darkness would soon fall, for Dona Gracia was being held under house arrest to make certain she, and her fortune, didn't vanish into the Ottoman Empire. He hurried down to the canalside where their boatman awaited, as the mist floated above the water like spectres in the torchlight. He was stepping into the boat when he heard a commotion from inside the house: shouts and cries.

'What now?' he muttered, running back inside.

Catarina had been caught leaving the Ghetto as the Christian guards – which the Jews were made to pay for as Catarina had told him many times – were closing the gates to lock the Jews in overnight. She was of course accused of being a Marrano, Crypto-Jew, Judaiser, relapser, apostate... it didn't matter which term was used for they all meant the same thing: imprisonment. And to be found guilty would likely mean death.

Mainard ungripped Mama's clutching hand from his arm. 'I was on my way to Joao's anyway. 'Tis better I see him first, for if anyone can help he can.' He ran back to the gondola.

'Someone has informed on us, for Catarina has been visiting the Ghetto almost since she arrived here. She was working with one of the printers assisting in the production of the Talmud,' he told Don Juan.

'This isn't too difficult to resolve,' said Joao. 'Some funds to the city coffers, a few letters to the right people, and we shall have her released.' He leant forward in his chair, wagging his finger at Mainard. 'But tell her to stay out of the Ghetto after that.'

'I have told her.'

'Then I will tell her. If she wants to save her people there are better ways. And look, we have a first copy of the new Bible from Ferrara that Samuel Usque's been working on.'

He passed the book to Mainard, who ran his hand over the rich brown leather and then opened the clip and spread it wide on the board, turning the thin pages carefully.

He lifted his head and gazed at Joao. 'It's in Judeo-Spanish,' he said in wonder.

'The Christians are not the only ones who can translate the Bible into a language that all may read. Now we can teach our people what they lost after we were forced to convert.' Joao stood up and placed his small hand lightly on Mainard's shoulder. 'I can say to you thoughts that I would not speak before another.'

Mainard wished Joao had kept his thoughts to himself.

'Of more urgency, at this time, is word that Brianda is planning a match between her daughter and some Venetian nobleman. I cannot allow the family fortune to fall into Venetian hands. I've spoken to the Doge's men about the information you gave me.'

Mainard looked blankly at him.

'About Brianda's physician and how she's likely a secret Judaiser herself, but I've yet to see it acted upon.'

'What about my sister?' said Mainard abruptly.

'I've told you that we'll soon have her out. I'll speak with a few people as soon as we've finished here. But I may need your assistance in return, for I think I must marry La Chica.'

'What!'

'I've spoken to Dona Gracia about it.'

'And did she agree to it? The girl cannot be more than twelve years of age.'

'She's thirteen, old enough to be married.'

'Barely,' said Mainard, then shut his mouth. It wasn't wise to antagonise Joao when he needed his help to extract Catarina.

But Don Juan was as good as his word, and a few days later Mainard found himself before the Inquisitor pleading his sister's case. Catarina stood arms folded and glaring at the judge in a most unfeminine way. Mainard expelled air through gritted teeth. What was she thinking not to display a suitable meekness? If she could but be humble and apologetic it would help her case immeasurably.

'If she is a Jew then she should wear the yellow badge,

281

and her brother too,' said the accuser pointing to Mainard. 'What's he doing in the black hat of a Christian? Where is *his* yellow hat?'

When Mainard was called he spread his hands wide. 'My sister is curious, that's all. How many among us here have not visited the Ghetto at some point to see how these Jews live? Have we not gone to watch the plays performed there and visited one of the many printers? We all wonder at their otherness and leave more committed than ever to a life before Christ.' He felt his stomach knotting as he spoke but resisted the feeling of shame to so deny his ancestors, for he had a family to protect.

Catarina glared at him as though he was Judas – although presumably she denied Judas along with Jesus. But his arrow had hit its target, for the judge shifted in his seat and grunted. Mainard sat down.

The judge conferred. 'You make a good argument, my friend, but I wonder at such a young woman being left to wander alone in a place where her feeble mind may so easily be corrupted. I'll treat this as a girl's nonsense; that she knew no better.' He stared at Catarina, who stared back.

Mainard could feel his own body tensing at her boldness. Then, praise be to the good Lord, she dropped her eyes.

'I release you into your brother's care and you must obey him. If I find you before me again, it will *not* go well for you.' The judge waved his hand.

Mainard let go the breath he'd been holding in. He took Catarina's arm and hurried her out into the spring sunshine.

She stood for a moment face upturned, eyes blinking in the brightness. 'I'll not stop, you know. I cannot stop, for they are my people.'

'Then you're a fool. Sooner or later we must leave Venice, for the forces against Conversos, never mind Jews, grow stronger. Bide your time till then. What will it profit you to openly become a Jewess now?'

'It will profit my soul.'

'God's blood, Catarina, can you not hold off.'

She shook her head vehemently. 'I cannot.'

An anxious Mama and Bethia awaited them at home. Mainard had absolutely forbidden both to attend the court, saying, 'It will not assist, and may indeed harm, her case.' He was grateful that they'd not argued, and acutely conscious that his wife was now almost as vulnerable as they to inquisitorial forces, given her brother's espousal of Lutheranism or Calvinism or whatever sect he was now a part of. He didn't sleep that night, but then that was no different from any night since he was arrested; could not remember the last time he did sleep through the night.

His foot was unaccountably painful – and it had been so much better of late. He arose, limped around the bed, and went out onto the balcony in his nightshirt. It was cold beneath his bare feet, but solid. Somehow the cool helped, so his head, which had felt hot and muddled, began to clear.

He bent and pressed his forehead against the cold stone of the balustrade to unravel the knot of his thoughts. Finding a husband for Catarina here was impossible. Perhaps he should have her shut up in a nunnery. He snorted at the idea. There was another option though... and it all hinged on Dona Gracia.

When it happened, it happened fast. Joao sent a message that Mainard must come immediately. He hastened round to the grand palazzo which Joao had rented close to his aunt's home. He was brought into the salon to find Don Juan seemingly at his ease, although Mainard knew him well enough to notice Joao's fine fingers curling and uncurling. Next to him sat an equally small man wearing a tall turban of dazzling white, and flowing robes. They all rose and bowed.

'De Lange, I am delighted to present you to Huseyin

Bey of Constantinople.'

Mainard inclined his head. He'd done business with Turks, Moors and Saracens since arriving in Venice but, by the richness of his clothes and the size of the jewels on his be-ringed fingers, this man was clearly no ordinary merchant.

'Huseyin Bey is special envoy come from the court of Suleiman the Magnificent. The Sultan is most concerned to ensure the safety of Dona Gracia and has sent his ambassador to speak with the Doge on this very matter.'

'And I have had fruitful discussions with the Doge,' said Huseyin Bey softly.

They were speaking in French and Mainard was impressed how confident the envoy was. He must learn Turkish and probably Persian too; it would be of use for trade regardless of where the family went next.

'The Doge clearly doesn't want to lose such a valuable person as Dona Gracia,' the envoy continued.

'But equally he wishes to retain the friendship of Suleiman,' said Joao.

'And I understand Dona Gracia has still the safe conduct from the Pope.'

'It is so. And I think the combined weight of the Pope and Sultan Suleiman should be sufficient to release Gracia from house arrest so she may gain safe passage to Constantinople.'

'Then she is ready to come?' the envoy said.

'She is indeed.'

The men bowed to one another and the envoy departed. Joao dropped back in his chair and mopped his brow.

'She is truly leaving Christendom?' said Mainard.

'Gracia has an instinct which is best not ignored. She escaped Portugal and then Antwerp at the very moment when their kings were ready to swoop in and seize our all.'

'But she has a safe conduct from the Pope. What

greater protection should she need?'

'Her safe conduct from the Pope,' Joao snorted, 'which begins... *to our cherished daughter in Christ...* is a valuable document to her freedom of movement but will become worthless the moment the increasingly elderly Pope dies and yet another takes the helm. She's awaiting some assurances from Suleiman, in particular that she be given permission to dress as a Venetian lady while she's living under his dominion, and then she'll go. She's anxious to leave before Brianda comes up with some new ploy to hold her here – and to relieve us of more funds.'

Mainard stood up and walked about the room. His back felt stiff, bent by the weight of family he was carrying. 'My sister?' he asked, although he already guessed where this conversation was leading.

'I'll need to agree it with Dona Gracia, but I think she'll have no objection to your sister forming part of her escort.'

He should feel sad at the thought of losing Catarina, of her going so far away from the family, but all he could feel was an overwhelming sense of relief. He stood taller, his back suddenly less constrained.

He held out his hand to shake Joao's. 'Thank you, my friend.'

Chapter Forty-Three

Family

It was late spring now. The days were bright with sunshine, the flowers in bud, with a hint of the colour that would soon burst forth, and cool enough at night that the air stayed fresh and without the summer stench of the canals. Bethia was eager to escape the cares of domesticity for an hour and go out into the light. The burden of familial responsibility fell almost as heavily on her shoulders now as on Mainard's, for Mama was gone.

The arguments had been fierce but Mama had prevailed. She would go to Constantinople, or wherever in the Ottomans Dona Gracia intended, with Catarina. She could not allow her daughter to travel unattended.

'Nor would I, ever,' said Mainard in return. 'Dona Gracia will keep a close eye upon our Catarina.'

But Mama wasn't reassured. 'She cannot go alone.'

'She won't be alone. And will be held on a much tighter rein by Gracia than we've ever managed.'

Bethia watched and wondered why Mainard wasn't simply acquiescing to what Mama clearly wanted. They argued back and forth and eventually Mainard bowed his head, although not before Bethia saw the tears glinting in his eyes, and said, 'Mama, if you feel you must go with Catarina, then so be it.'

Mama looked more frightened than relieved at these words.

'I think we need Mama more than Catarina does,' said Mainard later to Bethia.

She understood that he was fearful of the birth. But Bethia, although sad to see Mama depart, felt a certain joyfulness that she and Mainard were alone with their children for the first time in their married life – although only if their many servants were discounted.

Gracia departed with much fanfare, leaving the city for Ancona where she would embark for the Ottomans, both preceded and followed by a great trail of carts, the Ottoman envoy riding on one side of her carriage and the Venetian ambassador to the court of Suleiman on the other. Catarina hung out of the carriage following Dona Gracia's, waving her handkerchief with aplomb while Mama had hers pressed to her face. Bethia herself shed more than a few tears at Mama's departure, Catarina's less so, for she'd long since grown exasperated by her good sister's stubbornness, although a tiny corner of her recognised that was unfair. She'd not cared for being forced to espouse Protestantism in Geneva, when the true faith was with the Virgin and the Pope. She shook her head. It was all too confusing.

A few months later and Bethia was less sanguine about their departure when she was again brought to bed with child and no Mama there to support her. Venice was replete with midwives but still it was not the same as having Mama's loving care during her time of need. This time she refused the birthing stool until near the end, instead walking around the chamber, and didn't suffer the same agonies in her back. She also wrote her will, something Mama had forbidden before her previous confinements, saying it would call down the *mal ojo*. But Bethia was more concerned to die intestate than any threat of an evil eye being tempted into taking her. In any case, her time of trial was short and she was sooner than expected cradling the newest bairn in her arms.

Grissel and Ysabeau had charge of the nursery. Johannes had become one of the gondoliers that served the family and was no longer following Grissel around like a wee dog terrified of losing sight of its master. He'd also developed an increasing attachment to Ysabeau, which Bethia had no objection to.

Bethia tended to her new son, who was yet unnamed. Mainard, usually so decisive, seemed uncertain what to choose. Bethia wondered at it.

'What do you think of Mordecai?' he asked her one day.

Not a lot, she wanted to say, but she should at least give him the courtesy of appearing to consider it.

'It seems very...' Her voice faded away.

Mainard sighed. 'Yes, I know. It's Jewish.'

She looked at him over the top of their baby's head. 'Are you going to relapse, as Catarina has?'

'Why would I want to walk around wearing a yellow hat?' But she could hear the jocularity was forced. 'In any case, I cannot be a Jew married to a Christian, the punishment is vicious.'

'What do they do?'

He made a swiping motion at his groin.

'Cut off your pizzle?' she said, puzzled.

'No, castration.'

Bethia swallowed.

Neither of them were eager to discuss the subject further and the baby remained nameless.

'Wee lamb,' she called him.

'My name,' said Samuel-Thomas stoutly.

'You, Jacopo and the baby are all my wee lambs.'

'No! Me the big lamb.' He stood on his sturdy feet with his chest thrust out and Bethia reached over and drew him close.

'Hello, big lamb,' she said, kissing the top of his dark, curly head.

The days grew cooler as autumn waned and Bethia was pleased to spend them unburdened by pregnancy. She'd produced three sons in four years. Mainard said that this was enough to find livings for, and he would not risk his wife's life, nor have her made old before her time, by continuous pregnancies. And so Bethia consulted a midwife who advised the precaution of an ointment of honey, oil and salt.

'Remarkably sticky,' said Mainard, dipping his finger in it. 'I think we may find ourselves glued together like mating dogs.'

Bethia felt the laughter bubble up from deep inside. 'And someone will have to throw a bucket of water over us to effect a release.' She remembered Grissel doing just that to a yelping pair of conjoined dogs long, long ago when they lived in St Andrews.

'The midwife said that root of lily might be efficacious.'

'So I will have to find my way in past a root?'

Bethia giggled again. 'I doubt that's how it works.'

'It's best if I withdraw and spill my seed, as told in the Bible.'

'Where in the Bible is such specific advice given?' said Bethia, who was laughing so hard she could barely get the words out.

'In the Book of Genesis; Onan did so because he wanted to have congress with Tamar – but presumably without any consequence nine months later.'

'I doubt it's worded quite like that.'

'You're right, my love. But now, while our children are not making demands upon you, shall we slip away and practise the way of Onan?'

In response, Bethia grabbed Mainard's hand and they ran to their chamber.

Overseeing the household proved to be more complicated than Bethia had expected. Mama did everything with such calm serenity that Bethia had assumed it required little effort. And the servants were testing her, she soon realised, bringing their small squabbles and larger ones too. The Venetian housekeeper was constantly at Bethia's door with yet another question that only *la Signora* could answer.

'What is she about?' asked Bethia of Grissel one day.

'Och she's a richt one!' said Grissel tossing her head. 'She's aw aboot putting ye in yer place.'

Bethia raised her eyebrows while Samuel-Thomas ran around in circles shrieking *'putting ye in yer place'* and wee Jacopo tottered after him.

'Ye hae to speak in Scots else they micht understand you. There's some here that ken English although they pretend otherwise. We hae many watchers in this hoose.'

'I wish I could put you in charge, Grissel. Not much escapes you.'

Grissel threw her hands up in horror. 'God's death, dinna dae that. I'm much more use to you in among them.'

'You're right, of course. Dear Grissel, what would I do without you?'

Grissel blushed as red as the carnations on the windowsill and shuffled her feet. But before Bethia could say more they were distracted by the bairns, for Samuel-Thomas, in his wild capers, had run into the back of Jacopo and knocked him flying – not entirely accidentally, Bethia suspected. The howls from Jacopo set the baby off and Samuel-Thomas observed all with a degree of satisfaction that had Grissel promising to 'give him a good skelp' if he didn't mend his ways.

Nevertheless, Bethia pondered on what she and Grissel had spoken of and determined to replace any servants who adopted a sullen or sly demeanour towards her with ones of her own choosing. There was a certain satisfaction in knowing that she might do this without reference to anyone, for Mainard had told her more than once that the house was her domain. And she would start with the housekeeper; indeed wondered if it was her who informed on Catarina.

Another letter came from Will about Servetus, who seemed to be all that was talked of in Geneva these days...

I've been most curious to read of his ideas and understand why they're considered so dangerous. I feel it's important to know of them so I can refute anything my congregation might hear or wrongly attest to.

Will was himself treading a perilous path, and she quickly replied urging him to stay away from contentious material, not to risk antagonising John Calvin and find himself again thrown out. But she knew her brother and his curious mind, certainly where doctrine was concerned. Of course, he didn't rest until he'd acquired a copy of Servetus's banned book, *Christianismi Restitutio*.

I knew that which I earlier mentioned to you would be available somewhere. And I found it hid within the library where I work.

Bethia exhaled a great outrush of air. If Will thought that he was writing in code that a spy reading the letter would not decipher, then he was wrong. She was surprised by his lack of sense given what he'd already suffered in pursuit of his faith. And Calvin had a copy of the banned book – this should not surprise her either. Calvin would want to 'know mine enemy' as the Psalm directed. But really she had enough troubles on her doorstep. Her brother must fend for himself, which he was eminently capable of doing, and she should stop worrying about him.

There were Conversos arriving in Venice every day, fleeing Portugal and Antwerp, and Pelegrina and Guistina had taken to grumbling about it in front of her... 'There are so many of them we shall soon be outnumbered if something is not done to halt the flow. And most are poor and dirty. The Council of Ten must act.' The women looked to one another and shuddered. Then seemed suddenly aware of Bethia watching them, tight-lipped. 'Of course, we do not mean you, *piu dolce* Bethia, and in any case you are not one of them… really.' Their voices faded away.

'But I am,' said Bethia. 'And I'm also a follower of Christ, like my husband and all Conversos.' But her heart failed her as she spoke.

Then suddenly all Venice was in an uproar of delicious gossip and satisfactory outrage about the actions of one Converso family. Don Juan had eloped with Brianda's daughter La Chica… who was also his cousin. But for Bethia it was more than gossip; Mainard had vanished at the same time.

Chapter Forty-Four

Elopement

Two sleepless nights passed before a weary Mainard reappeared. She ran into his arms.

'Whoah,' he said, taking a step back. 'You nearly had me over.'

She gazed up into his face anxiously. 'Where have you been? Why did you leave no message?'

She could see by the deepening twin furrows between his eyebrows that he was thinking carefully before speaking. He opened his mouth and suddenly she couldn't bear to hear, shaking her head and covering her ears with her hands. 'Don't tell me. You're caught up in this abduction. Don Juan has dragged you in.'

Mainard closed his mouth and walked around the salon. Bethia heard the sound of running feet and the shrieks of her children from the floors above – Grissel and Ysabeau no doubt engaging them in a most exciting game.

Mainard rubbed his hand over his face. 'I've seen a side of Don Juan that I didn't overly care for.'

Bethia sat down on the tall chair that was once Papa's and folded her hands in her lap.

'I hadn't realised until two days ago that he has no wealth of his own, is entirely dependent on the funds that Dona Gracia gives him. Of course, he does earn them, for he's her most faithful, and favoured, adviser.' Mainard dropped down into Mama's old chair – which was low to the floor making his knees almost level with his face. He didn't seem to care and rested his forearms on his lap.

Bethia felt a rising impatience and burst out, 'So is it true, has Don Juan really abducted La Chica?'

'He's eloped with her, that's *different* from abducting her.'

'She's so young. She cannot have gone willingly.'

'Joao can be most charming. And why would she not go with him? He's younger and handsomer than the fat old Venetian noble that Brianda was planning on marrying her to.'

'It's that stupid book she was reading – La Chica has persuaded herself she's in some great romance. But this will not be about love, not on his part anyway.'

Mainard shrugged. 'He's fond enough of her. Love has no place in a wise alliance. Of more import is that her dowry will remain within the Mendes family and not disappear into the hands of Christian nobles who'll care nothing for Conversos.'

'There was a time when love was important to you.'

Mainard stood up and walked over to where she sat. He reached down, took her hand, then bent to kiss it. 'There are few who are as fortunate as we – or who have the indulgence to be so.'

'And what has your role in all of this been? Were you with Don Juan?'

Mainard gazed at the floor and circled his foot, outlining the pattern of the mosaic. 'His brother is helping him.'

'He has a brother! Why have I never met him?'

'Bernardo has only recently come from the Ottomans. He too is part of Dona Gracia's network.'

'Where are the brothers, and La Chica?'

'I'm not certain. In the Papal States somewhere.'

'You do know there are decrees posted all over the

city that anyone found to have given assistance to, or harboured them is to be hanged and forfeit their possessions. There's a reward of one thousand ducats for information leading to their recovery.'

Mainard paled beneath his brown skin. 'No,' he said slowly. 'I was unaware of this.'

Bethia lowered her head into her hands. 'What have you done?'

'Very little... and La Chica went willingly, eagerly even.'

'What! You took her to Ancona?'

'I arranged the transport.'

'Mainard,' she shrieked, drawing out each syllable of his name. She took a deep breath. 'It is enough that we are known to have connections with Don Juan. We must have no further involvement in this.'

But her determination to stay uninvolved was in vain, for a message came the next day from Brianda asking Bethia to attend her. Indeed, reading it, Bethia considered the tone to be more of a summons than a request.

'Where should I say you were, should she ask?'

'Say I had business in Ancona, which is true... in a way.'

Bethia was not reassured. 'I don't think I should go. She must suspect you had some involvement in this elopement.'

'You must go, for if you do not she'll know that I did.'

Bethia dressed with great care in her green satin with the pearls, the tallest headdress she possessed, and the ring Mainard gave her when Jacopo was born, and went reluctantly.

Brianda was wearing red satin, the huge sleeves lined with ermine, and as many jewels as one not very large woman could display. She had all the anger of a wronged mother and none of the despair.

'This is all her doing. Gracia is plotting to steal *my* daughter's dowry. It's not enough that she already

295

controls me,' she clasped her hands together in pretend supplication, 'that I must go begging, on my knees, for the small amounts that I need to sustain me.' She swept her hand around the vast chamber whose ceiling was so high that it wasn't easy to make out any detail of the elaborate murals painted on it, beyond lots of billowing clouds with large men trumpeting among them. 'Look where I have to live, in a palazzo so small there's barely room for more than twenty servants. And look where Gracia lived. In a grand palazzo, large enough to contain her husband's tomb and at least fifty, most probably one hundred, servants.' Spray flew from her mouth as she spoke.

Bethia sat well back while Brianda strode up and down before her, as much as a small woman with short legs wearing an overfull skirt could be said to stride.

'And as for her *assistant*, Don Juan Micas is the most devious, manipulative, lying, slippery seducer. Gracia may think he acts only in her interest but he does not. He is all about what he can get.' She waggled her finger. 'Gracia better beware. If he could steal my Chica, my beautiful baby, then he's capable of anything. He will turn on her like the serpent he is.'

Bethia realised she needn't have been nervous, for all Brianda wanted was to vent her fury. Although she was handsomer than Gracia her face was not overly attractive at this moment, puffed out and reddened with rage. Brianda paused for breath and looked to Bethia, who realised she was expected to say something and could not think what.

'Perhaps La Chica might be happy with him,' she mumbled.

'Happy, happy,' Brianda's voice rose to a shriek. 'What has happiness got to do with it? This is all about control.'

The door opened and a servant ushered in the Doge's man. Brianda sank onto the nearest chair, hand to her brow while Bethia surreptitiously wiped the perspiration from hers.

'Signore Verde,' Brianda said faintly, offering her fingertips as he bowed low over them. 'How very kind of you to come.'

Bethia rose and curtsied. 'I will go now so you may speak in private,' she said.

Brianda acknowledged her words with a flick of the hand, and Bethia, as she descended the stairs, worried that she should've lingered longer. Brianda was not a woman to get on the wrong side of, and she might have learned something of advantage.

Mainard was waiting when she returned. 'What did Brianda want?'

Bethia reached up to smooth the creases from his brow. 'An audience,' she said.

Chapter Forty-Five

Letters

It was a good day, for letters had come. Mama, Catarina and Will had written, and there was even a scribbled note from Geertruyt, who was a most dilatory correspondent. Bethia sat down with the pages spread before her feeling as rich as though she'd been given a casket of sparkling rubies. She twisted the ring on her finger that Mainard bought after Jacopo was born. He'd promised her more but she'd told him that one was sufficient. Mama had intervened saying that a woman could never have too much jewellery, for it was her safeguard; should something happen to her husband then it was there for her to sell at need. Bethia smiled, thinking she must remind Mainard she had had no gift to welcome the weeist lamb, but perhaps her husband was waiting until he eventually named the bairn.

Geertruyt's note announced the birth of her latest child. Three sons and two daughters in five years, no wonder she never had time to pen more than a few lines. Mama's letter was full of Constantinople, which they'd finally reached, and Bethia was glad to read that she was happy there. When she picked up Catarina's letter, Bethia's anger simmered, although it was never far below the surface where her sister-in-law was concerned. The letter was full of the rabbi and Catarina's studies towards becoming a

Jew. Unwise to write so openly; she'd clearly not thought of the danger she would place her family in by doing so – and when they had enough troubles with this elopement. But Catarina was like Will, she didn't care what damage she did to her family as long as she lived by her faith.

There was a postscript in the letter which had her running to the workroom to find Mainard. 'Dona Gracia has found Catarina a husband,' she said breathlessly, flapping the pages before his startled face.

It was only much later she got to Will's letter, which was dated *16 May 1553*; she could hardly believe it was near three years since she last saw him. Reading it was like sitting on a keg of gunpowder close to a blazing fire. It began well enough, with much talk of his ministry in the small parish close by Geneva. Bethia could sense, even from the great distance that separated them, Will's joy in having parishioners who sought his counsel.

The rest of his letter was devoted to Servetus, who was deluging Calvin with letters, if Will was to be believed, and was now imprisoned in Lyon.

Farni brings each letter from Servetus held between his fingertips, as though to touch the paper will contaminate him, and Calvin shakes his head slowly when he gazes on it. 'The man is a menace. How many letters has he written to me in the past few months?'

'It must be thirty at least.'

'And he has nothing new to say, it will only be a repeat of the same heresies. He wants to take everything down. It makes little difference if you're Protestant or Catholic, Servetus wants to poke us all in the eye. You may peruse the latest diatribe if you wish. I do not have the strength.'

I was of course most curious to do so.

And so I broke the seal and unfolded the page. Servetus's handwriting is cramped and I had to squint to follow the words. But, Bethia, you would not believe what he claims. Firstly he says that the world will end by the year 1600.

I read this aloud to Farni, who raised his eyebrows as he responded. 'Ah yes. He's most certainly apocalyptic in his thinking. Does he say the Archangel Gabriel will come then?'

Bethia, he did! Then he compounded such heresy by stating that the soul sleeps from death until the resurrection. Farni says this is a favourite subject of Servetus and, of course, in direct contradiction to what Calvin has expounded in his tract Psychopannychia. I do not know if you have read it but I would urge you to do so.

Bethia sighed. She wondered if her brother would ever accept that she was not to be tempted from the Virgin.

It's one of Calvin's earliest published writings, and what he says there more than contradicts Servetus's false interpretation of the texts. Farni agreed with me but added that it all links with Servetus's argument that there is no separation between God and the world, for Servetus says that God is manifested in every living thing.

I didn't say this to Farni, yet I do have some sympathy with this idea, but when I read what Servetus had to say next any sympathy I had evaporated. I quote it for you here, Bethia, for it is very shocking. 'The doctrine of the Trinity can be neither established by logic nor proved from Scripture, and is in fact inconceivable.' He denies the Holy Trinity, how can that be?

Farni says he fears that the man must be executed. He's too dangerous to leave unchallenged, for who knows what rebellion he may foment.

There was a break in the letter and the remainder was dated a few days later.

News has just come. Servetus has escaped from prison in Lyon. Take care, for he may even be headed your way; there are rumours he's making for Italy.

Bethia, I know it may be wrong, but I pray that they do not capture him. Bearing witness to one man burning in this life is

300

enough, and although Servetus is very wrong thinking, I do not think he's evil.

A few days later and another epistle came from Will to say that there would be no need to recapture Servetus for he'd walked into the lions' den unbidden.

I was in the church listening to Calvin, and holding my own copy of the Bible open in my hands as I followed the passage that Calvin was expounding. In those moments I know what a truly great teacher Calvin is, for he explains, slowly, carefully and without a hint of impatience to his flock. He truly wants us all to understand and connect directly with God. I cannot tell you the fondness I have for him.

There was only quiet reflection, then suddenly Calvin was shouting. 'Remove him. Remove that man from the holy presence. He has no place here.'

All was confusion as we looked around to see who Calvin was pointing at. Farni rushed forward waving to me. He leaned in close, hissing, 'It's Servetus.' Some people stood up, but Calvin commanded everyone to stay seated. Then I saw who he was pointing at.

Servetus sat there, his eyes fixed on Calvin almost as though he hoped to be welcomed. I was surprised that he didn't try to start a debate, but he was behaving quietly and respectfully, as any other member of the flock.

Farni and I reached him and I took one arm and Farni the other. Servetus is a tall man but I easily eclipsed him. He didn't resist but came almost willingly. We have him in prison now. Oh, my dear sister, I fear what may happen next.

And so do I, thought Bethia as she refolded the letter slowly, for her hands were shaking very much.

But soon she had too many worries piling up on her own doorstep to spare much thought for events in faraway Geneva.

Chapter Forty-Six

Talmud

'They have found Don Juan and his bride,' said Mainard, coming into the chamber where Bethia was feeding the baby. They'd tried a wet nurse this time. Mainard, who had so strongly objected to Samuel-Thomas being fed by anyone but her, seemed less fierce with this third child. Bethia herself was not certain she wanted to be tied to the nursery for months on end, especially since Jacopo still had need of her. More than one of her Venetian acquaintances treated the whole idea of breastfeeding with such revulsion that Bethia had become embarrassed to admit she did something so elemental. And so not one, but two wet nurses were found and Jacopo took happily to the substitute – which Bethia felt surprisingly hurt by – but the new baby screamed the place down and would have no one but his mother.

'This one is a most determined fellow,' said the fond father.

'He'll need to be, given that he's still nameless,' said Bethia.

'All in good time,' Mainard had responded.

She looked up now from tending to the baby. 'And?'

'They were married in front of Ravenna Cathedral before a large crowd. It's rumoured that Joao declares the marriage was consummated that night and La Chica's dowry must be released to him. Of course, the authorities, who have it in trust for La Chica after all the in-fighting between Brianda and her sister, don't want to give up ten thousand ducats.'

'But what can they do?'

'The Doge's men are on their way to Ravenna to retrieve La Chica and arrest Don Juan and his brother.'

'But if the marriage has been consummated…'

'The Doge says it matters not what has transpired, Don Juan must return her immediately, for her mother is beside herself with grief and…'

'And this way the Doge retains a hold on the dowry.'

'At least until La Chica is sixteen.'

'And what of La Chica, what does she want?'

'She too declares she's no longer intact and is Don Juan's true wife. It seems she has no desire to return to Brianda.'

'Don Juan can certainly be most charming, if he wants something.'

Mainard shrugged. 'And why not, women are not the only ones who can play that game.'

'But men have many more options than women – they hold the power.'

'Not in this case. The one who's tugging on everyone's strings is Dona Gracia. Joao wants his own fortune to play with.'

Several weeks later, La Chica was returned to Venice under armed guard. This provoked a fresh wave of gossip and many visitors to Brianda's home in the hope of catching a glimpse of the girl, but Bethia stayed away.

'Where is Don Juan? How did he escape?' Bethia asked.

Mainard laughed. 'Joao is most persuasive. He managed to gain agreement from the papal officials that he should go to Rome to plead his case. It's fortunate for him that there's no love lost between the Pope and the

303

Doge. The Doge has now increased the reward for Don Juan's capture to three thousand ducats. At the same time he's forbidden from entering Venice and if caught doing so is to be hanged between the columns at San Marco and then beheaded and quartered, and his various parts displayed around the city.'

'Well La Chica would certainly be safe from further encroachment, but it does seem an overly harsh punishment.'

'Joao has written to me; there are some business matters that I need to attend to with da Molina.'

'I wish we didn't have to have dealings with either.'

Mainard tugged on his ear. 'Da Molina is necessary since we're Conversos. The Venetians will not permit it any other way. And as for Joao… he's astute enough to survive anything. I understand he's already in communication with the French king asking him to intervene on his behalf.' He gazed over her head. 'He's also asking that I go to Rome to meet with him.'

Bethia sucked in air.

Mainard spread his hands wide. 'I'm sorry, my love. I've no choice. I must respond to his summons.'

Bethia tried to hold back the tears; she knew Mainard's hands were tied and she must support him. But in the end Don Juan removed to Ancona where the Venetians had no authority.

'Don Juan has been given a safe conduct from Suleiman, supported by the French king, that he can be let go to Constantinople,' Mainard told Bethia. 'So I need only go there.'

Off Mainard went, leaving Bethia puzzling over how the French and the Turks, normally enemies, were united in their desire to see Don Juan freed. Was there nowhere the Mendes money, connections, and spy network did not reach?

'You've never seen anything like it,' Mainard told Bethia on his return. 'The Sultan sent his elite personal guards to protect Joao. The clothes these janissaries wore – you wouldn't miss them in a fight! Crimson satin jerkins with gold buttons over a crimson shirt and the widest black velvet pantaloons; as Grissel would say, they thought themselves very braw fellows.'

Bethia felt no desire to laugh, couldn't even raise a smile. 'What did Don Juan want of you?' She could see by the deepening twin lines between Mainard's eyebrows that he would prefer not to say. Then he played with his ear, which confirmed it, but she couldn't let it go. 'We are a team, you said. Whatever happens to you will affect me and our children.'

'This is most secret and it's not wise you should know.'

'Tell me.'

'Don Juan gave me information that I will pass to the Portuguese ambassador for him to pass to his king.'

Bethia knew that her utter confusion must show on her face. 'But why would the Mendes, who had to flee the Inquisition in Portugal, be sending secrets to its king – for I assume it's sensitive?'

'Oh yes, most sensitive: about Turkish interests in Portuguese held lands in India.'

'May the Blessed Virgin guard and keep us.'

'But he *has* a very good reason for doing so.'

'This I cannot wait to hear.'

'There are still far too many of our people left in Portugal. This is a simple exchange; a personal favour in return for letting Conversos leave the country unmolested.'

'Then on this I cannot fault Don Juan.'

Mainard grinned. 'And there is one other thing I'm to make certain is sent to the king of Portugal. It seems he's most partial to the Parmesan cheese of Italy, which is to be included in the package I deliver to the ambassador.'

Bethia wrinkled her nose. 'It will reek by the time it arrives in Portugal.' She grinned back at Mainard. 'I hope it stinks his palace out.'

305

Dona Gracia was gone, Don Juan was gone, Mama and Catarina were gone. Life was remarkably tranquil, thought Bethia. She hoped now that they might live peaceably as a Converso family who had truly converted. By the time her children were grown perhaps it would be forgot that they were ever Conversos and they would be treated as true Christians. And she liked living here, for the most part. The city was voluptuous to the point of excess, but who could fault its light, colour, and the Virgin watching out for its inhabitants from every corner, wall, house, and grand building.

But then some clouds again began to form in her perfect blue sky. The Doge had ordered the tribune responsible for punishing blasphemy, moral offences, and printed violations to examine the Talmud. In a way Bethia was not surprised when a 'concerned' Venetian neighbour brought her the story. She'd been far more surprised by the plethora of Jewish texts openly printed here, many of them funded by the all-encompassing Mendes.

'You will be worried to hear of this action by the tribune,' said the neighbour, tilting her head to one side.

Bethia felt a stab of fear for her children. 'I'm from Scotland. We have no Jews nor Conversos there and I've been held in the arms of Mother Church since birth.'

The neighbour raised her eyebrows. 'Of course, *mia cara*. No one could suppose anything else, especially with your blue eyes and beautiful alabaster skin.'

Bethia felt a hot flush of shame to so deny her husband's family. I'm no better than the disciple Peter denying Jesus, she thought, as she glared at the neighbour's departing broad back.

'I have heard,' said Mainard when Bethia went running to tell him. 'The tribune claimed that the Talmud was filled with blasphemy and slander against Our Lord.'

He sounded utterly weary and she didn't press him to say more but instead wrapped her arms around his waist and leant her head against his chest. He spoke again and

306

she felt the rumble of his voice vibrating in her ear.

'Don Juan tried to buy an island off the coast here, did you know that? It was to be a homeland for Jews where they would rule supreme. No directives, blasphemy laws, nor Christians. Can you imagine such a place, where Jews would control their own destiny? Of course, the purchase was not permitted but, for a moment, there was hope.'

Bethia could hear a child wailing in the passageway. 'Let's also hope this fuss about the Talmud will soon be forgot,' she said as she hurried out of the chamber.

Chapter Forty-Seven

A Book Burning

Another summer tipped into autumn, which was the season she liked best in Venice: balmy days, warm evening and cool nights. There were rumours of the Inquisition, a few found guilty and quietly drowned – for Venice did not like a spectacle that might upset its merchants and traders. Then the stories began to circulate of what was happening elsewhere. One day, Bethia's Venetian ladies came to call twittering as loud as a flock of sparrows gathered along the apex of a roof.

'*Mia cara*, have you heard?'

Bethia, hands resting in her lap, wide skirts draped to advantage, the large lapis lazuli hung on a thick gold chain, which Mainard had gifted her only last night, resting on her bosom, smiled serenely at them. She knew no answer was required.

Pelegrina halted, raised hand in the air and her eyes narrowed. She leant towards Bethia. 'Oh my heavens, is that what I think it is?' She nudged Guistina, who raised her eyebrows.

'Lapis lazuli, and such a big stone. Are you setting out to rival the Medicis, *mia cara*?'

Her companion leaned forward, reaching out to take the stone in her hand. Bethia drew back in her chair, instead lifting the chain over her neck, but it caught in her headdress and she let it drop back.

The women looked at her with new respect. 'You have a most generous husband.' They paused, turned to one another and laughed behind their hands... 'Or is this the gift of another benefactor?'

Bethia was annoyed at herself for flushing. 'I'm hardly likely to openly wear the necklace if it was.'

There was another peal of laughter. 'Very true, very true.' They looked to one another once more. 'We all have our secrets.' Yet another peal of laughter was interrupted by Grissel, who'd finally arrived with the wine and sweet biscuits.

Bethia hoped they wouldn't stay much longer.

'Where was I?' said Pelegrina, brushing the biscuit crumbs from her lap, although she would've done better to wipe them from her around her mouth.

'Oh yes,' her face grew solemn, 'the books.'

'What books?'

'My sister who lives in Rome, you know, wrote to tell me all about it.' She shook her head slightly, eyes never leaving Bethia's face. 'They went to the printers and the synagogues and into the homes of the Jews and they took them. There was much crying aloud among the Jews, but they could do nothing.'

Bethia felt shaky but tried to control her voice. 'What exactly did they take?'

'You know, the books those Jews pray to, so many of them – books I mean, not Jews – although there is an excess of them too. The Pope decided that there must be an end to it. Really, it's surprising he permitted such open heresy for so long...' Her voice trailed away, and Bethia, following the women's glance, saw Mainard leaning in the doorway, arms folded.

The women rose together and shook out their skirts. 'We must away, *cara Bethia*, we have hindered you too long...' they smirked at one another, '...and husbands must not be kept waiting.'

Mainard bowed, the ladies curtsied and slipped out the door, their voices loud in the stairwell. Bethia opened her mouth to speak but Mainard put his finger to his lips and shook his head. She waited until she heard the sound of the heavy door leading to the portico closing.

Mainard pulled a chair close to her, sat down and took her hands in his. 'There's been a reaction in Rome which is all about countering the creeping power of the Protestants. It's unfortunate that the Jews of Italy, who've lived alongside their Christian neighbours peaceably for a very long time, are getting swept in with the reformers. So the Pope has ordered the seizure and burning of the Talmud. It'll not affect us and is unlikely to happen here, for the Doge wouldn't risk upsetting the fine balance we have that works to the advantage of everyone.'

'I pray you may be correct,' was all she said in reply, although the weight of fear was like carrying a pilgrim's crucifix on her back.

It was Friday. She was leaving church with Mainard by her side, trailed by Grissel and Johannes, when there was a great rumbling of noise all around them – and those who knew them as Conversos were glancing their way, whispering to one another behind their hands.

'What is it?' Bethia clutched Mainard's arm tightly.

He hailed da Molina, who was walking away from them in a great hurry. Mainard set off after him, dodging around the crowds in the square. Bethia waited, while Grissel and Johannes drew close.

'Whit now?' Grissel muttered.

Bethia sent Grissel and Johannes home. Mainard returned and took Bethia's arm once more. 'There's to be a burning. No, not of a person,' he amended quickly when he saw her horrified expression. 'Books.'

Bethia stopped and stared up into his face. 'It's the same as in Rome. They've seized the Jewish books,

310

haven't they? Grissel told me that Johannes said there was great commotion in the Ghetto the other day.'

'Yes, that's so.' He sounded relieved that she was remaining calm. 'The Pope insisted that the Doge impound them, but we hoped it would end there, and after a while the Talmud would be quietly returned, for it's big business here and many Christians make good money from selling it. But the burning is going ahead.'

She and Mainard followed the crowd to the piazza before San Marco's and saw the mound of books piled high. The soldiers came with lit torches, the wavering heat visible in the sunlight.

'Such a terrible waste,' murmured Bethia.

The paper was dry and the flames crackled, leaping higher and higher. The crowd encircled the fire, for there was no wind and little smoke to set anyone coughing. People watched silently; perhaps they felt as she did that it was a crime to burn such sacred materials. But then the masks came out and soon devils and demons danced around the blaze, their bodies contorting as though they truly were come from Hell.

'Was this all just the Talmud?' she asked as she and Mainard slowly left the square.

'Mainly, for it is a mighty set of books. However, I believe the Pope was not overly specific and it may also include the Tefillot and other sacred Jewish texts.'

Bethia would be happy if she never heard of the Tefillot again, but looking at Mainard's drawn face she decided not to voice that thought.

'Guistini is furious, da Molina says.' He turned to take a last look at the fire. 'He'll have lost over twenty thousand ducats in these flames.'

'But he's not a Jew, is he?'

'No. Printers go where there's money to be made and there was much in selling the Talmud. Da Molina does say that if the Pope is provided with sufficient *persuasion* he may allow the commentaries to be published after expurgation.'

'What does that mean?'

'There's already a friar and a Converso working together to follow the papal book of corrections and take out the sections considered heretical. Once they're cut out, any Talmuds left unburnt can then be returned.'

'And I assume by *persuasion* you mean the Pope is to be bribed.'

'Hush, Bethia, not so loud. But yes, you have understood correctly.'

She rubbed her eyes: dry and itchy. 'What a world we do live in.'

But this was not the end of her tumultuous day. When they reached home and climbed the curving stairs to the salon, they were met by Grissel.

'You have a visitor, mistress,' Grissel said breathlessly, capering up the steps in front of her.

'Who?' said Bethia wearily. She hoped it was not Guistina and Pelegrina come to chatter over the book burning.

Grissel swung the salon door wide and a tall figure rose to his feet.

'Will!' said Bethia.

Chapter Forty-Eight

Michael Servetus

Will knew he would surprise Bethia and de Lange but hadn't expected the shock on their faces.

He stepped forward and took Bethia by the hands. 'What's happened?'

She gazed at the floor and it was his good brother who spoke.

'There are troubles here in Venice. A burning of Jewish texts this very day.'

Will sighed heavily. 'It seems as though the whole world is on fire. You will, of course, know that the young King Edward of England has died?'

'Yes,' said Mainard, gesturing at him to take a seat. He spoke over his shoulder. 'Some refreshments, Grissel.'

Grissel, who'd been hovering in the doorway, left slowly.

'Now that Queen Mary has ascended the throne there is little doubt she'll enact terrible retribution on any so-called heretics and all Protestants in England fear for their lives.'

'What will John Knox do?' said Bethia.

'He's coming to Geneva. It's not safe for him to stay in England now.'

'And he'll bring his wife,' said Bethia.

'That is *not* why I'm here. Marjorie Bowes is as nothing

313

to me.' The words burst out of him and Mainard looked startled. Will rubbed his face. 'God's blood I wish it was so simple a reason made me leave Geneva. Do you think all my journey across Europe was running away because Marjorie Bowes chose Knox over me?' He sniffed. 'Not that her mother would've permitted it any other way.'

Bethia gave him a knowing look.

'I'm certain your departure had little to do with any woman,' said Mainard calmly.

The door opened and Grissel appeared with a silver tray of glasses and decanter. Will was impressed to notice her proficiency in both carrying and serving and winked at her as she poured his wine.

'The dinner is ready,' said Grissel in her usual abrupt manner. Some things never change, thought Will. Already he was glad he came; was beginning to feel better if only he could block from his head the terrible sight he'd recently witnessed.

'Let's eat and exchange tales thereafter,' said Mainard. 'For I fear it will ruin our digestion otherwise.'

He looked to Will for agreement and Will nodded. Whenever he told them of Servetus, it would not change the outcome so he might as well eat first.

Bethia led the way and they sat down at the wooden board polished to the highest degree, beneath a chandelier whose crystals sparkled in the dancing sunlight. He gazed at the large paintings on the wall opposite and pressed on his belly.

'Are you ill?' Bethia leaned forward anxiously.

How could he explain that there was something about the brightness of colour, the voluptuousness of the figures, the over-imagination of the artist and the general setting of mosaic floor, marble pillars, and ornate cornicing which made him feel as if he'd over-eaten on sweet pudding. This assault on the senses he could not but find repugnant after living in a plain, sober, God-fearing Geneva where all surroundings were about enabling quiet reflection and right-thinking.

'I'm fine,' he said, knowing he didn't speak the truth.

He saw her frown as the first course was served, and gazed at the long white creation decorated with flowers: fish. But, of course, it was Friday and he was back in Catholic country.

'Baccalà mantecato,' Bethia said. 'It's a creamed cod. I take it you're still not a fish lover.'

'No.'

'Ah well, we have soup.'

He ate the soup, for he was hungry, although there were slimy lumps of starch within it that he'd never encountered before and he didn't much care for the large beans either. The next course was served and he stared at the black sauce.

'It looks like ink.' He lifted his head from the study of his plate in time to catch Mainard and Bethia exchanging glances.

This is *Seppie col Nero*,' said Mainard heartily. 'The ink comes from a sea creature – but it's not a fish, I do assure you.'

Will placed his elbows on the board and cradled his head in his hands. After a moment he became aware of Bethia standing beside him, her hand resting on his shoulder.

'I am sorry,' he said, lifting his head. 'They burned Servetus and I can think of little else.'

The family left the half-eaten meal and returned to the salon.

Will began to talk, the words pouring out of him like a river in spate. 'Of course, Servetus was wrong thinking, yet he didn't seem dangerous. But then thoughts are dangerous of themselves and lead to sedition.'

He stood up and paced around the room while Mainard and Bethia watched him. 'Calvin wanted Servetus sent back to Vienna, for they were the ones who arrested him first, and then allowed him to escape. *Let them deal with him,* he said. But the magistrate insisted that Servetus must remain in Geneva, saying that he'd already escaped from prison in Vienna once, and what was to stop him from doing so again. Calvin was most distressed and we didn't have Farni to help us.'

He looked at his family, who were watching him intently. 'You see, Farni was being held along with Servetus because of a most peculiar Genevan law, which meant the accuser was confined, as well as the accused.' He shook his head. 'Quite how Farni and not Calvin was labelled Servetus's accuser I do not understand, but given Calvin's uncertain health, it was as well. And really, how could they have had the leader of the church in Geneva incarcerated?'

Will knew he sounded as though he was trying to excuse Calvin. He spread his arms wide. 'I do promise you, although Calvin had determined that Servetus must die, he never ever wanted him burned at the stake. Again and again he responded to Servetus's demand for a debate telling him he must *not* come to Geneva because he could not assure Servetus's safety.' He shook his head. 'I think Servetus was intent on martyrdom.'

'Like George Wishart,' said Bethia, quietly.

Will nodded, glad she understood. 'So Servetus gave Calvin no option but to call for his execution.'

There was a long sigh from Mainard but Will was bent on telling his story now and would not be distracted. 'Calvin was determined it would be a quick beheading.' He looked to his sister. 'Bethia, his compassion heartened me greatly.'

'I don't understand, Will,' said Mainard gruffly. 'Surely all Servetus wanted was an honest debate?'

'How can you debate with a man who denies there is original sin? It was impossible.' Will shook his head trying to clear it. 'It was not all down to Calvin in any case. For all his spiritual leadership he's not the determiner of everything that happens in Geneva. Farni said that it was

Calvin's enemies who had incited Servetus in yet another attempt to undermine Calvin. You'll remember, Bethia, all the things that were done to provoke him.' He turned to Mainard. 'They even played skittles outside the church while he was preaching. He didn't deserve such ill-mannered treatment. And the death of Servetus will damage Calvin's legacy. It's most unfair.' He was aware he was rambling, couldn't seem to stop himself.

'Why have you left Geneva?' asked Mainard.

Will stiffened then threw himself into a chair. It was a reasonable question if he could only formulate the answer.

'I couldn't stay, not after the burning,' he said simply.

There was a sudden thump from the ceiling above followed by a child howling. Bethia jumped up. 'Excuse me,' she said and, lifting her skirts, hurried out of the chamber.

Mainard opened his mouth to speak but Grissel appeared in the doorway. 'Signor da Molina is here.'

A man slid in behind her and spoke in French. 'I told your servant not to trouble herself, de Lange, for we do not stand on ceremony.'

Mainard rose to his feet.

'Ah,' said da Molina, holding his bonnet against his chest, its long white feather waving in the breeze from the open window, 'please forgive me. I didn't know you had a visitor.'

He looked to Mainard, who after a moment said, 'This is William Seton. And Seton, may I introduce Niccolo da Molina.'

Will rose and they bowed to one another. The fellow was small, dapper, and wore a bright red doublet slashed with gold, and his breeches too were decorated with gold thread.

'Have you travelled far?' asked da Molina, clearly made curious by the abruptness of the introduction.

Will saw that Mainard looked anxious, but his good brother need not fear, Will knew enough to dissemble, and certainly not to mention that he had, until recently, lived in a Protestant city state. 'I've come from Antwerp,' he said, scratching the back of his head. It *was* the truth, in a meandering kind of way.

'And how was the journey?'

'All went smoothly.'

'That is fortunate. Is your visit of long duration?'

Will noticed that Mainard had cocked his head awaiting the response.

'It depends on how my business goes.'

'You're a man of business. What line of work?'

Will wondered how long he'd have to fence with this sharp-nosed fellow who seemed most determined to extract more information. There was a pause while he tried to think of an appropriate response, which Mainard thankfully cut across.

'Come, da Molina, let us to my workroom and leave Seton here in peace. He'll be tired, having only recently arrived.'

Da Molina bowed again and Will was left alone with his thoughts.

Bethia soon returned. 'Where's Mainard?'

'A man came, name of da Molina.'

She frowned.

'You don't like him,' he asked, although her expression said it all.

'I don't trust him, but he's necessary for us to do business here.'

Will stood up and she took his arm. 'Let's forget our cares for the moment. You must come and see the children. They'll be excited to meet their uncle.'

He would be glad of the distraction.

'You have been busy,' he said, ensconced on the low nursery chair watching as Samuel-Thomas swung his wooden sword dangerously close to Jacopo's face and the smallest child crawled behind. 'But where's Katheline?'

'Katheline is now Catarina, a married woman who lives in the Ottoman lands.'

318

His eyes grew big. 'But how did I not know this?'

'It wasn't information I would entrust to a letter.'

'Ah, I see there's a story here.' He fell silent. 'Did she marry a Jew?'

'She did.'

He swallowed. Truth to tell, he was far sadder about this than any thought of Marjorie Bowes, for Katheline was a knowledgeable woman of spirit who would've made a most remarkable wife.

'You look tired,' said Bethia softly.

And suddenly he felt exhausted.

'Come I'll show you to your chamber.'

She left him in a comfortable room with a view of the canal way below. He stood gazing down upon the waters, watching the boatmen manoeuvre their long oar skilfully and calling out to their fellows as they did, a system that miraculously worked, for they slid past one another in the narrow canal with barely a finger's breadth between. His shoulders sagged and he sat down on the bed, tugged his boots off, lay back, and was asleep within minutes. But his dreams were very terrible.

He awoke to darkness and became aware of someone shaking him. He sat bolt upright, saw Mainard's face in the glow of a candle, and flinched from the flame.

'Hush,' said Mainard. 'You're safe here.'

It was as though he was soothing a child, but Will didn't take umbrage, was still too caught up in the tangle of his nightmare.

'I find it best to rise and walk around the chamber when demons torment me in the night.'

Will rose and found himself still fully clothed. 'I'm sorry if I disturbed you.'

'I was on my way to bed; Bethia's already asleep.'

Will followed Mainard as he limped over to the long window.

'This never happened to me before. Indeed, when I

was a galley slave I learned to sleep when I could.' Will snorted. 'My fellow forsares congratulated me on my ability to snatch rest at every opportunity.'

He could see Mainard smiling.

'And you, what disturbs you in the night?' Will raised his hand. 'Forgive me, that was a foolish question after what you suffered at the hands of the Inquisitors.'

'I'm working to free myself from their grip,' Mainard sighed, 'but it's not easy.'

'No, it is not. And for me it hits at the core of my faith. I keep questioning if Calvin was right to insist that Servetus must die, regardless of the means of his death.

'I too have had an unquiet heart since my time of torment,' said Mainard as he placed the candleholder atop the mantlepiece. He moved the two chairs in the chamber to the window, which he opened wide, then blew out the candle.

Will sat down on one and Mainard on the other. They gazed out at the tall houses on the other side of the canal, the convolutions of the roofline and the high funnel of the chimney pots a dark line against the blue-black starry sky.

Will began to speak slowly at first and then the words tumbled from his lips. He needed to tell what he saw, to bear witness, and then perhaps he might be released from the grip of its horror.

'Servetus was not a citizen of Geneva so could've been banished.' He glanced at Mainard. 'Just as your sister was.'

Mainard shifted in his seat but said nothing.

Will continued. 'But Calvin was most unhappy at this prospect, saying that Servetus shouldn't be permitted to continue to spout false doctrine and a sentence of death must be passed. Always, though, he wanted a quick beheading and preferably far from Geneva. He was distraught that we must all attend the public burning, said it rewarded Servetus for his blasphemy to receive a martyr's death and we'd do better to foil his intent and give him a more mundane end.'

Will knew it sounded as though he was trying to persuade himself of Calvin's goodness, but as he spoke it came to him that Calvin wanted to spare himself, not Servetus – or so it sounded. Perhaps both were true.

'What were Servetus's crimes?'

'He was found guilty of denying the Trinity and repudiating infant baptism.' Will turned to Mainard. 'Of course, he could have repented and then his sentence would likely have been commuted to a beheading, so in the end Calvin was quite right. Servetus did choose a martyr's death and was burned atop a pyre of his own books.'

He heard Mainard sigh again. He was grateful that his brother-in-law said nothing but continued to stare into the night, allowing Will to unburden himself in the sheltering dark.

'We had to send to his printer in Vienna to gather sufficient books. Calvin had copies in his library – but he didn't give them up.' Will rubbed his head. 'You will know that Bethia and I witnessed the burning of George Wishart, although it's more than seven years ago now.'

'I know,' said Mainard. 'We met soon after.'

Will swallowed. 'Very early on the morning of Michael Servetus's death I went to the place of execution, a small field close by the city called Plateau de Champel. There were men preparing the pyre as I arrived. I assumed they'd use well-seasoned wood and had left building the bonfire until then so that the firewood was kept under cover overnight and would burn quick. I was most surprised to find them dragging branches of oak still covered with leaves. I spoke to the overseer saying that the wood was too green to burn well. He said that the leaves would create plenty of smoke so Servetus would likely suffocate before he burned. They would pack the pyre with straw, as well as books, and use sulfur by Servetus's head to get it going. He promised all would be over quick.'

Will paused, noticing he was twisting his hands together. He placed them deliberately one on each thigh before continuing. 'Of course, it did not go to plan. Servetus's agony was longer than anyone, even his worst enemies, would've wished. The fire was slow to take, just as with George Wishart, the wind capricious and the green wood hissing and smouldering rather than burning: even the books seemed reluctant to catch alight. More straw was brought. He showed exceptional bravery and cried out only once. *What did he say*? was passed among the crowd. No one seemed certain, but in the end it was determined that Servetus's last words were *Jesus, Son of eternal God, have mercy on me.*'

Will turned to Mainard. 'Calvin said the words were most fitting. Then he said we should get back to work now it was done with. But I could hardly bear to look upon John Calvin. I could not stay. And that's why I'm here.'

Mainard touched him lightly on the shoulder. 'We can speak more in the morning. Are you ready for sleep now?'

Will, feeling slightly less oppressed after his unburdening, nodded. 'I am.'

Chapter Forty-Nine

A Place of Safety

Mainard awoke the next morning to find Bethia shaking his arm. He blinked. It was full daylight and the sun bright.

'What time is it?' he groaned, and rolled onto his back stretching.

'It's past ten bells, and Mainard, you must rise quickly. Da Molina is below waiting for you.'

'Tell him to come back later.' Mainard sat up and rubbed his eyes with the palms of his hands.

'He's most insistent, says he needs to speak to you urgently.'

'What's happened now?' said Mainard wearily. He lifted the covers and climbed out of bed.

'You were up late talking to Will.'

He nodded.

'Did he tell you what his plans are?'

'We didn't get that far.'

'Servetus?'

'Sadly yes. A terrible story.'

Bethia lifted a clean shirt from the kist and handed it to him. 'He won't go back to Calvin, will he?'

'I believe Will is done with Geneva.'

Bethia chewed on her lower lip.

'And he cannot stay here.' He saw her jump. 'I'm

sorry, my love, that came out louder than I meant.'

'I understand. Protestants are no more welcome in Venice than Catholics are in Geneva.'

Mainard splashed his face in the basin of water and smoothed his beard, glad he'd given up all the shaving pother. 'I'm ready. Let me go and find out what's so urgent and then we'll have a talk with Will.'

Bethia reached out and tugged his face down to kiss him. 'I'm sorry my brother might bring trouble to our home.'

Mainard shrugged. 'He'll be gone before anyone notices.'

He wasn't feeling so sanguine after his meeting with da Molina. The man was lolling in a chair when Mainard entered the salon and, making no effort to stand, waved Mainard to another chair.

Mainard had never much cared for da Molina. Now he was ready to take him by the scruff of the neck and boot him out of his home. He chose to stand, feet planted wide and arms folded, gazing down on the smaller man.

Da Molina grinned lazily in return and swung his foot. 'You have a very interesting visitor.'

Mainard tapped his foot slowly.

'I understand he's a follower of Calvin's recently come from Geneva.'

Mainard waited.

Da Molina sat up suddenly and leaned forward. 'I don't want much for my silence. Only a greater share of the profit, which really, for all the work I do, I'm entitled to.'

Mainard raised his eyebrows.

'You Conversos have plenty. You'll barely notice it. You're a man who thinks highly of his wife, I well remember. I shouldn't think it will be conducive to marital harmony should her brother be taken.'

Mainard clenched his fists, hidden beneath the fold of

his arms, but somehow kept his face impassive. 'Are you done?'

Da Molina shrugged. 'I've said all that needs to be said.'

'I will think on it and let you know.' He opened the door wide.

Da Molina paused at the top of the stairs. 'Don't take too long.'

Mainard found Will and Bethia awaiting him in the workroom.

'What did he want?' asked Bethia anxiously.

'To squeeze out of me as much as he can.' He turned to Will. 'Da Molina is a sly creature, just how cunning I didn't realise until now. He knows all about you.'

He looked to Bethia. 'I fear we may have a spy in our home, for I cannot think how else he got the information and so quickly.'

Bethia put her hand over her mouth.

He turned back to Will. 'Do you have a plan?'

Will started. 'I do. You were only a stop along the way. I'm going to Ferrara. Calvin had much correspondence with its duchess and indeed once visited there, although I believe he was in disguise. Renée of France seems most sympathetic to the Protestant cause and Calvin has given me an introduction.'

Mainard blinked. 'Jews live in Ferrara freely but,' he looked to Bethia for confirmation, 'we met no Protestants during our brief sojourn, and the duchess wasn't there either. I don't think the duke is sympathetic to Protestants. Indeed, Dona Gracia once mentioned the duke was intending to root it out of the French court which surrounds the duchess.'

Will was silent for a moment. 'She still corresponds regularly with Calvin. I've seen the letters. She is a true believer.' He looked down, rubbing his forehead gently. After a moment he said, 'what will this Italian do with the information about me? You'll likely be in danger?'

'I'm going to write to Don Juan Micas and apprise him of what's happening, he's due back in Venice soon anyway. And I'll seek new trading partners. Da Molina's a fool; there are plenty others who'll be very happy to work with us.' Mainard straightened his shoulders. 'But I think you are correct. We should remove from Venice, or at least be prepared to do so quickly.'

'I am sorry I've brought this trouble upon you.'

Mainard was silent. What could he say for Will had brought trouble to their door. He contained his sigh. 'It is never far away,' he said softly.

Will nodded and strode from the room.

Grissel appeared in the doorway and Bethia told her to start packing. Mainard watched as his wife hesitated, then she stepped forward and took Grissel by the hand.

'You will come with us wherever we go?'

Grissel looked startled.

'Only I thought there was a gondolier…'

'Ach there's more than one. Dinna go away without me, mistress. I must ay come with you.'

Mainard watched as Bethia squeezed Grissel's hand, and Grissel's eyes filled with tears.

'Johannes and Ysabeau, too?' said Grissel.

'Of course.'

Mainard squeezed Bethia's shoulder in turn and went to write his letter to Don Juan. He found her later, packing linens. She was composed, had not even yet asked where they were to go.

'I've finally decided on a name for the weeist lamb.'

She looked up. 'About time. When he passed his first birthday nameless I despaired for him! What's it to be?'

'Abram, from the Old Testament, where all life originates. It's a good, strong name for our strong lad.'

She gazed at him searchingly.

He tugged on his ear. 'Abram is Ortelius's name and he is *not* a Jew.'

She sat back on her haunches. 'I've heard it said that

someone who was not a good Jew cannot be a good Christian. The reverse may also be true.'

'I was a good Christian, but other Christians were not good to me.' He lifted his foot. 'I bear the scars still.' He paused. 'But truly, I don't know what to think any more. I have no plans to follow Catarina's lead.'

'But if we go to the Ottomans?'

'I will not leave Italy yet. There's too much business to attend to.'

'Can we go to Ferrara too then? I liked it there.'

'I do not think that wise. If Will wasn't going then yes, that would've been my choice but we cannot get drawn into his likely seditious activities.'

Her face drained of colour. 'I am sorry,' she whispered.

Mainard shrugged. 'Your brother, my sister. Both have brought peril to our door.'

'Do you think Will came here because he needs funds?'

Mainard paused, then shook his head. 'No. He needed to unburden his soul and I can understand that. But… he's probably hoping we'll offer some support.'

He reached down and took her hands, bringing her up to stand and wrapping his arms around her. 'What I do know is that Venice is no longer our place of safety. We must be brave and go on, my love. But wherever we go, our family will hold strong and stay together.'

Bethia pressed her face against his chest and held tight. Mainard held her back, even tighter.

'Together,' she whispered.

* * *

Find out what happens next for Bethia & Will....

.....the next book in the series is underway
& continues their story,
due out November 2023.

Please leave a review

If you enjoyed this book please take a moment to share your thoughts in a review. Just a rating and/or a few words are perfect.

Reader reviews help sell more books and keep your favourite authors in business!

Acknowledgements

I'd like to say a big thank you to my friends and family for their ongoing support and encouragement. And readers and bloggers, thank you for your kind reviews, and especially for inquiring when this next in series would be out... and pre-ordering it too.

To my beta readers humble thanks for their great suggestions and for challenging me to make this a better book – Sandra Greig, Mercedes Rochelle, Zoe Masters, Mike Masters, Jonathan Posner and Serra Deacon. Serra also suggested the title: huge thanks. Esther Mendelssohn is not only a fantastic friend and beta reader it also feels like she's on the journey with me and she regularly comes up with ideas and suggestions.

My developmental editor Margaret Skea thanks for your excellent guidance, and friendship. And Richard Sheehan thanks for your rock solid editing.

I want to very gratefully acknowledge the resources I'm able to access through the National Library of Scotland and in particular Jstor articles which provided me with some wonderful nuggets including whether animals have souls as well as lots more in depth on the remarkable Mendes Family. Thanks also to the Bibliothèque de Genève for their helpful assistance.

Hugest thanks of all, as ever, go to Mike for all his love, support and help... including doing the cover again.

Historical Note

I've tried to follow historical events as faithfully as I can, and the dates when they happened – Servetus was burned at the stake in 1553 and Don Juan Micas did elope with La Chica (and had to return her). Sometimes dates are slightly flexed for the needs of the story, for instance Gracia Mendes left for Constantinople a year later than I have her doing, although with the same pomp and ceremony as I describe. And I try to stick to known facts about real historical characters so Nostradamus's grandparents were indeed Conversos but the jury is still out on whether Albrecht Durer came from a family of Conversos – although given he was one of Hitler's favourite artists, it would be excellent if he had.

* * *

Let me know if you do spot any glaring inaccuracies, or want to chat about my books. I love a good blether with readers.

You'll also find a couple of stories delving more into the Seton Family, that are free to download from my website.

You'll find me at www.vehmasters.com.

The Castilians is Book
One of the Seton
Chronicles

The Conversos is Book
Two of the Seton
Chronicles

Printed in Great Britain
by Amazon